THE CROWN CONTEST

The Usurpers Saga, Volume II

A NOVEL BY:
JOHN R. PHYTHYON, JR.

COLUMBUS, OHIO

Also by John R. Phythyon, Jr.

The Usurpers Saga
THE KRAKEN BONE
THE DRAGON SWORD

MAGIC & MONSTERS: A COLLECTION OF SHORT FANTASY FICTION

Modern Fairy Tales
THE SECRET THIEF
LITTLE RED RIDING HOODIE
BEAUTY & THE BEAST

Wolf Dasher Novels
THE ARMAGEDDON CLOCK
TWICE IN A LIFETIME
GHOST OF A CHANCE
ROSES ARE WHITE
RED DRAGON FIVE
STATE OF GRACE

For Knute Pittenger, the best friend a person could hope to have.

THE CROWN CONTEST

CHAPTER 1:

The Hand of Destiny

L ILIANA GRAY HAD NEVER seen a crucifixion before. She hadn't planned to see one today. She'd been riding along the road to Twin Falls, hoping to make the city by nightfall, when she'd perceived strange magic off to the north. It floated towards her mind like a foul scent on the breeze, cloying at her thoughts, drenching them in fear. She'd had no idea what sort of sorcery this was, but it was soaked in darkness. She'd decided to investigate, driving her horse, Percy, towards the source of the vile magic, despite his reluctance to get any closer.

Approximately half a mile later, in a small woods comprised largely of evergreens hardy enough to grow in the frozen ground of the tundra, she discovered a giant, black cross with a naked man nailed to it. His body was in fine shape – well muscled and broad – but his skin was red with frostbite, and his head hung lifelessly on his neck, with a long mane of brown hair flowing down from it, obscuring his face. Liliana could only tell he was still alive by the way he shivered and by the six goblins, who surrounded the crucifix, staring reverently as though transfixed.

The cross hummed and throbbed with dark magic. It permeated the wood and infected the entire clearing with a palpable wrongness that screamed at Liliana's eyes, nose, and mouth. Malice poured off it, affronting her senses.

Stranger still, the spell seemed to be sucking the life, the soul, from its victim and channeling it into the ground. Crucifixion was a long, agonizing means of execution, but Liliana thought he would die before the exhaustion or the cold got him. Whatever was happening here was unnatural.

She'd never heard of goblins working this type of sorcery. And while she was no expert on the region or the species, she'd thought goblins were confined largely to the mountains, many leagues north of here. But there they stood, their leathery, green skin covered in animal pelts, gripping spears as the cold air turned their excited breath to steam.

Liliana had no idea what she'd stumbled upon, but she was certain she should stop it. The dark magic on the cross and the presence of goblins were enough to tell her no good would come of allowing them to continue their ritual.

She raised her right hand, pointed four fingers at the fiends, and summoned eldritch energy from the ether around her. Four bright, red arrows of light shot from her fingertips and hit four of the goblins. Each exploded in red fire, eliciting screams and breaking their trance.

Two died instantly, while their companions ran in circles, shouting in their strange language and wailing in pain. The two she hadn't attacked looked at her, horrified and frightened. One threw his spear at her. She waved her hand, and the weapon turned to marigolds, which fell harmlessly on the frosty earth in front of Percy.

That was all the convincing the goblins needed. Both turned tail and raced into the woods. One of those she'd attacked followed after them, still burning. The other had fallen over dead like his comrades.

Liliana was tempted to give chase, but goblins were clever, and they had the advantage of knowing the territory. She didn't want to risk an ambush. Besides, the man on the cross needed her assistance immediately if he was going to survive, assuming he could be saved at all.

She spurred Percy forward, but he took two only steps before he stopped again and refused to get any closer to the crucifix. He whinnied nervously. Clearly, he could feel the darkness too and didn't want any part of it.

"It's okay, boy," she said. "I won't make you go farther."

She dismounted, pulled a large blanket out of her supplies, and approached the cross. It still hummed with darkness. The goblins may have scattered, but their spell was still operating.

Hoping the enchantment wasn't securing him to the tainted wood, she raised her hand and summoned her own magic, commanding the nails to withdraw. They obeyed without resistance, sliding easily out of the cross, the man's wrists, and his feet.

Before he could fall, Liliana raised her other hand, drew more eldritch energy to her, and levitated him softly down until he was floating just a few feet off the ground in front of her. She swaddled him quickly in the blanket and then guided him over to Percy, bringing him to a rest on his back.

"There, Percy," she said. "You can hold our guest, can't you?"

Percy grunted quickly, as if to say, "Sure, can we get out of here now?"

Liliana agreed with him. Whatever was going on here was bad, and there was every chance the goblins would come back with reinforcements. She needed to get everyone away as quickly as possible.

She took Percy's reins and led him from the clearing and back towards the road. She stopped at the edge of the woods and made camp. She'd rather have taken the man all the way to Twin Falls, but she wasn't sure he would last that long. She didn't relish staying among the trees, since the goblins might pursue them, but she thought he needed the shelter of the evergreens instead of being out in the open where the wind could chill him further.

Liliana built a small fire, feeding it magical energy to get it going quickly. Then she laid the man down next to it and examined his wounds. She was no healer, and she didn't have any draughts or salves with her. But she laid her hands on the ugly holes in his wrists, imagined them closing, and then drew eldritch power to her from the air, infusing it into the wounds. The punctured skin and muscle moved slowly together, knitting and fusing until the damage was largely undone.

The seal wasn't perfect. Liliana did little more than sew the cuts shut with sorcery. But it would speed his recovery and prevent infection. Once he was well enough to travel, she could get him better treatment.

She moved to his feet and repeated the process on the wounds there. When she was finished, she was exhausted. It had taken considerable magic to mend his hurts. She needed rest.

But first, she had to take care of Percy and feed herself. The man shivered intensely for awhile, but by the time she'd gotten Percy tied up and fed, her patient was doing better. He remained unconscious, though, so she couldn't ask him any questions.

Ah, well. That could wait for later. For the time being, he was alive. She broke out some rations and had dinner as the sun went down. Whoever the strange man was, whatever reason he'd been crucified by goblins, she knew she had stumbled onto something important – maybe as important as that day two years ago when she'd woken up to discover Gothemus Draco's last instructions lying on her chest. Just as she had then, Liliana Gray felt the hand of destiny upon her.

CHAPTER 2:

The Sting of Cowardice

"WHAT DO YOU MEAN he was rescued?" Gursh demanded. The goblin king scowled at Krellnor, the lieutenant he'd trusted with the mission of crucifying the human. Krellnor cowered before him. His two surviving soldiers also shook with fear. Their green skin trembled, their yellow eyes were dim and downcast, and their large noses ran with snot – all signs they were scared; all signs they had no reasonable excuse for their failure. Gursh put his hands on his hips and thrust his stomach at them.

"Please, mighty lord," Krellnor said. "We were ambushed by a sorcerer."

Gursh shot an inquisitive glance at Kraven. His chief advisor and shaman shrugged the slight shoulders that could barely hold his bear pelt tunic. His thin face, dominated by a crooked nose, offered no opinion. Gursh turned back to the soldiers.

"What sorcerer?" he said.

"A human," Krellnor answered. "I'd never seen her before. She came out of the woods and started blasting us with magic."

"What about Grunk?" Gursh asked. "He's a magician."

"He was killed in her initial attack," Krellnor replied. "The woman had strange powers. She used neither wand nor staff to cast her sorcery. She simply conjured magic from the air."

"Impossible!" Gursh said.

He turned to Kraven for confirmation. His assistant shrugged again.

"I swear!" Krellnor said. "Magic arrows sprang from her fingertips. They killed Grunk and two others. Poin-Poin here was struck too."

Gursh turned his attention to the badly burned soldier. The goblin king was impressed he was still alive given the state of his injuries.

"It's true," Poin-Poin whimpered, both afraid and in pain. "They were magic arrows. When they struck us, they exploded in red fire. Grunk and Tabwa died instantly."

Gursh looked over his soldiers. He knew magic was difficult to fight, especially when the attack was a surprise. If Grunk had indeed been killed right away, they would have had difficulty fighting off the ambush. Still, there'd been six of them, and only two died in the initial onslaught. Why were three of them here, two uninjured?

"So what happened after she assaulted you?" he asked.

The other three looked at each other before responding. Gursh thought he knew the answer before he got it.

"We ran," Krellnor said.

"You didn't even fight back?" Gursh roared.

"Please, mighty lord," Krellnor pleaded. "There were six of us. We were struck without warning by a woman using magic we'd never seen before. Our own sorcerer was murdered. Three of us died in the initial onslaught. We—"

"Fled like cowards!" Gursh shouted.

He was disgusted with them. He doubted they'd have been effective against this unknown sorcerer, but he'd expect them to at least show some resistance before retreating.

"The human was being sacrificed to Gruul!" he said, still shouting. "We needed his essence to infuse Gruul's spirit, so he can break the chains that bind him. His blood was rare. Do you know how hard it was to find and kidnap him? Now Gruul may remain imprisoned.

"It's bad enough you allowed this to happen, but you didn't even *try* to stop it?"

"Please, mighty lord—"

"Enough!"

6

Gursh stood over them and glared. All three trembled before him.

"Flog them," he pronounced. "Let them feel the sting of their cowardice. I shall consult Lord Kremdor. If a sacrifice is required, they shall be on the altar. Take them away."

Guards hauled Krellnor and his soldiers off to be flogged. The failures wailed miserably, especially Poin-Poin, who, given the extent of his injuries, was unlikely to survive whipping. Gursh turned to Kraven.

"What do you think?" he said.

"About what?"

"What does this mean in terms of our plans?" Gursh said, irritated.

Kraven chewed his thumbnail and thought for a moment. Gursh tapped his foot impatiently.

"It depends on when the ritual was interrupted," Kraven replied at last. "Lord Kremdor told us to crucify the human to drag out his death. If he was on the cross long enough, we might have enough of his essence, even though he didn't die."

Gursh nodded. He understood the specifics of this scheme and how it all worked, but he didn't comprehend magic. That was Kraven's specialty.

"What about this sorcerer?" Gursh asked. "What does her appearance mean?"

"I'm not sure," Kraven said. "It's unlikely her coming along was accidental. Someone sent her, probably the gods. They don't want us to unchain Gruul, and they probably are against us conquering Twin Falls."

"That's not exactly what we're doing," Gursh said.

"True. But if this sorcerer doesn't need a staff or wand to cast her spells, she's really dangerous. Gods-sent probably."

"Is that really possible?" Gursh asked.

"I wouldn't cast dice on it."

Gursh nodded. Krellnor had been afraid. He knew his king would be furious with him for fleeing without a fight. He probably made up the part about her not needing spells to make her seem more powerful and frightening. It was an understandable lie. The ambush probably came from a regular magician.

But who was she, and why was she here? He supposed it could have been a member of the wizards' guild out on some excursion. Perhaps she was gathering spell components or seeking a good tree limb for a staff or wand.

The guild wouldn't have sent a master to do that, though. It would have been some novice, and Krellnor and company wouldn't have fled before a mere initiate. Assuming the story about being attacked by a single sorcerer was true, whomever it was would have had to be pretty capable to take out six goblins.

Which brought him back to the idea she was sent by the gods.

"You'd better report this to Lord Kremdor," Kraven said.

"Yes," Gursh said. "He's likely to be angry, but he needs to know what happened."

"And he may be able to answer any questions you have about the efficacy of the spell, even if the sacrifice didn't die," Kraven added.

"He might be able to tell us who this sorcerer is too," Gursh said. "But let's get back to Twin Falls. I don't like the idea of being out here with a powerful magician capable of slaughtering goblins with minimal effort."

Now it was Kraven's turn to nod.

"I'll summon us an escort," he said. "Just in case we run into her on the way back."

"If she's in the tunnels, we've got a much bigger problem," Gursh said.

"An excellent point."

Gursh grimaced. Until now everything had been going perfectly. They'd held up their end of the bargain, and Lord Kremdor had taught them the magic necessary to conduct the ritual. The goblin king didn't like that something was going wrong. He had a dark god to free and a city to sacrifice. Interference from a human sorcerer, especially if she'd been sent from Mt. Elysium, was a problem he didn't want.

CHAPTER 3:

Magic and Wish Fulfillment

A S THE PINK LIGHT of dawn broke through the pine needles, Liliana bent over the man she had rescued from a mysterious execution yesterday. He slept, but not peacefully. She could see his eyes shifting back and forth quickly beneath tightly closed lids, his brow furrowed in distress. Whether he dreamed or was remembering what happened to him, the vision wasn't pleasant.

He was attractive, whoever he was. She had little interest in sex or romance – it had never appealed to her. But she could see his face had ruggedly handsome features – the long, brown hair, three or four days' growth of beard, chiseled jawline, and large nose. His skin was still red and cracked from exposure, but she expected it would return to a nice healthy pink complexion that would charm other ladies.

Why would goblins want to kill this man? Why would they use dark magic to do it? Was he a randomly chosen sacrifice, or did they want him specifically? He was a mystery – the biggest one she'd encountered since she'd helped Calibot lay to rest his father, her former master.

The rabbit she'd been cooking looked as though it might done. She hadn't slept well last night, fearing an ambush from the goblins. Weariness and the strain of using so much magic the day before combined with the smell of roast coney to make her ravenous. She removed it from the fire and started withdrawing the spit, when her patient gasped, came suddenly awake, and tried to sit up. The blankets she'd wrapped him in fell away, and he immediately shivered against the chill of the early morning air.

"Here now," she said. "Take it easy. You're still injured."

She moved to him, and he flinched at her approach. Then, having apparently spent all the energy he had, he collapsed back onto the makeshift bed she'd constructed for him.

"It's okay, I won't hurt you," she said, smiling at him. "I rescued you."

He looked confused and shivered harder. She grabbed the blankets and tucked them around him, continuing to smile kindly.

"My name is Liliana," she said. "Liliana Gray. You've had quite an adventure. Can you speak?"

He opened his mouth, tried to form words, but he only was able to croak.

"Here," she said, holding out a wineskin. "See if you can drink something."

She lifted it to his lips and raised his head to assist. He took several sips before drawing away. She lowered him back to the earth.

"Better?"

"A little," he managed. His voice was still raspy.

"I was just getting ready to have some breakfast," she said. "Do you think you can eat?"

He nodded. She smiled at him again and returned to the coney. Grabbing her knife, she cut off a leg, and handed it to him. He took it weakly, but when he got a taste of the meat, he attacked it with relish.

"Well, I'm not a healer," Liliana commented, "but it looks like I've repaired you sufficiently for your appetite to return."

"Thank you," he said between bites.

"You're welcome," she replied.

She gave him the wineskin again and then cut up some rabbit for herself. Once she was satisfied he was cared for and her own breakfast was ready, she resumed questioning him.

"If you don't mind my asking," she began, "who are you?"

"My name is Garrick Tremaine," he answered.

"Well, Mr. Tremaine, why would goblins want to crucify you?"

He didn't answer at first. He just chewed his rabbit thoughtfully.

"I don't know," he said at last. "They ambushed me. I was traveling west *en route* to Twin Falls, when they sprang a trap. I don't know what happened to my friends. Slaughtered, I suspect. But they bound me, put a bag over my head, and carried me off.

"The next thing I knew, they were nailing me to a cross. They raised it, and then a goblin wizard started chanting. It felt like something was reaching through my back into my heart, pulling out . . . I don't know what."

Liliana turned what he'd said over in her mind. It fit with what she'd seen – some sort of black magic. But what would goblins be doing? She'd *never* heard of goblins engaging in a ritual this elaborate.

"You're lucky to be alive," she said. "They crucified you naked. With the cold, you could have died of hypothermia long before the crucifixion got you. Plus, it looked like they were drawing out your soul or energy or something."

"That's what it felt like," he said, his voice haunted. "Like they were siphoning away my life."

Yes. Whatever they had been doing, it was designed to get some ethereal piece of him they couldn't extract by spilling blood. She suspected that was why they'd crucified him – they'd wanted his death to take as long as possible.

"Why were you traveling to Twin Falls?" she asked.

He didn't answer immediately. His eyes darted away, avoiding her gaze.

"You won't believe me if I tell you," he said at last.

"Why not?"

"Because it doesn't make sense to me," he answered. He stared into the fire for a few a moments. "It sounds too much like magic and wish fulfillment."

Liliana smiled at him again. She brushed a lock of blonde hair out of her face, tucking it behind her ear.

"I believe in magic," she said. "I'm a wizard."

His eyes widened, and she chuckled.

"How do you think I was able to rescue you from six goblins?" she said. "Even with the element of surprise against them, goblins are tricky and fierce fighters. I ambushed them with my magic. My initial attack was so effective, three died and the others fled immediately.

"And that cross was drenched in dark sorcery. So if you tell me some eldritch source drew you to Twin Falls, I will not be skeptical. Given what happened to you when you were close, I would practically expect it."

He met her gaze at last, staring at her for several moments. His expression was impossible to read, but his eyes were haunted. Liliana had no idea if it was a reaction to the trauma he'd suffered, her revelation that she was a magician, or something else.

"Do you suppose that's what it was," he asked at last.

"What what was?"

"Do you think I was drawn to Twin Falls on purpose? That it was a trap?"

"I don't know," she answered. "I don't have enough facts. I need to know more about what happened to you and why you were journeying to Twin Falls."

Once again, he didn't answer right away. He gnawed the bone of his rabbit, tearing off the last of the meat. He washed it down with more wine and then looked at her again.

"I had a dream," he said. "The Duke of Twin Falls called out to me, saying I must come to visit him. He said it was important, that my destiny was at hand. I had no idea what it meant. I laughed it off in the morning, figuring it was just some wishful thinking on my part.

"But then I went to the blacksmith that afternoon. He'd been forging me a new sword, but it wasn't ready. He apologized, saying he'd burned his hand yesterday and so hadn't been able to work. It would be a few days before he was healed enough to complete the job.

"When he said that, I remembered something else from the dream. The duke told me I would see three signs to know his message was real. The first was, 'The weapons of old will have to suffice.' The fact that my new sword wasn't ready made me think of that.

"The next sign came true almost immediately afterward. I asked the blacksmith for details on his accident, and he pointed to his furnace and said his apprentice had over-stoked it.

"The second clue leaped into my mind. His hand was red and sore from the burn he'd sustained. The sign from my dream was, 'The man with the red hand points to danger.'"

Fascination blew through Liliana's mind like a strong wind. She'd been right. This was every bit as intriguing as unraveling the mystery of Calibot Middleton's mission to inherit his father's legacy.

"What was the third sign?" she asked.

"'A friend stands by without question,'" he answered.

"What does that mean?"

"Well, I was already disturbed by the first two things coming true," Garrick said. "I met my friend, Marcus, at our favorite tavern, but I was afraid to say anything about my vision."

"Why?"

"Because I didn't want him to think I was crazy," he said. "Strange dreams that come to pass may be everyday occurrences for a sorcerer, but for soldiers like us, they are signs that madness is setting in. Especially in the army of Lord Malach. You must know how he feels about magic."

"But you did tell," she said.

He looked away from her again. His gaze drifted into the fire, as though whatever he was seeking could be found in the glowing coals.

"Yes," he admitted.

"Why? What changed your mind?"

"When I first sat down," Garrick said, returning his attention to Liliana, "he said he had news. He told me the Duke of Twin Falls was ill. Furthermore, he told me the duke has no heirs. If he died without a successor being named, it would plunge the city into chaos. Marcus intimated there could be a war."

"But how did that make you think your dream was coming true?" she said. "What did that have to do with the third sign?"

"When I heard the duke was dying, I couldn't help but think about the dream," Garrick said. "He told me to come to Twin Falls to fulfill my destiny. I'd never thought about having a destiny before, but after seeing all these things from my dream coming true, it made perfect sense.

"So I said to Marcus, 'We should go to Twin Falls.' And he said, 'Okay.' No questions. No hesitation. He was just willing to do it. That's when I knew all this was real."

He fell silent again. His eyes practically begged Liliana not to tell him he was crazy. She let what he said drift through her mind without trying to knit it together. She just absorbed it.

"And you were ambushed when you got to Twin Falls?" she said after a minute.

"We never made it to the city," he replied. "We were a day's ride from Twin Falls when they fell on us. As you said, goblins are tricky, and they are fierce fighters. There were four of us – my friends Kaladriel and Benmark came too. But despite the fact that we were four experienced warriors from Lord Malach's guard, we were no match for them.

Marcus was killed in the first assault. Seconds later, they were all over us. Their shaman petrified me with magic. Then it was like I already told you. They threw a sack over my head and knocked me out. I don't know what happened to Kaladriel and Benmark, but I assume they are dead too.

"I awoke when the goblins started driving nails into my wrists. . . ."

His voice trailed away, lost in the horror of the memory. Liliana continued to let his story whirl around her mind.

"Where were you coming from?" she asked after another moment.

"Lord Malach's fortress," he answered. "We were soldiers-for-hire in Lord Malach's guard."

She nodded. She sensed everything she needed to know was contained in the story he told. At the moment, though, the vision wouldn't crystallize.

"I believe you do have a destiny, Garrick," she said. "You were summoned from an ordinary life as a soldier for Lord Malach to come to Twin Falls. On your way, you were ambushed by goblins, who slaughtered your friends but spared you so they could sacrifice you in a dark ritual. Before they could succeed, I happened to come along and rescue you, preserving you for whatever this destiny is. That all speaks to some higher purpose. I don't know what you're supposed to do or why. But I believe we need to get you to Twin Falls."

Garrick nodded. He drank another swallow of wine.

"If you say so," he said. "I don't know what's happening, but I have friends to avenge."

"Your friends are dead because someone wanted you," Liliana said. "Any vengeance is best served by first understanding why you were to be sacrificed in the first place. And the answer to that question lies in Twin Falls."

He nodded again. Then he made a move to get up, but he only rose a few inches before he collapsed again.

"For the moment, though," Liliana said, "you need to convalesce. Whatever they did to you on that crucifix clearly requires more treatment than simply feeding you. Rest now. I'll watch over you. When you're well enough to travel, we'll go find your destiny."

This time, he didn't nod. He only nestled back into the blankets. A moment later, he closed his eyes and was asleep.

Liliana's heart pounded with excitement. While she felt sorry for her new friend, given his loss and trauma, and while she was worried about a goblin ambush, the prospect of digging into a new mystery was appealing.

After turning away from his father's legacy and giving *Wyrmblade* to Sear, King of Dragons, Calibot had married Devon Middleton and settled into a quiet life as Duke Boordin's *poet laureate* in Dalasport. She was happy for him, but she'd eventually grown bored and set off in search of new adventures.

She'd found one at last.

Chapter 4:

Finish the Sacrifice

KREMDOR STOOD BEFORE THE magical fire in the *sanctum sanctorum* of his tower and fortress, The Krem. The flames shifted between blue, green, and purple, and the smoke drifted upward and out a vent at the top in blue-grey curtains. Glowing on the vapors were the images of Gursh, King of Goblins, and his chief advisor, Kraven.

They were an amusing contrast. Gursh was enormous, thick at the waist and the shoulders, a combination of powerful muscle and soft fat. The former was a testament to his youth, beating and scratching his way up the hierarchy of the tribe. The latter spoke of his allowing the comforts of his position to get to him. If he continued on this path, a younger lieutenant would one day become ambitious enough to supplant him.

For the moment, he wore his iron crown proudly on a head that resembled a boulder – round and hard. He had a small nose for a goblin, and that allowed his large, yellow eyes to gleam imperiously over all he surveyed. In middle age, he remained a fierce warrior whom no one yet dared to challenge.

Kraven, on the other hand, was rail thin. Where Gursh was muscular, he was slight. Where Gursh's head was round, his was elongated.

He had an enormous nose that dominated his face, and he looked like a threat to no one. But he was wise and crafty and clever, and he was the most accomplished sorcerer Gursh had at his disposal. He might have been a runt by goblin standards, but Kraven was in no more danger of being challenged than his king.

If their physical forms were contrasting, though, they appeared united in purpose. The two stood before their scrying station, looking both humble and defiant as they reported to their ultimate master.

"Explain to me again," Kremdor said, "how Garrick Tremaine was able to escape."

"My soldiers were ambushed," Gursh said.

"By a sorcerer," Kraven added.

Kremdor contemplated that. Goblins were crafty as a species, and Gursh was cleverer than most. If he said his minions were defeated by a single sorcerer, there was every reason to believe him. A talented magician could make short work of a goblin band.

Of course, goblins were also inveterate liars, so Kremdor was certain there was something he wasn't being told.

"Why would a sorcerer ambush your soldiers?" he asked.

"I don't know the answer to that," Gursh said. "I'm torturing the soldier in charge to make sure I know what happened. He claims they were gathered around the cross, when she attacked them with magic."

"He also claims half their number were killed instantly," Kraven said.

"But why would she attack them in the first place?" Kremdor asked.

"He says he doesn't know," Gursh said. "They were caught completely unawares."

There was disgust in his voice. Kremdor wasn't surprised. Gursh prided himself on being the trickiest goblin of them all. It must have galled him for a single human to have successfully ambushed his soldiers.

That didn't answer the question, though, and it was that mystery that worried Kremdor. He supposed it was possible that the woman had just happened upon the crucifixion and decided to intervene. A band of goblins was murdering a human, after all.

But Kremdor didn't believe in accidents. For a powerful wizard to come along just as the goblins were conducting a dark ritual in a secluded grove off the main road smacked of some other force at work. If that were true, the whole operation might be in trouble. Perhaps the gods themselves opposed Kremdor's ultimate plan.

He decided, though, that there was no sense worrying about such things. If the gods were aligned against him, there was little he could about it. The only options were to abandon his plans or move ahead anyway. Given that he couldn't know if otherworldly forces were working against him, it seemed foolish to give up his goals. That would be a waste of a lot of effort over probably nothing.

Still, there were variables he needed to control.

"This is an unfortunate failure, Gursh," he said. "I need Tremaine dead."

"I understand, my lord," Gursh said.

"No, you don't," Kremdor countered. "I sent him a dream, enticing him to Twin Falls. I made him believe in a destiny he didn't know he had. If I'd left him where he was, he'd have been no danger to my plans.

"But I drew him out, because you needed the Essence of Royalty to infuse Gruul's corporeal form, to make it possible for him to escape his bonds. I held up my end of the bargain. I delivered the sacrifice you needed. You were supposed to kill him, so he would not be able to interfere further, so he could not fulfill the destiny that lies before him. You failed me."

"You're not the only one at a loss here, Lord Kremdor," Gursh said. "The escape of the human jeopardizes my plans too."

Kremdor raised his eyebrows. Gursh must have been feeling especially bold today to speak so disrespectfully. He probably thought he was safe, since he was in his lair beneath Twin Falls. Fool. He had no idea how far Kremdor could reach.

"Don't address me in that tone, Gursh," Kremdor growled. "You may be King of Goblins, but I command the forces of the universe. And I have grander plans than releasing your foul god from his chains."

"We mean no disrespect, Lord Kremdor," Kraven simpered. "King Gursh only means this failure is as hurtful to us as it is to you. Without the human's essence, we may not be able to accomplish *our* objective of freeing Gruul."

Kremdor smiled to himself. Kraven was well named. He wanted no part of a contest with Kremdor.

"Your situation is not a dire as you think," Kremdor said. "You obtained some of Tremaine's royal essence. It may be that you have enough to satisfy the first requirement of breaking your god's chains."

"But we can't know for sure," Kraven said.

18

"Then I suggest you recapture Tremaine," Kremdor said, restraining himself from shouting. "Prevent him from fulfilling his destiny and instead have him serve ours."

"But how?" Gursh said. "We've no idea where he is."

Kremdor shook his head. Gursh was both intelligent and crafty, but he had no vision. He was a deadly instrument, but he had to be aimed.

"He will continue to Twin Falls," Kremdor said, "likely accompanied by the sorcerer who rescued him. If he was on the cross as long as you say, he will be extremely weak. She'll have to nurse him back to health, and he'll be vulnerable when he does make it to the city. Find him, kill her, and finish the sacrifice. Then you'll be certain you have the essence you need, and he'll be out of my way."

"Twin Falls is a large city, my lord," Gursh said. "How will we find him?"

"He'll be at the feast, you idiot!" Kremdor shouted, finally losing his temper. He took a moment to compose himself. "If he is not, he will go to the palace shortly after arriving in the city. He believes he has been summoned by the duke to fulfill his destiny. He will therefore naturally seek his answers from the throne. When he shows, kill him.

"I want Garrick Tremaine dead, Gursh. That was your part of the bargain. The duke has died with no apparent heirs. That is creating chaos as the guilds, the military, and the court all vie for control of Twin Falls's future. If Tremaine discovers his birthright, they'll unite behind him. And that dashes my plans.

"So find him. Find the last heir to the throne of Twin Falls and sacrifice him on the altar of your dark god. That way, we both get what we want."

"Yes, my lord," Gursh said.

"Now go. I have work to attend, and so do you."

Kremdor ended the spell before Gursh and Kraven could sign off. He was tired of talking to them. He had no objection to working with goblins or any other creature to accomplish his ends, and his recent failure notwithstanding, Gursh was a useful and reliable ally.

But the presence of this sorcerer concerned him. Whomever she was, she needed to be eliminated quickly. She had not been part of the original scheme, and that made her a wildcard that could destroy everything.

"What do you make of this sorcerer, Isadore?" he asked his familiar.

The giant bat detached herself from the rafters overhead and dropped neatly onto a nearby table. She flapped her wings once and then settled comfortably next to an iron bowl.

"It is a chance encounter," she screeched. "The woman happened along at the perfect time."

"The crucifixion was staged well off the road," Kremdor countered. "What was she doing there?"

"Who knows? Perhaps the guild sent her out to fetch something?"

"Maybe," Kremdor said. "But whether she was there by design or chance, she interrupted the ritual. Now, Garrick Tremaine is still in play."

"Gursh will recapture him," the bat replied. "He's quite capable."

Kremdor nodded. Isadore soothed his fears. This was likely an extraordinary piece of bad luck.

But he needed it undone. If Garrick Tremaine learned who he really was, the entire operation would fall apart.

CHAPTER 5:

A Contest of Succession

GARRICK AWOKE THE NEXT morning feeling more like himself. His wrists and feet still ached from the wounds of his crucifixion, and he was ravenously hungry and cold. But his strength had returned somewhat, and he was tired of lying in blankets wondering what would happen to him. He was ready for action – any sort of action at all.

The sorcerer, Liliana, did not have a rabbit roasting over the fire this morning. However, she had apparently caught two small birds she was cooking for their breakfast. Whatever else this woman was, she was an excellent hunter.

"Ah, you're awake," she said. "How are you feeling this morning?"

"Much better, thank you," he said.

He studied her for the first time with a mind that wasn't addled with fever or trauma. He'd never met a magician before – he was a soldier-for-hire in the employ of a warlord. Lord Malach didn't like wizards. His fortress was too close to the tower of the late Gothemus Draco, who had dominated the world with his sorcery. Indeed, Malach had established a garrison at the ruins of the tower to prevent anyone from looting it and inflicting more of Gothemus's horrors on The Known world.

Malach's home also bordered the Wild Lands, where all manner of fell creatures, including dragons, lived. He had no love or trust of magic, so he did not allow it within his walls.

And even before working for Lord Malach, sorcerers were not the sorts of people Garrick associated with. He was a simple man. He understood steel and battle. Mysterious, eldritch power was best left to be contemplated by those with the intellect to do so. And even then Garrick wasn't sure harnessing it was a good idea.

He didn't know what he should have expected in a sorcerer. He'd heard all the *clichés* about robes with stars on them and pointy hats. Liliana didn't look anything like that. She had long, thick, curly, blonde hair that was poorly groomed. She looked as though she hadn't washed or combed it in weeks. Her skin was pale and her eyes were bright green, but her face was plain. She wore a long, brown, woolen dress with an "X" cross-stitched over the bodice, and a blue, heavy, traveling cloak. A small, grey stone bound with a leather cord hung around her neck. She could have been anyone. She didn't look at all like a woman who could command the forces of the universe.

"Breakfast should be ready soon," she said. "And then, if you're feeling up to it, we should probably move out."

"Where?"

"Twin Falls, silly," she said. "We need to find out about this destiny of yours."

Garrick sighed. He still wasn't completely sure he believed in this destiny, and given that it had resulted in the murder of his friends and his own near-crucifixion, he wasn't sure he wanted any further part of it.

"I don't suppose you found my clothes when you rescued me," he said.

"I'm sorry, no," she replied. "You were naked on the cross. There were six goblins around you, but the only clothes were the animal pelts they were wearing."

She removed the birds from the pan, inspected them, and decided they were done. He stared incredulously at her. She didn't seem to have anything to add to her comments about the absence of his clothes.

"Well, I'm not sure I can travel then," he said.

"Why not?" she said, offering him a bird.

Garrick couldn't believe it. Was she serious?

"Because aside from the fact that it's too cold to go around naked," he answered, "polite society frowns on public nudity. I won't be allowed into the city without clothes, and I'd be arrested if we somehow managed it."

"Oh," she said, as though it were some casual fact, not an actual concern.

She put the bird back and turned to him. She waved her right hand, which glowed green for a moment. Then the blankets he was swaddled in did too, growing warm. They floated up into the air, molded themselves to him, and with a final flash of light, became a tunic and a pair of trousers. The fit was perfect.

Garrick stared at his new garments, astonished. He looked back at Liliana with his mouth agape.

"How did you do that?" he said, even though he knew the answer.

"I told you," she said. "I'm a wizard. It's magic."

She smiled at him and offered him the bird again. He took it cautiously. He was grateful to her for rescuing him, healing him. But he'd never seen sorcery before, and it scared him.

"Thank you," he said.

"You're welcome," she replied. "I'm not sure I can do boots for you. I don't really have anything for decent soles, and fitting them is much harder. But I've got some wool socks we can put on you to keep your feet warm, and you can ride Percy to Twin Falls, so you don't get wet. I'll buy you some boots and whatever else you need once we get to the city."

"Thank you," he said again. "But you're under no obligation."

"Well, of course, I am," she said. "If I don't take care of you, you'll likely die out here in the wilderness. If I was going to let that happen, I may as well have left you on that cross."

Garrick didn't know what to say. He was not used to accepting charity, and it wasn't like he was a rich man or a lord who could repay her. Helpless to do anything else, he thanked her again.

They ate in silence. The bird tasted good, but it was way too small to satisfy his appetite. When he'd finished it, he was still hungry, and he yearned for more. But he didn't dare to ask for anything. He was already too much in this woman's debt.

When she was finished, she dug into her saddle bags and produced the socks she'd promised him. They were indeed warm, but they itched a little, and they irritated the wounds on his feet. The flesh had closed and scar tissue was forming, but they were still sore, and the socks were

23

uncomfortable over them. He thanked her anyway, because it beat having his extremities exposed to the cold.

Standing proved more difficult than he'd imagined it would. If he'd thought the socks irritated his wounds, standing on them was worse. It was difficult to put weight on his feet. Additionally, while he did feel better, especially after breakfast, he remained weak. He'd taken only two steps before dizziness assailed him, and a desire for rest beckoned him to collapse.

Liliana caught his arm and draped it over her shoulder. She assisted him over to the horse and helped him into the saddle. By the time he was mounted, he had no energy left.

"Here," she said, handing him the blanket she'd used as a bed. "You can use this as a cloak."

He accepted it gratefully and at least felt warm as she doused the fire and broke camp. Then she took the horse's reins and led him out of the woods and back towards the road to Twin Falls.

They reached the city in mid-afternoon. Garrick had never seen it before, and it was even more amazing than he'd heard.

It sat on a large butte that overlooked the plain. Gargantuan in size, Twin Falls covered the entirety of the rise with walls that were rumored to be thirty feet high. Garrick couldn't say if they were indeed that tall or if they just seemed that way due to the mesa on which they sat, but any enemy would have difficulty scaling them to reach the city within.

The spires of tall buildings rose over its ramparts, gleaming in the afternoon sun. The palace was visible too. Garrick had never seen one so enormous – from this distance it appeared to dwarf Lord Malach's entire fortress.

As magnificent as the city itself appeared, though, the natural feature for which it was named dwarfed its splendour. To the east, the Rapid River and to the west the Winding River flowed south from the Northern Range Mountains. They nearly met at Twin Falls, but before they could join, both spilled over a great precipice that dropped two hundred feet into Crystal Lake below. The roar of the water over the falls was deafening.

The city sat between the two rivers and against the cliff. It was only approachable from its northern face. Assaulting it would be nearly impossible. As a solider, Garrick was impressed with Twin Falls's strategic positioning. As a man, it took his breath away.

"I'm glad we got here when we did," Liliana said. "They take the gates up at night."

By "gates," she meant a massive drawbridge that spanned the Rapid River. Garrick presumed it had a twin on the western face that enabled access across the Winding River. Here too his soldier's mind approved. The city could be approached unimpeded only from the north. Therefore, no gates were placed on that wall. You could get in only by crossing one of the two rivers.

Liliana led the horse across the bridge and through the arch. The brilliant defenses continued. Iron portcullises flanked the arch, which was approximately fifty feet across. Holes in the roof allowed defenders to pour oil down on invaders who somehow managed to penetrate the first portcullis. Garrick could not imagine this city ever falling.

Inside, it was typically fast-paced. Garrick had been to Dalasport, and inside the walls, Twin Falls reminded him greatly of Duke Boordin's city-state. Every kind of merchant was working the streets – some of them charlatans, some of them with legitimate stands. Armed patrols weaved among the people, and everyone seemed to be moving.

Liliana was unbothered by the constant commotions swirling around her as she led her horse, with Garrick atop it, through a maze of streets. Garrick couldn't tell if she knew where she was going, or if she was wandering wherever her feet took her. She didn't push her way through crowds or look for a particular turn or intersection. She just walked, a beatific expression on her face as she turned her head back and forth, gazing at the sights.

Before long, she found a livery stable and paid a boy to take the horse from her. She assisted Garrick down.

Despite not having to walk all morning, it was still painful to stand. Garrick limped slowly to a block outside the stable, and Liliana eased him down onto it.

"I'll be back," she said and started off.

"Wait!" Garrick shouted. She turned back. "Where are you going?"

"You're still too weak to walk," she answered as though he hadn't noticed. "I'll get you some salves and maybe a healing potion. Twin Falls has a powerful wizard's guild. I should be able to buy everything we need to fix you up."

He didn't like being left alone, but he didn't see that he had a choice. He couldn't go on as he was, which meant Liliana had to find care for him. He felt vulnerable, though, and he watched every single person who went past, assessing them as threats.

Half an hour later, she returned wearing a smile.

"Good news," she said. "I got more than I was hoping for. There's a healing draught, which should take care of your immediate needs, and I also picked up some cakes and a salve we can apply when we get you to an inn. They'll make you sleepy, so you can't take them right away, but you should be much better in the morning."

She handed him a gourd. He looked at it uncertainly.

"I know you worked for Lord Malach," she said, "but don't worry. Just because it's magic doesn't make it dangerous."

Trying to look braver than he felt, he unstoppered the small jug and sniffed. His nose wrinkled in disgust immediately.

"This smells like sewer water," he said.

"That's the herbs," she replied. "It tastes worse, I bet."

Garrick glared at her, but she continued to smile.

"Drink up," she said. "It'll make you feel better, and then we can get going. We need to get you some supplies and find an inn before nightfall."

He sighed and lifted the gourd to his lips. She'd been right. It tasted worse than the smell – like flowers that had been rotting for the better part of a month.

"Don't spit it out," she said when she saw his face twist in disgust. "And make sure you drink it all. You were hurt badly, and I still don't know the full extent of what they did to you."

Garrick struggled to obey. He putrescence and rot filled his nostrils, assaulted his taste buds. Gooseflesh popped on his skin, and his gag reflex warned him that, if he continued, he would vomit it all back up.

Somehow, he managed to keep going. He summoned the very last of his will to force the final revolting drop down his throat.

He threw the gourd to the ground and wiped his mouth. Then he spit, trying to get rid of the disgusting taste.

"That stuff better work," he said. "That was one of the worst experiences of my life. In fact, being crucified is the only thing I can think of that was worse."

"With any luck, you won't have to repeat either," she replied. "How do you feel?"

He opened his mouth to retort, when he realized he was indeed feeling better. He'd been exhausted and weak before. He suddenly felt as though he could do something.

Carefully, he stood. His feet didn't hurt in the same way. They were still sore, but the pain was manageable. He took a few tentative steps forward. He was steady. It wasn't agony to walk.

"Better," he said. "Much better, actually."

"Good," she said. "Let's get you outfitted before the sun goes down and all the shops close."

Garrick nodded. He didn't know what else to do but follow her orders. He remained astounded. She'd rescued him from an horrific death. She'd tended him in his initial convalescence. Now she had healed him further at her own expense and was planning to buy him supplies to get him back on his feet. She was extraordinary.

"Liliana," he said, "don't think me ungrateful, but how are you affording this? You don't look like a rich woman."

She laughed. He was beginning to enjoy that sound. Liliana Gray sounded happy whenever she found something amusing. In his grim life as a soldier, that was a rare personality trait.

"I served in Duke Boordin's court in Dalasport," she answered.

"Really? You don't seem like a courtier."

"I'm not really," she said. "I tried it for about two years, and decided it wasn't the life for me. But the duke was extremely grateful to me for returning his *poet laureate* to him, and he didn't have a magician to advise him when I arrived. He figured having Gothemus Draco's former apprentice was a boon."

Garrick's heart stopped. Had she just said what he thought she had?

"Wait," he said. "You were Gothemus Draco's apprentice?"

"Mm-hmm," she said as though it were nothing.

"You're the Liliana who brought Gothemus's son, Calibot, *Wyrmblade* and helped him defeat the Council of Elders?"

"Yes," she said, still looking at him placidly.

Garrick blanched. He hadn't witnessed any of these events, but everyone knew about them. Gothemus had been murdered by Eldenberg's Council of Elders in an attempt to wrest the Eye of the Dragon and control of The Wild Lands from him and his warlord brother, Zod. Calibot stole his father's body, transported it to Silver Lake, and then cast some sort of spell that let him into the tower. When he emerged, he was powerful enough to

27

conquer the world, but he chose instead to give the sword to the King of Dragons.

And Liliana had been by his side the whole time? Just how powerful was she? And why was she interested in Garrick?

"We need to get going," she said. "The sun is already getting low in the sky. If we don't hurry, we won't be able to get it all done before nightfall."

Wordlessly, he followed her. He'd found himself admiring Liliana Gray up until this point. Now he was afraid of her. What kind of trouble had he gotten himself into?

They spent the rest of the afternoon visiting several craftsmen. Liliana bought him fresh clothes and took him to a cobbler, who sold Garrick a comfortable pair of boots. Then she brought him to a smith, who didn't have any armor in Garrick's size, but he had a nice selection of weapons. Garrick found a sword that was weighted correctly for him and felt guilty when Liliana shelled out fifteen silver coins for it.

The smith sized them up as he took Liliana's money.

"I suppose you're here for the contest," he said.

"What contest?" Liliana said.

"And what makes you say that?" Garrick added.

"I've never seen either of you before," the smith said. "Most of my customers have been coming to me for years. Especially the ones who want armor and weapons. Unless you're new in the military and someone recommended me, you're strangers."

"You're very observant," Liliana said.

The smith scowled at her. Like most people of his trade, he was covered in soot and grease. He had a broad face and a receding hairline.

"What about this contest?" Garrick said.

"You must have just got to town if you haven't heard," the smith answered.

"Actually, that's true," Garrick said. "We just arrived this afternoon. We're resupplying because we were ambushed by goblins."

The smith stared at him, apparently trying to determine if he were telling the truth. After a moment, he nodded.

"You're lucky to be alive then," he said. "Goblins aren't renowned for their mercy."

"No," Garrick agreed. "Three of my companions didn't survive."

"My condolences," the smith said. "Dirty, little bastards. They've been bad lately. There's rumors they're in the city."

Liliana stopped examining his wares when he said that. She turned to him.

"Really?" she said. "Goblins within the city walls?"

"They're just rumors," he said, trying to put the issue to rest. "No one I know has actually seen one. With the duke's death, there've been a lot of crazy things said. Everyone's spooked, fearing there'll be some sort of succession war."

"The duke's dead?" Garrick said.

He was unable to hide his astonishment. He'd assumed his dream meant he was called here to serve the Duke of Twin Falls. To hear that he was dead threw out completely what little understanding Garrick had of this strange situation.

"Yes, may the gods bless his soul," the smith said. "He'd been sick for weeks. He passed away three days ago."

"Long live the duke," Garrick said.

"Well, that's the problem," the smith replied. "We don't have one."

"What!" Garrick and Liliana said in unison.

"There is no heir," the smith said. "So right now, no one is in charge officially. Well, that's not true. Chancellor Bismarck is running the government until a new duke is named. But he won't be able to do it forever."

"Why not?" Liliana asked.

"Because with no clear line of succession, everyone with a stake in Twin Falls's future wants a shot at taking over," the smith explained. "The military, the guilds, and the courtiers all think they have the best vision for where to go from here. The chancellor can hold them at bay for awhile, but you know how power-hungry people get when there's a vacuum. Sooner or later – and you can bet it will be sooner – someone's going to get itchy. Someone's going to decide they can take the throne for themselves. Then there'll be a war."

"So how long do you figure the chancellor has?" Garrick asked.

His nerves were singing. His soldier's mind was sharp and focused. He knew this wasn't his problem, but he couldn't help assessing risk and determining strategy.

"Well, he's bought himself some time with this contest," the smith said. "If that comes out okay, there probably won't be any trouble. But if it doesn't resolve quickly . . ."

"You keep mentioning a contest," Liliana said. "What is it?"

"A Contest of Succession," he answered. "Chancellor Bismarck has made an open call to any who would aspire to be Duke of Twin Falls. He will gather them together, and then ask a riddle. The person who can solve it will show he or she has the wisdom to rule and be awarded the crown."

"What is this riddle?" Liliana asked.

"No one knows," the smith said. "He's been very cagey about it, but the rumor is it will involve more than just knowing the answer. The winner must also show courage and cunning and strength. It's not just a puzzle; it's a whole task you have to figure out and complete."

"How does one do that?" Garrick asked.

"No one knows," the smith said again. "And that's the problem. The chancellor is holding off a succession war temporarily. But it's not clear how one wins this contest or how difficult it will be. If it takes a long time for someone to solve the riddle, or if no one solves it all, you can bet there will be a war.

"And of course, there's no guarantee everyone will accept the outcome. If the crown is earned by someone the rest of the interested parties don't like– if the guilds or the military or even the courtiers don't respect the winner – there may be a war anyway."

Neither Garrick nor Liliana offered comment. The smith's tale was so extraordinary it hardly seemed it could be true. Garrick had never heard anything like it – a monarch with no heir dies, and his crown is put up in a contest and awarded to whomever can solve a puzzle? Who would do such a thing?

"When is the chancellor expected to call together all the aspirants?" Liliana asked.

"There's a feast at the palace tonight," the smith replied. "That's why I assumed you were here for the contest. I figured you thought you had a shot to be duke and were looking for a fancy new sword to wear to dinner."

"So *anyone* can apply?" Garrick said. He remained astounded.

"Officially," the smith said. "Of course, it's only an open contest technically. The guilds are each backing a particular contestant, and General Calavan intends to compete as well. I'm sure at least one of the nobles is also planning to participate. Any freelancers will get squeezed out."

"What do you mean?" Garrick asked.

"Neither the guilds nor the military is going to willingly cede control of Twin Falls to a stranger," the smith said. "If someone they don't know, like, or trust enters the contest, that person will surely meet with a bad end *before* getting a chance to solve the riddle."

"That makes sense," Garrick commented.

"Assuming the so-called freelancer isn't too powerful for them," Liliana said.

Garrick and the smith both stared at her. She didn't seem to notice. Her expression was faraway, as though she were sifting all the details of what she'd heard.

"Thank you, my friend," Garrick said. "These are strange times, indeed."

"Yes, they are," the smith said. "If I were you, I'd take that fancy, new sword and the rest of your supplies and get out of Twin Falls before it becomes a very dangerous place. Until this is settled once and for all, strangers are unlikely to be welcome."

Garrick nodded. He tied the sword Liliana had bought him onto his new belt, thanked the smith again and walked away. Liliana raced after him.

"I think we've found your destiny," she said, when she caught up.

"What?"

"Think about it, Garrick," she said. "The late duke came to you in a dream and told you to come to Twin Falls to find your destiny. You were ambushed by goblins on your way here, your friends were killed, and you were crucified in a dark ritual. I just happened to come along in time to save you. Now we arrive on the eve of this contest to determine a new duke. I think that's why you're here."

"Why?"

"To win the contest!" she said. "To become the new duke!"

"I don't know anything about ruling a city," he protested. "Especially this one! I've never even been here before."

"That doesn't matter," Liliana countered. "You were called here by the late duke. He meant for you to succeed him."

"You don't know that!" Garrick said. "He said to come to Twin Falls. He said to find my destiny. He didn't say to become the new duke."

"Now you're just splitting hairs."

"I'm not," he argued. "And even if I were, you heard what the blacksmith said. The powers-that-be will make certain a stranger doesn't win the contest. If I attend that feast and attempt to solve the riddle, I'm as good as dead."

31

"I'll protect you with my magic," she said.

"Damn it, Liliana," he said, "I'm not the son of Gothemus Draco or anyone else important. I don't *have* a destiny. I'm just a soldier-for-hire. And I don't want to put my nose where it doesn't belong. That only leads to trouble."

Her green eyes searched him. A sad expression camped on her face.

"You already made the decision 'to put your nose where it doesn't belong' when you left Lord Malach to come here," she said. "And you've already got trouble. Your friends were murdered because the goblins wanted *you*, Garrick. If you weren't important, they wouldn't have preserved you for a dark ritual. They'd have just killed you with the rest.

"I don't know whose son you are, but there is some magical force at work on you, Garrick Tremaine. The duke summoned you here, and you answered. Goblins attempted to stop you. It all means something.

"Even if it isn't your destiny to become the new duke, I believe you must enter this contest. The answers to whatever's happening to you are found within it."

Garrick wanted to strike her, wanted to rage in her face that she was mad and that he was not the sort of person this happened to. But she had saved him. He'd be dead if it hadn't been for her. Moreover, she'd paid to re-outfit him. And unless he left right now before the gates were closed for the night, he would need her to provide him with accommodations.

He sighed. Why was this happening to him? He was a mercenary, not a hero. Not a prince. He supposed it didn't matter, though. Destiny, if that's truly what it was, was upon him.

"All right," he said at last. "What do we do then?"

"First, we need to attend that feast tonight," she said. "That means we need to go to the palace. We'd better hurry."

The sky had turned pink with the setting sun. It would be night soon. He put a grim expression on his face.

"I hope the food is good at this thing," he said.

CHAPTER 6:

The Blessing of the Fey

T HE FEAST WASN'T AS crowded as Liliana had expected. She'd have thought, with an open tournament to determine who would be the next duke of one of the Known World's giant city-states, there'd be a large crowd of hopefuls. Aside from whomever the various factions within Twin Falls's political circles were putting up, she'd have thought there would be any number of adventurers, fortune-seekers, and would-be tyrants applying.

But besides Garrick, whom she had to practically force to enter, there were only eight other candidates. The easiest to spot was General Calavan. He wore a smart, sky-blue jacket, with gold epaulets and a grass-green cloak that was also fringed with gold. His white trousers were tucked into black boots, and he had fifteen or sixteen medals pinned to his left breast. He wore a ridiculously fancy sword on his left hip attached to a large, black belt. The only sword Liliana had ever seen that had beat it for ostentation was *Wyrmblade*.

Calavan strutted around the great hall of the palace with his chest thrust out and a disapproving look on his face. A large entourage of adjutants and honor guards followed him wherever he went. He looked both proud and uncomfortable.

Four other contestants were clearly backed by Twin Falls's powerful guilds. A wizard, who reminded Liliana a lot of Gothemus – long, white beard and hair, blue robes with tiny, white stars, a matching conical hat – stood among others dressed similarly. He nodded politely to everyone who passed him and spent the rest of his time attempting to look smarter than everyone else in the room.

There was a large man, built even more powerfully than the smith who'd told them about the contest. He wore a sleeveless green tunic and a tan pair of pants tucked into sensible, brown boots. Liliana thought he was a little underdressed – both for the occasion and the weather – but the only part of him that wasn't covered in thick, black hair was his head, which was completely bald. A bushy beard, with just the first traces of steel-grey, grew from his face in every direction and looked like it hadn't been combed since his first day of adolescence. He stood with his arms crossed and glared at everyone, surrounded by others who were obviously laborers.

A third man was covered in rich clothes, a broad hat with a giant feather, and enough gold chains and rings to buy virtually everything his competitors for the throne owned. He had a long, blonde mustache he had waxed into curls. Liliana wanted to laugh at the sight of him, he was so ridiculous.

And finally, there was a short woman with close cut, red hair. Dressed in nondescript clothing, she talked amiably with a small group of strange-looking characters. One was lanky and had hair going in every direction. Another was nearly as short as she, with perfectly braided, blonde hair. A third was Garrick's height but rotund and with restrained mid-length, grey hair with a leather headband. All of them wore all-black, kept their hands on the hilts of their swords, and watched everyone else in the room.

Liliana had heard rumors that Twin Falls actually supported a thieves' guild. If that was true, this woman absolutely had to be their representative.

Aside from the five candidates who obviously had a powerful organization behind them, there were three freelancers. One man associated with no one. His eyes darted furtively around the room, and he fidgeted nervously with a coin.

Another was a warrior with a group of friends. They talked loudly and drank a lot.

But the eighth and final contestant caught Liliana's eye as soon as she entered the great hall. It was Vicia Morrigan. A former member of Eldenberg's Council of Elders, she had masterminded Gothemus's murder. When the tide turned against her, she'd offered to betray the Council and become Duke Boordin's magic advisor. Calibot and Devon had turned her down. As expected, she'd been expelled from the Council and had had to flee Eldenberg to escape justice.

She was an accomplished sorcerer, and she was as wicked a woman as Liliana had ever met. She was also power-hungry. If Vicia was here to compete for the crown, she would stop at nothing to win. And Liliana could well imagine the sort of tyranny that would result from any reign as duchess by Vicia Morrigan.

When she spotted the disgraced Elder, Liliana immediately attempted to slide behind Garrick, so she wouldn't be seen and recognized. She and the former Lord Vicia had never spoken, but Liliana had been by Calibot's side during their final contest. If Vicia got a good look at her, she would surely recognize her.

"What are you doing?" Garrick said.

"Shh!"

Garrick looked alarmed. He turned and faced her.

"What's the matter with you?" he said.

"Don't look," Liliana said.

"Don't look where?"

"Directly behind you."

As if he hadn't heard her, Garrick started to turn. Liliana grabbed his shirt and pulled him back.

"I said, 'Don't look!'" she hissed.

"Don't look at what?"

"One of the competitors is the woman who murdered Gothemus Draco," Liliana said.

"What!"

Garrick's voice carried through the giant room, and several people stopped talking to look at them. Liliana wanted to kill him. She gave him an exasperated look.

Garrick smiled uncomfortably at the room and tried to act like nothing important had happened. When everyone had returned to their individual conversations, he turned back to her.

"What did you say?" he asked more quietly.

"The black-haired woman in the purple dress and blue cloak with the staff is Vicia Morrigan," Liliana answered. "She's the woman who murdered Gothemus Draco."

Garrick glanced to the side, trying to get a look at her. Liliana pulled him back again.

"*Don't look!*" she growled. "I don't know want her to know I recognized her."

"You know her?" he said.

"Not personally," Liliana said. "But after she murdered my master, she tried to kill me on two separate occasions."

"What's she doing here?"

"Probably the same thing as us," Liliana said. "She aspires to be Duchess of Twin Falls."

"Damn it, Liliana," he whispered. "What have you gotten me into?"

"*I* haven't gotten you into anything," she said. "I rescued you after you got yourself into it. I'm just helping you find the destiny you seek."

Garrick opened his mouth as though he were going to say something, but he snapped it shut again. He sighed heavily.

"Come on," she said. "Let's move away from her."

She took Garrick's arm and led him gently across the floor. A moment later, she engaged the wizard in the blue robes in conversation.

Pomposity poured off him at her approach, although he gave her the same polite nod he'd offered everyone else.

"Hello," she said when they were only a few feet away from him.

The others had all turned to stare at her and examined her dismissively. Liliana smiled pleasantly. She didn't look like a magician at first glance, and she suspected that, even if she had, anyone not a member of Twin Falls's wizard's guild would be viewed as inferior.

"Greetings," the man in the blue robes said.

"So are you one of the contestants?" she asked.

His eyes narrowed, and his already conceited expression grew frosty. His mustache rose and his beard seemed to elongate.

"I am Zalachorus ir-Bedlam Donovian," he replied.

"Wow," Liliana said. "That's impressive."

"Quite," he said. "And, yes, I intend to succeed Duke Evonin."

"So are you the head of the wizard's guild?" Liliana asked.

As irritated as he was when she asked if he was one of the aspirants, his face seemed to radiate frost in response to her latest question. Garrick shifted uncomfortably from foot to foot, as if he wished he were anywhere else.

"No," Zalachorus said. "I am too young for that honor. My master, Ephraim Vendaya, holds the title of Guildmaster."

"Too young?" Liliana said.

"I am only forty-three, miss," he said, his tone growing more and more condescending. "The Illustrious Guild of Sorcery and Wisdom values experience and understanding. Any fool can become powerful. A tempered approach to applying it only comes with age. One must be fifty to be considered for such an august position as Guildmaster."

"You're only forty-three?" Garrick said. "You look at least twenty years older."

Zalachorus ir-Bedlam Donovian turned his withering gaze on Garrick for the first time. He looked on him as though he were a very stupid child.

"Magic is more than parlor tricks," Zalachorus said. "It is mastering the fundamental forces of the universe. Such things require a powerful mind, and there are prices to be paid."

"Very true," Liliana commented.

She often wondered just how much Gothemus Draco had suffered in his mad quest to dominate the Known World.

Zalachorus returned his attention to her. For the first time, he seemed to be sizing her up.

"I'm sorry," he said. "I didn't get your name."

"Oh, forgive me," she replied. "I've forgotten my manners. I'm Liliana Gray."

She watched as the pompous sorcerer studied her. He was obviously attempting to determine if he should know her name. Liliana wasn't sure if he would or not. Everyone knew who Gothemus Draco was, but the identity of his apprentice wasn't common knowledge. *Her* role in Calibot's mission to lay Gothemus to rest wasn't the part of the story people remembered.

"A pleasure," Zalachorus said at last. He showed no sign of recognizing her. "And are you also – How did you put it? – a contestant?"

"Oh, no," Liliana said. "That's not my destiny."

"Quite," Zalachorus pronounced.

"It's his," Liliana said, pointing her thumb in Garrick's direction.

If her companion had been uncomfortable during this entire conversation, he was mortified at being made the subject of it. Shock seized

Garrick's face, and he took one involuntary step back before returning to his original position.

The sorcerers, who had all dismissed him when he asked about Zalachorus's age, now looked him up and down. Each of them, but especially Zalachorus himself, gazed on Garrick as if he were a coiled snake trying to decide if he should strike.

"Destiny?" Zalachorus said at last.

"Well, I think 'destiny' is a rather strong word," Garrick said.

"Oh, no," Liliana said. "He was visited by the duke in his dreams."

Zalachorus's eyes widened. Garrick shot Liliana a glance that said, "Shut up." She ignored it.

"Duke Evonin told him to join him in Twin Falls," Liliana continued. "He said Garrick would find his destiny here."

"Hmph," Zalachorus said. "It'll take more than dreams to become duke, Mr. –?"

"Tremaine," Garrick replied. "Garrick Tremaine."

"'Tremaine,'" Zalachorus said. "I've never heard that name before."

"There's no reason you should have," Garrick replied.

"Well, Mr. Tremaine, I think you'll find being duke is more than having a dream," Zalachorus went on. "Twin Falls is a complex city, and it takes someone with wisdom *and* power to rule it."

"And I take it that's you," Garrick said, a strong hint of irritation in his tone.

"Look at the competition," Zalachorus said. "If you can call it that. Bram Dover." Zalachorus indicated the bearish-looking laborer. "A mason and Guildmaster of the Brotherhood of Craftsmen. He knows bricks and mortar and how to hold a customer hostage over price for projects. But what does he know about running the business of the city? What could he hope to do in the face of an attack?

"Or Lindsay Grunvilio," he said, nodding towards the fop with the waxed mustache. "The Twin Falls Chamber of Commerce backs him because he's rich and he owns five successful businesses. But he's only interested in *his* wealth. As long as he's making money, he doesn't care whom he exploits or what the consequences are. How could such a man be relied on to protect the people in times of need?

"And then there's Levinia Mordecai." He barely looked at the short woman Liliana believed to be part of the rumored thieves' guild. "She's a criminal. Is this the sort of person Twin Falls wants ruling? She'd empty the government's coffers for herself and her band of smugglers."

"What about General Calavan?" Liliana asked.

Zalachorus sniffed disdainfully. His eyes drifted across the room in the direction of Twin Falls's top soldier.

"He's more qualified than the others," Zalachorus allowed. "But he has no vision. He sees things only in terms of battles and wars."

"I find accomplished soldiers to be good rulers," Garrick said. "They have a keen mind for strategy and for anticipating problems that helps them solve crises."

Zalachorus gave him another of his trademark withering looks. Liliana was convinced the man thought no one in the Known World was his intellectual peer. She wondered what a meeting would have been like between Zalachorus ir-Bedlam Donovian and Gothemus Draco.

"And then there are the opportunists like yourself, Mr. Tremaine," Zalachorus went on. "Fortune-hunters with no appreciation or understanding of the intricacies of Twin Falls and its complex politics.

"It takes wisdom to rule any city-state in the Known World, and this one requires the vision and the skill to balance varied needs."

"And I suppose you're the only one smart enough to do that," Garrick said, his voice nearly a growl.

"Quite," Zalachorus said.

Liliana wasn't sure if he'd missed Garrick's sarcasm or if he didn't care. However, she thought they'd learned what they could from this conversation. It was going to become damaging if she allowed Garrick to say much more.

"Well, it was nice meeting you," Liliana said, hooking her arm in Garrick's and drawing him away. "Enjoy the feast."

"Good luck finding your . . . destiny, Mr. Tremaine," Zalachorus replied.

"That guy is an asshole," Garrick said after they'd taken only a few steps.

"A sadly not-uncommon trait among wizards," Liliana said. "One of the prices of being able to harness the fundamental forces of the universe seems to be a loss of social niceties."

"Arrogance is a deadly character flaw on the field of battle," Garrick said. "That's among the reasons Lord Malach doesn't trust sorcerers."

"I think you'll find arrogance throughout this room," Liliana commented.

"Ladies and gentlemen," a valet called. "Abrodien Bismarck, Chancellor of Twin Falls!"

The chancellor entered wearing rich robes in the same sky-blue and grass-green of General Calavan's uniform. He looked old and haunted. White hair flowed elegantly to his shoulders and was restrained by a surprisingly modest gold torq on his brow. His cheeks were flaccid and his gait hobbled, as though his bones ground in his joints with the slightest movement.

Liliana could see he was in no shape to rule for long. His mind might be bright – she didn't know yet. But his body was frail. She scanned the room quickly, looking over the major players in the succession contest. Those that gazed on him did so contemptuously. Among them was General Calavan, who stood at attention, a picture of military respect. But his eyes and expression suggested he was honoring protocol, not the chancellor. There was no enthusiasm or solemnity on his face.

Four of the aspirants, including Zalachorus ir-Bedlam Donovian, didn't even bother to pay attention. They stopped their conversations and observed the minimum decorum of silence, but that was all.

Liliana understood the smith's concern over the political situation. Chancellor Bismarck had everyone in line for the moment. But it wasn't going to last. None of Twin Falls's power brokers respected him. If this contest didn't end quickly, with a successor everyone could accept, there would be a civil war.

And since no one knew the nature of the competition, the whole thing could unravel tonight when the announcement was made.

"Please take your seats," Chancellor Bismarck said.

Everyone dashed to the grand table. Seats were not assigned, aside from the chancellor's spot at the head, so there was a mad rush for position. Vicia swept into the throng of sorcerers, and forced her way into the chair next Zalachorus Donovian. Several of his guildmates frowned, and two looked as though they might unleash vengeful magic on her right then.

General Calavan took the seat across from Zalachorus, and his retinue forced the other freelancers out of the way. Calavan sat to the chancellor's right, and Zalachorus to his left.

Bram Dover, scowled at being unable to secure a spot near the chancellor, and was forced by Calavan's officers to sit no closer than seven seats away. Lindsay Grunvilio managed to impede two of the sorcerers from taking chairs near Zalachorus and thus made it closer to the chancellor and the other leading candidates.

Liliana drew Garrick to two open seats towards the foot of the table. At least for the moment, she didn't want to get into a contest with anyone else over who was more important or who was going to win. She wanted to be unassuming, non-threatening. Garrick had already made an enemy of Zalachorus, which was fine. He was arrogant and unlikable. But she didn't want to encourage any other aspirants to hate Garrick before the contest even began.

She also wanted an opportunity to observe everyone during dinner to see if alliances were forming or if anyone appeared to have the early favor of the chancellor. Since they had just arrived in the city and were entering the contest virtually on a whim, she wanted as much information as she could gather before they had to commit.

Garrick didn't object. He simply followed her, still looking out of his depth. For the moment, she was content to let him be that person. If he appeared not to know what he was doing, no one would take him seriously. That allowed them to keep a low profile. Eventually, though, his behavior would have to change.

As soon as everyone had a place at the table, servants came out in large numbers bearing food. There were roast turkeys, venison, cheese, three kinds of bread, beans, grapes, apples, beer, wine, and cider. Liliana hadn't seen a feast like this since her days in Duke Boordin's court, and she'd never attended one on this scale. Garrick's eyes popped open at the amount of food served, and he seemed a little ashamed to take as much as he liked.

Most of the others showed no reservation. In particular, the hangers-on and the freelancers helped themselves to enormous portions, often stuffing it in their faces as fast as they could. The wealthy attendees and the powerful ate with more restraint, but the rest looked like this was more food than they expected to see in a year.

Garrick's own humility didn't last long. After a few bites of turkey, his appetite took hold of him. His body was still recovering from his ordeal, and the prospect of loading up on nutrition seemed to inspire him to eat heartily.

Liliana was hungry too, but she spent more of her time watching the other aspirants than eating. Calavan and Zalachorus spent most of the meal ignoring each other despite sitting directly opposite. When their gazes did meet, both offered the other a frosty expression of utter contempt. Likewise, Dover and Grunvilio spent much of the meal glaring at each other. Liliana supposed that rivalry made sense. Working-class craftsmen and wealthy merchants tended to have opposite views of what was good economic policy.

Levinia Mordecai didn't speak with anyone during the meal. Like Liliana, she hadn't rushed to find a seat at the table. She'd walked calmly to the feast and taken the first available chair. She ate quietly and observed the others, her eyes darting from person to person, her ears clearly tuned to multiple conversations.

She was dangerous. Indeed, she was likely the most threatening person at the table. Her dimunitive size and placid demeanor belied a sharp mind backed by a criminal organization. Calavan and Zalachorus were strong and intelligent, but Levinia was cunning. Liliana could easily imagine Levinia Mordecai outwitting everyone to get to the throne.

Of all the contestants, the most gregarious was Vicia. She spent a lot of time talking with anyone who would listen. In particular, she attempted to draw Zalachorus and Calavan into discussions. It was too noisy for Liliana to understand them. But she suspected Vicia sought to engage Zalachorus in discussions on magic and Calavan on military strategy. Having been on the Council of Elders, she had experience in both arenas.

When most of the attendees' plates were empty, a servant rang a bell. The dinner conversation died down, and Chancellor Bismarck pushed himself painfully to his feet.

"Ladies and gentlemen," he said. "On behalf of the interim government of Twin Falls, I welcome you to the grand palace. Many of you we know. Some we do not, but you are all welcome."

The chancellor's voice sounded as weak as the rest of him looked. The man appeared to be surviving on sheer willpower. Liliana wondered what would happen if he also expired before the contest concluded.

"As you know," the chancellor went on, "Duke Evonin died without naming a successor. There are no known surviving members of the duke's family. He therefore drafted a plan to provide for a proper transfer of power."

There were a number of grumblings around the table. Liliana wasn't sure if they were commenting on this being a proper transfer of power or if they didn't believe this was legitimately the duke's plan.

"According to the duke's will," Bismarck went on as though he hadn't heard the protests, "Twin Falls shall hold a Contest of Succession. Any who feel they are worthy and are willing to assume the mantle and responsibilities of serving as duke of our fair city are invited to submit their names.

"The time has come for all who wish to participate to declare their candidacies. Aspirants to the title of Duke of Twin Falls, please rise and state your name."

Vicia leaped to her feet as though her chair had bitten her. Bismarck looked startled. Zalachorus rolled his eyes.

"Vicia Morrigan," she said. "Former Elder of the Council of Eldenberg, master sorcerer, slayer of Gothemus Draco."

Liliana gaped. She'd have thought Vicia would have downplayed her role in Eldenberg's power play. Being expelled from the Council of Elders was no honor, and she hadn't slain Gothemus, she'd poisoned his drink.

But Vicia seemed to think these accomplishments would cause others to either fear or respect her, possibly both. Liliana wasn't sure if Vicia's game was reckless or calculated, but it made her more dangerous than Liliana had first believed.

"Thank you, Lord Vicia," the chancellor said.

Liliana stifled a humorless laugh. The Council had stripped Vicia of her honorific when it expelled her. Chancellor Bismarck was showing her undue respect.

"Bram Dover," the bearish laborer said, rising. "Guildmaster of the Brotherhood of Labor."

Each contestant followed Vicia's lead. They stood, gave their name, and then offered some title or remarkable accomplishment as qualification for the job, despite the fact that the chancellor hadn't asked for it. General Calavan noted he was the supreme commander of all of Twin Falls's military forces, making the position sound like a threat. Zalachorus listed his lengthy rank within the wizards' guild. Lindsay Grunvilio enumerated each of his positions with the five businesses he owned or ran, as well as his job as treasurer for the Chamber of Commerce.

The unbacked warrior introduced himself as Demetrian Tumet and claimed to have slain several monsters and fought in two battles Liliana had never heard of. His friends applauded him. The loner who'd been fidgeting with the coin earlier claimed to be Lance Edger, Master of Illusion. He didn't elaborate on what that meant.

Only Levinia Mordecai didn't affix a title or any accomplishments to herself. She stood up, gave her name, and sat back down – a welcome departure from the pomp and arrogance of the others.

When everyone else had gone, Chancellor Bismarck looked over the table. The room was quiet.

JOHN R. PHYTHYON, JR.

"Anyone else?" he prompted.

Liliana nudged Garrick. He looked at her as if to say he still didn't think this was a good idea. Then he pushed his chair back and stood up.

"Garrick Tremaine," he said. "Lately of service to Lord Malach."

He seated himself again, casting a steely gaze over the table. Now that he was in, he wasn't about to let anyone intimidate him. Good.

No one else rose. Bismarck looked around one final time.

"Last call," he said.

There were no takers. The Contest of Succession would have nine competitors.

"Very well," the chancellor said. "Entry is hereby closed. The tournament is officially open."

"Perhaps you could tell us how to play," Zalachorus said.

"Perhaps you could hold your tongue and let me explain," Bismarck shot back.

The wizard's eyes flared murderously. Liliana thought he might assassinate the chancellor on the spot and begin a war.

But he held his temper and gripped the edge of the table to steady his patience. His eyes continued to bore hatred into Bismarck's soul.

"As you know," the chancellor continued, "you will all be in direct competition with each other to prove your worthiness as monarch. However, Duke Evonin was disinterested in strength as a measuring stick. Ruling a city takes cunning and wisdom and insight.

"To that end, the late duke calls for you to solve a riddle."

Murmurs went through the great hall. The various attendants began whispering among themselves. Zalachorus had a smug look on his face, no doubt certain he could solve it tonight. Vicia also appeared confident.

"The riddle, however, is more than simply deciphering an intellectual puzzle," the chancellor went on. "You must figure out what it means, and then act appropriately.

"So here is your challenge: Bring the Blessing of the Fey to Twin Falls. The person who can do this will be duke."

Silence followed immediately. Stunned by the late duke's orders, they looked at each other in confusion.

Then the room burst into complaint. Practically everyone shouted at the chancellor for some explanation.

"What does this mean, 'the Blessing of the Fey'?" Grunvilio said, echoing the general sentiment.

44

"That's the riddle," Bismarck replied. "You must determine what the Blessing of the Fey is, how to get it, and then act to bring it to me."

More shouting followed. Everyone wanted a more thorough explanation. Bismarck only raised his hand for silence. After a few moments, he got it.

"I have given you all the instruction there is," he said. "Bring me the Blessing of the Fey for the city. The one of you who does so will become Duke of Twin Falls. The contest is now officially open. Begin your quest."

Liliana's mind raced. She wasn't sure what the enigmatic Blessing of the Fey was, nor was she sure exactly how to bring it back to Twin Falls. But she thought she knew where to begin, and she believed her abilities gave Garrick an advantage over the other candidates. This was as clear as sign as the gods ever offered. Her destiny was linked to Garrick's in the same way it had been to Calibot's.

"What now?" Garrick said, looking irritated.

Liliana smiled at him.

"I have a plan," she replied. "Let's go."

CHAPTER 7:

An Unexpected Entry

A
S SOON AS CHANCELLOR Bismarck signaled the feast was over, Vicia rose from her seat and swept from the room. She didn't even bother saying goodbye to the people she'd been associating with or to make excuses for leaving suddenly.

She didn't understand why this kept happening to her. Why did every scheme of hers go horribly wrong? Was Gothemus Draco *still* mocking her from beyond the grave?

Two years ago, she'd successfully assassinated the world's most powerful magician with the aid of the vengeful gnome, Elmanax. He'd promised her that, with Gothemus dead, she could get the Eye of the Dragon, master it for Eldenberg, and ascend to the presidency of the Council of Elders.

But he'd been wrong about so many things. The first was that Gothemus's magic had lived on after his death, preventing anyone from getting into the sorcerer's tower to actually retrieve the Eye. When she couldn't deliver what she'd promised, the Council lost faith in her. Then Gothemus's brat son had turned up with the dragon sword, *Wyrmblade*, demanding his father's body.

Things had spiraled out of control from there. By the time it was over, she'd been expelled from the Council and couldn't go back to Eldenberg, since there was a warrant out for her arrest. She didn't fancy spending the rest of her days in one of the Council's dungeons, possibly awaiting execution.

Now, it was happening again. She and Lord Kremdor had set up a perfect plan for her to seize control of Twin Falls, make herself the duchess, and form an alliance that would make them the most formidable tandem in the Known World. Together, they'd be able to conquer anyone they chose, including her former home of Eldenberg.

She didn't care that Kremdor employed goblins and monsters. She didn't care he might not even be human. After all, she'd worked with Elmanax. What mattered to her was he was willing to help her achieve her ambition.

So why wasn't it working? Why, once again, was a perfect plan unraveling before it really got going? Did the gods hate her? Why? What had she ever done to offend them?

She entered the small guest chamber she'd been assigned when she came to the palace a few days before to begin her part in Kremdor's master plan. She barely spent time closing and bolting the door before striding straight to the full-length mirror.

"*Spatium loqui*," she said, waving her staff and pointing it at the mirror.

Silver sparkles flew from the end, struck the glass, and caused the whole thing to shimmer. A moment later, her reflection was replaced by swirling fog.

"Lord Kremdor," she chanted. "Lord Kremdor, I call out to thee. / Lord Kremdor, Lord Kremdor, show thyself to me."

Vicia waited impatiently for him to answer. She tapped her foot in irritation while the seconds ticked away.

She was about to repeat her summons when his image finally appeared in the glass. As usual, his face was covered with a black metal helmet decorated with cured leather bat's wings on each side. Two eye slits revealed only dots of red light that glowed malevolently. Vicia was never sure if this was just magic designed to make him look more sinister or if they were truly his eyes. His communication vessel was the smoke from an eldritch fire, and Vicia could see the flames dancing just below his head.

"Greetings, Lord Vicia," he said in a voice that sounded both metallic from the helmet and otherworldly. "How went the feast?"

"Poorly," she said. "We have a problem."

"What is it?"

"There's a new, unexpected entry in the contest," she said.

"Garrick Tremaine," Kremdor said.

"Yes," she replied. "How did you know?"

"Gursh's soldiers failed to kill him two days ago," Kremdor answered. "He was supposed to be their sacrifice. Before they could complete the ritual, they allowed him to be rescued."

Bile rocketed up Vicia's esophagus and exploded on the back of her throat. She could feel everything unraveling all over again.

"That makes it even worse," Vicia said.

"Garrick Tremaine is no threat to us," Kremdor said. "Gursh is under orders to kill him as soon as he is spotted in Twin Falls. If he entered the Contest of Succession – which I fully anticipated – he is already dead. The goblins were watching the feast and will be seeking to capture him and finish the sacrifice at the earliest opportunity."

"Garrick Tremaine isn't the problem!" Vicia shouted.

Kremdor's red eyes grew brighter for a moment. At first he said nothing. Vicia didn't know if he was trying to control his temper, but she didn't care. The situation was worse than he understood.

"Tremaine is just some soldier who used to work for Lord Malach," Vicia said. "I could easily kill him myself if it were necessary. That's not the issue."

"Then what is?"

"He has an ally – a sorcerer named Liliana Gray," Vicia said.

"Gursh mentioned Garrick was rescued by a magician," Kremdor said.

"Yes, well, in case the name doesn't ring a bell for you, Liliana Gray was Gothemus Draco's apprentice," Vicia said. Kremdor didn't comment, so she went on. "When she first came to Eldenberg with Gothemus's son to claim the body, she was a bumbler. She didn't appear to have any understanding of magic at all. But she was extremely clever. She helped them escape our guard with simple parlor tricks.

"She went into Gothemus's tower with Calibot to retrieve the Eye of the Dragon. When she emerged, she was incredibly powerful. She undid all my magic, changing my spells to something harmless as soon as I cast them. She enhanced *Wyrmblade's* fire, turning it into a deadly weapon capable of slaying tens of soldiers, even from a distance. She protected

Calibot from all harm in the battle at his father's tower. She can do the same for this soldier-for-hire.

"I don't know how she does it, Lord Kremdor. She doesn't need a staff or a wand. She doesn't cast spells. She just commands eldritch forces as though she were some kind of god. She's exceptionally dangerous – almost as big a threat as her master was when he was alive."

"That would explain how she was able to so easily defeat Gursh's minions," Kremdor mused.

He fell silent, evidently contemplating what Vicia had told him.

"Yes, well, she's capable of doing more harm than defeating a simple band of goblins," Vicia said. "If she's protecting Tremaine, she can undo everything we're trying to accomplish. Your plans for conquest, Gursh freeing his god, and me sitting on the throne of Twin Falls are all in jeopardy as long as she's involved."

Kremdor still didn't speak. Vicia tapped her foot impatiently as her partner considered all the implications.

"She'll need to be eliminated," Kremdor said at last.

"You think?" Vicia said, sarcasm burning like acid in her tone. "We need to kill her as soon as possible, Kremdor."

"Stop worrying," Kremdor said. "I know you have history with this woman and know what she is capable of. I take your concerns seriously. I will instruct Gursh to deal with this problem tonight."

"Gursh?" Vicia said in shock. "Kremdor, he couldn't deal with her the first time. Why would you think he can do it now?"

"His men were ambushed in the first meeting," Kremdor countered. "She came upon them and attacked before they knew she was there. This time, the situation will be reversed. It is the goblins who will have the element of surprise. Few people can survive such an attack."

"And if she's one of the lucky ones?" Vicia said.

"Gursh and his army are not the only servants at my disposal," Kremdor replied. "If the goblins fail, I will escalate."

Vicia wasn't convinced. This was exactly the same sort of assurance Elmanax had given her. He went on and on about his fairy earth magic and how no one would be able to withstand it once Gothemus was out of the way. That had proven to be completely false. Calibot had killed Elmanax – an extraordinary feat, since fairies were immortal. Kremdor's promise sounded like the same overconfidence the gnome had suffered from.

"I hope so," she said. "We can't afford to mess around here. Liliana Gray is dangerous. The longer she's alive, the greater the chance for our plans to fail."

"Relax, Lord Vicia," Kremdor said. "Everything has proceeded just as I have arranged. Duke Evonin died of disease. Chancellor Bismarck is under my spell and executing my will. He has asked a riddle few if any of the other aspirants are likely to solve. I have given you the answer and enchanted the trials so they will yield to you. All you need do is continue to execute your part of the plan."

"You're wrong, Lord Kremdor," Vicia said. "You may have set everything up according to our design, but not everything has proceeded as you arranged. Garrick Tremaine was supposed to die on that cross. He didn't. Liliana Gray wasn't even supposed to be involved. She is. I'll relax when she's dead and everything is back on track."

"Suit yourself," Kremdor said. "Just remember to fulfill your part of the scheme. Don't do more than you're asked or change the plan. You get the Blessing of the Fey and claim the throne. I'll handle Tremaine and Gray."

"See that you do," Vicia said. "I'm leaving Twin Falls tomorrow morning for The Enchanted Forest. I'd prefer if I didn't have to worry about Liliana and her pet following me."

"I tire of this conversation, Lord Vicia," Kremdor said, a dangerous tone entering his voice. "I've given you my assurances the matter will be taken care of. There is no further need for you to insist it be done.

"Please keep me informed of your developments. I don't want any surprises in the execution of our plans. Farewell."

The mirror went dark. A moment later, Vicia was looking at her own reflection again. She scowled.

He could tell her all he wanted that everything was under control. She would believe him when Liliana was dead. Until then, everything was in jeopardy.

She sighed in frustration. Why did this keep happening to her? It just wasn't fair.

CHAPTER 8:

Goblins Inside City Walls

G ARRICK'S HEAD WAS SPINNING as they left the palace. The Blessing of the Fey? What the hell did that mean? And why was Liliana so sure she knew?

And what about all those other contestants? General Calavan had looked furious when Chancellor Bismarck finally revealed the nature of the competition. Zala-whatever-his-name-was appeared smug, the Chamber of Commerce guy seemed confused, and the mason alarmed. Only that thief, Levinia Mordecai, seemed to carefully consider the question and what it might mean. She was dangerous.

Perhaps as dangerous as the sorcerer Liliana had pointed out. Garrick was already worried about her. If Liliana thought she was someone to be feared, then Vicia Morrigan needed to be viewed as a severe threat, especially since she'd bragged in front of everyone about murdering Gothemus Draco.

The brash sorcerer had gotten up and left swiftly as soon as the chancellor ended the feast. Everyone else stayed, discussing the competition and the clue. The other two freelancers – the warrior and the illusionist – conferred, perhaps forming a temporary alliance.

But not Vicia. Her face had been impossible to read. Garrick had no idea if she thought she already knew the answer and was hurrying out to solve the riddle before anyone else or if she'd decided to give up, thinking the task was impossible.

Garrick thought it was. If Liliana hadn't insisted she had a plan, he'd have given up the whole thing as a bad idea right then.

She hurried down the darkened street towards the inn where she'd lodged them. She was much shorter than he, but he was still having trouble keeping pace with her.

"In the name of the gods, slow down, Liliana," he said.

She turned back, saw she'd outdistanced him, and stopped. An embarrassed smile lit up her face in the dim torchlight.

"I'm sorry," she said. "I keep forgetting you still haven't fully recovered from your ordeal. The effects of the meal and the healing draught are probably working on you too."

He grimaced at her. He didn't need her reminding him he wasn't at his best.

"As long as we're on that subject," he said, "has it not occurred to you that, with me still recovering, I may not be in position to actually win this thing?"

"Nonsense," she said, in an irritatingly cheery tone. "We've got salves for you back at the inn, the huge meal you ate will awaken your body's natural healing process, and you've got me to help you solve the riddle."

He sighed at her. She continued to smile at him as though nothing could possibly be wrong.

"Liliana," he said, "I don't know anything about the Fey, except that they're tricky and not to be trifled with. And I certainly wouldn't know where to look for one to get its blessing."

"Where to look is easy," Liliana replied. "The Enchanted Forest is only a few days' ride from here. We'll have to get you a horse."

"The Enchanted Forest?" Garrick said, shocked. "Liliana, that place is supposed to be filled with all sorts of magical beings!"

"It is," she enthused. "But it's not like The Wild Lands. The Enchanted Forest is more mysterious but far less malevolent. We'll be safe as long as we're careful."

"Even if that's true," he said, growing increasingly frustrated, "The Enchanted Forest is a big place. Do you know where to find fairies?"

"Not exactly," she said. "I need to do a little research."

"So we're going to a mysterious, magical forest, where we'll wander around until we find a fairy to give us a blessing we can take back to the chancellor."

His tone was not friendly. Garrick remained grateful to Liliana for rescuing him, but she'd been leading him on a mad quest ever since, and he had had just about had enough of it. He wanted to finish healing and then return to Lord Malach's fortress, where his life made sense.

"No, silly," she said. "We won't 'wander around.' I'll know more or less where to go when we leave the city."

"Liliana," he said. "I'm out of patience for this. I don't like mysteries. I prefer things I can understand – battle, defensive formations, strategy. I don't want to be duke, and I certainly don't want to go off on some strange quest to The Enchanted Forest to seek a fairy and beg for its blessing."

She continued with that infuriating smile of hers. If she didn't stop soon, he was liable to shout at her or worse.

"Garrick," she said. "It's neither as simple nor as complex as you're making it."

"Oh, well, then!" he said, throwing up his hands.

"The answer to a riddle is both obvious and obscure," she said. "You can't think about it literally. The language is code. Whatever we're meant to bring back, it's not actually a blessing. That's an audible thing you can't verify. 'The Blessing of the Fey' means something else."

"And do you have any idea what it is?"

"No," she admitted.

Garrick bit his cheeks to keep from losing his temper. He walked in circles several times.

"Twin Falls must have some connection to the Fey in its past," Liliana said. "Otherwise, it would be meaningless for a prospective duke to bring it to the city. Once I know what that is, I'll know where in the forest to look and how to find it."

He sighed again. What she said made sense in a cryptic, wizardly way. But that didn't make him feel any better about it.

They started walking again.

"What about the others?" Garrick asked.

"What others?"

"The other contestants," he answered.

"What about them?"

"What if they already know what this connection is?" he said, feeling his irritation rise again.

"Ha!" she laughed. "No one knows what it is. You could tell by their reactions. Zalachorus might have a clue, but I think the smugness he showed was just him thinking no one else would be able to figure it out. Levinia has a plan. You could tell by how she was studying everyone else and thinking about everything that was said. But she doesn't know exactly what it means either. And the rest of them have no clue."

"Not even Vicia?" Garrick prodded.

Liliana walked in silence, chewing on what he said. He watched her, waiting for her answer.

"She sure left in a hurry," Liliana said.

"Yes," Garrick said. "You don't think that means she knows exactly what she's doing?"

Again Liliana didn't answer right away. She contemplated the possibilities.

"That might be exactly what it means," she allowed. "Although it doesn't seem possible. No one knew the nature of the contest until the chancellor made his announcement."

"Do we know that for sure?"

Liliana stopped and looked in his eyes. Alarm spread across her face.

"No," she said. "Actually, we don't."

"So it's possible Vicia only showed up tonight because she had to to participate," Garrick said. "As soon as everyone was in and the riddle announced, she left."

"Which means she could be on her way out of the city right now," Liliana said.

"No," Garrick said. "They close the gates at night, remember? No one gets in or out. She'll have to wait until morning."

"Which gives us a little time to figure out what it all means," Liliana said.

"We also need to consider that Vicia isn't the only one who knows," Garrick said.

"Do you think any of the others might already have known?" Liliana asked.

"No," Garrick said. "But both Zalachorus and Levinia had different reactions from the rest. Neither of them looked shocked, worried, or confused. You may be right that they're as in the dark as everyone else. But if we are considering that Vicia understands, both of their reactions present the possibility."

"So three people might be ahead of us," Liliana mused.

"Or none," Garrick said. "Or any combination in between. We don't know."

Liliana nodded thoughtfully. Then she started walking again.

"Tomorrow morning, we need to get you a horse right away," she said. "Then we need to watch the gate to see who leaves."

"If we get the horse first, we might miss someone leaving," Garrick countered.

"Right," Liliana said. "We'll have to split up. One of us will need to watch the gate, while the other gets the mounts."

"Agreed," he said. "I'm afraid I'm still penniless after having been robbed."

"So you're on gate duty," Liliana said.

"I'm sorry."

"Don't be," she said. "It's all part of your destiny. You can pay me back when you are Duke of Twin Falls."

He started rolling his eyes at her when a lasso snaked out of the darkness and dropped neatly over her shoulders. A second later it was pulled taut, and Liliana was yanked away from him towards an alley.

"Hey!" he shouted.

But before Garrick could react further, a second lasso came from the opposite side of the street, also found its mark, and was pulled tight so Liliana was held in the middle of the street with her hands pinned to her sides.

Things continued to happen faster than he could respond. Sinister snickering surrounded them. Goblins ran into the street from all directions.

Two more lassos ensnared Liliana. All four goblins holding a rope ran to equidistant anchor points and pulled hard so she couldn't move.

Garrick took one step towards her, when heavy whistling reached his ears. A moment later, a weighted net dropped over him, knocking him to the ground. He struggled to rise, but the ropes were thick, and the weights held everything firmly down. He was able only to make it to his knees. Several more goblins rushed to his position, and started working the net to drag him off.

Meanwhile, with Liliana held fast, two goblins had set up in front of her with spears. They pointed their weapons at her and grinned in malicious delight. Uttering guttural war cries, they charged her as their companions pulled tighter on their lines.

"No!" Garrick cried.

But Liliana wasn't as helpless as she appeared. She raised her head, and the four ropes holding her glowed with yellow light that lit up the street brighter than the dim illumination of the torches. The goblins holding her floated off the ground, looking surprised and scared. She gave them no time to react.

Liliana twisted her body and spun, magic propelling her around like a millstone. With no way to resist, the goblins sailed through the air, still clinging to their ropes. The two charging her were moving too swiftly to stop. One of the "flying" goblins collided with the first spear-wielder, knocking him off his feet and into his partner, who also crashed to the cobblestones.

With the immediate threat countered, Liliana spun a few more times to maximize the speed of her captors. Then a burst of red magic caused all four lassos to vaporize, sending the ropers sailing away from her in four directions.

Garrick was so stunned by Liliana's sorcery, he didn't immediately realize he was being dragged away from her. Then he was pulled off his knees as the goblin bushwhackers got full control of the net and proceeded with abducting him.

One of the goblins who had attempted to gore Liliana was on his feet, and he lunged at her, forcing her to dodge. Distracted by the fiends trying to kill her, she couldn't see Garrick being dragged away. If he didn't do something soon, he would be carried off to an uncertain fate, possibly another crucifixion.

He struggled against the net, but his efforts were in vain. He was still weak from his first encounter with goblins, and the snare this group employed was well constructed and seemingly impenetrable.

"Liliana!" Garrick shouted, unable to do anything else.

She threw her cloak over the goblin she was fighting as the second made it to his feet. Then she turned quickly to see what Garrick was shouting about.

Alarm ran briefly across her face when she saw the situation. She waved her arm at him, and a ball of red light shot from her hand in his direction.

"Oh, shit," he said.

Liliana was forced to turn back to face the two goblins on her before her magic did its work. Garrick closed his eyes, expecting to be destroyed in a wayward spell.

Instead, the sorcery struck the net and caused a bright flash of heat that made him feel warm. When he opened his eyes again, he saw eldritch energy eating a hole in the strands until the whole thing fell away from him. His captors stopped and stared, stunned at the new development.

Garrick got to his feet and drew the sword Liliana had bought him that afternoon. Realizing he was armed and probably dangerous, the four goblins who had been abducting him, drew short swords of their own and then fanned out and surrounded him.

Panic began to flood his mind. The little bastards had already proven tricky, and he fully expected them to team up on him.

He bit down on the rising fear and allowed his training to take over. He scanned them briefly, and then charged the one closest to him.

It looked scared for only a moment. Then it flung itself to the ground rolling under Garrick's attack with a maddening chuckle.

Garrick turned and saw the other three racing towards him. He swung his blade in a wide arc, just trying to slow them down. The sword sliced the shoulder of the goblin on his right flank and then connected with the weapon of the center fiend. He managed to dislodge the blade from his opponent's hand, and the flat of it hit the third goblin in the shoulder, causing him to flinch and arrest his charge.

But the one who'd ducked away from him initially, sprang up and attacked. Garrick barely parried the blow in time.

The two uninjured goblins moved to join their companion, while the fourth nursed his wound. Garrick stepped back to give himself some room to fight them.

Before they could strike, though, three arrows of red, magical light flashed into the fray, each hitting a separate goblin and exploding in eldritch fire. The goblins screamed as they died, and the one Garrick had cut gaped in shock at the sudden and unexpected demise of his friends.

Garrick charged forward and drove his sword into the fiend's throat while he stood slack-jawed. He appeared to be as surprised by his own death as his companions'. The look on his face as he slid off Garrick's sword was darkly comical.

Liliana and Garrick stood panting for a moment.

"Thanks," he said to her when he'd recovered enough of his breath to speak.

"You're welcome," she replied. "I think we'd better get out of here before any reinforcements arrive."

Garrick agreed, and they moved off without him sheathing his sword. He wanted to be ready in case there was a second ambush.

When they made it to the inn, they went straight to their room, and Liliana inspected Garrick to make certain he hadn't been harmed in the attack. When she was satisfied he had no new injuries, she got out the healing salves and applied the thick, green cream to his prior wounds. It smelled as bad as the draught she'd made him drink had tasted.

"Don't magicians know how to make things that don't stink?" he said.

She chuckled at his joke and then washed the residue off her hands. When she was finished, she smiled again.

"You better lie down," she said. "The sedatives in that salve are pretty strong. You should be feeling much better by morning."

"Liliana," he said, "what have you gotten us into?"

"I keep telling you," she replied. "*I* haven't gotten us into anything. This is your destiny. You are the one who elected to follow it."

"Fine," he said. "What have I gotten us into? We were just ambushed by goblins *inside city walls*."

"I know," she said, frowning. "It seems our friend the smith's rumors were correct after all. That's alarming. How did they get in? Why are they are after you?"

"Are we sure they were after me?" he asked. "Maybe the city is so chaotic with the duke's death, they are operating as a street gang, attempting to steal from drunkards out after dark."

"They netted you and tried to carry you off, Garrick," she said. "Me they just tried to kill. They wanted you alive. Given that you were captured while your friends were slaughtered on the way here and now they've tried a second time, I'd say it is you specifically they want."

"But why?" he said.

"That's the question," she answered. "That crucifixion I rescued you from wasn't just an execution. There was magic involved. Maybe they needed you to die on that cross and are trying to get you back up on it.

"They're up to something, Garrick. If anything, this proves beyond any reasonable doubt that you have a destiny to fulfill here."

She fell silent. He tried to think about the implications of what she'd said, but he was already feeling sleepy. His mind struggled to connect one thought to the next. He lay back on the straw mat.

"But what is it?" he said with a yawn. "What's my destiny?"

If Liliana answered him, he didn't hear it. He was prone only a few seconds before the magic of the salve carried him off to a world of dreams he didn't understand.

CHAPTER 9:

The Crown of Silence

KREMDOR LOOKED OVER the list of names Chancellor Bismarck had given him and smiled cruelly behind his iron mask. Vicia's warnings about Liliana Gray notwithstanding, everything was proceeding exactly according to his design.

Each of the guilds had put up a predictable representative to try to wrest control of Twin Falls in its direction. General Calavan had also decided he wanted to rule. And there were a few fortune-seekers who didn't know they'd signed their own death warrants by pursuing their ambition.

Garrick Tremaine's candidacy was vaguely concerning. If the fool discovered who he was, it could throw the whole scheme into chaos. But Gursh was ensuring that wouldn't happen. Once Tremaine was out of the way, it wouldn't matter if Gray lived or died. She'd be out of the picture.

There was nothing here he couldn't handle, nothing to cause him any real worry. It was time to launch the next phase of his plan, especially since he had only a few hours of night left.

Kremdor strode deliberately across his *sanctum* to a table on which rested a large wooden box. It was polished mahogany, and it shone in the moonlight that poured through the open window at the top of his tower.

Ancient sigils were carved on its lid, and an elegant, gold clasp held it shut. Kremdor smiled on it and lightly flipped the catch.

He put his hands on the side and gently lifted the lid. Resting within, surrounded by blue crushed velvet, was the Crown of Silence. The mystical artifact was made of dull grey iron and was tipped with four peaks at equidistant points around it. Each of these contained a single stone – ruby, orange opal, yellow sapphire, and emerald.

Kremdor reverently lifted the crown out of the box and placed it on his head, sliding it over the metal slope of his helmet to create a snug fit. Then he returned to the center of the *sanctum* and prepared to summon the crown's deadly servants.

"*Venite ad me,*" he chanted, raising his arms. "*Venite ad me. Conjuro te. Lusso meo. Venite ad me.*"

A smoky mist surrounded Kremdor's head, drifting out, formless at first. But then it split into four separate tendrils of grey fog. The vapor floated briefly in the air before turning towards the floor, as though it were being poured into some invisible container. Seconds later, there were four pillars of substanceless smoke standing before Kremdor. They swirled, then hardened, congealing into bodies.

The transformation took a full minute. And then four warriors in black tunics and leggings, and black cloaks with black hoods stood before him – the servants of the Crown of Silence, the power behind its purpose, the Silent Knights.

They bowed softly before Kremdor, their master so long as he wore the crown. Wordlessly, they awaited his bidding.

"I have enemies I need eliminated," Kremdor said. "There are five. I will give you their names, and you will destroy them."

The Silent Knights only bowed again in response. They did not speak. Silence was their nature – they acted in it, and they delivered it. Kremdor raised his right hand to the crown, made contact, and then intoned the names of his intended victims.

"Bram Dover," he chanted. "Lindsay Grunvilio. Levinia Mordecai. Demetrian Tumet. Lance Edger."

He left the other names deliberately off his hit list. Zalachorus ir-Bedlam Donovian had a different role to play in this drama.

The goblins were taking care of Garrick Tremaine. Not only was Liliana Gray a danger to the Knights, freeing Gruul from his metaphysical prison would be more certain if Kraven had all of Tremaine's essence.

As for Blake Calavan, Kremdor needed him where he was at the moment. If he was assassinated too soon, Twin Falls would descend into chaos. Someone needed to be in charge of the military, and whomever succeeded Calavan might decide it was time for a *coup*. Plus, the death of the leading authority figure in the wake of the duke's demise might trigger a panic. Calavan would get his in due time, but Kremdor needed to exercise patience first.

And of course, he couldn't give them Vicia's name. He needed his puppet refugee in place to rule Twin Falls in his name.

The rest, though, were in his way, obstacles that might challenge Vicia's rule if they didn't get what they wanted. They needed to be eliminated so they didn't cause problems and didn't interfere with her winning the contest.

"Go," Kremdor commanded. "Fly swiftly to Twin Falls and kill these people as I desire."

For a third time, the Silent Knights bowed to him. Then they returned to their smoky, vaporous forms and flew out the window into the night sky, speeding north to Twin Falls.

Kremdor watched them go. Death was coming to the competition he'd organized. And it would arrive on the night air with no sound to give warning.

CHAPTER 10:

A Good View of the Gate

LILIANA SHOOK GARRICK AWAKE before dawn. It was just as well. He'd been having a strange and intense dream, wherein goblins danced around him gleefully. He'd watched them in confusion, unable to understand why they should be so happy. Then he felt something weighty on his head. He reached up and discovered a crown on his brow. This seemed to delight the goblins even more.

The after effects of the dream and sedatives in the healing salve combined to leave him groggy. He didn't understand why she woke him. Wasn't he supposed to be convalescing?

"You need to get dressed and get over to the west gate," she told him.

"Why?"

"To watch," she reminded him. "We need to see who leaves and who doesn't. The portcullises are raised and the drawbridge lowered at first light. You need to be there before that happens, so we don't miss anyone."

Yes. Last night's planning finally returned to him. They expected Vicia knew the answer to the riddle and would leave for The Enchanted

Forest. It was possible Zalachorus and Levinia also knew what was up and would get a jumpstart on the competition.

Wearily, he dragged himself off the straw mat and put on the boots and sword Liliana had bought him yesterday. He had just thrown on his cloak, when a thought occurred to him.

"Liliana," he said, "what if I'm ambushed by goblins again?"

"That seems unlikely," she said.

"It's still dark," he countered. "If they're in the city in any force, they could conceivably attack me before I make it to the gate."

She studied him for a moment. Then she nodded.

"I'll walk you there," she said. "That way you'll have my magic to protect you. But then I've got to leave you. I've a lot to accomplish before we head out ourselves. I think you'll be safe on your way back here. There may be goblins in the city, but I very much doubt they'll show themselves during the day. They can't want anyone to know they're really here."

That made sense to Garrick. He had no idea how or why goblins were inside the walls of Twin Falls, and he had even less idea why they were so keen on capturing and sacrificing *him*. But he agreed that the fiends didn't want anyone to know they were here – at least not yet. Whatever their endgame, it had to require secrecy until they were ready to move.

Liliana donned her cloak, and the two of them made their way out into the waning night and across town.

Thirty minutes later, he was standing in a side street with a good view of the gate. He leaned against the wall of a stable, enshrouded in a shadow made from the still-dark sky.

There was minimal activity for him to observe. Soldiers patrolled the city wall, and the occasional person moved through the streets. A block down was a bakery, and Garrick could smell bread whenever a breeze blew past him. It made his stomach rumble despite having gorged himself at last night's feast.

After only a short time, he noticed his shadow had moved off him. He turned around and saw soft, pink light above. Dawn had arrived.

As he moved back into the gloom, someone cried out orders from the wall. A moment later, the distinct clinking of chains cut through the early-morning silence, and the drawbridge rumbled as it made its way to the ground. Lowering it took the better part of a minute, and it came to rest across the river with a thunderous thud.

With the bridge down, the rushing of the water and the roar of the falls came loudly to Garrick's ears. Facing west, little light came through the gate, but the sounds of Twin Falls's water features were as clear as though he were standing next to them.

"All's clear," someone called from the parapet over the gate.

At that announcement, chains clinked again. The inner portcullis rose slowly, the heavy, iron bars lifting from the ground and disappearing into the archway above. When it was fully open, the outer one began its ascent. Before long, Twin Falls was open to the world again.

Garrick's heart picked up pace. How long would he have to wait before one of the competitors showed and made a move? Who would it be? Would anyone show at all?

As daylight broke across the city, traffic near the gate picked up. Shopkeepers made their way to their businesses, milkmen and bakers delivered wares, and farmers went out to work the fields beyond the wall.

The livery Garrick had chosen for his stakeout opened for business. A stable hand saw him and approached. Before he could say something, Garrick moved off. He found shelter at a general store that hadn't opened yet. It sat at the end of the side street he'd been on, leaving him feeling a little more exposed, but he didn't see that he had much choice.

Ten minutes later, a man dressed in a leather hauberk, with a heavy cloak that didn't quite conceal the sword on his left hip, walked over to the wall about thirty feet away from the gate. He leaned against it, brought out an apple, and proceeded to eat it slowly while keeping an eye on the city's west exit. His hood was up, so Garrick couldn't observe his features, but it was easy to figure out he was here on the same errand Garrick was – he wanted to see who left town.

Garrick wondered who he was. He was too large to be the self-described illusionist, Lance Edger. The braggadocios warrior, whose name was eluding Garrick, didn't seem like the type to hang out like a spy, although Garrick supposed it could have been one of his entourage. His body frame fit Bram Dover, but Garrick thought it would be strange for a mason to lurk by the wall, especially with a sword, even if he did have the wisdom to figure Vicia was up to something.

Short of asking him his identity, though, Garrick didn't see a way to find out for sure whom this new arrival was or to whom he was reporting.

He returned to watching the gate himself, glancing at the new arrival occasionally to see if anything had changed.

Nearly an hour passed without incident. Traffic at the gate increased, and more of the shops opened. The other man had finished his apple and now sipped occasionally from a flask as he kept the same vigil as Garrick.

With daylight fully on the city, Garrick wondered if he and Liliana had overestimated Vicia's or anyone else's understanding of the challenge. But then a horse ridden by a woman in a blue traveling cloak approached the gate. Garrick was behind her and couldn't see if it was Vicia or not. Her hood was up masking both her face and the color of her hair from his vantage. But she carried a staff in her right hand.

He left his post at the general store, circling around to the rider's left, trying to catch a glimpse of her face. He put up his own hood to conceal his identity. Despite that limiting his view, he didn't want her to recognize him if she glanced his way.

Trying to look as casual as possible, he drew even with her horse. He glanced sidelong at her. Long, black hair trailed out of the blue cowl, waving gently in the morning breeze. It had to be her. It had to be!

The wind picked up, and her hair swirled into her face. She let go of the reins and brought her left hand up to brush it aside, opening her hood enough that Garrick got a good look at the sharp features underneath. It was indeed the former Elder of the Council.

As soon as he was sure it was her, Garrick turned, putting his back to her and meandering away from the gate. He didn't want to give her the same opportunity she'd given him. The other spy had his eyes focused on Lord Vicia. He didn't seem to notice Garrick.

Ducking to his left, Garrick slipped off the main street and into a shop selling tack. He watched as Vicia nodded to the guard and continued through the gate and out of the city.

"May I help you?" a man said behind him.

"No, thank you," Garrick replied without looking.

He left the shop and walked back towards the gate, slipping into an alley so he could resume watching unobserved. His first instinct was to run straight back to Liliana and tell her what he'd seen. But he was interested in the other man keeping watch. There were two other people he and Liliana thought might be wise enough to head straight for The Enchanted Forest. For whom did the back-garbed stranger work?

Ten minutes later, Garrick got his answer. A woman and two men leading four horses approached the gate. The spy left his post to join them. The woman was short, and she put down her hood at his approach. It was Levinia Mordecai.

Garrick watched as they spoke. Levinia nodded several times. Her companions leaned in so they could hear better. After a brief conference, they all mounted their horses and rode off quickly through the gate.

So, two of the three aspirants Garrick and Liliana thought might be onto the game had proven worthy of their estimation. What about Zalachorus?

Garrick decided to wait to see if the sanctimonious sorcerer also left the city. Another hour passed. Traffic increased out of the gate.

But Garrick saw none of the other competitors. General Calavan did not come to check on the troops or leave the city himself. Zalachorus or the guildsmen did not arrive and exit the gate. Neither of the other freelancers showed. Only Vicia and Levinia seemed to have a clue about the nature of the strange riddle Chancellor Bismarck had posed last night.

After another half hour passed with no contestants showing, Garrick figured it was safe to report back to Liliana. Anyone who thought the answer lay in The Enchanted Forest would have wanted to get an early start. The fact that none of the others were here or had obviously sent agents to observe what happened told him they had no idea what to do or how to solve the riddle. Realizing the pompous windbag, Zalachorus, was in the dark made Garrick smile.

He left the gate, heading back to the inn. Hopefully, Liliana would have everything they needed and be ready to go. He didn't know why, but he was suddenly looking forward to leaving Twin Falls in search of the Blessing of the Fey.

CHAPTER 11:

Peaseblossom

GARRICK FOUND LILIANA PACKING things into her saddle bags. She looked at him in surprise.

"I didn't expect you back so soon," she said.

He cocked his head, concerned. Had he done the wrong thing?

"I have the information we need," he said. "I figured I should come help you get ready, so we can move out."

"Oh," she said. "I thought I was picking you up at the gate."

Garrick continued to stare at her. She returned it with an impassive expression.

"I'm not sure that was clear to me," he said, feeling defensive.

"Oh, well," she said. "What did you learn?"

"Vicia left the city as soon as the sun was fully up," Garrick replied. "She was traveling by horseback."

"Was anyone with her?"

"No," Garrick said. "She appears to be operating completely on her own, despite her efforts to make friends at last night's feast." He thought for a moment. "That might explain why she was hobnobbing so much – trying to gain some allies in the quest."

"Or she was trying to establish relationships with key players, since she's convinced she's coming back with the title of 'Duchess of Twin Falls' in her hand," Liliana said. "She's an unknown here. She'll need to secure some support to rule."

"I figured she'd just dominate everyone with her magic," Garrick said.

"That's not enough," Liliana said. "She can get to the throne with magic, and she can suppress some of her enemies with it. But she'll need at least one and probably three or four factions on her side if she doesn't want to fight a war to hold onto her position."

Garrick nodded. That made sense to him. He was no politician, but as a soldier, he understood strategy, and he knew you couldn't command troops who didn't want to follow you.

"Was Vicia the only person you saw?" Liliana asked.

"No," Garrick replied, grinning slightly. "Levinia Mordecai left about twenty minutes or so after Vicia."

"So she thinks she knows too," Liliana mused.

"I'm not sure that's true," Garrick said. "Before Vicia showed up, a man I'd never seen before arrived and started watching the gate just like me. Levinia appeared with two other men after Vicia left. The first man approached her, they conferred, and then all four of them left on horseback together."

Liliana chewed on that information. Garrick watched as she churned possibilities in her mind.

"Those men are clearly part of her gang," Liliana said.

"Right," Garrick said. "My thought is this: Levinia doesn't know what the riddle means, but she believes Vicia does."

"So she's following her," Liliana finished.

"That's my bet," Garrick said. "I think Levinia is smarter than some of the others. She may not know how to solve the puzzle, but she's clever enough to track the person she thinks does."

"And then steal the blessing from her," Liliana said. "And she must be smart enough to know as much as we do – that to secure a blessing from a fairy, the most logical place to go is The Enchanted Forest."

"Which is why she sent her man to the gate to watch for Vicia."

"Just like we did," Liliana said.

She fell silent and thought some more. Garrick had questions of his own.

"So are we essentially following the same strategy?" he said.

69

"What do you mean?"

"Are we just going to follow Vicia to see what she does?"

"Yes and no," Liliana said. "I have a little more information than Levinia. Well, I guess I don't know that for sure, but I believe I know more than she does.

"I spent some time poking around in the wizards' guild libraries this morning. Zalachorus wasn't there, so no one hassled me. I think if I'd been recognized from last night, I'd have met resistance.

"As you know, The Enchanted Forest is filled with fairies. Indeed, it's the densest population of Fey in the Known World. According to my research, there are numerous breeds and clans."

"I don't see how that helps us," Garrick said. "If anything, that makes it harder."

"I wasn't finished," Liliana said. "As you might expect, because it's a magical forest, there are a lot of dryads."

"What's a dryad?"

"A tree spirit," Liliana answered. "They're fairies who inhabit trees, imbuing them with magic. One in particular, Peaseblossom, will grant a boon to any mortal who performs a service for her. This boon is bestowed in the form of a favor – a branch the holder can use to summon Peaseblossom's magic. I believe this favor is 'the Blessing of the Fey' Chancellor Bismarck seeks to win the throne."

Garrick let that wash over him. It all made sense. Liliana had said whatever "the Blessing of the Fey" was, it had to be a play on words, a pun of some sort. And since this contest was crowning a new Duke of Twin Falls, there would need to be some sort of proof the winner had actually achieved the goal. Thus, a magical tree branch capable of summoning fairy magic was a good token.

"But how will we find this Peaseblossom, and what sort of service do we need to perform to get her boon?" he said.

"I don't know the answer to either of those questions," Liliana said. "But I bet Vicia does."

Which was why they needed to follow her. It all made sense – except for one thing.

"Liliana, as right as all this seems, how do we know for sure this is what we're after? All Chancellor Bismarck said was to secure the Blessing of the Fey. If The Enchanted Forest is as full of fairies as you claim, how do we know this is the right one?"

"Well, I can't know for absolute certain," she answered. "That's another reason we should be tracking Vicia. If it isn't Peaseblossom, she'll lead us to whomever it actually is.

"But I think I'm right about the identity of the fairy we need. I found all this out, because there was a story about a prince from Twin Falls rescuing Peaseblossom from an evil sorcerer four hundred years ago. To repay him, she told him Twin Falls would enjoy her favor for as long as his line ruled the city.

"There's just too much in common. A fairy blessing the city? A duke being chosen by receiving said favor? If anything, the true meaning of the riddle is that the winner must reclaim the Blessing of the Fey to be worthy of the throne."

Garrick nodded. Liliana was right. There were too many coincidences for this to be the wrong answer. He didn't know anything about magic or fairies, but he knew you didn't ignore clues that added up. One doubt niggled at his mind, though.

"Four hundred years ago?" he said. "This is the same Peaseblossom?"

"Fairies are immortal," Liliana said with a smile. "They can be killed, but they do not expire. And it takes a lot to destroy them. The only time it's ever been done to my knowledge was when Calibot killed Elmanax. He cut him in half with *Wyrmblade*. If he hadn't been using an enchanted sword, and a legendary one at that, I'm not sure he would have succeeded."

Garrick shuddered at the thought of a creature so formidable it couldn't be slain without a powerful artifact. It also unnerved him that Liliana had been witness to that particular piece of history. It was another reminder how dangerous this whole adventure was. If Liliana Gray and Vicia Morrigan were involved, this was clearly a high-stakes event. And that didn't include some of the other potent people like General Calavan, Levinia Mordecai, and Zalachorus ir-Bedlam Donovian. As confident as he'd felt an hour ago, he was once again doubting this was actually his destiny.

"So now what?" he said.

"Now we pick up supplies for our journey, get over to the livery to collect our things and rent you a horse, and then we hit the road. Vicia has a head start, which is fine. The road from Twin Falls goes through The Enchanted Forest, but we don't want to fall too far behind. The longer we wait, the harder it'll be to make up ground."

"Assuming she takes the road," Garrick said.

"I think she will," Liliana replied. "It's the safest passage to the forest, and it follows the precipice. If she left via the west gate, which you report she did, she'll have to follow it until she makes it down the slope. She can venture off after that if she wants to, but until then, she's hemmed in by the drop-off.

"Furthermore, staying on the road will make it easier for her to determine if she's being followed."

"It'll also make it easier for her to *be* followed," Garrick said. "What if she's thought of that, and leaves the road at her first opportunity?"

"I'll track her with my magic," Liliana said. "It's not foolproof, but since I know whom I'm looking for, I'm pretty confident I'll be able to keep us on her trail."

"All right," he said. "I guess we better move out."

It took them over an hour to get everything Liliana thought they needed. She bought rations, blankets, and a bow for Garrick, reasoning he could use it to hunt if they needed him to. He wasn't an outstanding archer by any measure, but he accepted the weapon and her logic. Since the smith they'd visited yesterday hadn't had any armor, she got him a studded-leather jerkin too.

She also purchased more healing salves and draughts. She liked how Garrick's wounds were progressing, but she thought it wise to have more supplies on hand in case he had a setback or if they ran into trouble out in the wilderness and needed to recover. He saw a lot more wisdom in this than the bow, especially since they were trailing a dangerous sorcerer and a gang of thieves.

Finally, they went to the livery by the east gate and retrieved Percy. Liliana also rented a large, black stallion for Garrick. He looked a little long in the tooth. Garrick wondered how much endurance he had. But he was well muscled and seemed fit enough.

Saddled and with their gear packed away, they mounted up and wound their way through the city to the west gate, where first Vicia and then Levinia had disappeared off in the direction of The Enchanted Forest.

It took almost an hour to pick their way through the heavy traffic to reach their initial destination. With the day in full swing, Twin Falls was bustling with business of every kind. Garrick grew frustrated at the constant roadblocks and having to wait, but Liliana smiled serenely, as though there were no urgency to their errand or nothing could bother her.

By the time they went through the gate and crossed The Winding River, it was early afternoon. The sun was high in the sky. There were no clouds, and the air was cold. Steam puffed from their mouths as they set off west on the long journey in search of the dryad Peaseblossom.

"It'll take a day or two before we reach the bottom of the precipice," Liliana said.

"Well, at least Vicia and Levinia won't be able to get there any faster either," Garrick commented.

Just past the drawbridge, the road entered a woods. Garrick shuddered involuntarily. The memory of his last encounter in a woods leaped into his brain, causing fear to crawl over his thoughts like spiders.

"Are you cold? Liliana asked.

"Yes," he lied. "Now that we're out of the sun, it's chilly."

He put up his hood to complete the prevarication and hoped not to see any goblins along the way. Given the attack they'd survived in the city last night, he wasn't very optimistic.

Zim-Zam watched the two humans leave the city through the west gate. No one had taken any notice of him. Kraven's magic had worked as promised. Everyone saw a human child running through the streets, not a goblin spy.

It had been difficult to follow the sacrifice and his pet sorcerer from the east side of town to the west, but they were held up frequently by carts crossing the roads, crowds milling about merchant booths, and pedestrians jamming the streets. A small child could easily slip through these obstacles, and Zim-Zam was cleverer than any human brat.

They bought a lot of supplies before leaving town. They clearly planned to be traveling for some time. Not that they would reach their destination. King Gursh would make certain they were unlikely to see another sunrise.

When he was sure the humans had crossed the drawbridge and were fully on their way, Zim-Zam left his post and returned across the city towards the secret portal. He would report what he'd seen to the king, and he would be rewarded. And tonight, if he were lucky, he'd get to be part of the ambush party that would kill the sorcerer and recapture the sacrifice. That would be a lot of fun.

CHAPTER 12:

An Incident at the Temple of Design and Glory

ZALACHORUS SAT AT HIS desk, drawing patterns with his finger on the polished wood. Calavan stood officiously in front of him, his back ramrod straight as usual. Zalachorus appreciated the general's discipline – it was something he understood himself. Discipline was necessary to master sorcery.

But he also knew how to relax. Blake Calavan wouldn't have relaxed if his bones had been removed. He'd still have found some way to salute, perfectly rigid.

"So three left the city?" Zalachorus said.

"Yes," Calavan said. "The former Elder, Mordecai, and the soldier with the female assistant."

"Tremaine," Zalachorus said.

"Yes."

"Interesting," Zalachorus said.

"Why?"

"Last night at the feast, the woman accompanying him told me it was his destiny to become duke," Zalachorus answered.

Calavan snorted. Zalachorus shared the sentiment.

"Destiny is made, not predetermined," Calavan commented. "Only fools believe otherwise."

And only fools believe fate doesn't play a role, Zalachorus thought.

Calavan was a brilliant strategist, but he was too earthly. He didn't understand there were unseen powers working on the world at all times.

"So that leaves the two guilders still here, as well as the fortune-seekers," Zalachorus said.

"Yes," Calavan said. "And us."

"Right," Zalachorus said. "Edger, the self-proclaimed master illusionist, has been in the libraries researching fairy lore all day."

"Do you think he'll find something?"

"Anything's possible," Zalachorus said. "But I doubt it. Liliana Gray was there this morning, and she left after only two hours. Then, according to your men, she departed the city with Tremaine."

"What are you saying?"

"That Edger doesn't appear to have the wits to find the answer," Zalachorus replied. "If Gray found it after only a few hours of searching, but Edger's been in there all day, he doesn't know what he's doing."

Calavan's brow furrowed as he thought.

"What is this answer Morrigan, Mordecai, and Gray all seem to know?" he said. "Where are they going?"

"Our librarians are going over the tomes Gray read to see if they can find the answer to the first question, but the latter is easy to answer," Zalachorus said. "You said they all left through the west gate and continued west on the road?"

"Yes," Calavan said.

"Then they're undoubtedly heading for The Enchanted Forest," Zalachorus said. "It's teeming with fairies. They must believe they can get the Blessing of the Fey there."

"But how?"

"That," Zalachorus said, "is the mystery we need to solve."

Calavan frowned. Zalachorus suppressed a smile. He didn't know the answer to the riddle himself, and he was certain none of the cretins who left the city in search of it did either. But it amused him that Calavan was worried. The man was out of his depth.

"What do you know about the others?" Zalachorus asked.

"Dover and his laborers have been holed up in their temple all day," Calavan answered. "Occasionally, a functionary leaves or arrives, but the entire guild appears to have their heads down over a table trying to divine a solution to the riddle's meaning.

"As for Grunvilio, he's doing what you might expect – paying people to do research for him. In fact, you should check with your own agents in the libraries to see if anyone else is researching fairies. They're probably working for Grunvilio."

"And the warrior?"

"Hmpf. He's been in a pub all afternoon."

Zalachorus nodded. At least they didn't need to worry about him.

"I don't like this, Zalachorus," Calavan said.

"None of us does. This entire Contest of Succession is moronic."

"That's not what I meant," the general said. "But I agree with you. The duke should have named someone to succeed him before he expired.

"But I don't like this mystery about a blessing from a fairy, and I really don't like the implication that it can only be achieved outside Twin Falls."

Of course, you don't, Zalachorus thought. *It takes you away from your power base into a world you do not understand.*

"Don't worry, Blake," Zalachorus said. "The duke was untraditional, but he wasn't insane. I am certain he had the city's future well in mind when he arranged this contest."

"That's just it," Calavan countered. "He *wasn't* like this. Duke Evonin was cagey, and he was sometimes unconventional, but this isn't the sort of thing he favored. From the moment he became ill and Bismarck started doing the talking for him, the duke's orders have been very unlike him. I see a darker hand in this, and I can't identify to whom it belongs.

"But the fact that the solution to this 'riddle' lies outside the safety of the city walls bodes ill. Something fell is going on here."

Zalachorus stroked his magnificent beard and pondered that. He was reasonably certain Calavan was just being paranoid. It was his job in a way. As Twin Falls's general, he was tasked with defending the city, and that meant looking for threats under every stone. Most likely, he was only jumping at shadows.

But Zalachorus had to admit that there was truth in what he said about the duke. Evonin had been many things, but he had never been an eccentric, and this whole Contest of Succession was the conception of a madman. Between the strange malady that had struck him down – the disease no healer or magician could find a cure for – and his odd commands leading up to his death and culminating with his unusual game for the throne, something – several somethings in fact – had not been right with him.

On top of that were the rumors that swirled around the city streets. Curses being worked by home-schooled shamans, predictions for famine and blight, and goblins operating within the city walls, were all spoken of in hushed whispers and circulated as credible facts that had the population looking over their shoulders at every turn, especially after dark.

One thing was certain: Zalachorus needed to solve this riddle and ascend the throne as quickly as possible. Until he was the unchallenged duke, he would not be able to establish order in any meaningful way. And that was why he needed Calavan.

"Take heart, my friend," he said. "We'll solve this. As long as we keep cooperating and keep track of the unworthy competitors, one of us will become duke, and we'll establish a new dynasty."

Calavan eyed him warily. Zalachorus hid his lies behind a smile.

"I hope so, Zalachorus," he said. "Twin Falls needs wise, strong leadership from someone experienced and prepared to give it. The other guilds have no vision, and the opportunists don't care for the city; they just want the power. We need to ensure our future."

Zalachorus was about to give him another round of assurances, when one of Calavan's aides ducked his head in.

"Excuse me, sir," he said. "You're needed. There's been an incident at the Temple of Design and Glory."

"An incident?" Zalachorus said.

The aide flicked his eyes to Calavan to see if he should answer. Calavan turned back to Zalachorus.

"Let me see what this is about," he said. "I'll fill you in with all the details when I have them."

"See that you do," Zalachorus replied, a terse note in his tone.

He was holding out on Calavan to an extent. He'd prefer it if the general didn't reciprocate that behavior.

"I'll be in touch," Calavan said.

Then he turned on his heel and went out. Zalachorus wondered what kind of an incident could be going on at the Brotherhood of Craftsmen headquarters that required the attention of the general of the military.

He supposed it didn't matter. If it was that big, Calavan wouldn't be able to conceal it from him. In the meantime, he had a mystery to solve and a throne to claim.

Bram Dover rubbed his bald head wearily. They'd been at this all day. Every scholar the Brotherhood of Craftsmen had access to had been poring over legends, fables, and obscure religious texts since dawn to attempt to unravel the mysterious meaning of "the Blessing of the Fey." So far, they were no closer to understanding than they were last night when Chancellor Bismarck first announced it.

He sat in the general meeting room of the Temple of Design and Glory, with his hope for a breakthrough diminishing. The tall columns and intricate carvings dedicated to the worship of Gogolus, God of Design, and Forge, God of Labor, offered no inspiration, no insight into this strange riddle. He began to fear it was impossible.

"Master Dover," Lucretius, their chief archivist, said, "we've finished our research on fairy divinity. We find no evidence fairies have any gods. They have a king and a queen, who quarrel and war as often as not, but there is no god the Fey serve.

"Furthermore, despite having monarchs, there is no fairy kingdom *per se*. While most fairies live in The Enchanted Forest, they are not confined there exclusively, and there are so many different breeds and types of fair folk that their frequently feuding king and queen do not speak for them all. Indeed, there are some fairies who claim allegiance to Auberon the king, others who swear fealty only to the queen, Titania, and more that acknowledge both as King and Queen of the Fairies but pay them no tribute.

"I'm afraid 'the Blessing of the Fey' is not something that exists — at least in terms of a grant from the fairy nation as a whole."

Bram sighed. Of course. It would be logical to assume one could obtain a favor from a fairy king like you could from any human monarch. Therefore, it could not be done.

"Thank you, Lucretius," Bram said.

Bitterness welled in his heart. When this unusual Contest of Succession had first been announced, Bram had thought there was at last a chance for the commoner to have a say in the rule of the people. If a laborer could become duke, it would finally be possible for everyday people to be considered in tax policies, work laws, commerce, and more. The wealthy and the erudite wouldn't be the only ones to benefit from government. There wouldn't be a constant battle between the labor guild and the throne.

But it seemed the duke had designed this contest so that only an educated man could win it. The promise of the throne being open to anyone was a sham.

"I think our next recourse should be to explore alternate meanings of the words, 'blessing' and 'Fey,'" Lucretius said. "This is a riddle, so it stands to reason that 'Blessing of the Fey' is code for something else."

Bram nodded. He was about to reply when he heard shouts outside the door.

"What was that?" he said.

Lucretius and the two temple soldiers standing guard at the chamber entry all turned their heads to see what the source of the disturbance was.

Before anyone could react further, though, the door burst open. A man dressed all in black and wearing a black cloak with the hood up and carrying a bow walked confidently into the meeting room. He turned, dropped to a knee and took aim at one of the soldiers.

Bram noticed the weapon wasn't strung, but that didn't faze the man in black. He made a motion with his right hand, as though he were drawing the bow. A glowing, golden arrow and string magically appeared. The archer released the "string," and the arrow shot towards the guard hitting him in the chest and killing him instantly in a flash of yellow light.

Bram leaped to his feet. Lucretius recoiled in fear. The other soldier brought his spear to bear, but the black-hooded archer turned and shot the second guard, killing him just as he had the first.

The assassin stood and walked into the room. Three more men dressed just like him followed. One held a sword composed entirely of red light just as the arrows of the first man had been yellow. He pointed it at Lucretius and steered the archivist away from the table.

A third man held a whip of orange light. He snapped it over his head and then sent it snaking towards Bram. Before Bram could appreciate what was happening, the strange weapon wrapped around his shoulders. Its wielder pulled it taut instantly, and Bram found himself caught with his arms pinned to his sides.

The fourth and final killer walked straight to the table, carrying a spear of green light. He leveled it at Bram and gored him.

Bram cried out and looked down in pain at the magical spear penetrating his stomach. Horror raced through him, stripping any logical thoughts from his mind.

With a savage pull, the assassin withdrew the spear from Bram's belly. Blood gushed out after it. Bram's hands raced to his guts, vainly trying to staunch his wound.

The killer wasn't finished, though. He re-aimed his weapon and shoved its lethal tip into Bram's throat.

Fear, pain, and confusion all warred for control of his mind. Seconds later, he lost consciousness. He never got a chance to pray for salvation.

CHAPTER 13:

Intended as a Sacrifice

LILIANA THOUGHT IT BEST to camp just inside the woods, gaining shelter and cover from the trees. They'd be better protected from the weather that way and more invisible to either of the two parties they were following.

She spent a little time hunting, figuring that, once they got out onto open ground, food would be scarcer. If she or Garrick could catch something to eat tonight, that would extend the rations she'd bought a little further. She caught sight of a deer but elected not to kill it. It was too large for a single night's meal, and they had no practical way to take leftovers with them.

Eventually, she found a pair of rabbits and felled them with a quick blast of magic. Then she and Garrick set to skinning and roasting them. It was well past dark when they finished eating.

"We'd better sleep in shifts," Garrick said.

"What do you mean?"

"We need to have someone stay awake to keep watch," he answered. "We were attacked by goblins inside the city, and I was abducted on the road to Twin Falls. Whatever is happening, those goblins seem to have it in for me. There's every reason to believe they'll assault us again tonight."

"You have a very suspicious mind," Liliana said with a smile.

"I find I live longer that way," he replied.

Liliana grinned wider. He was so serious, this soldier-for-hire destined to become a duke. But underneath the worry and the paranoia, she saw someone with a sense of humor and some charm.

"You're much better company than Calibot was," she commented.

"What?" he said, furrowing his brow in a way she could only think of as cute. "What do you mean?"

"Well, as you may know, he's a poet," she said. "A pretty good one actually. At the time he was writing this epic comedy. What was it called? Oh, yes! *Drake and Drudger's Journey: A Canticle to Knavery.* He'd just finished the third canto when I met him.

"Of course, I was bringing him news of his father's death. That would shake anyone, but Calibot and his father were estranged. They hadn't spoken in five years, and so Calibot was shocked when he heard his father was dead."

"I think the whole world was shocked by that," Garrick said. "It was Gothemus Draco after all."

"Right," Liliana said. "But because they didn't get along, Calibot was even more upset than you might expect. When he found he had to go to Eldenberg to retrieve his father's body and return it to Gothemus's tower to be cremated, he was even angrier.

"So the whole time we were on the road, he was in a black mood. Everything I said or did made him mad. He was really unpleasant company.

"Then, after we had to break out of Eldenberg, Gothemus's magic had begun working on him. That made him *really* dark.

"Anyway, it's kind of ironic, when you think about it. A man who writes comic poetry is someone you would think you would want on a journey with you. Instead, he made it miserable."

"Yes, well, as I've heard the story told, he had some cause to be wretched," Garrick said.

"Oh, I agree," Liliana said. "I'm not blaming him or saying he was unjustifiably gloomy.

"But you have some cause to be grief-stricken too. Three of your friends were murdered, you barely survived a crucifixion, and you've been thrust into a quest you really didn't want a part of. Yet, except for complaining about what I've allegedly gotten you into, you're generally easy to get along with. You're not a dark, storm cloud blackening up everyone's day."

He cocked his head. Confusion drifted around his face before spreading into a smile.

"Really?" he said. "I've always thought I was pretty gruff."

"You're a little gruff," she said. "But you're a warrior – a man hardened by battle. I expect that. You could be angry or depressed or insane after what happened to you on the way to Twin Falls. Instead, you're just rolling with the circumstances as they come."

"Well," he said, his face a mask of both confusion and amusment, "thank you."

"You're welcome," she said.

They gazed on each other wordlessly for a few moments. A pleasant sensation washed through Liliana's chest. She had no idea what it was, but it made her return his smile.

"Why don't you get some rest?" he said, breaking the silence. "I'll take first watch."

"Are you sure you're up to it?" she asked. "You're still recuperating from your ordeal, we were attacked last night, you were up early this morning, and it's been a long day."

"All the more reason for me to have the first watch," he said. "Once I fall asleep, I won't want to wake up."

He grinned at her, and she couldn't help but return it. He made her feel strange in the most wonderful way.

"Very well," she said. "I hope you—"

She stopped in mid-sentence, cocked her head, and listened intently. There was rustling in the evergreens overhead.

"What?" Garrick said. "What's the matter?"

"Do you hear that?" she said.

"Hear what?"

She scanned the trees, searching for the source of the sound. Glowing red dots lit the branches over Garrick's head. There must have been ten or twelve of them. Her heart stopped when she realized they were eyes.

The recognition almost came too late. A net dropped from the tree.

"Get down!" she shouted.

His soldier's instincts kicked in, and he flung himself to the ground as she summoned magic to her hand and sent a bolt of yellow energy at the net. It struck the snare just above Garrick's prone form. The ropes turned instantly to sparrows, and they flew away in every direction.

She heard a crack above her and turned, whirling her hand above her head and encasing herself in a dome of purple light. This too she managed just in time. Arrows poured out of the tree and smashed against the eldritch energy. Curses rained down from above when she was unharmed.

Garrick was on his feet and raced to his sword, sheathed on the rented stallion. Five ropes dropped from the tree he'd been standing under, and a goblin slid down each of them. They hit the ground and brought short swords and shields to bear. Liliana opened her hand and sent four red arrows of light at them from her fingertips. The goblins raised their shields, and Liliana was astonished to see her magic bounce off them harmlessly.

The fiends all grinned at her in wicked delight. One of them said something in his guttural language, but she couldn't make it out.

She turned to warn Garrick and saw she had problems of her own. Six more goblins were sliding down the tree above her. They too brought out shields and short swords.

Before she could even think to panic, one of them raised his shield in front of him and charged her with his sword raised. Ensorcelled to repel her magic, the shield pushed a hole in the protective dome she'd made, and the goblin charged through it.

Liliana aimed her palm at the ground and sent another blast of yellow energy at it. The earth in front of her attacker turned to quicksand, and he plunged in headlong, disappearing beneath the surface.

Two more goblins had penetrated her shield, but they pulled up short when they saw what she had done to their companion. A fourth goblin crashed through the barrier, ran into one of his friends and knocked him into the quicksand.

"Liliana!" Garrick cried. "I need help!"

She risked a look in his direction and saw the goblins had him surrounded. He was trying to fight them all off, but they kept rushing him from behind. He wouldn't last long.

The problem was, she couldn't attack them herself. They would repel her magic. She could wait to pick off the ones with their backs to her, but the goblins attacking her absorbed too much of her concentration. They were already working their way around the quicksand she'd made.

An idea occurred to her. She couldn't fight the goblins for Garrick, but she could help him repel them.

With a flick of her hand, she sent a silver ray of light in his direction. It struck him in the head. A second later, he started moving at five times his normal speed.

She didn't have a chance to see how well it worked, though. The remaining two goblins that had shot at her broke through her shield from behind. One slashed at her and nearly made contact.

Liliana snapped her fingers, and the quicksand returned to frozen ground, killing the two fiends who'd fallen into it. Then she charged across it between the two goblins who'd been working their way around the trap to get to her, dropping the energy dome as she went.

She spun back to face her attackers. She let the two that had been behind her get a little closer as the ones flanking her skidded to a stop.

This time, she waved her hand at the campfire, and a burning log came sailing out of the pit and smashed into the back of the head of one her pursuers. He sprawled before her, whether unconscious or dead she didn't know.

His partner put up his shield, lowered his head, and barreled straight for her. She sent another yellow ray at the ground in front of him, and the earth sprang up, snaring his foot. He too crashed headlong into the ground, and his face connected hard with the shield he'd raised to protect himself. She heard a sickening snap as his neck broke.

She risked a look back at Garrick and saw him decapitate a goblin, leaving only one left of the lot that tried to immobilize him.

Meanwhile, the remaining two raced to flank her. Both hid behind their shields and looked for an opening. She enchanted the ground at their feet. Fists of dirt reached up and gripped their ankles holding them fast.

In a blur, Garrick zoomed over and killed them both before she could think to tell him they should leave one alive for questioning. She sighed and disenchanted him. He collapsed to the ground, completely spent.

"As much," he panted. "As much as I appreciate you making it . . . possible . . . for me to kill them all, . . . let's find another way . . . next time."

She nodded, although it would require some thought to come up with a different solution. If they were going to come ready to combat her magic, it would make things extremely difficult.

"They're learning, Garrick," she said when she'd caught her own breath. "Their shields were enchanted to repel my magic. They were ready for me this time."

"Sneaky, little bastards," he said.

"They want you badly," Liliana said. "This is the third time they've tried to capture you. Me they want dead, but you they want for that dark ritual they were conducting when I first found you. Something very big is at stake here."

"I suppose," he said, "you're going to tell me it's all got to do with my destiny."

"I can think of no other explanation," she replied.

"But why would goblins care about how whom the Duke of Twin Falls is?" he asked. "Why wouldn't they want me to ascend the throne?"

"There are two possible explanations," she said, "and I think they are both true. First, someone is controlling them. Someone who seeks the crown has thrown in with goblins to eliminate the competition. I'd say the other contestants will be facing them too."

"But why would they have attacked me on the way to the city? I didn't even know about the Contest of Succession, and I had no plans to enter until you forced me."

"That's the second reason," she said. "You're intended as a sacrifice. I don't know to whom or why, but those goblins are determined to make you the blood to fuel their black magic. You're important somehow, Garrick. You're important in a way we don't understand yet. We need to make sure they don't accomplish whatever it is they're up to."

"Well, strictly speaking," he said, "I'm pretty dedicated to the idea of not dying on a cross. Or in any other manner, actually."

Liliana chuckled. There was that sense of humor again. They'd just been attacked by goblins, their lives were in extreme danger, and he found some comedy. Garrick Tremaine was incredibly appealing.

"We'd better clean up this mess," he said. "We don't want any of their friends finding them, and the carcasses will attract scavengers."

"Good point," she said.

They set to piling up the goblins and then digging a hole for the bodies. Liliana used her magic to make it easier.

However, the exertion of wielding so much magic, the stress of the fight, and the length of the day all combined to make her weary. When they were finished, she sat down with her back to a tree and fell almost instantly asleep.

She dreamed of being Garrick's duchess in Twin Falls. A smile blanketed her face as she slept.

CHAPTER 14:

Lord of Goblins

KREMDOR SIGHED SOFTLY. GURSH'S troops had once again failed to capture Garrick Tremaine and kill Liliana Gray. This was becoming irritating – largely because he couldn't understand how the soldier and his sorcerer kept surviving. Gursh was no fool. It wasn't like he and his soldiers were bumblers. Instead, Tremaine and Gray were crafty – cleverer even than the goblins trying to dispatch them.

That boded ill.

It was time for a change in strategy. The longer Tremaine remained alive, the more likely it was the whole operation could be jeopardized. If necessary, he would send the Silent Knights to kill them, but he didn't want to pull them off their current mission of eliminating the other contestants in Twin Falls, and he feared Gray's magic. He had another plan. He just didn't like it.

"I suppose I must, mustn't I, Isadore?" he said.

"You won't be happy," she screeched from her perch in the rafters.

He looked up and met her gaze. She looked ridiculous, giving him advice as she hung upside down. But she wasn't wrong.

"I'll be perfectly happy if he gets the job done," he said.

"No," she replied. "If he's successful, he'll be worse than if he fails."

"If he fails, he'll be dead," Kremdor said and tossed summoning powder on the fire.

He waited as the flames turned purple, then green. Then he raised his arms.

"Gremsh," he intoned. "Gremsh, Lord of Goblins, hear me."

Kremdor waited a few moments. When he got no response, he repeated his summons.

"I command you, Gremsh," he said. "Hear me."

This time, he felt his presence. A moment later, the self-styled lord appeared in the smoke.

Gremsh was uglier than any goblin Kremdor had ever seen. His green skin was pock-marked. He had several scars from battles, and his nose seemed to fill up his entire face. He leered into Kremdor's communication spell with one angry, yellow eye.

"Lord Kremdor," he said. "What an unexpected surprise."

Kremdor bit his tongue. Gremsh liked to sound important, but he wasn't intelligent enough to pull it off. Of course the surprise was unexpected. It wouldn't have been a surprise otherwise.

"I have a mission for you," Kremdor said.

"I thought you already had a mission for me," Gremsh countered.

Irritation rose in Kremdor's mind like bile. Gremsh needed to shut up and listen.

"This mission is in addition to the one I've already assigned you," Kremdor said.

"My, but we have many needs of late," Gremsh said.

If he didn't stop talking, Kremdor might kill him instead of enlisting his aid.

"I need you to capture Garrick Tremaine and sacrifice him," Kremdor said.

"I thought Gursh was doing that."

"He has struggled to complete the task."

"Heh," Gremsh said. "I'm not surprised."

"Your cousin has not failed due to incompetence," Kremdor said. "There has been an unforeseen complication."

"Go on."

"Tremaine was rescued from Gursh's forces by a sorcerer," Kremdor explained. "We have made two attempts to recapture him since then, but in each case, the sorcerer's magic has proved superior. She must be eliminated so Tremaine can be caught and sacrificed."

"Understood," Gremsh said. "But where do I come in? Twin Falls is a long way away."

"They are *en route* to you," Kremdor said. "They left Twin Falls yesterday and are traveling to The Enchanted Forest. When they arrive, make sure they don't leave."

"Heh. Roll out the unwelcome mat, eh?"

Kremdor shook his head at the joke. Gremsh may have been clever on the field of battle, but he needed to cease trying in his dialogue.

"Just make sure they do not leave the forest alive and that they do not interfere with Lord Vicia before you dispatch them," Kremdor ordered.

"Consider it done," Gremsh said.

"I will when it is *actually* done," Kremdor retorted.

"I'm not my cousin," Gremsh said, sounding angry. "I can be counted on."

"So can Gursh," Kremdor said. "I cannot overemphasize the craftiness of the sorcerer, Liliana Gray. Last night, Gursh sent soldiers with shields enchanted to repel her magic. The shields were effective, but she still found a way to defeat your cousin's warriors. She is easily the more dangerous of the two. You need to neutralize her to have a chance at netting Tremaine. As long as she's able to act, your mission is in danger."

"I understand," Gremsh said. "We'll prepare something special for her."

"Don't overthink it, Gremsh," Kremdor said. "Put an arrow through her throat before she even knows you're there. Make it quick and unanticipated. That's the only way to get her."

"Yes, my lord," Gremsh said, sarcasm dripping from his tone.

Kremdor scowled behind his mask. The goblin lord wasn't taking this seriously enough. He needed an incentive.

"If you can manage this," Kremdor said, "if you can kill Liliana Gray and sacrifice Garrick Tremaine, then I will make you my general instead of Gursh."

"I thought you said the failure wasn't his fault," Gremsh said, his scarred, ugly face twisting in a wry leer.

"It wasn't," Kremdor said. "But I need results. If you can do what he could not, I'll have to give the mantle to you. I need more than someone to lead my armies in the coming days. I need someone who can conquer in my name."

Predictably, Gremsh swelled with pride. His biggest weakness was easy to exploit. Stroke his ego, and he fell right in line.

"This will be my first accomplishment as your strong right hand," he said.

"See that it is," Kremdor replied. "And remember the task I've already assigned you. No one frees Peaseblossom without my leave."

"I haven't forgotten," Gremsh said. "Everything will be as you designed."

"Excellent. I look forward to your updates."

Kremdor ended the spell and sighed.

"I told you so," Isadore said.

"He hasn't succeeded yet."

Kremdor wasn't entirely certain Gremsh *could* succeed. The Lord of Goblins was too overconfident, too smug. But he was a sinister bastard. Kremdor hoped his cunning would win the day.

Even if it did, he very much doubted he was going to have to make good on his promise to elevate his status. Gremsh was going to get in Vicia's way. The Lord of Goblins was not privy to that part of the plan, but Vicia would have to rescue Peaseblossom from *someone*. Gremsh was unlikely to survive such an encounter.

No, it was a near-certainty Gursh would remain Kremdor's trusted general, and that was good. His inability to nab Garrick Tremaine notwithstanding, he was smart and reliable. And loyal. That was very important too.

The problem with everything continued to be Liliana Gray. She had interrupted the sacrifice, keeping Tremaine's royal blood in play. Now, her magic continued to outwit Kremdor's goblin allies. He needed to get rid of her, and he wasn't sure how.

Based on the descriptions of her work Gursh reported, he was beginning to think Liliana Gray was no sorcerer at all. She didn't use a wand or a staff. She reacted too quickly to the ambushes with magic. She was able to adapt her spells to the needs of the moment.

It sounded like wild magic.

Yet Kremdor had never heard of any human able to master wild magic before. It was too powerful, too primal, for the human mind to command. Only fairies, the gods, and certain dragons could keep it under control.

Of course, that wasn't entirely true. There had been one human wizard, who *had* been a wild magician – Gothemus Draco. Few knew that was the secret of his former mastery of The Known World. The Council of Elders had never been able to understand how his spells were so much more potent than theirs. Kremdor was perhaps the only person alive who *wasn't* surprised when Gothemus's charms lived on after Vicia murdered him.

And Liliana Gray had been his apprentice. By all accounts, she'd been a bumbler, completely inept, before his death. Vicia herself reported Gray to have been pitiful when she arrived in Eldenberg accompanying Calibot Draco and his lover, Devon Middleton.

But after she went into Gothemus's tower with Calibot and his uncle, she emerged a different woman. She'd countered all Vicia's spells and those of the gnome Elmanax. Kremdor had seen it himself, watching from afar with scrying fire.

So maybe Gothemus had taught her his secrets. Maybe he had given her some sort of gift that enabled her to control the magic coursing through her.

That was a problem Kremdor wasn't sure how to solve. If Liliana Gray was a wild magician in control of her power, she was more formidable than Vicia or Gremsh or Gursh. It was possible she was stronger even than Kremdor.

He didn't like that thought. If Gremsh couldn't deal with her – and Kremdor wasn't sure he could, now that he thought about it – he was going to have to find a solution himself. As far as Kremdor could tell, Liliana Gray was the most dangerous woman in The Known World. If she was what he thought she was, she could destroy all his plans.

That night, in Twin Falls, Demetrian Tumet stumbled out of the Nag's Head Saloon, with Darius and Sirillian with him. The three of them sang loudly, drawing shouts to be quiet from several windows.

"But when are you planning on finding out what this Blessing of the Fey is and doing something about it?" Darius said after they'd finished their song.

"My good man," Demetrian said, putting an arm around his friend to keep himself from falling over. "I told you. The gods will send me a sign. As soon as they do, I'll know how to proceed. Until then, there's no profit in worrying over it. Let the others madly scramble to solve this mystery."

"But what if one of them solves it?" Darius said.

"Then we'll be there to benefit from their labor," Sirillian said.

"Precisely!" Demetrian said. "Let them do the work, and we'll claim the reward. That's what being a duke's all about!"

The three of them laughed and continued to stumble towards the inn. Demetrian missed his step and lost pace. He was about to call out to his friends to wait, when a whip seemingly made of orange light wound around his throat and was pulled taut.

Demetrian was yanked off his feet and onto his back. A moment later, he was drawn into the alley, skidding across the cobblestones.

There, a man dressed in black raised a sword made of red light and plunged it into Demetrian's stomach. He screamed.

The sound got the attention of his companions. They raced back to see what had become of him. Another man in black knelt at Demetrian's side and drew back a bow. An arrow of yellow energy magically appeared, and the archer let fly.

At the same time, yet another black-garbed warrior hurled a glowing, green spear out of the alley. It impaled Sirillian through his heart. He clutched at it, and then fell over dead. The golden arrow hit Darius, killing him instantly.

The man who had stabbed Demetrian withdrew his sword. Demetrian stared at them all in horror. Then the whip around his neck was drawn up, lifting his head and shoulders off the ground. The man with the magical sword brought it down.

"No!" Demetrian yelled just before he was beheaded.

CHAPTER 15:

Wild Magic

LIGHT WAS COMING FULLY through the pine trees when Liliana woke. Worn out from the previous days' events and from using so much magic, she'd slept later than she'd wanted. Garrick was also still unconscious, recuperating from his ordeal on the cross and the exertion of two consecutive nights' fighting.

She got up slowly, stretched her muscles, sore from sleeping on the ground and riding a horse, and then went over and shook Garrick awake. She almost hated to. He looked peaceful for the first time since she'd met him.

He roused quickly, though, and set to helping her break camp. They ate what was left of last night's dinner for breakfast, bundled themselves against the cold, and then mounted their horses and set off.

When they broke out of the trees onto open ground, the wind blasted down off the mountains, chilling them. They both put up their hoods and gathered their cloaks as tightly around them as they could manage.

With her head enshrouded, she couldn't really get a good view of Garrick. She saw the head of his horse and so knew he was keeping pace with her, but she didn't know how well he was managing the weather.

An hour into their journey, a light snow started to fall. It might have been pleasant if the wind hadn't whipped it around. Despite her best efforts, the icy breeze drove some of it inside her hood, stinging her face.

With the flurries and wind, it was impossible to see very far. She had no idea if Vicia or Levinia were still ahead of them. She had to hope they both remained on the road, or if they had ventured off it, that they were still going to The Enchanted Forest.

By day's end, she and Garrick were chilled and miserable. Liliana worried about the horses, since they didn't have a good place to shelter them from the wind.

They camped on the side of the road and tried to build a fire. But even with Liliana's magical assistance, the wind was too strong to keep it lit. She gathered some large stones together and enchanted them to radiate heat. Then she brought the horses near to them, made them lie down, and threw blankets over the animals to aid in their warmth.

She and Garrick ate in silence and then cuddled up to their mounts to share body heat. Neither of them slept very well that night.

They awoke the next morning to find themselves dusted with snow. The sky was clear, and the wind had abated. It was still cold, but at least it wouldn't be rotten weather for traveling. They breakfasted quickly and then broke camp and were on their way.

The sun shone, setting the snow on the ground ablaze like diamonds. Liliana found her mood improving rapidly.

At midday, they came upon tracks in the snow. Garrick stopped and examined them.

"There are at least three horses here," he said. "Probably four."

"Levinia and her men?" Liliana said.

"That would be the most likely scenario," Garrick said. "The snow would have covered the progress they made yesterday, but this must be where they set off from this morning. At least we know they're still on the road."

"But is Vicia?" Liliana said.

They had their answer an hour later. Garrick was certain he'd picked up a fifth set of horse tracks on the road. He also spied something else.

"See those craters in the snow?" he said, pointing to depressions off the path.

"Yes," she answered.

"They look like they were made by someone lying on the ground," he observed. "Notice too how there are footprints moving to and away from them."

Liliana looked further, seeing what he meant. The tracks were clearly made by a biped.

"I'd say Levinia is sending advance scouts to spy on Vicia," Garrick said. "Mostly likely, they're dressed in white, so they'll blend in with the snow. They're not just following Vicia; they're tracking her to make sure she doesn't alter course, and they're staying at a safe distance, so she won't detect them. My bet is they're a half-day behind her, to make it hard for her to notice them."

"That makes sense," Liliana said. "Not only would they not want her to know they're trailing her, she'd probably attack them if she was aware."

"Right," Garrick said. "We should be careful."

"What do you mean?"

"Well, if they're scouting ahead to keep an eye on Vicia, it stands to reason they're also watching their own backs," he answered.

"Which means they know *we're* following *them*," Liliana said.

"I think that's a safe assumption," he said.

Liliana cursed silently. She hadn't really been trying to be stealthy, but they'd left hours after Levinia and her men. She'd thought they wouldn't have to worry about that. She was more worried about *losing* them than being spotted.

"Oh, well," she said. "Nothing we can do about it. We've repelled two goblin ambushes. We should be able to deal with a few thieves if it comes to it."

Garrick nodded, but he didn't look comfortable.

"Let's hope we don't have to," he said. "It's not like we really have a plan."

She looked at him as they moved on.

"That bothers you, doesn't it?" she said.

"Yes," he replied.

"Why?"

"Because it means we can't be ready for whatever comes," he said.

Liliana laughed. She couldn't help it. He gave her a cold stare.

"I'm sorry, Garrick," she said. "I'm not trying to mock you. But you can never be prepared for 'whatever comes.' It's just impossible. You can't imagine every scenario, so you can't prepare for them all. Even if you could envision everything that could happen, it's extremely unlikely you could be ready to deal with it all."

He continued staring at her, incredulity pouring off him. Liliana chuckled.

"What are you saying?" he said.

"That worrying over every possibility isn't going to help," she said. "We've left the city, we're out in the middle of nowhere with no place to hide, and we don't know what our enemies are doing. All we can do is keep going forward and react as best we can to what develops."

He looked at her as though he had never heard anything more ridiculous.

"That's not the way I like to do things," he said.

"Of course not!" Liliana said, laughing again. "You're a soldier. You want to know exactly where everyone is and what the plan is for each scenario."

"Exactly," he said.

"Except that you can only plan so far, Garrick," she said. "The unexpected is a part of life. You have to be able to adapt. You need to learn that if you're going to be duke."

He didn't reply right away. She watched as he turned that idea over in his head.

"Yes," he said at last. "But that doesn't mean you shouldn't plan for what you *can* foresee."

"I never said it didn't," she said, smiling at him. "Just that you have to accept that no matter how well you plan, things are likely to go differently than you expected."

They chatted amiably for the rest of the afternoon, and Liliana found herself enjoying the journey again. They stopped periodically for Garrick to examine the tracks, but it was fairly obvious that both Levinia and Vicia were staying on course.

By nightfall, they'd just made it to the bend in the road where it turned south. The tracks were difficult to see, but Garrick was fairly certain both parties were still headed for The Enchanted Forest.

"If we quicken our pace, we may be able to make the forest before sundown tomorrow," Liliana said. "Let's make sure we give the horses plenty of food and water tonight. I want to push them a little harder tomorrow."

"What about Vicia and Levinia?" Garrick asked. "Aren't you worried we'll overtake them?"

"I don't think so," she answered. "We'll have to work to make it to the forest by day's end. Vicia should easily make it inside before then, and I would think Levinia would too."

Garrick nodded, and they moved off the road. It remained cold, but they were at lower elevation now, and Liliana pushed them back slightly east, so they could use the ridge for shelter. They were warmer and much more comfortable without the wind cutting through them.

"Why did you become a soldier?" she asked him after they'd eaten and bedded down by the fire.

"It was what I was good at," he said. "I got into a lot of fights as a boy. My father was the town undertaker. The other kids made fun of me, said I talked to the dead. I didn't like that, so I started fighting. My father tried to tell me there was no shame in what he did, that people needed his services. But that didn't change the way I was treated.

"Well, if you're going to be fighting all the time, you had better get good at it. It got so no one wanted to mess with me. Sometimes there would be amateur competitions, and I'd enter to earn some money.

"My father wanted me to apprentice with him, but I had no desire. I'd been mocked too much. I didn't want to actually start working with the dead.

"When I was fifteen, an adventurer was putting together a band of soldiers to go off into The Wild Lands to slay a dragon. I was dumb enough to volunteer. I didn't know anything about swordsmanship or other weapons. All I was practiced at was fisticuffs. But I went anyway.

"As you might imagine, venturing into The Wild Lands to take on a dragon is a fatally stupid idea. We were routed quickly. The dragon scorched us and tore the adventurer who hired us to pieces in front of our eyes. I was one of only two survivors. The other was the cook for the expedition.

"But I'd been taught swordsmanship and archery, so I thought I could make a name for myself as a hired warrior. That led me to enlist as a mercenary for several plunderers. I acquired a little money and a lot of skill. Eventually, I found my way to Lord Malach and signed on with his guard. I was there until Duke Evonin called out to me in my dreams."

Liliana lay on her back, looking up at the stars. The fire warmed the side of her face pleasantly. Garrick's tale reminded her a little of herself.

"So you never made a conscious choice to become a soldier?" she said. "You just fell into it?"

"More or less," he said. "I didn't go out looking to become a soldier-for-hire. I just discovered it was the thing I was good at, so I pursued it."

She chewed on that. It was interesting he should have come by his career so randomly, when he had explicitly said before he liked to have everything planned out. She supposed, though, that people changed as they grew.

"What about you?" he said. "Did you always want to be a sorcerer?"

"Yes and no," she answered. "I don't really remember what I wanted to be when I was a little girl. My parents were servants in Eldenberg, so I guess that's probably what would have happened to me."

"What *would* have happened?" he said.

"If I wasn't unusual," she said. "You see, I'm not really a sorcerer."

"What?"

"Well, I didn't understand it at the time," she explained, "but I have a special kind of power called wild magic. I'm not like other wizards. They have to use spells. I can just summon the magical energy and make it do what I want.

"But that ability is extremely rare in humans, and I had no idea that's what I was doing. I kept causing strange things to happen. My will was changing the environment, and there would be accidents – plates exploding with no warning, walls changing color. Once, the floor turned to mud right in front of my parents' employer. He twisted his ankle when he stepped in it and hurt himself when he fell. Not to mention his best suit was ruined.

"Anyway, when I was twelve, my parents made me leave. They were afraid of me. I don't really blame them. I'd have been scared of me too.

"By then, I knew this was some sort of magic, so I thought I should become a sorcerer. Since I lived in Eldenberg, it seemed like the perfect choice.

"The thing is, though, wild magic works completely differently than regular sorcery. I'd try to cast the spells they taught me, but I would make a total mess of it. The wild magic would change the eldritch power, and things would go horribly awry.

"I studied under three different masters, over the course of five years, and each one eventually turned me out, saying I was hopeless and would never learn. They told me no one could teach someone as inept as I.

"Well, I got to thinking about that, and I knew I was magically inclined, so it had to be possible for me to learn sorcery. So I thought that, since I was so inept – there really was no denying it; even I could see it – I would need the finest teacher in The Known World. I would need someone extremely gifted, who could figure out why I kept blowing things and fix it.

"So I packed up what little I had, and I traveled to Gothemus Draco's tower. I explained my situation to him and asked for him to take me on as an apprentice. He agreed.

"But the funny part was he couldn't teach me any better than the others. I still made all the same mistakes and all my spells went wrong. He just never got frustrated by it."

"So what changed?" Garrick asked. "You're extremely accomplished now."

"After he was murdered, I woke up with a note from him on my chest, saying I was supposed to gather up this box, take it to Dalasport, and find his son, Calibot. I was to give Calibot the box and tell him Gothemus had been murdered in Eldenberg and Calibot was supposed to go get the body. The box contained *Wyrmblade*, and you know what became of all that.

"However, before we went into the tower, Gothemus came to me in a vision and said he had left something for me. Inside, in my room, I found a grey stone on a pendant. When I picked it up, there was another vision, wherein Gothemus explained that I was a wild magician just like him. He told me that the wild magic had been spoiling my spells, and as long as I wore the pendant, it would enable to me to control the energy and work it the way I wanted.

"So naturally, I put it on, and I was able to fight by Calibot's side during the big battle at the tower, protecting him from Vicia and Elmanax.

"When that was over, I went back to Dalasport with Calibot and his husband. I served Duke Boordin for awhile before I got bored and set off to find some other purpose.

"So in a way, I've always wanted to be a sorcerer, but in another way, I just sort of fell into it like you did with soldiering. And in another way, I'm *still* not a sorcerer, because the magic I work is completely different."

"Fascinating," Garrick said.

"You're the first person I've told about being a wild magician, Garrick," she said. "Aside from Calibot and Devon, of course, since they were there. But I've kind of kept it a secret. I don't know why, but it seems important to keep that knowledge as an advantage, especially since other wizards don't think it's possible for humans to control wild magic."

She fell silent. The stars glittered down at her. Garrick didn't comment for a bit.

"Why did you decide to tell me?" he asked, breaking the silence.

"Because I'm your ally," she said. "You're here fulfilling your destiny, and I believe I was sent by someone – the gods or another power – to assist you. You need to know who I am, so I can serve you best. It's fate."

He didn't reply right away again. Liliana smiled up at the night sky. A sense of trust she wasn't quite familiar with descended on her. She'd trusted Gothemus, because he'd been patient with her. She'd trusted Calibot and Devon, because she felt she was supposed to.

But nothing was driving her feelings towards Garrick. He did nothing to make her feel as though she owed him her faith. He just made her feel right.

"Thank you," he said at last.

"You're welcome," she said.

She closed her eyes. Happiness enshrouded her like a warm blanket. Soon, she was fast asleep.

CHAPTER 16:

Strange Killers

B LAKE CALAVAN LOOKED ON Lindsay Grunvilio with disgust. The Chamber of Commerce's candidate prostrated himself before Blake, begging him for protection as though bandits were about to attack him at any moment.

"Please, General," Grunvilio whined. "You've got to help me."

"You're overblowing this, Mr. Grunvilio," Blake said, turning away and rolling his eyes at his adjutant, Errol, who smirked back.

"Am I?" Grunvilio said. "Every single night, since the contest began, one of the contestants has been murdered. Three nights ago, it was Bram Dover, assassinated in the very heart of the labor guild's headquarters. Then that braggart, Tumet, was killed in the street, despite being accompanied by two of his cronies. And last night, the illusionist, Edger, was murdered in the libraries while conducting research.

"These are not coincidences, General. This is a coordinated attack on all the aspirants. You're in as much danger as I am! You've got to protect us all!"

"*I'm* in danger?" Blake said, rounding on Grunvilio and making his incredulity plain. "I'm in danger? I'm the supreme military commander in

Twin Falls, Mr. Grunvilio. I am surrounded by trained soldiers, and I'm a master swordsman. I'm virtually untouchable."

Grunvilio's eyes narrowed. For the first time, his trademark contemptuous smile appeared.

"These are not mere soldiers or ordinary assassins, General," he said. "According to witnesses, they materialize from nowhere – as though they were made of vapor and suddenly become flesh. They wield magical weapons no mundane blade can equal. And they fight with a savagery and skill unmatched. They are not hired assassins, General Calavan. They are monsters summoned to kill."

Blake regarded him carefully. The richest man in Twin Falls had a wild look in his eyes. Fear burned in his mind. He was absolutely sincere.

And this was so unlike him. Grunvilio typically had a confident nonchalance brought on by the knowledge he could buy anyone or anything he liked. These murders had him spooked.

Blake admitted to himself he didn't know who was committing them. The only link was that all three victims were participants in the Contest of Succession. Given that they were murdered in three different locations, it could be coincidence.

But it probably wasn't. The descriptions from the survivors all matched. They all told of four lethal men dressed in black tunics, leggings, boots, cloaks, and hoods. Each wielded a strange weapon that glowed with unnatural light.

So given that all the victims were contestants and they were each killed by these same mysterious warriors, it stood to reason that someone was eliminating the competition. Someone was trying to make sure no one else could obtain the enigmatic Blessing of the Fey.

It wasn't him. And given that Grunvilio was here begging for protection, it wasn't him either. And it wasn't Dover, Tumet, or Edger, unless something had gone horribly wrong. So that left Zalachorus, Mordecai, Morrigan, and Tremaine. He'd spoken to Zalachorus this morning, and the sanctimonious magician had sworn he knew nothing about it. The other three left the city three days ago.

Blake sighed. It could be any of them, including his alleged ally. He was going to need to investigate further.

"If you're right, Mr. Grunvilio," he said, "if this is an attack on the aspirants to the throne, why don't you drop out? I'm sure you could save your life if you were no longer a candidate."

Blake wasn't sure that was actually true, but he wanted to see the merchant's reaction.

Grunvilio's expression soured. He glared at Blake, regarding him with suspicion.

"Because I am not a coward, General Calavan," he spat. "I would be unworthy of the title of Duke of Twin Falls if I were."

"Then why are you here?" Blake said.

"Because you're the law!" Grunvilio shouted. "You're supposed to protect the people of Twin Falls, and I am one of its foremost citizens. And because I came to warn you, General. Someone is trying to kill us. Someone wants to make sure only he or she can succeed. I thought you would want to know.

"Unless of course, it is you who is behind it. Perhaps these mysterious warriors with their magical weapons are soldiers of yours."

Blake smiled thinly at the accusation. He wasn't surprised. He'd gotten exactly the response he'd expected. Grunvilio was sincerely afraid. This wasn't some show. And he had no idea who was behind this. He just thought his life was in danger, and he wanted someone to help him.

"Calm down, Mr. Grunvilio," Blake said. "If I wanted to kill you, I wouldn't have to concoct some elaborate scheme. I'd just gore you now and be done with it. Do you think I couldn't arrange to have you disappear with no one knowing where you went?"

Grunvilio looked at him, horrified. Blake smiled wickedly. After a moment, the merchant's face broke into a grin, and he started to laugh, sounding just the slightest bit insane.

"Oh, very good," he exclaimed. "You had me going for a moment there. I'm sorry, General. I must be becoming paranoid."

Blake was about to say something sarcastic, when they heard yelling from without. He looked at the door and cocked his head. Someone shouted, and then there was a wail. Blake turned to Errol and flashed him a look that said, "Do you know what that is?"

"By the gods!" Grunvilio shouted. "They're here!"

Errol looked concerned. He drew his sword and stepped forward.

"You two," he said, addressing the soldiers who stood guard at the door. "See what that is. And use caution."

They turned to the doors, and one of them put his hand on the knob.

"Are you mad?" Grunvilio shouted. "You'll let them in!"

But the guard didn't listen. He pulled the door open as his partner set up with a spear.

There was a bright yellow flash, and the spearman fell over with a golden arrow buried in his chest. It vanished in another burst of yellow light before he hit the floor.

Blake couldn't help but gape. He'd never seen anything like this before. A black-garbed warrior knelt down the hallway with a bow in his hand. It didn't have a string.

Another assassin, dressed exactly the same, hurled a spear through the open door. It glowed with an otherworldly, green light. In fact, it seemed to be made purely of emerald energy. It embedded itself in Errol's chest, killing him instantly. Blake's adjutant fell over with a look of total surprise permanently set on his face.

"It's them!" Grunvilio squealed. "They've come for us!"

The spineless merchant turned to run. Blake had no idea where the fool thought he was going. But before he could take three steps an orange whip shot into the room, wrapped around Grunvilio's shoulders, and was pulled taut.

"Help!" he cried as he was yanked off his feet.

Blake watched in horror as the guilder was dragged across the floor to the door. There, a third warrior held the whip, while a fourth, with a sword made of Hell-red light, stood over Grunvilio and prepared to gore him.

That spurred Blake into action at last. He snatched his own sword out of its scabbard and rushed the assassins. He had no angle to parry the killer's attack on Grunvilio, so Blake settled for lowering his shoulder and body-checking the man to the floor before he could complete his murder.

The one holding the whip turned to Blake, but if he was surprised, Blake couldn't tell. There was no face visible under the black hood. There appeared to be nothing but darkness.

Regardless, Blake brought his blade around in a wide arc, intending to decapitate the killer. The strange assassin ducked the blow by throwing himself to the floor inside the room. He tucked and rolled and came up behind Blake, still holding the whip. Then he pulled Grunvilio into the room.

By then, the sword-wielding killer had regained his feet. He surged towards Blake, bringing his hellish blade around savagely. Blake got his own weapon up just in time to parry the blow. He was mildly surprised his sword was able to check the fiend's strike. Tremendous heat came off the red blade, as though it were made of hot, malevolent fury that no mere steel could deny.

But his sword protected him anyway, and Blake was at last in his element. He didn't know anything about acquiring blessings from the Fey, and he didn't understand whom these magical assassins were or why they were here. But fighting was something he knew a lot about, and he was good at it.

He pushed back and counterstruck. The black-hooded warrior was a keen swordsman. He easily parried Blake's thrust, then advanced, driving Blake back into the room.

The two hacked and slashed at each other, with neither able to gain advantage. The assassin appeared to expend no effort matching Blake blow for blow. Like his companion with the whip, he had no face Blake could detect. There was only cold, empty darkness under his black cowl.

A yellow flash behind him was followed by a scream. The bowman had shot the other soldier guarding the door. Blake grimaced as his man fell to the floor.

Out of the corner of his eye, he saw the second warrior withdraw his spear from Errol's chest. Damn! He was outnumbered, and Grunvilio was no help. If he didn't get reinforcements soon, they were done for.

"No!" Grunvilio cried.

Blake turned to see what was happening – a move that cost him. The swordsman's red blade bit into his shoulder, burning him as though it were made of fire. The force of the blow knocked him to the floor.

He had a perfect view of the spearman driving his weapon into the merchant's gut. Grunvilio screamed as he was gored. The killer pulled out the weapon and then drove it into the guilder's throat. He died with a terrible gurgling.

Blake shoved the horror of it from his mind. If he panicked, he'd be next.

He jumped to his feet preparing to resume his duel with the red-bladed swordsman, but the strange warrior only held out his weapon to keep Blake at bay. His companions gathered behind him and then went out.

When they had made it through the door, the swordsman backed out of the room. When he was across the threshold. He lowered his blade. A second later, it dematerialized, as though the source of its crimson light had been extinguished. Before Blake could think to charge him, the black-garbed killer turned to smoke and drifted away down the hall.

Blake was left standing in a room filled with four dead bodies. The hallway without was littered with several more.

Once again, Blake couldn't help but gape at the scene. What the hell had just happened here?

It was obvious that the assassins had struck again, that this time their target had been Lindsay Grunvilio. It was further obvious that they were indeed killing off the other competitors in the Contest of Succession.

What didn't make any sense was why they had spared *him*. He was an aspirant to the throne too. He hadn't hired these strange killers, so if their mission was to murder everyone but their employer, why hadn't they taken him also? That swordsman was besting him, and after killing Grunvilio, Blake was outnumbered four to one.

It just didn't make sense. Something very odd was happening.

He needed to get this cleaned up. He also needed to get some help, find out what everyone knew, and get the dead down to the morgue.

And then he was going to pay a visit to Zalachorus ir-Bedlam Donovian. His so-called partner had some questions to answer.

CHAPTER 17:

Barring the Way

FOUR DAYS AFTER SHE left Twin Falls, Vicia arrived at The Enchanted Forest. She'd seen it looming on the horizon ever since the road from the city turned south, but its appearance in front of her still seemed sudden. A thin layer of snow covered the plains leading up to it, and then, as abruptly as a city wall rising from the earth, it stood towering before her, with trees reaching high towards the heavens.

Despite the season, the forest was verdant. Winter seemed to exist only outside its borders. Within, the magic kept it eternally summer. Green light glowed with livelihood. Warmth crept softly from its edges.

Vicia smiled. Inside, was the dryad Peaseblossom. She waited in her vernal prison for someone to release her. Someone with magic, who could overcome the bonds placed on her. Someone like Vicia. And then she would grant her the boon necessary to claim the throne of Twin Falls.

That thought made Vicia warmer than the magical glow radiating from The Enchanted Forest. Lord Vestran and the rest of the cowardly Council of Elders had made her the scapegoat for the failure of the plan to obtain the Eye of the Dragon. They'd expelled her and attempted to have her executed. Those weak fools hadn't had the vision to eliminate the bane of their existence – Gothemus Draco. Only Vicia had had the courage to attempt it, and the Council had gone along.

She'd done it because she'd planned to become President of the Council of Elders – arguably the most powerful sorcerer in The Known World. With the Eye in hand and The Known World at their feet, she'd have driven Vestran from the office and destroyed anyone who opposed her.

Well, now she was going to become Duchess of Twin Falls. Then she and Kremdor were going to show the Council its folly. Eldenberg would become property of Twin Falls. Afterward, she would turn her sights to Dalasport, avenging herself on Calibot and his husband.

Everyone who'd crossed her was going to pay. The Known World would tremble before her. Vicia Morrigan would be queen over all, and her name would be both feared and revered.

But first, she had a few details to attend to. She had to rescue Peaseblossom and secure the Blessing of the Fey. Before that, though, she needed to deal with the people following her.

Levinia Mordecai and three of her stooges had been trailing her since she left the city. They'd been stealthy, creeping across the plains at a distance, hoping she wouldn't notice them. They'd kept an advance scout on foot and dressed in white, so he wouldn't be as easy to detect in the snow.

They were fools. Even if she hadn't expected someone to shadow her, her magic was easily enough to reveal them. Vicia knew she was the only one who understood Chancellor Bismarck's riddle. Kremdor had given it to her before the contest began. She also knew at least one competitor would be clever enough to trail her, thinking she would be foolish enough to lead them to the prize, so they could steal it.

Vicia had no intention of allowing anyone to jump her claim to the throne. She was not about to be denied her rightful place of rulership again. Fortunately, Kremdor had a solution – a spell he'd taught her to make certain all pursuit ended here. It was time to leave Levinia Mordecai behind.

The road led directly through the trees. Branches sprouted over it, forming a natural arch of leaves – a sort of vernal gateway. Vicia spurred her mount to canter into the magical forest. A curtain of pleasant warmth fell over her as soon as she crossed the threshold.

However, she had just penetrated the forest, when she pulled on the reins. She wheeled the appaloosa around so she faced the entry. Then she raised her staff.

"*Crescere*," she said.

The end of her staff radiated yellow light. A moment later, the branches of the trees were illumined with the same golden glow.

"*Crescere,*" Vicia said again, with more authority.

The yellow light brightened. Slowly, the branches expanded, growing before her eyes. Vicia fed the spell more eldritch energy and pointed her staff at the ground.

"*Crescere!*" she cried, and her voice echoed off the trees as though she had shouted into a cave.

The branches obeyed her will, growing down from on high like some giant, wooden portcullis, barring entry to The Enchanted Forest. Vicia continued to pour energy into the spell, delighting as the natural magic of the trees enhanced and amplified her sorcery like the bell of a horn. Unsatisfied with simply covering the arch, she wove the branches together until the limbs and leaves were so thickly entangled that passage into the forest was absolutely impossible.

Still she wasn't done. The golden light intensified until Vicia could barely see as she fed the spell more power. She extended the growth as far as she could manage in both directions, creating an impasse over five miles both east and west. Anyone coming after her would travel for an hour before finding entry. And then they'd be hopelessly off-course.

Even that wasn't enough. Walling off her competition was good, but she wanted better. She wanted them dead.

"*Spinas venenosa,*" she said.

The light of her staff changed from yellow to crimson. A ray of blood-red energy shot from it to the branches. Thorns as sharp as daggers grew from the thick branches, pointing in every direction.

At last, the light returned to normal, and Vicia lowered her staff and rested. She was a conjurer, not a transmutationist. Kremdor had taught her the spell, but she was unaccustomed to working that kind of magic. It drained her, especially since she had altered so many of the trees.

But Vicia smiled in satisfaction. Let them try to cut their way through that.

She removed her warm, winter cloak. She was already sweating in the humid air of the forest, and the exertion of that much sorcery had made it worse. She took a few moments to pack away the cloak and catch her breath.

Then she wheeled the horse around and spurred her down the road. Based on the directions Kremdor had given her, she needed to travel south for roughly another hour. Then it would be time to veer off to the west and a date with destiny.

"I'm coming, Peaseblossom," she said aloud. "Our mutual suffering is nearly at an end."

The sun was low in the afternoon sky when Levinia and her companions at last made it to the forest. Merrick was standing at the edge of the trees, looking worried and nonplussed. That alone was enough to tell Levinia something was wrong.

Her next clue was that the road seemed to end.

The road to Sothernia went straight through The Enchanted Forest, branching off to Lord Alavair's and Lord Kremdor's fortresses along the way. So it was definitely strange that there were thick tree branches and nasty-looking thorns completely barring the way. Had things changed? If so, why wouldn't she have heard about it? Enough trade came up this road that the Chamber of Commerce and the Brotherhood of Labor would have said something. She had spies everywhere. She would have known if the road had closed.

So there had to be some other explanation for this obstacle. This was a recent development, and it didn't portend well.

"Where's Vicia?" she asked Merrick without preamble.

"Inside," he answered, thumbing his hand over his shoulder in the direction of the trees.

"How?" she said, packing all of her inquiries into a single word.

"She arrived a few hours before you," Merrick explained. "Around midday. The road was clear then. When she went in, she cast a spell. The branches grew before my eyes. They completely covered the road."

"Yes, I can see that."

"They wove among themselves to further bar our entry," he went on. "And then I heard her cast a second spell. The thorns you see grew from the branches."

Levinia examined them. They looked lethal.

"Did she see you?" she said.

"I don't believe so," Merrick said. "Although, I suppose it is possible she did. But I was well-hidden."

"Hmm," Levinia said. "So she either knew we were following her, or she was taking precautions."

"Have you scouted to see how far this barrier extends?"

"Yes, ma'am," he said. "It's over a mile in both directions. We'll have to go considerably out of our way to penetrate this mess."

Levinia swore silently. Vicia knew what she was doing. She must have planned for this all along. Who knew how far the blockade went? If it was more than a few miles, there would be almost no chance of tracking her unless they got lucky.

"Maybe we can cut our way through," Stephen said.

She turned and looked at her chief lieutenant. He didn't appear to be offering sarcasm. His expression suggested it was a legitimate option.

"Thoughts?" she said.

"I think it's worth a try," Kanyon said. "We have axes."

"I disagree," Merrick said. "This was done by magic. It therefore cannot be undone simply. Furthermore, this is The Enchanted Forest. The trees here are said to be sentient. Chopping at them may be a mistake."

"They're just wood," Kanyon countered. "Wood yields to steel. And sentient or otherwise, it's not like the trees can stop us."

Levinia thought about it. He made an interesting point.

"Stephen?" she said, asking for another analysis.

"I agree with Kanyon," he said. "Merrick is correct that magic creates problems of its own, but assuming this is wood, even *intelligent* wood, it should not be able to withstand an axe blade."

She considered it a little longer. She decided they would not know who was correct without trying.

"Very well," she said. "Kanyon, try your axe."

"Yes, ma'am," he said.

He dismounted, unpacked his supplies, and withdrew the hand-axe from his bag. It was really only intended for cutting small wood for fires, but Kanyon was both large and strong. Levinia had chosen him to test the theory not because it was his, but because he had the greatest chance for success.

Kanyon approached the wall and then gazed on it for a few moments, studying it for a place that might be ideal to strike. When he thought he had one, he raised the axe high above his head and brought it crashing down on the barrier.

The blade sank into the soft wood, and several splinters of bark flew off. Kanyon smiled, wrenched the blade out of the branch, and then raised it and struck again.

This time, though, he cried out. He let go of the axe handle, and his left hand flew to his right forearm. He turned back to Levinia in pain and horror, and she saw that he had gashed his arm open on one of the thorns. She was about to ask how bad it was, when his eyes rolled up into his head, and he fell to the ground.

"Kanyon!" she cried.

Merrick rushed over to him. He examined him, calling his name several times. Kanyon didn't answer. After several moments, Merrick looked up at Levinia, blank terror on his face.

"He's dead," he said, astonished.

"Dead?" Levinia said. "How?"

No matter how severe the wound had been from that thorn, it shouldn't have been enough to kill him that quickly.

"Poison," Stephen answered. "And an extremely potent toxin, judging by how quickly he succumbed."

"Magic?" Levinia said.

"I've no doubt," Stephen replied. "There are plants and animals with highly lethal venom, but for it to act that quickly, there has to be magical enhancement."

Damn. If that was true, then it was Vicia's doing. Not only had she barred the way, she'd made certain to kill anyone who tried to undo her interference.

"Now what?" she said.

"Fire?" Stephen suggested.

"No," Merrick said, his voice adamant. "My mother used to tell me stories about this forest when I was little. She very specifically said the trees are sentient, and the fastest way to earn their wrath is to bring fire to The Enchanted Forest."

"Was your mother a loremaster?" Stephen snorted.

"It doesn't matter," Levinia said. "Everyone knows this forest is magical and everything here is different. For the gods' sake, look at it. It's winter, and the trees are green. They're not conifers; they're deciduous. That shouldn't be. No matter what his mother knew or didn't know, it's clear the usual rules don't apply here. And given that we just lost Kanyon due to attempting something Merrick thought was risky, I think we should err on the side of caution."

No one said anything for a bit. They all stared gloomily at Kanyon's body.

"Since this is a problem created by a magician, perhaps we need a magician to solve it for us," Stephen said.

"What do you mean?" Merrick said.

"Garrick Tremaine and his sorcerer have been following us nearly as long as we've been following Vicia," Stephen said. "They haven't veered off the road. They no doubt have the same plan we do – allow Vicia to lead us to the blessing and then steal it from her once she has it.

"Since she's a sorcerer, she may be able to undo Vicia's magic. I suggest we lie in wait for them and allow her to solve the problem for us."

"Suppose she isn't willing to help us?" Merrick said. "She's helping Tremaine. She'd want to thwart us."

"If we hide from them, it will be logical to assume we've already gone in," Stephen said. "So we let her undo Vicia's magic, and then we follow them in."

Levinia nodded. That was sound logic. She didn't believe for a moment Tremaine and his lieutenant could be trusted to cooperate. But if they didn't know Levinia and *Res Nostra* were waiting for them, relying on them to gain passage to The Enchanted Forest, she might be able to use them as unwitting allies.

"All right," she said. "That plan makes sense. Stephen, get Kanyon. We'll need to find a place out of the way to bury him. Merrick, make us a place where we can hide but still observe the road."

"Yes, ma'am," they both said.

She regretted losing Kanyon. He was a good man, and he was their best tracker. His skills would be hard to replace. She would remember to reward his family richly when she was duchess.

In the meantime, they had a lot to accomplish. Tremaine and his sorcerer would be here in two hours or less.

CHAPTER 18:

Strength in Numbers

GARRICK AWOKE THE NEXT morning feeling more like himself than he had in a week. He was still sore from sleeping on the ground, but Liliana's idea to move off the road far enough to use the ridge for shelter had been a good one. The wind passed over them, and they slept warmly for the first time since leaving Twin Falls. Moreover, there had been no goblin attack the night before.

This was the closest he'd come to rest since before he was abducted and crucified. His wounds had largely healed, and his energy had returned. His only complaint was hunger, and that was easily sated.

Liliana was in equally good spirits, and she moved about camp, humming tunelessly as she prepared their breakfast. The wind blew her blonde hair into her face multiple times, and he found himself charmed by that silly look and the way she wouldn't fix it right away, instead waiting until virtually half her hair was completely obscuring her vision.

The startlingly frank conversation they'd had the night before returned to his mind. She was a lot like him in some ways. She'd struggled to fit in, to find her place. Garrick hadn't really felt at home until he'd settled in as one of Lord Malach's hired swords. He found friends and camaraderie there. Liliana's story of bouncing from one master to the next and only truly discovering her gifts after Gothemus Draco died, reminded him of his own struggles to like who he was.

Whatever else this strange journey had brought him – and there had been a lot of misery already – he enjoyed Liliana Gray's company. At least if he had to follow a destiny he wasn't sure was his in the first place, he had someone he liked with whom to share the road.

Like she had promised, Liliana drove them at a good pace all day. Garrick wasn't able to watch the tracks as carefully, but it didn't matter. They clearly led to The Enchanted Forest.

By midday, he thought he could see it off in the distance. The horizon had been blue and gray with faraway snow, but it started looking green by noon, which surprised him. At this time of year, he would have expected the forest to be stark and bare, enchanted or otherwise. He told himself it must be a trick of the light or that there were a large number of coniferous trees.

But as the day wore on, the emerald light at the edge of the sky grew brighter. By three o'clock, it was still a ways off in the distance, but he could clearly see a large, deciduous forest before them. An hour later, he was certain they were deciduous trees.

His suspicions were confirmed half an hour later. They came at last to the forest as the light was starting to fail. Leafy, green trees stretched as far as he could see to the east and west. They were tall and thick and majestic, and they seemed to glow from within with a soft luminance that made them appear friendly and comforting.

But Liliana frowned as they got close, and he, too, could see something was wrong. The road ended abruptly at the trees. Large branches twisted and wove across it in both directions. It was completely impassable. Worse, the wood was covered in thorns the size of daggers. They pointed at every angle, and Garrick saw no way to cut through the branches without being sliced to pieces.

"That's strange," he said. "I thought the road went through the forest to Sothernia and The Krem."

"It does," she replied. "And to Lord Alavair's fortress. Something has happened."

She frowned at the barrier. Then she dismounted and walked straight to it. She cocked her head and examined the twisted limbs. She leaned in so closely, Garrick was afraid she might decapitate herself on the thorns.

"This is sorcery," she pronounced after pulling her head back out. "The magic here is different than the natural enchantment of the forest. This was done deliberately to prevent anyone from entering."

"Vicia," Garrick said.

"Almost certainly," Liliana said. "Although I suppose it's possible this is part of the contest somehow – that you have to defeat the barrier to enter and get the blessing."

Garrick had another look at the edge of the trees. He saw thorns to the edge of his vision both east and west.

"Well it was definitely done to prevent entry," he said. "I can't see a way in in either direction. My guess is we'd have to walk a very long way to find one."

Liliana didn't say anything. She continued to stare at the forest.

"What do you recommend?" Garrick asked.

"I believe I can undo this," she said after a pause. "At least enough for us to penetrate the forest. But it will take a lot of energy and time. We'll need to wait until tomorrow."

"What about Vicia?"

"There's nothing we can do about her," Liliana said. "This is almost certainly her work, and she surely did it so she couldn't be followed. But it's going to take me some time, and I'll need to be able to see what I'm doing. We'll have to wait until morning. In theory, she won't be traveling tonight. So she won't have more than a day's jump on us."

"What if that's enough time?" he said.

"Garrick," she said turning to him, "we know we must perform a service for Peaseblossom to receive her favor. When we find her, we will do whatever is necessary. We can only manage this at the pace we can. Vicia has cleverly slowed us down, but we are not defeated. We'll have to locate Peaseblossom, earn her boon, and then try to overtake Vicia on the way back to Twin Falls.

"In the interim, we need to rest. This is powerful magic. I need to be fresh if I'm going to defeat it."

He nodded. There was no arguing with her. He was completely out of his depth here, and this whole plan had been her idea.

"Whatever you say," he said. "You're the wizard."

She regarded him curiously. He smiled at her to show he trusted her.

"Come on," she said. "Let's make camp. It'll be dark soon."

Garrick had just finished his dinner when he and Liliana heard shouts in the distance. They both turned to look. It was too dark to see what might be happening, but there was definitely a commotion to the east, and it was a lot closer than Garrick had initially thought.

A second later, a bright, yellow flash briefly illuminated the scene. Three people were under attack. One lay on the ground, a golden arrow embedded in his chest. It was difficult to see whom they were fighting.

"Come on!" Liliana shouted as she took off at a run in the direction of the skirmish.

Garrick leaped to his feet, snatched his sword from its scabbard, and raced after her.

More eerie light rose from the snow. A line of orange stretched away a short distance, while a second, shorter green light rose up from the ground.

"Help!" a woman's voice cried.

Garrick thought he detected someone else moving to her aid, but a third line of light, this one thicker and red, materialized and flashed back and forth. A moment later, Garrick realized it was some sort of magical sword, and its wielder was dueling one of the people in the other camp.

When he reached the fight, he saw four strange men dressed all in black. The orange line turned out to be a whip held by one of them, with which he had ensnared Levinia Mordecai. A second warrior moved to gore Levinia with the green light, which Garrick now saw was a spear.

Before the assassin could strike, Liliana opened her hand, shooting a ball of red light from it that struck the spearman in the back. A terrifying, otherworldly shriek ripped through the darkness, causing Garrick's flesh to ripple in horror. The fiend's spear exploded in a blast of emerald light so bright, Garrick was dazzled. When his vision cleared, all that was left of the would-be killer was a pool of viscous, black liquid on the ground.

A fourth warrior Garrick hadn't seen before wielded a bow. He turned towards Liliana and took aim.

"No!" Garrick shouted.

He rushed the black-garbed man as the fiend drew back his bow. An arrow of golden light magically appeared in it, nocked and ready to shoot.

Garrick chopped at the pristine wood. His blade made contact with the bow, spoiling the shot. The arrow launched harmlessly into the ground and disappeared in a flash of yellow light.

Liliana cast another spell, this time at the man holding the whip. He flung himself to the ground, rolling under it. He came up on one knee right next to Garrick. With a savage swing of his sword, Garrick sliced neatly through his neck.

But his head did not roll off. Instead, the killer turned to smoke and rose up into the sky. A second later, the man with the bow and the warrior with the red sword, who was dueling Levinia's companion, did the same. They gathered briefly overhead and then shot away to the southeast as though propelled by some powerful wind.

Everyone stood panting and staring after them in astonishment.

"Who . . ." the man gasped, "who *was* that?"

"Assassins," Liliana answered. "Commanded by someone with a powerful artifact."

"Are they demons?" the man said.

"Not exactly," Liliana said. "They are called the Silent Knights. Four powerful killers, each with a unique weapon. They never speak a word, only murder their intended target without mercy."

"But who—" Levinia began, but Liliana interrupted her.

"The identity of the person who sent them is unknowable," she said. "Although, we can hazard a guess. But they serve the Crown of Silence. Whoever wears it may give them the name of an individual. Once uttered, that person is doomed. The Knights will not rest until he or she is silenced forever."

No one spoke for a moment. They all stood around, gazing fearfully off towards the southeast.

"Will they be back tonight?" the man asked.

"I've no way of knowing for sure," Liliana said. "But I doubt it. We've done what is not supposed to be possible. We've killed one of them."

Everyone's attention turned to the black mess in the snow. The oily substance smoked as though it had been burning and was only recently extinguished.

"How?" Levinia said.

"They must be vulnerable to magic," Liliana said. "I hit this one with a fireball, and it screamed and left these remains. By contrast, Garrick beheaded one, but it turned to vapor like its comrades and fled."

"But why were they after us?" Levinia said.

119

Liliana looked at her for the first time. She gazed coolly on her.

"You are Levinia Mordecai, are you not?" Liliana said.

"Yes," Levinia said, a note of caution in her tone.

"And you are a contestant for the throne of Twin Falls," Liliana said. "It is logical to assume then that you were targeted by someone who does not want you to succeed."

"Zalachorus?" the man said.

"As logical as that would be," Liliana replied, turning to him, "I do not believe he left the city."

"So?" the man said.

"The Knights fled to the southeast. That would take them *inside* The Enchanted Forest. Assuming they were returning to the Crown, the wearer would have to be inside the trees. Which means either this is an obstacle designed as part of the Contest of Succession—"

"Or Vicia Morrigan wears the Crown of Silence," Levinia finished.

Garrick cursed. Of course. Vicia had arrived in the forest earlier in the day. She had used magic to bar the rest of them from entering. Then she'd summoned her killers to murder them.

"But why wait to attack us until now?" the man said.

"The Silent Knights can only be summoned after dark," Liliana said. "The magic does not work in the daylight."

"It's a good thing you happened along," Levinia said.

"We didn't just happen along, Ms. Mordecai," Liliana said. "We were doing the same thing you are. We were following Vicia to see if she can lead us to the Blessing of the Fey. She seems to know more about it than the rest of us.

"And you were here because she made it impossible to gain access to the forest."

No one said anything for a moment. Liliana calling out Levinia left uncomfortable admissions lying in the open unspoken.

"Perhaps we should work together," Levinia said at last.

"What do you mean?" Garrick asked.

"We've been tracking Vicia for exactly the reasons you say," Levinia said. "But I've lost two of my men today – one to the thorns and a second to these Silent Knights. I cannot gain entrance to the forest without magic, and if these killers return, they seem to be vulnerable only to sorcery. So it makes sense for Stephen and me to throw in with you."

"And what's the advantage for us?" Garrick said.

He still wasn't sure he wanted to be duke, but he knew a power play when he saw one. Levinia realized her own campaign was dead and was trying to revive it by clinging to his.

"Strength in numbers," Levinia answered. "If the Silent Knights have come for me, they will surely come for you, Garrick Tremaine. And your sorcerer here can fight only one of them at a time. The rest of us can at least hold them off while she works her magic.

"Additionally, I brought Stephen, Merrick, and Kanyon with me, because they are expert trackers. If we are to overtake Vicia and prevent her from securing the Blessing of the Fey, whatever it is, for herself, we'll need to know which way she went.

"So you see, we can help each other."

Garrick nodded. It made sense, but he still had questions.

"What about the throne?" he asked. "Assuming we defeat Vicia, how do we settle that?"

"I'm sure we can work that out once our other rivals are defeated," Levinia said, a wry smile on her face.

Garrick didn't like it. Levinia was being too cagey.

"How do we know we can trust you, Ms. Mordecai?" he said.

"You saved my life," she said as though it should be obvious. "I owe you."

He studied her, trying to determine if she were sincere. She offered him a smirk in return.

He sighed. In the end, there was no way to know if she would betray him or not. She was a criminal, she had her own agenda, and she aspired to the throne. It seemed likely she would sell him out eventually.

But her logic was sound. For the moment, at least, they made better allies than rivals.

"Very well," Garrick said.

"So now what?" Stephen asked.

"We need to get into the forest," Levinia said. "Can you manage that?"

"I think so," Liliana answered. "But I need to rest. Given the enormity of the job, it's going to require a lot of energy. I can attack it in the morning."

"Then I suggest we merge our camps and establish a watch," Stephen said.

"Good idea," Levinia offered.

"I'll take the first one," Garrick said.

Levinia smiled broadly.

"Ah, Mr. Tremaine," she said. "I can see you're willing to cooperate, but trust will be slow to establish."

"I would think you of all people would understand that, Ms. Mordecai."

"Quite," she said, still smiling.

Garrick still wasn't sure he liked the arrangement, but there was nothing for it. For now, at least, they were all on the same side.

CHAPTER 19:

The Dangerous One

KREMDOR SIGHED REGRETFULLY. HE gazed on the Crown of Silence. The emerald in its fourth spire was shattered. Someone had killed the Green Knight. He had no way of knowing whom, but he could guess. The only way to dispatch the Silent Knights was through magic. It was almost certain Liliana Gray was responsible.

Vicia had been right. The woman was considerably dangerous. And since all the evidence to date suggested she was what didn't seem possible – a wild magician – she was clearly the biggest threat not only to his current scheme, but his ambitions as a whole.

The other three gems on the Crown lit up, filling his *sanctum* with a strange mix of red, orange, and yellow light. He turned to the window, and moments later, three swift streams of smoke blew in, came to a halt, and then formed into the dark bodies of the surviving Knights.

"You've lost one of your number," Kremdor said.

The Red Knight bowed his head in acknowledgement.

"This occurred while you were attempting to assassinate one of the targets?"

A second nod.

"Was your mission otherwise successful?" Kremdor asked.

The Red Knight shook his head. Kremdor frowned behind his mask. They had eliminated Dover, Tumet, Edger, and Grunvilio. He had given them five names.

"You were attempting to kill Levinia Mordecai?" he prompted.

The Red Knight nodded again.

"Was there a sorcerer present?"

A fourth nod. Kremdor thought about it. Mordecai and Tremaine had both left the city in pursuit of Vicia. They must have joined forces. That complicated matters.

"How many people survived your assault?" he asked.

The Red Knight held up four fingers. So, Mordecai was still alive, and it stood to reason two of the others were Tremaine and Gray. The fourth must have been one of the goons Mordecai had brought with her.

"The sorcerer survived?" he prodded.

The Red Knight nodded again, confirming Kremdor's suspicions. So Mordecai and Tremaine were working together now. And Liliana Gray was their ally. Vicia had at least a day's head start on them, but could they overtake her or overwhelm her if they teamed up? It would be better not to find out.

"Return to your home," Kremdor said. "I release you from your current contract."

All three Silent Knights bowed their heads deferentially. Then they turned to vapor and drifted into their stones on the Crown.

It was time to alter his strategy slightly. With Liliana Gray capable of destroying his best minions, he needed to deal with her first. Everything else could wait.

He went to the fire and tossed summoning powder into it and waited for the flames to turn green. Then he raised his arms.

"Gremsh," he called out. "Gremsh, Lord of Goblins, hear me."

He had to repeat the command three times before he finally felt Gremsh's presence come through the fire. The Lord of Goblins was getting more impertinent. He would need to fix that in the future.

"What do you want, Kremdor?" Gremsh said as his ugly visage appeared in the flames. "If you want me to catch Garrick Tremaine for you, you'll need to give me the time to actually do it."

Kremdor frowned. Gremsh definitely thought he was more important to the plan than he was. If Kremdor hadn't needed him for the task at hand, he'd have killed him for his insolence.

"There has been a development of which you need to be aware," Kremdor said, controlling his temper.

"What is it?" Gremsh said, leering at him through his lone, yellow eye.

"Tremaine has joined forces with another of Lord Vicia's rivals," Kremdor said. "There are now four in his party instead of two."

"I thought you were dealing with the rivals," Gremsh said.

"That's the development," Kremdor said. "There has been a complication."

"I thought the development was the new alliance," Gremsh sneered.

"Shut up and listen," Kremdor snapped. "The problem is the sorcerer, Liliana Gray. Her magic is much more powerful than we anticipated. That is how she freed Tremaine from your cousin, how he has managed to elude recapture, and how my work on eliminating Vicia's rivals has been set back.

"She is the dangerous one, Gremsh. She must be killed above all others. Even if you have to let Tremaine escape, you must dispatch Liliana Gray. Do you understand?"

"I understand what you are saying, Lord Kremdor," Gremsh said. "But not why. We must have Tremaine's essence to free Gruul. To do that, we must sacrifice him. If we let him escape just to kill this sorcerer . . ."

Kremdor bit his lip to keep from shouting. The goblins did not grasp the entirety of the situation. Freeing their god was an important piece of things, but it wasn't the only consideration.

"That may not be true," Kremdor explained. "We have a good bit of Garrick Tremaine's essence already. The sacrifice was in process when he was rescued. We might not need him to break Gruul's chains. I am only being thorough in seeking him.

"But even if that isn't true, even if we *do* need more from him, we cannot get it while Liliana Gray lives. She will track him down and use her magic to destroy us. If you allow Tremaine to escape while ensuring her death, he can be easily hunted with no magician to protect him. But while she lives, Garrick Tremaine is all but lost to us, and she is a direct threat to the rest of the operation.

"So find Tremaine as you were planning. Be aware that his numbers are doubled. But whatever you do, make sure you kill Gray. Your entire ambush should be keyed to getting her. Don't let her escape, and don't let her live."

Gremsh stared at him with his one-eyed gaze for some time, assessing Kremdor's words. He put a green hand to his greasy chin and stroked it thoughtfully.

"If she's that powerful," Gremsh said cautiously, "what makes you think we can take her? She's defeated every other goblin war party dispatched to bring in Tremaine. It sounds like she's defeated whomever you sent after the other contestants. Why do you think I can succeed?"

Kremdor smiled behind his mask. This was the goblin he knew – calculating, clever. Gremsh suspected he was being set up.

"You will have the element of surprise," Kremdor explained. "Every expedition thus far has been aimed at bringing in Tremaine. Gray has been an afterthought – just someone to deal with to get the true objective.

"Your assault will be aimed at her. The whole purpose will be her death. They will not suspect this. They will focus their efforts on keeping Tremaine safe. That will leave her vulnerable."

Gremsh grinned fiendishly. Kremdor could see he liked the misdirection. The idea of tricking the humans into defending the wrong person appealed to his diabolical mind.

"Very well," he said. "If they enter the forest, they will pay with their lives."

"They will," Kremdor said. Vicia's magic wouldn't hold them forever. "See that you water the trees with their blood. And don't forget – Liliana Gray is to die, even if the others do not. The only thing that matters is her demise. Everything else follows from that."

"I won't forget," Gremsh growled. "Whatever you may think, I'm not stupid."

"If I'd thought you were stupid, I wouldn't have hired you, Gremsh," Kremdor replied. "*That* would have been stupid."

Of course, Kremdor *did* think he was arrogant, and that was a weakness that would lead to the downfall of the so-called Lord of Goblins.

All that could wait, though. For the moment, Kremdor needed someone to murder Liliana Gray, and Gremsh was his best option. Kremdor feared everything else would be in jeopardy if Gursh's cousin failed.

CHAPTER 20:

The Soul of the Woods

VICIA STARED AT THE small cluster of holly bushes in disgust. She was certain this was the third time she'd seen them. She'd thought they'd looked familiar last time, but she hadn't wanted to believe it was true. It was time to admit it, though. She was going in circles.

She cursed Kremdor. His magic was too clever, keeping Peaseblossom hidden well away, causing someone seeking her to continue passing by without noticing her vernal prison. It would ensure none of the other contestants could free her to gain her favor.

But Vicia was *supposed* to find her. She *had* to penetrate the spell. Why the hell hadn't he designed it so she wouldn't have to work so hard?

She contemplated calling him for help. He created the damned thing; he should have to get her through it. But she was not about to beg him for assistance. This was her part of the mission, and she had to prove she was worthy of the title Duchess of Twin Falls.

Besides, she hated groveling.

She sighed. Then she raised her staff, closed her eyes, and spoke.

"*Locant* Peaseblossom," she said.

Silver sparks crackled from the end of her staff, flew out in front of her, and landed in a splash on the ground. Then they stretched away to form a shimmering path leading off in the same direction she had already traveled twice.

Muttering another curse, she spurred her horse forward. Kremdor had said the gate was overgrown with holly. Vicia had seen this one patch only. Hopefully this time, the spell would reveal it. She was tired of seeking her destiny. She wanted it now.

Liliana stood before the entangled impasse, studying it. In theory, this was simple to undo. Vicia had just enchanted the branches to grow and weave, and all she had to do was reverse that sorcery.

But the magic here was potent. She could feel it pouring out of the wood, heating her face like a bonfire. It wasn't clear how much power this would require.

She closed her eyes and reached out her other senses to the air around her. The tendrils of eldritch energy she normally felt were stronger, thicker, and concentrated in the forest. Indeed, she saw not so much sorcery in the tangled wall but wild magic, coursing through the branches like a raging river rushing relentlessly toward its mouth. It was this power she needed to tap to unmake Vicia's blockade.

Still with her eyes closed so she wouldn't be distracted by her outer vision, she raised her arms and slowly opened her hands. She drew the wild magic into her body, felt her insides become hot, as though she had a deadly fever. Sweat poured off her brow, and her hair dampened and stuck to her skin.

"Are you okay?" Garrick said.

"Hush," she managed before returning her full concentration to the task at hand. She needed all her focus.

When she thought she could absorb no more of the forest's potent energy, she turned her hands so her palms faced the trees. Then she passed the magic back to the branches along with her will.

The enchanted wood did not yield. It stayed stubbornly in its tangled condition. She realized she was holding her breath and gasped for air.

An unvoiced call resounded in her head. She could make out no words, no feelings. But the trees beckoned her, invited her. An entrancing melody lilted through her mind over and over. Yes! Deep in her heart, she heard and understood their song.

Liliana rotated her palms back towards her head, once again drawing the magic into her body. The eldritch power seared her brain like a brand. She moaned painfully, desperately clinging to the energy, refusing to let it go, lest she be unable to regain it.

"Liliana!" Garrick shouted, but she ignored him.

She turned her hands towards the trees again, reversed the flow of magic. This time, in addition to her will, she sent her mind.

All at once, she felt every single tree, shrub, and blade of grass. She was alive in a way she'd never been. She was connected to the earth, could feel its breath on the wind and the beating of its stone heart. The thrill of being *in* the trees, in the forest's strange consciousness, quickened her heart rate.

Part, she thought. *I need you to part at the road. Allow travelers once again to pass.*

The blockade, previously hard as the wood of which it was made, softened, became like wet clay. Liliana reached out with mental fingers and gently pried it away from the road. The branches unwound and parted. The thorns fell off harmlessly. Liliana shaped and worked the tangled limbs until there was a wide hole through which mounted riders might pass.

My thanks, she thought.

The trees answered with a respectful song, a deep, luxurious melody resounding through her mind. When they were sure she understood their message, they fell silent.

Her mind slipped out of the wood, floating lazily back to her brain along rivers of wild magic. When she was once again in her own body, she released her connection to the forest. Then she collapsed to the ground, suddenly cold and spent.

"Liliana!" Garrick shouted again.

Strong hands were on her, rolling her to her back, supporting her head. She opened her eyes, but her vision was blurry. She perceived three faces, but couldn't make out whose they were.

"Are you all right?" Garrick said. "Speak to me!"

"Give her some air," a female voice said. "You're crowding her."

Liliana's sight cleared at last, and she found herself with her head resting in Levinia's lap, while Garrick and Stephen bent over her. Stephen's face was covered in astonishment. Garrick was worried.

"Oh my," Liliana sighed.

"Are you okay?" Garrick said.

"I think so," she answered. "I just need to rest a moment."

"What happened?" Garrick asked.

She wasn't sure how to reply. What could she say that he would understand? How could she explain it to him?

"I made a connection with the forest," she said. "It was like I was . . . in its soul."

Garrick continued to stare at her with worry. He was awfully sweet that way. Stephen glanced at Levinia as if to say, "Do you believe this?"

"Together, we overcame Vicia's sorcery," Liliana continued. "I asked, and it parted the branches for me."

Her eyes fell on the trees. She was somewhat astounded to see the hole she'd made. It was as if some giant creature had reached in among the thorns and torn the branches aside. She hadn't unmade Vicia's spell; she'd overcome it.

"I've never seen anything like that," Stephen commented. "You're the most powerful sorcerer I've ever encountered."

"Thank you," she said. "But just at this moment, I feel terribly weak."

"Liliana!" Garrick said, but his voice came from far away.

She drifted out of consciousness on a soft river of exhaustion.

She woke an hour later feeling vibrant and alive. Her eyes snapped open, and sunlight and cold poured into her mind, filling her with a sense of wonder and hope.

She sat up as Garrick came rushing over. Worry continued to seize his expression. She smiled beatifically at him.

"You're awake!" he said.

"Yes," she replied, amused.

"You gave us a scare," he said.

"Did I?"

"Yes!" Garrick said.

Hot anger flushed his face, reddened his tone. What was the matter with him?

"It really was frightening," Levinia put in. "You . . . glowed. Blue."

"Blue?" Liliana said. They all nodded. "Fascinating."

She stood up.

"Well, we'd better going," Liliana said. "Vicia's already got more than a day's jump on us. If we're going to have any chance of catching her, we'd better get after it."

She brushed past her three companions, walked over to Percy, and mounted him. She looked back on them. They each looked stunned.

"What?" she said.

"Liliana," Garrick said, "you nearly died."

"Well, of course I didn't, silly," she said. "I was just overwhelmed by the power. The forest is alive in a way I can't describe, but I tapped into that life force. It's what enabled me to open a passage into the forest. I'm quite fine."

Levinia shrugged. She walked over towards her horse. Stephen followed. Garrick continued to stare at her.

"Really," Liliana said. "I'm fine."

At last, he shook his head and approached his own horse. The same irritation that had flushed his skin before poured off him again, but she couldn't fathom why. Everything was perfect. Didn't he know?

They rode silently into the forest. As soon as they were through the aperture Liliana had made, the weather changed. The air went instantaneously from clear and cold to warm and humid. Within a minute, everyone was removing cloaks and loosening collars. Inside the trees, it was eternally summer.

Liliana rejoiced in the feel of the heat on her skin. She broke a sweat almost immediately and didn't mind. The life, the very heartbeat, of the forest reached out to her, welcoming her in. It felt like an old friend, one whose acquaintance she was glad to renew.

"This is amazing," Levinia said.

"Indeed," Stephen agreed. "I knew the forest was magical, but I didn't realize it defied the elements."

"It is a thing unto itself," Liliana said. "Just as your body stays warm no matter the season, so too does the forest's."

Stephen looked at her askance, as though he wasn't sure whether to take her seriously. She returned his gaze with a smile.

He shook his head and then dismounted and knelt to the ground. He examined the road for half a minute.

"Well, she followed the road, at least for awhile," he pronounced. "There are horse tracks here, and the animal was shod. Given that she sealed off the passage, it has to be her mount that made them." He climbed back up in his saddle. "They should be easy to follow for now."

He snapped the reins of his horse and moved off at moderate pace, his eyes trained to the ground. Liliana continued smiling.

As they moved along the road, all her senses expanded. A warm, yellow glow lit everything she looked at. Insects and birds called to each other. Every tree offered a welcome, a kindly smile, a reassuring wink. She was so entranced by these sensations she could barely pay attention to her comrades, could hardly even remember they were here.

"I'll say this for it," Garrick commented, "it lives up to its name."

"What does?" Levinia asked.

"The Enchanted Forest," he answered.

Liliana smiled more broadly. Yes, it did.

They'd been following the road for about an hour, when Stephen raised his hand, signaling for them to stop. Liliana watched as he dismounted, walked a short way ahead, and then knelt down.

He spent several seconds studying the road, and then got up and walked to his right. He looked at a few bushes, moving into the trees as he did. He disappeared for several minutes before re-emerging.

"She left the road," he pronounced. "Judging by the signs, I'd say it was around twenty-four hours ago. The tracks move off west."

"Wait a minute," Garrick said. "Last night, the Silent Knights disappeared to the southeast. If Vicia is wielding the Crown of Silence, west is the wrong direction to find her."

"The horse tracks we've been following leave the road here," Stephen said. "If they were made by Vicia, she's headed west."

"And it's unlikely they were made by anyone else," Levinia added. "We know Vicia was horse-mounted. We were tracking her here. The entry to the forest was blocked by her magic. Thus, no one else could have made those tracks."

"Liliana?" Garrick said, apparently seeking her support for his objection.

"There are any number of possible explanations," Liliana said. "For all we know, she left the road here, traveling west, and then doubled back to the southeast."

"And we're assuming Vicia is the one with the Crown of Silence," Levinia said.

"Well, who else would it be?" Garrick demanded.

"I couldn't say," Levinia replied. "It's probably Vicia, and I don't have an explanation for that. But Stephen says she headed west from here. If we want to track her, this is the way to go."

Garrick's shoulders sagged. He obviously didn't like the situation – probably he was uncomfortable allying with the head of a criminal organization, who was after the same thing he was. But he was out of arguments.

Liliana saw no reason not to continue following Stephen's lead for the moment. He seemed to have the skill to keep them on Vicia's trail, and they were as motivated to find her as Garrick and she were.

"Very well," Garrick said, resigned. "Lead the way."

"It'll be hard to track her now that she's gone off-road," Stephen said. "I'll need to proceed on foot from here."

"That's going to be a problem, isn't it?" Levinia said.

They were already towing the horses of their two slain companions. Bringing a third riderless beast along would indeed slow them further.

"You could leave the extra horses behind," Liliana suggested.

"Do you have any idea what a horse is worth?" Levinia said, turning to her. "I'm not leaving behind perfectly good mounts."

Liliana shrugged.

"It's up to you," Liliana said. "They're your horses. You might ask yourself if their value outweighs catching Vicia before she secures the Blessing of the Fey."

Levinia stared at her. Liliana could see her sorting through options.

"We can't abandon the animals," Garrick said, surprising Liliana. "We don't know what sorts of predators there are here or if the horses could find enough to eat. It wouldn't be right."

Liliana shrugged again. The trees would take care of the beasts. She was certain of that. But she didn't know how to explain that to the others.

"Here," Garrick said. "If we each take one that'll make it easier."

He cantered over to Stephen and took the reins of his horse. Liliana moved Percy over to Levinia and took a horse from her.

"Okay, let's go," Stephen said.

They moved off into the trees. Liliana felt both the soul of the woods and Garrick's destiny move closer.

133

CHAPTER 21:

Changing Approach

THE LIGHT WAS BEGINNING to fade as Liliana waited patiently for Stephen to investigate the bushes around them. Garrick sighed heavily at this latest halt. Liliana wished she understood his foul mood. Maybe he just didn't trust Levinia. Maybe he was angry about being overruled on which direction to go.

Whatever the case, he'd been surly all day, reminding Liliana much more of Calibot than of the amiable warrior with whom she had ridden from Twin Falls.

"Something's wrong," Stephen declared.

"Pardon me for saying so," Garrick sneered, "but would it be too much for me to note that this grove of trees looks exactly the same as the last two times you've stopped us?"

"No," Stephen said. "It wouldn't. I believe we've been traveling in circles."

"Great," Garrick muttered.

"Are you sure?" Levinia said.

"Yes," Stephen replied. "As Mr. Tremaine noted, we've been through this particular group of trees at least once today, maybe twice."

"So we've been on a wild goose chase all day?" Garrick said, irritation in his tone.

"Not exactly," Stephen said. "We are no closer to catching Vicia, and we are likewise no nearer to finding the mysterious Blessing of the Fey."

"Oh, for the gods' sakes," Garrick cursed.

"But neither is Vicia," Stephen said.

"What do you mean?" Levinia asked.

"Vicia is lost," Stephen pronounced.

"What?" Liliana said.

"It is a little hard to distinguish," Stephen said, "but there are multiple tracks through here."

"We've got six horses," Garrick said. "And we've been through here at least once. I would think that would account for it."

"But Vicia has only the one horse," Stephen countered. "The first time we were here, there was only one set of tracks. There are now two, maybe three, that are distinct from ours. As I said, it's a little hard to tell, but Vicia has definitely been through this same grove of trees more than once, and judging by how fresh some of the marks are, at least one of those trips occurred today. We're going in circles because she is."

"Are you absolutely sure, Stephen?" Levinia asked. "Couldn't the tracks have been made by someone else?"

"Theoretically," he said. "But it's extremely unlikely. Remember, Vicia walled off the forest after she entered it. So these would have to have been made by someone who was already here or came in after us.

"Additionally, the shoeprints that I find appear to be the same. It would be unusual for two shod horses to have identical prints."

No one said anything for a moment. Liliana smiled. Vicia might be ahead of them, but she was no closer to finding what they were all looking for.

"So now what?" Garrick said.

"I think it's time we changed our approach," Liliana said.

"How so?" Levinia asked.

"Following Vicia is keeping us just as lost as she is," Liliana answered. "We need to strike out on our own."

"Going where?" Stephen said. "We don't know what we're looking for. We were following Vicia, so she would lead us to it."

"I think it's time to share some information," Liliana said.

"Liliana?" Garrick said, clearly nervous.

"I believe Vicia is seeking the dryad Peaseblossom," Liliana went on, ignoring him. "Four hundred years ago, she gave her blessing to the ruling house of Twin Falls. My guess is that, to win the Contest of Succession, an aspirant must secure that blessing once again.

"Peaseblossom lives in The Enchanted Forest. Through means I don't understand at the moment, Vicia knows where to seek her. However, she has become lost. Thus, it is now possible for us to get ahead of her, and claim the blessing for ourselves."

Levinia and Stephen stared at her incredulously. Garrick looked at her as though she had lost her mind. She understood his feelings, but they were irrelevant. Had Vicia led them to Peaseblossom, Levinia and her man would have found out anyway.

"That's a fine plan you have there, Ms. Gray," Stephen said. "But where do we look? Do you know where this Peaseblossom can be found?"

"No," Liliana answered. "We were following Vicia for the same reason you were."

"Then how do you expect to find her before Vicia?" he said. "She may be lost, but she at least has some idea where to search. We're completely in the dark."

"Simple," Liliana answered. "We'll ask the trees."

"What?" Garrick and Levinia said together.

"Peaseblossom is here in the forest," Liliana said, thinking it should be obvious. "The trees must know where she is and how to find her. So we'll ask them."

Everyone blinked at her. The only sounds were the cries of the insects.

"Ms. Gray," Levinia said.

"Please, call me Liliana."

"Fine. Liliana, none of us is a sorcerer. We're ignorant of these things. How does one ask a tree for directions?"

"When I opened the road to us this morning, I was unable to do it simply on my own," Liliana explained. "The Enchanted Forest is much more than a large cluster of trees. It is an organism unto itself – a collective, if you will – with a heart and a soul. The trees in this forest are alive in a way that trees elsewhere are not, except perhaps in The Wild Lands.

"I drew on the life force of the forest itself to part the branches that denied us access. In doing so, I made contact with the intelligence the living things here share. I believe I can do so again to ask where we may find Peaseblossom."

Garrick stared at her with a look of absolute wonder on his face. His eyes shone brightly in the darkening forest. Liliana smiled at him. He had a magic to him that had nothing to do with sorcery.

"Can I ask why we didn't do this *first*?" Stephen said. "We've been tracking Vicia all day, when we could have just asked the forest where she was going. Pardon me for saying so, but I'm beginning to think Mr. Tremaine was correct when he described this as a wild goose chase."

"Tracking Vicia seemed the most prudent thing to do," Liliana answered. "Since she had a head start on us, it was unlikely we could get there ahead of her. The best thing was to allow her to lead us to Peaseblossom and then either prevent her from receiving the blessing or steal it from her after she'd gotten it.

"Things have changed. Vicia is lost. It now seems possible Levinia or Garrick could earn the prize before Vicia even arrives."

Stephen opened his mouth to protest and then closed it. He shook his head.

"Well, it's not my decision," he said. "Levinia and Tremaine are the contestants. It's up to them."

"I follow Liliana," Garrick said, his tone suggesting there would be no argument.

"Liliana and Mr. Tremaine have information we don't," Levinia said. "Without them, we'd be wandering around more lost than Vicia. I see no reason not to continue with our alliance."

"Very well," Liliana said. "Let's make camp."

"What?" Stephen said.

"The light is failing," Liliana said. "We're likely terribly off-course. We need to wait until morning."

Stephen scowled in disgust, but he didn't argue. He went to his horse and started unpacking supplies. Levinia dismounted without comment and went to assist him.

Garrick smiled at Liliana for the first time today. She wasn't sure what brought it on, although she suspected it was the irritation of their companion. Liliana thought he was taking a little too much pleasure in that. He distrusted their allies unnecessarily. Levinia and Stephen might betray them, but it wouldn't happen right away – certainly not before they'd located Peaseblossom and secured her boon. Until then, they would be staunch.

However, Liliana liked his smile. It warmed her heart. Garrick Tremaine was definitely getting under her skin. That made her happy.

CHAPTER 22:

Danger along the Way

L ILIANA AWOKE THE NEXT morning feeling excited. As draining as her first experience connecting with The Enchanted Forest had been, she was looking forward to renewing contact. She'd encountered dragons and a gnome on her adventure with Calibot, but this was different. The forest was exotic in a completely different way. She could commune with its intelligence, perceive its life force on a primal level she couldn't detect in any other living thing.

She barely had an appetite for breakfast. Her enthusiasm stole it. Her companions seemed likewise anxious to get started, so they ate quickly and packed up their camp.

"Are you ready?" Garrick asked.

"Very much so," she said.

"Let's get started then," Stephen said. "There's no guarantee Vicia is still lost."

Garrick threw him a glare, but Liliana only smiled. Her impatience far outweighed his.

Standing equidistant from three trees, Liliana closed her eyes and reached out her senses to the eldritch forces of the forest. Blue-green threads of magical power wove all around her, visible to her mind if not her eyes. A warm sense of security and strength wrapped her like a thick comforter.

Gently, she pushed her consciousness out of her mind and into the web of magic. Seconds later, she felt herself in every tree, every shrub, every leaf. She was connected to it all. The feeling of tranquility was nearly overwhelming. She wanted to give herself over to the vernal safety of the forest's collective consciousness.

With an effort, she fought off the desire for sleep it was inducing in her and asked her question.

Can you show me Peaseblossom? She thought.

Yes.

The voice was strong, clear, and booming in her ears. She started when she heard it. It came so fast, she could hardly believe it.

Please, she thought, *guide us to her.*

Guide you we can, but speak with her you cannot.

Why not?

Imprisoned she is. Strong magic.

I see, Liliana thought. *If you show us the way, we will free her.*

Open your eyes.

Liliana did as the forest told her. A line of trees stretching away from their present location glowed softly blue, forming a path.

Thank you, Liliana thought.

Danger for you. Threats to your life before you reach your goal. Show caution.

Thank you.

Liliana walked to Percy and mounted him. She turned to her companions.

"Follow me," she said. "I know the way."

"Extraordinary," Levinia said.

Garrick smiled broadly at Liliana. The three of them mounted up, and Levinia and Stephen took the reins of the riderless mounts.

"The forest has given me a path," Liliana said. "It has also warned me of danger along the way."

"What kind of danger?" Garrick asked.

"It didn't say," Liliana answered. "But it told me Peaseblossom has been imprisoned. I suspect freeing her is the way to earn the Blessing of the Fey. It therefore stands to reason that the threat we were warned of is whatever guardians have been placed to prevent her release."

"That makes sense," Levinia said. "Lead the way, Liliana. We'll keep our eyes peeled for trouble."

Liliana spurred Percy and steered him off in the direction the forest indicated. The path went east and was thick with trees and undergrowth. Yet the branches seemed to part and rise to give them access.

Hope flowed through her. Things were getting very exciting.

After two hours, they hadn't made it back to the road, and Liliana perceived they had turned slightly north. Assuming Peaseblossom's prison – whatever it was – was west of the road, Liliana guessed that Vicia had traveled too far south before venturing into the trees.

"Any idea how much farther?" Stephen asked.

"No," Liliana said. "I am simply following the trail they've given me."

"Can you ask them?" Stephen said.

She was about to reply, when she thought she saw something move out of the corner of her eye. She turned to her left and gazed into the greenery.

"What?" Garrick said, alarm in his voice.

"Did you see that?" Liliana asked.

"See what?" Levinia said.

"I thought I saw something move," she replied.

Everyone brought their horses to a halt. The four of them stared into the trees for almost thirty seconds.

"Maybe it was nothing," Liliana said, but she didn't believe that.

She was about to start Percy moving forward again, when she heard a distinct rustle behind them. Apparently, the others heard it too, because everyone turned to look. A few leaves from some bushes were waving. There was no breeze.

"There's something out there," Stephen said.

He and Garrick both drew their swords. The four of them scanned the trees and bushes looking for signs of trouble.

"Look out!" Levinia shouted.

Stephen turned just as an enormous, black wolf, bigger than any Liliana had ever seen, leaped at him, its jaws open. He got his blade around

140

just in time to impale the savage beast through the neck. It yelped mournfully, and spattered him in dark, red blood.

"Wolves!" Garrick yelled.

Five of them as large and as black as the first sprang from the thickets. They were the size of small ponies, and their teeth gleamed wickedly beneath burning green eyes. Two leaped at Garrick and two more at Levinia. The fifth launched itself at Stephen.

Liliana glanced around quickly, looking for the ones meant for her, but there were none. Garrick chopped one of his across the neck, wounding it, but the second knocked him from his saddle.

"Garrick!" she shouted, and raised her hand to aim death magic at it.

Before she could summon the energy, though, a noose dropped neatly around her neck and quickly pulled taut. A second later, she was yanked up out of her saddle. The rope choked the breath from her, bit into her skin. She looked up and saw goblins in the trees, grinning savagely at her.

Arrows rained at her companions in every direction. The goblins above her took aim. She threw up a magical shield in front of her just before the first arrows could reach her. They bounced off it harmlessly.

But she was still in danger of asphyxiating. She reached up and put her hands on the rope. Her vision swam in front of her, and she grew lightheaded. Seizing the rope tightly, she sent magic into it with the last of her strength. She felt more than saw it transform to smoke, releasing her from the goblins' bondage and certain death.

She dropped back to the earth and landed flat on her back with a painful bump that sent daggers of agony shooting all through her. She gulped desperately for air and tried to gather her wits.

Stephen screamed horribly, and Liliana rolled over just in time to see a wolf tear his throat open, stifling his cries. The horrid beast fell on him and began devouring him in the middle of the battle.

Liliana flicked her fingers and sent red sparkles at the wolf, which ignited into hot fire when they landed on its fur. It howled in agony and went dashing off into the woods.

Arrows struck the ground in three places around Percy. He reared up and nearly trampled her. She flung up her arm towards the goblins in the trees and sent arrows of red magic from her fingertips into the branches. She heard cries, and two goblins fell out, dead.

The situation was dire. Three of the wolves still lived, and there were more goblins than she could count shooting at them from partially visible positions. That didn't include the ones still in the tree, who had tried to kill her. Three horses were dead along with Stephen. Levinia was still mounted and fighting off a wolf. Garrick had managed to gain his feet, but he was still engaged with two wolves while trying to dodge the missiles of the goblin snipers.

Liliana risked helping him before dealing with her own attackers. She got to her knees and launched another round of magic arrows at one of the wolves snapping at him. All four struck the fiend in the flank, and it fell to the ground with a surprised yelp and didn't move.

With the odds temporarily even for him, she turned her attention to the tree above. Arrows fell from it again. She threw up another shield and stood. Percy reared up again, and she sent a ray of soothing magic into his brain to try to calm him.

Meanwhile, Levinia expertly wheeled her own mount around, and it kicked the wolf attacking her in the head, shattering its skull. She paid for the maneuver immediately. An arrow struck her in the thigh, and a second lodged itself in her shoulder, breaking her balance, and toppling her out of the saddle. She landed in a painful-looking heap, and her panicked horse nearly kicked her too. Liliana cast a shield over her to keep her safe for the few seconds it took for the animal to get clear.

She wanted to return her attention to Garrick, but another attack from the goblins in the tree demanded her attention. She ducked just as an arrow whistled past her and a second went wide left.

Liliana tried not to panic. They were badly outnumbered, and they couldn't see their attackers. The wolves were neutralized, but Stephen and Levinia were out of the fight. Sooner or later, the goblins' arrows would find their marks. She needed to do something to change the conditions of the battle.

As she scanned the scene looking for a solution, she saw blue-green lines of magical energy weaving through the trees. Of course! They had allies! It was time to get their assistance.

Liliana reached out to the tree containing the goblins, sending her own essence through the eldritch lines touching it. It began shaking as though rattled by an earth tremor. Two goblins fell out immediately. Then a third hit the ground. Soon, the tree was bending back and forth as though it were being assailed by a gale-force wind. Two more goblins were flung from its branches like stones from a catapult. They died on impact with other trees. Liliana shot the three on the ground with her magic, red arrows.

She turned in Garrick's direction and was nearly decapitated by an enormous axe. She jumped back just in time and found herself staring down the ugliest goblin she'd seen yet. They were an unattractive race as a whole, but this individual was profoundly disgusting. He leered at her with a single, yellow eye, and he snarled through rotten teeth.

Instinctively, Liliana threw up a shield to ward herself from him. He raised his giant battle axe and brought it down on the shield, which crumbled before it like shale smashed by a hammer. Liliana's eyes popped open wide in horror as he stepped through the magical shards and grinned disgustingly.

"Your puny spells are no match for *Grimblood*," he growled. "Now, die on its fell blade!"

He chopped at her, and Liliana was forced to dodge again. She stumbled backward as he advanced. Off-balance, she waved her hand at him, sending another volley of her magic arrows racing towards him. He swatted them aside with *Grimblood*.

"Is that the best you've got?" he taunted. "Your pathetic parlor trick may have been good enough against my cousin's rabble, but I am a true warrior with an arcane weapon. You can't stop me, you worthless human!"

He swung at her again, and Liliana was forced to backpedal. Her foot caught a tree root, and she tumbled over backward, an accident that saved her life. The fiend's blade narrowly missed her. He stood over her and raised his axe.

"Time for this charade to end," he said. "Die, witch!"

Help! Liliana screamed to the trees.

The one-eyed goblin brought down his battle axe. A low branch from an adjacent tree moved between Liliana and the blade, intercepting it only six inches from her chest. The axe embedded itself in the wood and held fast.

The goblin looked confused. Liliana took advantage.

She waved her hand at the grass, which grew rapidly, coiling up the goblin's body and wrapping around his throat. He pulled at *Grimblood* in desperation, but he could not yank it free.

After several attempts, he turned purple as the animated grass choked the life out of him. Realizing he was in serious danger, he let go of the axe and struggled with the vines garroting him.

Liliana summoned more magical energy to her hand and sent it sparkling over the dread weapon's handle. Then she grinned triumphantly at her attacker.

"Is this what you want?" she quipped. *"Grimblood?"*

With a wave of her hand, the giant axe flew out of the tree branch and buried itself in the goblin's skull. He looked terrified for one second before he sank to the ground, dead.

She wasted no time feeling satisfied. She got up immediately and surveyed the situation.

Garrick had slain his remaining wolf, but arrows volleyed out of the trees in his direction, and he struggled to find cover from them. One ricocheted off his sword and would have taken his eye out had the blade not happened to be in the right place.

So far, no one had attacked Levinia. The goblins had left her for dead.

Liliana reached out her hands and extended a blanket of purple magic over the three of them. Then she closed her eyes and put her mind into the forest.

Please, she thought, *I need more help.*

The response was nearly instantaneous. Goblins yelped in fear. Tree limbs thrashed them, knocking them into briars that stung them and refused to let go.

The goblins endured this torture for less than thirty seconds before they ran. Even then, there was no good escape. Wherever they went, trees assaulted them. Liliana watched as some goblins died, impaled on limbs that had not been in their way moments before, or had their brains dashed out by a strong blow to the head. The rest eventually got free, but not without a host of injuries for their trouble.

Thank you, she thought.

Free Peaseblossom. Rid us of this blight.

We will.

She dropped the protection spell and went to see to her comrades. Garrick limped over to her. He had a number of visible cuts, but he looked to be in generally good shape.

"Are you all right?" he asked.

"Yes," she replied. "I'm fine. You?"

"I'll live," he replied. "Though I won't be happy about it for awhile."

She turned to Levinia, who looked considerably worse. Not only were two arrows embedded in her, her right leg was twisted at an impossible angle. Her face was a gray mask of pain.

"I know this is a stupid question," Liliana said, "but how are you?"

"I'd like to tell you I've been worse," Levinia responded, gritting her teeth in pain. "But I'd be lying."

"That leg's broken," Garrick said.

"You think?" Levinia said, her voice full of both anguish and sarcasm.

Liliana knelt beside her and looked her over. Levinia was brave. She was fighting the pain as best she could. Something had to be done for her, though.

"Are these your only injuries?" she said.

"Are they not enough for you?" Levinia said in the same sarcastic tone she'd used with Garrick.

"Levinia, I need to know the extent of your wounds, so I can treat you," Liliana said.

"Sorry," she replied. "I've always found sarcasm to be good medicine for a bad situation. Yes, the broken leg and the arrow-wounds are the only injuries I'm aware of. I broke the leg falling off the horse. If I have bruises from that, the other pain is drowning them out."

Liliana nodded. She turned to Garrick.

"We've got to set her leg," she said.

Garrick grimaced at her. He rubbed the back of his head.

"I'm not a healer, Liliana," he said. "I can stitch a wound and soothe a fever, but this is a little beyond my experience."

"I thought you were a soldier," Levinia said. "Haven't you had battle experience?"

"Yes, but I've never had to mend a broken limb," he said.

"I bought salves and healing draughts before we left Twin Falls," Liliana said. "Healing her wounds isn't the problem. But the leg has to be straightened first, so the bones will knit together correctly."

Garrick stared at her for a moment.

"That's going to hurt," he said at last. "A lot."

"Great," Levinia said.

"All right," Liliana said, "let's attack this one problem at a time. We'll set the leg first, since that will be the worst. Then we'll get the arrows out. Levinia, I'm sorry, but you're going to suffer before it gets better."

"As long as it actually gets better," Levinia said.

Liliana searched the ground and found a solid stick. She went behind Levinia, knelt, and put the other woman's head in her lap. Then she handed her the stick.

"You need to put this in your mouth, so you have something to bite down on," she said.

Levinia grimaced and took it. She drew in a deep breath, and then put it in her mouth.

"Okay, Garrick," Liliana said, "I'll hold her shoulders. You need to take the leg, pull down, and then twist it back into position."

Levinia groaned at the thought. Garrick looked scared.

"You have to do it quickly," Liliana went on. "Make it fast."

She waited for him to kneel by Levinia's foot. When he had it in his hands, she waved her hand over Levinia, causing soft, blue sparkles to materialize in the air and then descend on Levinia's leg.

"That will ease some of the pain," she said.

Then she nodded at Garrick. He yanked Levinia's foot towards him, causing her to scream around the stick. Then he twisted it hard to the right, aligning her foot correctly. Levinia wailed more piteously. Liliana stroked her head.

"There," she said. "That's done it. The rest will be easier."

She directed Garrick to get the healing supplies out of her saddle bag. When he brought them to her, she tore open Levinia's pants leg and slathered a generous portion of salve over the break.

Then she turned and used her magic to remove the arrows. The skin and muscle pulled apart gently, allowing the missiles to slip out. Liliana applied more salve to each wound, watching them close immediately under the magic's power.

"Here, drink this," Liliana said.

Levinia was barely conscious. Liliana had to hold the gourd with the healing draught in it to her lips. Levinia spit out the first swallow.

"That's horrid," she said.

"I know," Liliana replied, "but it's medicine. It will speed your recovery."

Levinia fought the rest of it down, pausing frequently and grimacing the whole time. When she was finished, Liliana used more magic to levitate her to the shade of one of the trees. She finished by throwing a blanket over her.

"Now what?" Garrick said.

"First, you drink a healing draught yourself," Liliana answered. "You're in need of repair too."

"Ugh," he said, but he took the gourd from her, unstoppered it, and drank it all without stopping. Then he bent over and battled the urge to vomit it all back up.

"Next, we'll need to head out," Liliana said.

"What about her?"

Liliana turned and gazed on Levinia. She already looked better, but she was in no shape to travel.

"We'll have to come back for her," Liliana said.

"What?" Levinia moaned. "You're leaving me?"

"Only for a short time," Liliana said. "I'm sorry, Levinia. The healing salves will take care of your arrow wounds mostly before nightfall. But your leg is another matter. It will take several days for it to completely recover, and you won't be able to put any weight on it for at least twenty-four hours. The salve and the draught will accelerate your recovery, but it still takes time for bones to mend. I'll splint your leg and instruct the trees to protect you. You should be safe until we return."

"How . . ." she said, sounding sleepy. "How do I know . . . you'll come back for me?"

"I give you my word," Liliana said. "You will see us again."

"Unless we die," Garrick put in.

"Then I'll . . . see you in Hell," Levinia said.

"Fair enough," Garrick said.

Liliana found two sturdy dead branches and used a little magic to shape them straighter. Then she lashed them on either side of Levinia's leg. The other aspirant was asleep by the time she finished, sedated from the magic in the salve. Liliana left her a waterskin and some rations.

"What about the dead horses?" Garrick said. "And Stephen?"

Liliana sighed. She was growing weary from all the magic she'd used. Harnessing the forces of the universe wore on the body. She really wanted to rest.

But they were short of time. If they were going to reach Peaseblossom and free her before Vicia righted her course, they had to get going. And leaving the horse and wolf carcasses lying out would attract predators.

She knelt to the ground and sent more magic into it. Yellow light spread from her hand across the earth, and each dead beast sank in and was covered. For Stephen, she raised rocks and soil over him. He would be protected from scavengers, but he could be easily exhumed so Levinia could bury him properly when they returned.

"Okay," she said. "We have to go now. The day is moving on, and we don't know how much farther we have to travel."

"After you," Garrick replied.

They both mounted their horses. Summoning her resolve, Liliana once again spied the path the trees had set for her. Then she spurred Percy and moved off in search of the imprisoned dryad she had sworn to rescue.

CHAPTER 23:

Clasping Destiny

VICIA SAT ASTRIDE HER horse before the holly grove. This had to be it – it *had* to be! She'd been by the damned thing five times. Her spell indicated she should keep going, but each time she'd followed it, she'd ended up back here. Kremdor's magic had to be concealing the entrance to Peaseblossom's vernal prison. He'd said to look for a large grove of holly bushes. This was a large grove of holly bushes. This had to be it.

She dismounted and faced the bushes. Raising her staff, she chanted the spell Kremdor had given her. Gloomy grey light issued from the rod, and darkness descended on the grove.

"*Aperi*," she said, pointing her staff at the bushes. "By the authority of Lord Kremdor, *aperi!*"

The holly bushes trembled and glowed with the same grey light. The branches shook as if a storm were lashing them, and then they parted, peeling away to reveal a small path between them.

Vicia stepped through to a copse of oak trees. Like those she'd used to bar passage to The Enchanted Forest, the oaks' branches intertwined. There was no way through them without magic.

A row of goblins, all armed with spears, stood in front of the trees, leering at her. Wicked malice danced in their yellow eyes, promising violence and hoping she would provoke them.

"If you are wise," the lead one said, stepping forward, "you will turn around and go back to Twin Falls."

"I haven't got what I came for yet," Vicia said.

"And you won't," the goblin chief said.

Vicia frowned. The goblins were supposed to be working for Kremdor. Why the hell were they barring her way?

"Look, you miserable little fiend," she said, "I'm Lord Vicia. I'm the one Lord Kremdor sent to free the dryad. Move aside."

"Lord Kremdor instructed us that none shall pass," the goblin countered. "Unless your name is None, you're not passing. And since you've already told us it is Vicia . . ."

He leered again. Gleaming, yellow eyes set behind a giant nose undressed her with their gaze. Disgust and fury twisted her stomach.

"Move," she said, starting forward.

All of the goblins immediately brought their spears to bear. She looked them over. There were six of them. This would be no trouble.

"Very well," she said. She pointed her staff at the leader. "*Ardebit!*"

An orange ball of light shot from it and struck the lead goblin in the chest. He immediately burst into flames and screamed in agony.

The remaining five looked shocked. Vicia smiled grimly, and then turned her staff on the closest one. She directed a second fireball at this one with the same effect, and the goblin next to him cried out in alarm.

The others rallied, though. Two flung their spears at her, while the third charged.

Vicia rolled her staff in front of her, swatting the spears away. Then she spun, dropped to a knee, pointed her staff at the charging goblin, and launched a third fireball. He too disappeared in a gulf of orange flame.

She was about to dispatch the final two fiends, when an arrow whistled just past her nose. Two more followed it quickly, and she was forced first to duck and then to raise a shield of purple energy. Six more arrows hit it and disintegrated.

There'd been more than six goblins. The others had been hiding. Damn them and their clever ambushes. She was desperately outnumbered. She would need to change tactics.

With a wave of her staff, she summoned a pair of mountain lions that went charging into the archers' position. She heard screams as the beasts fell on the goblins, occupying them for the moment.

However, the two who had flung their spears at her now attacked with swords. She got her staff up just in time to check both blows. Hatred burned in their eyes as they hacked at her again and again, driving her to her knees.

When they raised their swords, she shoved the staff into their abdomens, pushing them to the ground. Then she rose and cast bolts of green, eldritch energy at the two of them, killing them instantly.

Before she could recover, a lasso looped over the end of her staff and yanked it out of her hand. Three more goblins charged her.

Trying not to panic, she drew her knife, and hurled it at the lead goblin, striking him in the eye. He plunged forward and tripped his mates, spilling them to ground.

She reached out with her right hand and summoned the staff back to her. It responded to her command, sailing through the air and dragging along the goblin who had stolen it.

Vicia caught the staff expertly and turned the butt towards its captor. Unable to stop, he charged forward, and Vicia planted the end of the staff firmly under his jaw, breaking his neck.

By then, the two goblins who had tripped were up again. They rushed forward. Vicia pointed her staff at earth in front of her and raised a magical shield. Like their comrade, the fools could not check their momentum. They crashed headlong into the purple wall and bounced off it. A quick pair of eldritch bolts finished them off.

She turned back to the mountain lions. The goblins had managed to slay one of them, and two of the little, green-skinned bastards were poking spears at the second. She shot them both with eldritch bolts as well, then waved her staff, causing the lion to dissipate.

Silence descended on the forest. Vicia spent a few moments panting and making sure there were no more goblins.

When she was she certain she was safe, she reclaimed her knife from the goblin's face and spent a minute to clean it. Then she approached the oak trees.

She studied the branches carefully. They were woven together tightly, more compactly than the spell she had cast at the entrance of the forest. Kremdor had likely done this one himself.

151

Once again, she enchanted her staff with the words he had given her. With a deep breath, she pointed it at the branches.

"*Aperi*," she said. "In the name of Kremdor, *aperi!*"

Just as the holly bushes had, the branches glowed with sickly, grey light. Then they began unweaving. Like tentacles, they disentwined themselves, retreating into the trees from which they had grown.

The process took fully two minutes. When it was finished, the branches formed a neat archway into a clearing. At the center, stood an enormous, gangly tree, covered in thick, woody vines. Bound to it by the vines was a woman Vicia could only assume was Peaseblossom.

Vicia had never seen a dryad before, but Peaseblossom fulfilled all her expectations. Her body was feminine but made of wood, a dress of ivy leaves covered most of it, but her arms and feet were bare. Tiny branches grew from her head and sprouted holly leaves to form hair. The dryad's head was bowed and her eyes were closed. She appeared to be held in an enchanted sleep.

Kremdor hadn't explained how to free Peaseblossom. Vicia assumed her own magic would be sufficient.

She stepped into the clearing, and black light poured from above, illuminating everything with an eerie glow. Then the ground turned red like lava.

It bubbled in front of Vicia. A soft column of red and black, molten stone rose up before her. The heat from the thing was terrific, and Vicia had to step back and put up a hand to ward herself.

The stone shifted and took shape, growing legs, arms, and a head. When it was finished, it was a stone elemental, and it glared down on her with two malevolent, red eyes.

"May the gods damn you, Kremdor," Vicia said.

The elemental brought a fist down at her, forcing her to dive out of the way. It struck the earth with a thunderous crash, causing the ground to shake.

Vicia rolled to her feet, pointed her staff at the thing, and launched an eldritch bolt at it. The green energy splashed harmlessly off its chest like a wave crashing against a cliff face.

"That's not good," she said.

The monster flung its hand at her, and the stone fist detached from its arm, sailing at her like a boulder falling from a cliff. Again she threw herself to the ground, and the giant missile passed over her. It crashed against the trees on the other side of the clearing, and shattered into tens of fragments. A new hand grew in its place on the elemental's arm.

"By the gods!" she swore.

How the hell did you fight an elemental? What magic did she have that would stop it? She was a conjurer; she evoked energy and objects and turned them into something lethal. What could she summon that would harm stone?

The giant lifted its foot and made to stomp her into the ground. She summoned a shield of purple, protective energy. The elemental's foot stopped when it made contact, but it continued to apply pressure. White fissures spider-webbed across the shield. Vicia realized it wouldn't hold.

Seconds later, the spell broke like a pane of glass, and Vicia barely avoided being crushed. The beast's foot came down on the hem of her dress, and she panicked as she realized she was caught.

The elemental reached for her. She cast a fireball onto the exposed part of her skirt. Heat licked at the backs of her legs, and her skin seared. The fabric gave way just before the stone hand descended on her, and she once again rolled away from certain death.

She got up and ran to the far side of the clearing, trying to buy some time. She needed an idea, any idea.

The elemental turned towards her, straightened up, and started crossing in her direction. She put the tree imprisoning Peaseblossom between the two of them. The elemental adjusted to go around. Vicia moved to keep the tree between them. Confusion crossed its stone face. It tried to go back the other way. Vicia moved again. The elemental stopped and looked frustrated. Vicia smiled. It may have been formidable, but it wasn't very smart.

Her mind raced. Kremdor had set up an indestructible guardian. But he also intended for Vicia to rescue Peaseblossom. She couldn't do that if she were dead.

Had he double-crossed her? Did he not intend for her to become Duchess of Twin Falls?

She supposed that was possible, but it didn't make sense. Every part of this complicated scheme involved him having Twin Falls as an ally. He'd murdered Duke Evonin with a magical illness and then set up the Contest of Succession. He'd told only Vicia the meaning of the riddle they had to solve, and he was supposed to be killing the other aspirants while she was garnering Peaseblossom's favor.

So it didn't make sense that this was a betrayal. The elemental was invulnerable, so far as she could tell, so there had to be some way to free Peaseblossom without killing the guardian.

Of course! She needed to free the dryad first. If Peaseblossom was no longer imprisoned, the elemental would have nothing to guard.

Vicia faced the stone giant again. She moved slowly, circling the tree, goading the monster into following her. When she was back in front and had a clear view of Peaseblossom, she aimed her staff at the vines.

"*Aperi!*" she cried. "In the name of Lord Kremdor, *aperi!*"

Grey light erupted from the woody bonds. They twisted, snapped, and fell away, releasing the dryad from their hold. Peaseblossom pitched forward and looked as though she would fall face-first to the earth, but before it was too late, she put a wooden foot out and steadied her balance. She looked up, and her eyes opened, revealing two bright, green stars that gazed on Vicia with gratitude and beneficence.

Behind her, the elemental fell to pieces. Vicia gasped in relief.

"My thanks to you," Peaseblossom said in a voice that made Vicia shiver with contentment.

"You are most welcome," Vicia replied, bowing slightly.

"I am indebted to you," Peaseblossom said. "Name a boon, and I will bestow it in thanks."

"Twin Falls is without an heir," Vicia said. "I ask for your favor, so I may once again bring the Blessing of the Fey to that fair city and claim the throne."

"It shall be as you ask," Peaseblossom said.

She reached behind her and plucked a branch from the tree that had imprisoned her. She gazed on it, and tranquil blue-green light engulfed it, before settling into a soft glow. She extended it to Vicia.

Her heart pounding with joy, Vicia took the favor. At last, her dreams were coming true. She would have power. She would have her revenge. When her hand closed around the proof of Peaseblossom's blessing, she felt she was clasping destiny.

An arrow sped past her, missed Peaseblossom, and struck the tree that had held the dryad. Vicia whirled to see Garrick Tremaine holding a bow, and Liliana Gray poised for battle at the opening of the clearing.

"Sorry," Garrick said to his companion. "I told you I'm a bad shot."

"Never mind," Liliana said. "I'll cover you."

No. That bitch was not going to steal Vicia's destiny again.

Liliana launched a spell, and Vicia threw up a shield, intercepting it. She didn't care if she had to burn down the entire forest to do it, those two interlopers were about to die.

CHAPTER 24:

Forest Fire

GARRICK RODE IN SILENCE with Liliana for several minutes after leaving Levinia behind. He hadn't recovered mentally. He'd been in fights before. He'd been in fights all his life. Since becoming a soldier, he was no stranger to battle.

But this one was affecting him. He'd thought he was going to die. Fighting off two of those giant wolves – he'd had no idea the beasts could get that large – and a host of goblins had made him think they were doomed. Seeing Stephen's throat torn out had terrified Garrick in a way he didn't like to admit. It was a grisly death, one unbefitting a soldier or even a thief like Stephen. Garrick hadn't liked him, but the man had been brave and capable.

Then there were the goblins. This was the fourth time he'd been assaulted by the fiendish, little bastards since he'd left Lord Malach's fortress. And like his first encounter with them, people had died. Horribly. Once again, only Liliana's magic had prevented his own demise.

Why did they want him? What did goblins have to do with this outlandish Contest of Succession? Were they in league with Vicia? Were they also assassinating aspirants to the crown just like the Silent Knights?

Or were there two separate events here that just happened to be converging on him?

Garrick didn't like it. Bile burbled up from his stomach and stung the back of his throat. This was bad business. Liliana liked to tell him this was his destiny, but he was becoming convinced that his actual fate was to die at the hands of goblins.

"That attack was different than the others," Liliana said.

"Yeah," Garrick said. "They used wolves this time. I'd always heard rumors that goblins knew how to train wolves to fight with them, but that's the first I've ever seen it. Although to be honest, I'd never encountered goblins before coming to Twin Falls."

"Those were no ordinary wolves," Liliana said. "They were *teufelhunden* – devil dogs. I'd always thought they were a myth. They're sinister – spawned by a demon, according to legend, for some fell purpose lost to the annals of time. They're intelligent. They make alliances with dark things, including goblins. Their presence in today's attack is a bad sign."

"Great," Garrick said, feeling more depressed.

"But that's not what I meant," Liliana said.

"What?" She had him confused.

"Today's attack was different from the last two you and I have endured," she said. "In the previous ambushes, the goblins attempted to kidnap you. They only fought me because I was with you.

"But today, they attempted to slaughter you like the rest."

"Lucky me?"

"I don't think so," she said. "Think about it, Garrick. We were attacked by six *teufelhunden* – two each assaulted you, Levinia, and Stephen. But none came after me. Instead, I was ensnared. They dropped a noose over me and pulled me out of my saddle."

"So you think they were trying to abduct you now?" he said.

"No," she said. "They pulled me up, so I was hanging. Then they shot at me with arrows. When that failed, their leader attacked me, trying to kill me with a magical axe. He gloated and taunted the whole time. If I hadn't gotten assistance from the trees, he might have killed me.

"I believe this was an assassination attempt. The wolves and the other goblins were there to engage the three of you, so you could not defend me. I was the target."

Garrick let that roll around in his head for a bit. If it was true, it was a strange development. Liliana was not a player in the Contest of Succession. Why would they want her dead?

157

Possibly because she was protecting him and, by extension, Levinia. If whoever was behind this wanted to eliminate them, getting rid of Liliana was paramount to getting it done.

But if it wasn't related to the contest, then something else was at work here. And that boded very ill. It all came back to the mysterious ritual he'd fallen victim to. Why had those goblins slaughtered his friends and crucified him? Why had they twice attempted to abduct him since – presumably to finish the job? And what did Liliana have to do with it now?

"Something has changed, Garrick," she said. "I'm not sure what it is, but these goblins were different than the ones we encountered outside the forest."

He was about to comment, when he heard someone shout up ahead. It sounded like a woman's voice, but he couldn't be certain. There was a thunderous crash that shook the earth.

"Come on!" Liliana said.

She spurred her horse and set off at a gallop. Garrick followed quickly behind her.

A minute later, they came to a strange sight. A grove of holly bushes sat before them, and they had a distinctive part in their growth – as though someone had cleared them to pass through. A few feet away, an appaloosa mare stood tied to a tree, stamping its feet nervously in the grass.

"Garrick," Liliana said, "the trail ends here."

He drew even with her and peered through the bushes. Another loud crash shook the ground. A woman's voice shouted again. A flash of purple light burst through the trees.

"Vicia," he said. "It has to be."

He dismounted and drew his sword.

"Wait," Liliana said. "Take the bow I bought you. We don't know what's happening in there, Vicia is a powerful sorcerer, and it'll be safer to fight her from a distance."

"I'm a terrible shot with a bow," Garrick confessed. "I'm a terrible shot with any weapon. I'm much better in close quarters."

"You may not get the chance for close fighting," Liliana replied.

He sighed heavily and sheathed his sword. Then he grabbed the bow off the back of the saddle, strung it as another crash reached their ears, and then slung the quiver of arrows over his shoulder. Liliana had dismounted by then.

"Come on," she said.

Garrick nocked an arrow and went after her. They pushed through the bushes into a clearing. Dead goblins lay all over the ground. A grove of oak trees stood on the other side, and it had an aperture in it the same as the holly bushes.

"Well, it doesn't look like the goblins are working for Vicia," Liliana said.

That seemed strange. If they weren't Vicia's minions, why were they after him?

"Assuming these are the same goblins that attacked us," he said.

"Good point."

They moved forward cautiously. It suddenly got quiet. Something had happened.

Garrick crept to the opening. He took cover behind an oak tree, and then peered around it. Liliana mirrored him.

Through the trees was another extraordinary sight. Vicia stood in her signature purple dress, which was missing a scandalous amount of material on the back of the skirt, addressing what looked to be a woman made of wood. Wearing a dress of leaves and with tiny branches of holly for hair, this strange creature smiled at Vicia beatifically.

"That must be Peaseblossom," Liliana said.

Garrick nodded. He hadn't really spent any time imagining what a dryad might look like. Now that he beheld one, she took his breath away.

He couldn't make out what Vicia and the dryad were saying. He moved out of his hiding spot and stole through the trees right to the opening of the clearing, so he could hear. In its center stood an enormous, vine-covered tree. A strange-looking pile of rocks stood at its rear.

"Twin Falls is without an heir," Vicia was saying. "I ask for your favor, so I may once again bring the Blessing of the Fey to that fair city and claim the throne."

By the gods! This was it! Vicia was obtaining the key to the contest right now!

"It shall be as you ask," Peaseblossom said.

A strange sense of tranquility went through Garrick. It sprang from his guts and spread out all through him like a warm bath. He couldn't remember a time when he'd felt so peaceful.

Liliana nudged him. He looked at her in shock.

"Now's your opportunity!" she hissed.

The spell broken, he shook his head, drew back the arrow, and stepped out of cover. The dryad was extending a small branch to Vicia. The sinister sorcerer took it as Peaseblossom smiled on her.

Garrick took aim, steadied himself, and let fly. The arrow sailed across the clearing, missed Vicia by a foot, and embedded itself in the tree. Garrick cursed as Vicia whirled to face them.

"Sorry," Garrick said. "I told you I'm a bad shot."

"Never mind," Liliana said. "I'll cover you."

She opened her hand and sent red, magic arrows at Vicia as she had done several times against goblins. But the other sorcerer was already moving. With a sweep of her staff, she cast a shield of purple energy that intercepted Liliana's magic.

Garrick drew another arrow, fitted it to the string, and then cut to his left, trying to flank Vicia. He figured his arrows had as much chance as Liliana's of penetrating Vicia's shield. Peaseblossom's wooden eyes were open wide in surprise, and they shone like a pair of green stars. Garrick had to look away to avoid being mesmerized.

Vicia sent a ray of energy through her shield at Liliana. Garrick was about to cry out, when Liliana simply waved her hand and turned it to a shower of posies. Unable to resist, he stopped and marveled. He'd seen Liliana work her magic before, but her ability to transform something deadly into something harmless was extraordinary.

With another sweep of her staff, Vicia summoned a bear that landed in front of her in a ball of yellow light and then charged Liliana. Garrick took aim at it with his bow, but he never got a shot off. Liliana responded with a yellow ray of her own. It struck the bear, transforming it into a puppy. Vicia cursed.

"Stop," Peaseblossom said, but no one was listening.

Garrick adjusted his stance, drew a bead on Vicia, and launched another shot at her. His aim was off again. He'd gauged the distance wrong, and the arrow floated well over her head.

The attack got her attention, though. She whirled in his direction and sent one of her green death-rays at him. He ducked and was fortunate to have the beam strike the bow. It shattered in his hand, causing a painful sting to shoot up his arm, but he was otherwise unharmed.

He tossed away the broken remnants of the weapon with little regret. It was the wrong tool for him. Keeping his eyes fixed on Vicia, he ripped his sword from its scabbard.

She prepared to cast another spell at him, but before she could complete it, the grass snaked up around her legs and waist. Vicia looked down, horrified. Liliana smirked. Seeing an opening, Garrick charged her.

With a scowl, Vicia pointed her staff at the ground. An orange spark shot from the end, hit the earth, and ignited the grass around her. Her bonds fell from her as Peaseblossom stared in horror.

"No," the dryad wailed. "No fire!"

Vicia ignored her. She stepped away from the flames at her feet and then launched another orange ball at Garrick. Before he could reach her, it struck the ground before him and ignited into a giant wall of fire.

Garrick flung himself backward, sliding into the grass and narrowly avoiding plunging into the conflagration. Hot flames licked at his feet, and he scooted backward swiftly to avoid being burned.

"Stop this!" Peaseblossom cried. "I gave you my favor! You cannot repay me by destroying my home!"

Garrick couldn't see Vicia's response. He was too busy trying to avoid being immolated. He got to his feet and backed away.

More fires ignited in the trees. Vicia was launching fireballs in every direction. Garrick couldn't see Liliana, but he spied Vicia darting out of the clearing through the opening in the oaks.

He charged after her. He wasn't about to let her escape with her prize, especially since she seemed willing to destroy the entire Enchanted Forest to get away.

But as he entered the short tunnel of giant oaks, Vicia turned and flung another fireball back at him. He dove for the ground, and while it passed over him, it struck another tree and exploded in a hot sphere of flaming doom. Within seconds, burning branches barred his path forward.

Garrick started coughing. Smoke and fire were everywhere. He wasn't certain which way to go. He couldn't see any way forward or back.

Once again, he feared for his life. Before it had been goblins and *teufelhunden*; now it was a forest fire.

He was about to pray for mercy when Liliana stepped into view, looking like a god. Her face was stony, serious. Her stature commanding. She waved her arms over and over again. Orange light flew from them to the trees.

And everywhere she cast her magic, the flames extinguished. One by one, she put out the fires until, at last, there was nothing but smoke.

She came forward, stood just in front of him, and smiled. She was the most beautiful thing he had ever seen. Tears lit his eyes.

161

"Let me help you," she said, extending him her hand.

He took it, allowed her to assist him to his feet. Then he pulled her into a tight embrace and kissed her.

CHAPTER 25:

Birthright

LILIANA'S EYES POPPED OPEN wide. He was kissing her! No one had ever kissed her before. She didn't know what she was supposed to do.

Alarmed, she drew back. She looked into his eyes, trying to figure out how to react. He turned crimson.

"I'm sorry," he said. "I didn't mean . . . I didn't want . . . I shouldn't have done that. I'm sorry."

"No, it's okay," she stammered. "I . . ."

But she didn't know what to say after that. It was a mistake? He hadn't meant it? Oh. That was disappointing. Was it disappointing?

They stood looking awkwardly at each other for a moment. No words would come to her mind.

"We should see if we can catch, Vicia," he said.

Vicia? He was thinking about her now? Well, that made sense. He had said kissing her was a mistake. It must not have meant anything.

"I was thinking we should talk to Peaseblossom," she replied. "She may be grateful to us for putting out the fire. Maybe we can get a superior blessing from her."

"Okay," he said. He refused to look at her. "What about Vicia?"

"We'll catch her if we can," Liliana answered. "But I think you can make a superior claim to the throne if you've done something other than just steal the favor Vicia earned."

"Whatever you think," he said, meeting her gaze at last.

She didn't move right away. Every time she looked into his eyes, the kiss flashed back into her brain. Embarrassment seized him again, and he looked away. Her heart sank, though she wasn't altogether sure why.

Liliana turned and made her way back into the clearing before things could become more awkward. Garrick followed. Peaseblossom stood in the center of the scorched grass looking profoundly sorrowful.

"Fire is the most devastating force in the world," she said.

"I'm sorry," Liliana said.

"When a thing dies naturally, it still has life in it," Peaseblossom went on as though she hadn't heard. "It goes to the earth and decomposes. It gives its body back to nature and is resurrected in other living things.

"But fire destroys utterly. It turns the living body to ash, where it blows away on the wind, offering nothing to anyone."

She fell silent. Liliana wasn't sure what to say to her. She felt as odd gazing on the distraught dryad as she had looking at Garrick after he'd kissed her.

"I'm so sorry, Lady Peaseblossom," Garrick said. "I feel we have failed you. We came here to seek your blessing, to free you from your imprisonment. Not only did we arrive after you were already released, our zeal to win your favor caused this tragedy."

Peaseblossom turned and stared at him. The green stars of her eyes glowed with sadness and wonder. She came forward.

"Why did you seek my blessing?" she asked.

"I am participating in a Contest of Succession for the throne of Twin Falls," he answered. Peaseblossom looked confused.

"Duke Evonin died without an heir," Liliana explained. "Before he expired, he organized a competition to succeed him. The person who can bring Twin Falls the Blessing of the Fey shall ascend the throne."

Peaseblossom came forward two more steps. She examined Garrick closely.

"I still don't understand," she said. "Why would you seek my blessing for Twin Falls?"

Garrick swallowed. He looked briefly at Liliana for help, but she wasn't sure herself what to say. He turned back.

"Because you once blessed the duke's line," he said, "my companion here thought you were the fairy to bestow it again."

"Yes, I comprehend that," Peaseblossom said. "What mystifies me is why *you* came to me to renew this favor when you already have it."

Liliana's mouth fell open. Was the dryad saying what she thought she was?

"I'm sorry," Garrick said. "Now it's me who doesn't understand."

"You say the duke has died without an heir," Peaseblossom said, "but here you stand before me."

"What?" he whispered.

"Garrick," Liliana said, "I believe Peaseblossom is saying you are the duke's heir."

He turned and gaped at her. Then he looked back at the dryad with the same confusion plastered on his face.

"But that's impossible," he said.

"Why would it be impossible?" Peaseblossom said. "I recognize your blood. I blessed the entire line four hundred twelve years ago."

"Because before a week ago, I'd never been to Twin Falls," he protested. "I'm no royal. I'm the son of an undertaker. I'm a soldier-for-hire."

"Your blood does not lie," Peaseblossom said. "My patronage flows through it."

"Garrick," Liliana said, taking his arm. He turned to stare at her. "Think about it. The duke came to you in a vision. He told you to join him in Twin Falls, where you would meet your destiny. This is it. You are his last surviving heir. The Contest of Succession is meaningless. You have a birthright."

He didn't say anything at first. He only blinked at her. His gaze fell away as he turned the thoughts over in his mind.

"Do you suppose that's why the goblins are trying to kill me?" he asked. "They want me dead, so I can't claim the throne?"

"I think that's a real possibility," Liliana said. "Although it still doesn't explain the mysterious crucifixion or why they keep trying to abduct you. If they just needed you out of the way, they could have simply killed you. But I think your royal blood has something to do with it, Garrick."

She watched as his mind reeled. She suddenly realized she found him attractive. She'd never thought of anyone that way before.

The memory of the kiss exploded in her brain, frightening her. She shook her head to clear it, reminded herself he'd said he didn't mean it.

"If it's true," he said, "if I am the heir, we need to get back to Twin Falls before Vicia. Before she can steal the throne."

"In theory, your claim would be substantiated despite her being in power," Liliana said.

"In practice, it won't matter a damn," Garrick replied. "If she's crowned duchess, we'll have a hell of a time deposing her."

Liliana thought about it. Calavan and Zalachorus didn't like the arrangement. They might support Garrick's claim. But he was right that it would be ugly. It would be far easier to secure his birthright *before* Vicia won the contest.

"Lady Peaseblossom," he said turning back to the dryad, "I apologize again for the harm we've brought The Enchanted Forest. I was unaware of my lineage. I'd have made a claim before had I known."

"Go with my forgiveness," she said. "I am saddened to have given my favor to the sorcerer. She was unworthy. See that she cannot make use of it."

"You have my word," Garrick said.

"Thank you for containing the fire before it destroyed more than it did," Peaseblossom said. "My gratitude shall be unending."

Garrick and Liliana both bowed to the fairy. Then they turned and left the clearing.

Liliana's brain was racing as they reached their mounts. There was so very much to consider. This new information changed everything.

It wouldn't be easy. They were going to need a plan. She intended to have one before they reached Twin Falls.

CHAPTER 26:

The Krem

VICIA BOLTED FOR HER horse. The wall of fire might have held Tremaine at bay for the moment, but Gray was still alive, and her magic could undo Vicia's. She still couldn't understand how the woman had gone from bumbling apprentice to master sorcerer, but it hardly mattered at the moment. All Vicia cared about was getting away. She had Peaseblossom's favor. She just needed to get back to Twin Falls to complete her rise to power.

She found the appaloosa already spooked from the flames. She was tromping back and forth, scratching at the ground and trying to free herself from the tree to which Vicia had tied her.

"Easy, girl," Vicia said.

She put a hand on the mare's neck to steady her. Then she untied her, held tightly to the reins, and mounted up. She spurred the beast to take off, but she needn't have. The mare was more than ready to leave.

Vicia drove her hard through the trees. She expected Gray to put out the fire Vicia had started, but she didn't want to take the chance it would get away from Gothemus Draco's former apprentice. If the fire did spread, Vicia wanted to be as far away from it as possible.

She rode due south. From here on, she didn't need to be worried about getting lost. As long as she kept moving south, she would find the road. Then it would be easy travel to the east until she reached The Krem.

For the moment, though, the going was difficult. The appaloosa expertly picked its way through the roots, bushes, and rocks. But Vicia constantly had to duck branches and sometimes large bushes as the horse raced through the trees. The paths seemed to narrow, and Vicia was swatted and scratched multiple times. The tranquil, happy light she had seen since first entering The Enchanted Forest was gone, replaced with an angry, grey glow. Indeed, she had the impression the trees themselves were attacking her as she passed.

By the time she found the road, she was bruised and battered. Every muscle ached. Dried blood stuck to multiple scratches. Her left eye was sore from a particularly vicious shot from an ash tree.

She directed her horse into the center of the road, where it would be more difficult for the branches to reach her. Then she stopped to rest for a moment.

She drank a long draught of wine and wiped sweat from her brow. Then she spent several minutes casting the few healing spells she knew. She wasn't able to repair much of the damage done to her, but she at least eased her hurts so that riding was no longer agony. After a quick meal for her and the horse, she moved on.

Fire and pursuit were no longer concerns. She'd seen no sign of anything burning for an hour now. There was no smell of smoke in the air. Likewise, Tremaine and his pet sorcerer were not behind her. Even if they were following, they would have to track her, and that would slow them down. She had a good lead.

But she didn't feel any safer. Too much could still go wrong, and it was clear the trees had it in for her.

She drove her horse swiftly east, keeping her pace short of a gallop but still at a fast trot. She didn't figure she could make The Krem by nightfall. It was too far, and it was too late in the day. But she wanted to be as close as possible.

Vicia rode on after dark. The trees, which looked angry during the day, looked positively fiendish once the sun went down. She had no desire to stop.

But eventually, the poor appaloosa could go no farther. If she continued to drive the beast, she would kill it, and then she would have to walk, slowing her escape from the forest.

She didn't make much of a camp, though. She was unwilling to go near the revenge-minded trees. She made the horse lie down in the middle of the road and refused to unsaddle her. She took only a blanket from her supplies and then curled up against the animal's flank, keeping her staff clutched tightly in hand.

Strange dreams visited her as she slept. A fairy with a handsome but sinister face, who called himself Robin Goodfellow, came to her and said Auberon had sent him to take back Peaseblossom's favor. He told her great tragedy would befall her if she didn't give it to him. She blasted him with an eldritch bolt, but he vanished in a flash of green light, and his laughter echoed through her mind the rest of the night.

She awoke at first light feeling cold and frightened. She checked her belt immediately and saw the token from Peaseblossom was still there. Relaxing only slightly, she breakfasted quickly and was on her way.

Like she had the day before, Vicia drove the horse at a swift pace. She had to restrain herself from commanding it to gallop. She wanted the hell out of The Enchanted Forest. The poor beast whinnied in protest frequently, and Vicia allowed her to slow her gait for a short while whenever she did. But it was never long before she snapped the reins to encourage more speed.

The light was failing when she at last saw the edge of the forest. It emptied out onto the cold plains to the north but continued to the south.

The temperature dropped as soon as they broke out of the trees, and Vicia immediately regretted losing part of her dress to Kremdor's stone guardian. A thin layer of snow didn't quite cover the grass, but the air was frigid, and Vicia shivered. She'd only gone a few minutes, when she stopped, unpacked her cloak, and put it on.

Fortunately, The Krem was just ahead. Sitting on the banks of Crystal River, it rose dark and imposing before her. Unlike Gothemus Draco's tower, which was smooth, perfect stone, The Krem appeared carved from a giant finger of black rock that rose at an angle towards the sky like an insult from the earth to the clouds. The rock face twisted maliciously, and the only part of the stone that was worked was the very top, where small battlements defended Kremdor's flag – a brown bat on a black field – which snapped in the breeze.

The road went all the way to the foot of the strange fortress, but gaining access to the tower was difficult. A path wound some fifty feet up the rocky outcropping, twisting around until it came to a stop at a large gate on the opposite side, facing the river. Kremdor's forbidding redoubt was nearly impossible to assault. The path was too narrow and steep, and soldiers in the battlements could rain death down on any army foolish enough to attempt to ascend.

Kremdor had carved the gate to look like a giant maw. The portcullis, which appeared to be made of the same black stone as the rock and the tower, was shaped like wicked teeth. Two enormous iron doors were just behind it.

On either side of the gate stood a soldier with an enormous glaive. They wore black hoods and tabards adorned with Kremdor's banner over silver mail. Feral, blue eyes glowed with sinister light beneath their cowls. When Vicia approached, each extended his glaive across the opening, barring her.

"Hail," she said. "I'm here to see Kremdor."

"Who seeks counsel with Lord Kremdor?" one of them said in a voice that sounded like a low growl echoing through a distant canyon.

Vicia shivered reflexively. She'd heard rumors that Kremdor used undead soldiers to serve as his guard. She'd only half-believed them, thinking they were legends designed to make him seem more forbidding. This was the first time she'd ever been to The Krem, and these fiends before her seemed to be the dark warriors Kremdor resurrected with his magic.

"Lord Vicia," she answered. "I am expected."

The guards gave no sign they had even heard her, let alone accepted her introduction. But the portcullis moved. Splitting in the middle with the top half rising and the bottom sinking, the bars parted like a mouth opening.

When it was clear, the guards pulled their glaives away, and the doors opened, spilling torchlight onto the path.

"Proceed," the guard said in that same horrific voice.

"Thank you," Vicia said.

She spurred her horse forward, and it moved into Kremdor's fortress despite whinnying in protest. She found herself in a large antechamber, where dirty servants came to assist her from the saddle and take her mount. Like the guards out front, they wore hoods, but their clothes were tattered, and they were covered in grime. Vicia couldn't say if they were human or not.

A woman with straggly, grey hair and haunted yellow eyes surrounded by wrinkly, sunken skin descended a set of stairs and came forward. She wore a black dress with Kremdor's symbol stitched on the chest. Gnarled, arthritic fingers knitted themselves together in front of her.

"Lord Vicia," she said in a cracked voice. "I am Esmerelda. My Lord Kremdor welcomes you to his abode. He requests I give you comfort while you await your audience."

"What does that mean?" Vicia asked, suspicious.

"I shall take you to quarters and provide you with hot water, fresh clothes, and food and drink," the woman answered.

Vicia nodded. All those things sounded divine to her, although given Kremdor's reputation, she doubted any of them were.

"Very well," Vicia said. "I accept Lord Kremdor's gracious hospitality."

"Follow me," Esmerelda said.

She turned and ascended the stone stairs. Esmerelda walked with a slight limp, but she did not seem to tire as the steps wound up numerous flights.

Vicia grew short-winded quickly. She was a fit woman, but she was exhausted. It had been a harrowing ordeal in the forest the last two days, and the entire journey from Twin Falls to here had been long and draining. When they at last reached a hallway and a wooden door through which Esmerelda ushered her, Vicia was worn out.

The chamber was spacious, and there was a soft bed with cotton sheets and a heavy, wool comforter. Vicia hadn't seen such luxury since she was on the Council of Elders. A large table was set with dried meat, fruit, cheese, and bread, and there was a tub with steaming water.

"You will find clean, warm clothes in the wardrobe," Esmerelda said, indicating the giant oak cabinet. "Does Lord Vicia wish someone to bathe her?"

"No, thank you," Vicia said. "I think I'd prefer a little time to myself."

"As you wish," Esmerelda replied. "Take time to bathe, eat, and rest. Lord Kremdor will send for you when he is ready."

Ordinarily, Vicia would have been irritated with that remark. She wanted to see Kremdor immediately. They had things to discuss, and she needed to move forward. Tremaine and Gray were doubtless still alive, and that meant they were in position to harm her and the plan. They didn't have time to mess around.

But she was so tired that she consented to Kremdor's schedule. It was late, and she needed rest.

"Thank you," Vicia managed before Esmerelda showed herself out.

Vicia went to the table and poured herself some wine from the jug. Then she grabbed a hunk of cheese and a loaf of bread and took the lot with her to the tub. She stripped off her clothes and eased her aching body into the warm water.

Relief streamed through her immediately. The pain ebbed away, and the steam relaxed her mind. She ate a bit as she soaked but didn't have much of an appetite. After ten minutes, her eyelids grew heavy.

Not wanting to fall asleep in the tub and possibly drown, she forced herself to rise from the steamy water and dress. The chilly air was bracing, but she found a warm sleeping gown in the wardrobe and pulled it on.

She went to the bed and slipped between the sheets. She was unconscious in less than a minute.

CHAPTER 27:

The Backing of the Thieves' Guild

GARRICK'S MIND WAS SWIRLING. He was heir to the throne of Twin Falls? He wasn't just a participant in the Contest of Succession? He wasn't here because Liliana had pushed him into it? He was *supposed* to be? This actually *was* his destiny?

He'd been no one his whole life. He was the undertaker's son – the kid who'd had to learn to fight if he didn't want to be bullied. He'd carved out a name for himself as a soldier, but it wasn't like he was anyone special. He was just a guy who'd earned the respect of his mates.

Now, suddenly, he was someone. Not just someone – someone important. Someone who held the key to the most powerful city-state in the northern reaches of The Known World.

He'd never really thought this was going to happen. He'd participated in the contest because Liliana had told him he was supposed to. He'd gone along because it seemed like something was happening. Why else would the goblins be after him?

But he hadn't believed he would win. Someone who actually knew something about ruling Twin Falls would come out on top. Liliana would realize this wasn't actually his destiny.

Liliana. By the gods, he'd kissed her! What had he been thinking? It had to be the emotion after the fight, didn't it? He'd heard of such things before. Men and women often went to bed before or after a great battle. It was a way of bonding, of coping with the stress. That had been it, right?

Except that he'd felt himself growing attracted to her before that. Her stark honesty, the way she had an answer for nearly everything, and her staunch faith in him had all combined to make him see her as more than an accomplished magician, more than a strong ally. He'd grown accustomed to thinking of her as a friend – perhaps as a special friend.

But she clearly hadn't been feeling anything for him. She'd been startled when he'd kissed her. She'd pulled back, shocked. He'd overstepped the boundaries of their relationship.

He had to say something to her about it. It was hanging like a lodestone around his neck and would interfere with their working relationship. He'd seen that happen too many times in the ranks. Men and women would get together, and one of them would assume it meant something more than the other thought it did. Then it was awkward, and they wouldn't trust each other in a fight anymore. He couldn't afford that. He and Liliana needed to have faith in each other until they had a fuller understanding of what was going on.

"Liliana," he said, summoning his courage.

"I know what you're thinking," she said.

She did? Was it that obvious?

"What?" he said.

"You're still thinking it can't be true," she said. "You've been a soldier your whole life. You're not a duke. I told you before, Garrick, this *is* your destiny."

"No," he said. "That's not—"

But she cut him off, going on as though she hadn't heard him.

"Listen, there are several complications surrounding this issue we're going to need to work out," she said. "The first and most important is establishing the authenticity of your claim. It's entirely possible and even likely that at least one of the other contestants will challenge it, demanding you produce some sort of proof."

Likely? Garrick was certain someone would challenge his claim. Zalachorus ir-Bedlam Donovian was dead set on becoming duke. Garrick figured him for the surest person to stand in the way.

"Now, I think Zalachorus might actually be some help on this," she said.

"You're kidding!" Garrick said. "He wants the position more than anyone, except maybe Vicia."

"Yes, but he's also a patriot," Liliana countered. "If you claim to be a lost heir, he'll feel compelled to investigate, and he's got influence with the libraries, which may be critical to tracking down your heritage."

"Doesn't that mean he could block our access to any documents we need?"

"Theoretically, yes," Liliana conceded. "But I don't think he will. He's ambitious, but I believe he is also honorable. In the end, he'll do the right thing."

"And how far away is the end?"

"That will depend on how well we persuade him," Liliana said.

"Now, next we'll also have to work to build you a coalition. Vicia has the Blessing of the Fey and a head start. Even if we beat her back to the city, it won't be by much. You need friends, and you're a stranger in Twin Falls. Fortunately, so is she, so that puts you on even footing.

"I suggest you approach General Calavan first. Whoever has his backing has the support of the military. You'll need that or all this is going to be nothing more than an elaborate charade. Based on what I saw at the feast, Calavan is less ambitious than Zalachorus. I bet he'll support a long-lost heir over a murderous former Elder. If we can convince him there's any legitimacy to your claim, I think you'll win him over."

She went through every idea she had, all the contingencies she'd thought of. Garrick marveled at how thorough her mind was.

But they never got around to discussing the kiss. She talked so incessantly about the details of his claim to the throne, he began to doubt the kiss had even happened. Perhaps he had only imagined it. Liliana certainly didn't give any indication she remembered it.

She'd just about worked out how to get Dover and Grunvilio onboard when they came upon Levinia. She appeared unmolested, and she woke when Liliana checked on her.

"Am I dreaming?" Levinia said when she looked into Liliana's face.

"No," Liliana said. "Unless you're also talking in your sleep. In any case, I can hear you."

"You came back for me," Levinia said.

"Of course," Liliana said. "I told you we would. Garrick gave you his word."

"Yes, but I didn't believe you," Levinia replied.

Her voice was weak. She was still in the throes of the powerful healing salves.

"Why not?" Liliana asked.

"Because we're rivals," Levinia answered. "We're after the same thing. It would have been easy for you to leave me here to die."

"I think if we were going to do that, we wouldn't have bothered to heal you," Liliana said. "It would have made more sense just to finish you off."

"Oh, yes," Levinia whispered. "I guess that's true."

"We've made an exciting discovery," Liliana said.

"Oh?"

"Yes. Peaseblossom has revealed Garrick is a long-lost heir to the throne," Liliana explained. "He's the rightful successor."

"That's nice," Levinia murmured.

Then she was asleep again. Liliana stared at her for a few moments before turning back to Garrick.

"The sedatives in the healing salves still have a strong hold on her," she said. "I'm not sure how much of this conversation she'll remember."

"It's just as well," Garrick said. "It's getting late. We'd need to make camp soon anyway. Levinia's in no shape to travel today. We'll have to sort it all out in the morning."

"Good point," Liliana said.

She got up and set to unpacking the horses and pitching camp. Garrick watched her for a moment before he dismounted and helped. It was going to be a very strange night.

Levinia's condition improved rapidly overnight. Most of her injuries were healed, although her leg was still mending, and it was too tender to put weight on it. Garrick was disappointed in that development, but Liliana had a plan to construct a sled for her, so they could transport her until the leg was strong enough for her to ride. Garrick thought that would slow them down when time was of the essence, but he didn't see that they had much choice.

"So what happened?" Levinia inquired. "Did you get the Blessing of the Fey?"

"Not exactly," Garrick said.

"What does that mean?" Levinia asked.

"Vicia was already there," Garrick said. He wasn't sure he wanted to discuss his newfound heritage just yet. "She'd already gotten the favor from the dryad."

"Damn," Levinia said. "So what did you do?"

"I attacked her," Garrick answered. "But it didn't go well."

He explained how he was a poor shot and had missed with his arrows, how Vicia and Liliana had fought with magic, and how Vicia escaped by setting the trees ablaze. Levinia looked fascinated throughout the tale and glanced over at Liliana in awe several times.

"So now what?" Levinia said. "She's got the blessing and a head start. How do we stop her?"

"Well," Garrick demurred. "We also learned something very interesting talking to Peaseblossom."

"What Garrick is too shy to come straight out and say," Liliana interjected, "is that Peaseblossom revealed he is a blood relative of Duke Evonin. Here's actually heir to the throne."

"What?" Levinia said, turning to Garrick in stunned surprise.

"Peaseblossom gave her blessing to the duke's line over four hundred years ago," Liliana said. "She recognized Garrick's royal blood when they spoke."

Levinia didn't say anything at first. She alternated between staring at Liliana and at Garrick.

"So that would mean the Contest of Succession is invalid," she said at last.

"Yes," Liliana said.

"Which would also mean that even if Vicia makes it to the city ahead of us, her claim to the throne would be illegitimate," Levinia said.

"Also true," Liliana said.

"But only in theory," Garrick added. "If she gets that crown on her head, I'd have to fight her to claim my birthright. That could cause a civil war."

Levinia nodded, clearly thinking the same thing. She turned possibilities over in her mind.

"Pardon me for asking," she said, "but do you have any proof?"

"To support my claim, you mean?" She nodded. "No. That's another problem. I can walk into Twin Falls and declare myself Duke Evonin's rightful heir all I want, but not everyone is going to believe me. In fact, I suspect no one will."

"We'll need to court support with key figures while we search for evidence to legitimize Garrick's claim," Liliana said.

"Well, I'll back you," Levinia said.

"Why?" Garrick asked, thunderstruck.

"Because you saved my life," Levinia said as though it should be obvious. "Twice. Both times you could have left me to die. The Silent Knights would have killed me if you hadn't intervened, and the wolves we fought yesterday nearly did. I'd be dead without the healing salves and draught you gave me. Plus, you could have left me to be eaten by predators, and instead you came back for me. I owe you.

"Whoever said, 'There is no honor among thieves,' was either ignorant or a liar."

"Thank you," Garrick said.

"No, thank you," Levinia countered. "It was obvious you didn't trust me, but you stuck by me anyway, Mr. Tremaine. You deserve to be rewarded for that, especially since we were rivals up to today. I think you'll find *Res Nostra* a powerful ally."

"Heh, well, I've got the backing of the thieves' guild," Garrick said. "That's a start."

"It's a better start than you think," Levinia said. "I control a powerful network, Mr. Tremaine. We don't just take a piece of the action of every crime in Twin Falls; we know virtually everything. We've got spies everywhere. Assassins too, if you need that sort of thing."

"Let's hope not," Garrick said, grimacing. "I prefer a straight fight to murder."

"Suit yourself," Levinia said. "Regardless, with my backing, you'll be a lot stronger than most people will suspect, and it will give you some leverage, since a lot of folks are afraid of us."

"I'd thought to go first to Zalachorus," Liliana said. "Since he has access to the libraries, I thought it might be wise to court him, so we can find proof of Garrick's legitimacy, but maybe we should start with General Calavan. A criminal-military alliance would give us a lot of power."

Levinia laughed.

"Calavan doesn't like me," she said. "I'm sure you can imagine why, what with my being a criminal and all. But he's more trustworthy than Zalachorus Donovian. That man has immense ambition. He's only interested in power for himself."

"That was my impression as well," Garrick said, shooting Liliana an I-told-you-so look.

"We need to bury Stephen," Levinia said. "Then we should be on our way. I'm already going to slow you down as it is, and we need to reach Twin Falls as soon as possible. If we're lucky we should be able to prevent Vicia's coronation. If not, we need her on the throne for as short a period as possible. We can't let her solidify her power base."

Garrick agreed. The less time wasted, the better. He still wasn't comfortable with the idea of being duke, but he needed to start acting like one if he was going to rule.

"All right," he said. "Liliana, would you use your magic to dig us a hole? We can get him buried, Levinia can say a few words over him, and then we need to get on our way."

"As you command, my lord," Liliana said with a wry grin.

She got to work immediately. Garrick watched her for a few moments. They still hadn't discussed the kiss. His heart ached.

CHAPTER 28:

Right about Her

LIGHT CREPT THROUGH THE shutters of her window and fell on Vicia's face when she awoke. She sat bolt upright in alarm. How long had she been asleep? What was happening?

She scanned her surroundings and remembered she had made it to The Krem and been given a room and "comforts," as Esmerelda had called them. Examining the table, she saw that the meal had been refreshed. There was fruit, a steaming decanter that smelled of coffee, bread, butter, and a silver, covered plate.

She got out of bed and padded over to the table. Lifting the cover, she discovered scrambled eggs, bacon, and sausage. Her stomach growled in response.

Pouring herself a mug of coffee, Vicia sat at the table and dug into the meal. She devoured the eggs and meat, had three slices of bread with plenty of butter, and ate half an apple before her appetite finally subsided.

She was on her third cup of coffee and beginning to feel like herself, when there was a knock at the door. It opened a crack and Esmerelda poked her head in.

"Ah, good," the old crone said. "You're awake. Excellent. His lordship will see you when you are ready."

"How much time has passed?" Vicia asked.

"Since your arrival? A little over eleven hours."

Vicia nodded. Good. She'd only slept through the night. She remained as on-schedule as possible.

"Please inform Lord Kremdor, I will see him as soon as I am dressed," she said.

"I am to wait for you, Lord Vicia," Esmerelda said.

Vicia nodded again. That was just as well. She didn't want to waste any more time.

She got up from the table and went to the wardrobe. She found a warm gown in her signature purple as well as fur-lined leggings. She got dressed and brushed her hair.

"All right," she said, turning to Esmerelda. "Let's go."

The old woman turned and led her out. They proceeded down the hallway back to the staircase that had brought them to Vicia's room last night. Once again, they ascended the steep steps.

Like last night, Esmerelda climbed the stairs without apparent effort. Vicia had gone what she thought were about two flights when she grew winded, and her thighs began to burn.

The tower seemed to rise forever. Vicia was uncertain how many levels they passed as they ascended. But just as she thought she couldn't take another step, they arrived on a landing. Vicia came to a stop on it and spent a few moments panting.

"Lord Kremdor is through the door," Esmerelda explained. "I will await you here."

She swept her arm towards the door. Vicia could only nod. She took two deep breaths, brushed her hair from her face, and then opened the door and went through.

Kremdor's *sanctum sanctorum* was impressive. She had seen bits of it during their communication spells, but this was the first time she had viewed the whole thing.

It appeared to encompass the entire top level of the tower. A fire burned in a large altar set near the far wall. She suspected this was where he did his scrying and communication.

A spectacular lab took up a good portion of the opposite side. Tables, vials, powders, scales, a cauldron, and tomes, covered the area.

Vicia could not imagine the spell Kremdor would be unable to cast, so vast were his resources.

A window looked out to the west and The Enchanted Forest, which appeared tranquil and majestic from this distance. An intricate, wooden box sat on a stool near the window.

She'd taken three steps inside the magnificent laboratory, when a giant bat the size of a small dog dropped from the ceiling and landed on the table next to her. Startled by its sudden appearance, Vicia jumped away from it as it looked on her large, curious, brown eyes.

"Ah, Lord Vicia," Kremdor said, stepping out of a shadow. "Welcome to my humble sanctuary."

Kremdor appeared as he always did. Brown leggings with black boots, a black, leather jerkin with his bat symbol stitched on it in brown, a black cloak, and the black metal helmet with a full faceplate and batwings mounted on the sides. He was shorter than she by half a foot. There were many rumors about whom Lord Kremdor was – a lot of conjecture suggested he wasn't human. His height made Vicia think that could be true.

"Nice to see you," she said, sarcasm dripping from each word.

"This is Isadore," Kremdor said, indicating the bat.

"Greetings, Lord Vicia," the rodent said.

Vicia scowled. She was already in a bad mood about the things that had gone wrong. Kremdor's parlor tricks and a talking bat were doing nothing to improve it.

"Hi," she said.

She knew she sounded gruff, but there were complications they needed to discuss.

"I take it by your presence here that you have rescued Peaseblossom and secured her favor?" he said.

"Yes," she said, coming forward. "And what the hell was the idea of trying to kill me?"

"What do you mean?"

"First, the goblins standing sentry refused to let me pass," she said. "Not only did I have to fight them, they had an ambush prepared. I had a hell of a time dispatching them.

"Then that damned elemental of yours was virtually undefeatable. It nearly killed me, Kremdor!"

"I apologize for the trouble I caused you," he said. Vicia didn't detect a lot of sincerity in his tone. "It was necessary."

"Why!"

"Because Peaseblossom needed to believe she was being rescued," he answered. "Had you been able to simply walk in and release her, she would have been suspicious. You would not have earned her favor. This way, she saw you fighting for your life to free her. She was therefore inclined to bless you for your efforts."

"You could have told me about that part of the plan!" Vicia shouted.

"No, I could not," Kremdor countered. "Had you known it was a charade, you would have acted differently. You would have had a plan in mind and been too casual. That also would have aroused suspicion. By forcing you to sincerely fight for your life, there was no way the deception could be detected.

"I apologize, Lord Vicia. I recognize this was stressful. It was, however, the only way to accomplish our objectives."

Vicia chewed on that. She wasn't pleased. Kremdor's logic may have made sense, but he'd put her at risk without telling her. That wasn't going to happen again.

"No more surprises, Kremdor," she said. "You either play straight with me, or I'll go it alone. Now that I've got the Blessing of the Fey, I can claim the throne without your assistance."

"Foolish," Isadore said. "And impertinent."

Vicia narrowed her eyes and glared at the bat. Who the hell did they think they were dealing with?

Kremdor stared silently at Vicia. There was no expression in his red eyes. She couldn't tell if he were smiling or scowling behind his mask.

"There's no need for threats, Lord Vicia," he said. "Our goals remain aligned. And you will find yours much easier to accomplish with my assistance. Whereas, they could be exceedingly difficult without it."

Vicia smiled unpleasantly at him. She was vaguely amused that he had told her there was no need for threats and then issued one only a moment later.

She wasn't afraid of him. She'd done battle with Gothemus Draco. She'd survived Elamanx's betrayal, Calibot's stealing the Eye of the Dragon, and the wrath of the Council of Elders. Lord Kremdor was no match for her.

"We've got a problem," she said. "Liliana Gray is still alive."

Kremdor didn't respond right away. He searched her, trying to read the details of what happened in her expression.

"Damn," he said, turning away. "That's unfortunate."

He wandered across the *sanctum* and ran his fingers over the box by the window. Vicia took a step towards him.

"You're damned right it is," she said. "She and Tremaine nearly killed me. Fortunately, he's a terrible shot with a bow. Even then, that bitch, Liliana, blunted all my magic again. I was lucky to get away."

"How did you manage it?" Isadore asked.

"I set the forest on fire," she said, irritated that Kremdor's talking pet had the gall to question her. "Liliana spent time putting it out."

"You were right about her," Kremdor said after another pause. "She killed one of the Silent Knights."

"What?" Vicia said. "As in one of the servants of the Crown of Silence?"

"Yes," Kremdor said. "So I tasked Gremsh with taking her out. It seems he has failed too. Even after employing *teufelhunden*. I should have known something was amiss when I hadn't heard from him."

"By the gods, Kremdor," Vicia said, "something has to be done about her. She can undo the entire operation."

"Yes," Kremdor said. "If Garrick Tremaine were to discover his birthright, it would threaten your claim to the throne."

"And as long as she lives, so will he," Vicia added.

"So it seems."

Kremdor fell silent again. Vicia was at a loss. Something had to be done. But what?

"We need to get you to Twin Falls as quickly as possible," he said. "Once you are crowned, the strength of his claim will wane."

"What if they get there ahead of me?"

"That will not happen," Kremdor said. "You will travel north across the lake. Gursh's soldiers will meet you at the falls. There is a cave that will grant you access into the city through his network of labyrinths. Tremaine and Gray will travel back the way they left, along the road. That will take them days out of their way. By the time they reach Twin Falls, you'll already be duchess."

"I have a better idea," Vicia said. "How about they not reach the city at all. They can't win a war of succession if they're not alive to fight it."

Kremdor turned and looked at her. He regarded her for some time before he spoke.

"Very well," he said. "I will send the Silent Knights to dispatch them. It's risky, but they are more competent than Gremsh or Gursh, and we need the goblins for the final phase of the plan anyway."

Vicia nodded. Liliana may have slain one of the Silent Knights, but even she wasn't good enough to get them all.

"You'd better get going," Kremdor said. "Even taking the direct route, it's still a long journey. We don't want to lose any time."

"Very well," Vicia said. "As long as you take care of your end of things, I'll handle mine. Just make sure Liliana Gray is out of the picture."

"I will," he said. "Go. Take whatever you need."

She thanked him and left. She had a knot in her stomach. This reminded her too much of how things went bad with Elmanax. Kremdor was more competent – he wasn't obsessed with revenge the way the gnome had been.

But Vicia wasn't about to take any chances. She would make sure she was installed as Duchess of Twin Falls. Once that was taken care of, she would worry about Kremdor and his grand plans to raise a god. Until then, his concerns were not hers.

CHAPTER 29:

Liliana Gray Must Die

GARRICK, LILIANA, AND LEVINIA traveled through the forest, slowed by the sled on which they dragged Levinia. Shrubs, bushes, trees, and roots all caused blockages. Often, they had to stop and clear a way or dislodge the apparatus from long branches.

Levinia apologized profusely every time this happened and cursed herself for being hurt and slowing them down. Liliana reassured her and told her it was no trouble, but Garrick grew frustrated. He could feel time slipping away from them. Even with Levinia's vast network, it would be extremely difficult to unseat Vicia if she were crowned, and she had a lead on them that grew larger every time they had to stop.

He feared the journey would prove too much for Levinia. She didn't seem to be doing well getting banged around in the undergrowth. She cried out when they would go over a bump the horses had avoided themselves but dragged her through. Levinia might be willing to put her entire network at Garrick's disposal, but she had to make it to Twin Falls alive for that to become reality.

They reached the road at last as night fell. Immense relief washed over Garrick, and Levinia practically cried with joy.

They made camp in the trees, preferring a little cover. Liliana salved Levinia's leg again, hopeful she would be able to ride tomorrow. Consequently, *Res Nostra's* guildmaster was out cold before they'd broken out rations for dinner.

Garrick tried to find the words to discuss the kiss, but Liliana didn't seem interested. She chatted strategy with him for a little while, and speculated on Levinia's recovery. Then she suggested they get some sleep and asked if Garrick would take the first watch because she was feeling worn out. He agreed glumly.

He watched her as she slept, his heart aching at the remembrance of their impromptu embrace. The more he thought about it, the more he was convinced it was not some strange urge fueled by surviving a great battle. He had kissed her because he'd meant it. He was falling in love with her. Her mind, faith, and conviction all appealed to him. He wanted Liliana for more than an ally, more than an advisor. He wanted her for much more than a friend.

But Liliana wouldn't mention the kiss, acted as though it had never happened. It was obvious his feelings were unrequited. Liliana remained loyal to him. She was determined to help him establish himself as Duke of Twin Falls. But she had no desire to rule by his side.

She smiled sweetly at him when he woke her for her watch. He tried to tell her how he felt, but once again his tongue froze. No words would come to him.

"Better get some rest," she said. "We need to get an early start tomorrow."

He nodded and lay down. Heartsick, he dropped into a troubled sleep.

The next morning, Liliana helped Levinia to her feet. The thieves' guild's master tried desperately to walk, but she couldn't manage it. The pain was just too great.

Garrick sighed. Liliana wished he wouldn't do that. Levinia felt bad enough as it was.

"I'm sorry," Levinia said, as if to give voice to Liliana's thoughts. "I'm ruining everything."

"It's okay," Garrick said. "It's not your fault. We've got the sled. We'll pull you for another day."

"Great," Levinia said, her voice full of disappointment.

"I'm sure it'll be fine tomorrow," Liliana said. "I've got a little more salve we can use on it tonight."

They breakfasted quickly and then got on their way. It was much easier going now that they were out on the road. The sled didn't get stuck on bushes and tree roots. They still couldn't travel very swiftly, though. The ride was too rough for Levinia that way.

Liliana tried to discuss strategy with her, but it was no use. The sled was too noisy for Levinia to hear well, and she constantly had to ask to have things repeated. After awhile, Liliana gave up.

With the struggle of getting through the trees past and no way to include Levinia in a conversation, Liliana was left alone with her thoughts. There was nothing to do but ride, and her mind turned to memories of Garrick kissing her.

She didn't understand it at all. He'd kissed her, which seemed to indicate he felt something for her. But then he'd said he didn't mean it. And he hadn't bothered to say anything about in the two days since, despite having plenty of opportunities, so he must have been sincere.

That saddened her. She liked Garrick Tremaine. She liked him more than any man she'd ever met. She didn't really know what it was to be in love. She wasn't sure she loved Garrick. But she liked him enough she'd have been willing to find out.

He wasn't interested, though. He'd made that perfectly clear with his apology for kissing her and his silence on the subject since. He evidently wanted her as an advisor but not as a duchess.

That was just as well. She'd been bored with court life in Dalasport. She would get Garrick set up as duke, make sure he was securely on the throne. Then she would leave again, looking for adventure somewhere else. That would be best.

In the interim, she resolved not to talk about the kiss. He had enough to think about with claiming the throne and building a coalition to hold onto it.

Still, it might have been nice to be his duchess. She enjoyed his company, and he made her feel special.

They reached the edge of the trees just as the light was failing. Liliana suggested they camp within the forest for additional shelter.

"Besides," she said, "the air is warmer here than without. We'll sleep better."

Garrick and Levinia both agreed. He dismounted, detached Levinia's sled, and helped her out. He set her gently under a large tree, while Liliana started making camp.

"I think we should have you drink another healing draught in addition to salving your leg," Liliana said. "It will speed your recovery."

"Ugh," Levinia said. "They taste like sewer water."

She relented, though, and Liliana gave her one that she choked down. Then Liliana started unpacking rations and hoped that tonight would be as peaceful as the last two. The serenity of the trees comforted her, but she would feel better when they were out of The Enchanted Forest. On the open ground, at least, they couldn't be ambushed.

Kremdor stared out the window of his sanctuary into the night. He didn't like this plan, was very concerned it would fail. Where would that leave him? If he lost the Silent Knights and Liliana Gray remained alive, would it spell the end of his ambition?

He'd spent years positioning himself for this. He at last had three of the major city-states in precarious political positions. He could topple Twin Falls now by putting Vicia on its throne, and then her lust for revenge would cause war with Eldenberg. With the Council of Elders too busy fighting their prodigal outcast, they'd be in no position to use their sorcery to stop Kremdor's ultimate goal.

Meanwhile, his plans against Sothernia were already bearing fruit. His agents would soon return from The Dread Islands with the power to topple Duke Contin. Then Lord Alavair would be isolated and outnumbered. Neither he nor Sothernia would be in any position to challenge Kremdor, especially since Alavair would have his hands full with the Vinshu. Then the real operation would begin.

But Vicia had to fulfill her ambition of becoming Duchess of Twin Falls first. Kremdor needed The Known World's northern-most city unable to oppose him and distracted by war. And that meant eliminating Garrick Tremaine, which in turn meant killing Liliana Gray. Kremdor wasn't confident the Silent Knights could defeat her.

If he lost them, it would make all the rest of his aims more difficult to accomplish. It would force him to reassess, reroute his resources.

And of course, if they couldn't kill Liliana, everything could fall apart in the next few days.

Kremdor supposed he didn't have a choice, though. The goblins didn't have the skill to murder her. Both Gursh and Gremsh had tried. His other allies were too far south and west to intervene. If he sent the Dread, his hand would be revealed in this, and he wasn't ready for anyone to know he was the one pulling all these strings. The Silent Knights were his best play.

He waited a moment more, feeling the cold night air cool his eyes through the slits in his faceplate. Then he drew in a deep breath and withdrew the Crown of Silence from its ornate box and placed it on his head.

"*Venite ad me,*" he intoned. "*Venite ad me. Conjuro te. Lusso meo. Venite ad me.*"

Kremdor turned to face the sanctuary as the three remaining assassins materialized in front of him. As usual, they bowed as one and then stood waiting for his instruction. He touched his hand to the crown.

"Liliana Gray," he said. "Take great care. She is the sorcerer who felled your companion. You must catch her completely unawares, so she has no chance to respond to your attack. Slay her before she can invoke any magic at all."

The three Knights nodded again.

"If you can kill her companions, that is better," Kremdor said. "But it is not your primary objective. Liliana Gray must die above all other concerns.

"Go swiftly. Slay her tonight. Time is of the essence."

The Silent Knights nodded a third time. Then they transformed into three pillars of mist and sailed out the window in the direction of The Enchanted Forest. Kremdor watched them go.

"Isadore," he said.

A giant bat dislodged itself from the rafters above and flapped down to him. He stroked its head twice.

"Follow them," Kremdor instructed. "Observe their work, and come back to tell me what you have seen."

"Yes, Lord Kremdor," the bat croaked.

Isadore took off after the three trails of vapor. He hoped he wouldn't need her report. He hoped the Silent Knights would return victorious. But in case they didn't, he needed to know what happened, so he could adjust his plans.

Garrick finished eating and looked at the women. Levinia was already asleep, once again pulled to slumber by the side effects of Liliana's salve. Liliana sat thoughtfully, illuminated by the glow of the magical light issuing from a stick she'd enchanted to act as a torch.

"There's a problem I haven't worked out yet," she said.

"What's that?"

"Well, Levinia's offer is generous, and it's the best thing we've got," she mused. "But we're going to need the military too. As long as General Calavan opposes you, there is no way you can maintain your grip on the city, even if you are able to depose Vicia. You'll need the backing of the army to maintain control and prevent a *coup*."

"So we need to figure out how to get Calavan to support you, even though you're working with criminals."

Garrick turned the question over in his mind. Calavan was a soldier. In theory, that made him a pragmatist.

"I'm a soldier, just like the general," he said. "I'll appeal to his sense of strategy. He and I will see eye to eye on security issues – he'll know he can trust me on that. I'll have to make him see that an alliance with *Res Nostra* was born of necessity and can benefit the city since I'll be able to monitor them more closely."

"Will he buy that?"

"I'm not sure," Garrick replied. "I don't know the man. But we're both soldiers. That ought to provide us some common ground."

"Let's hope so," she said, nodding thoughtfully.

Garrick's thoughts turned again to his burgeoning feelings for his companion. Lit up in the soft, blue glow of her magical light, Liliana looked hauntingly lovely.

"Liliana," he began, but his throat tightened, and he had to swallow. "Yes?"

"There's something . . . something I have tell you . . . discuss with you."

"What is it?" she asked.

A line of bright, orange light snaked out of the darkness behind her and wrapped around Liliana's throat, finishing with a sharp *crack!* A second later, her hands flew to her neck, and she was pulled backward.

Fear and recognition shot through Garrick's mind. This was the same attack they'd made against Levinia, only now it seemed Liliana was the target.

Indeed, he could see the black-garbed fiend behind her, pulling his magical whip taut. Liliana choked and struggled.

Garrick leaped to his feet, grabbed his sword, and charged. Before he took three steps, though, a second assassin appeared in front of him, summoned a sword made of red light, and slashed, forcing Garrick to parry the blow.

In the next instant, an arrow of yellow magic flew past him and struck Liliana in the throat. Garrick had no time to be horrified. An explosion of blue, magical fire engulfed Liliana and the killer with the whip, who shrieked in horrific agony, chilling Garrick's heart and freezing his blood.

"Liliana!" Garrick cried. "No!"

The fiend he was fighting didn't take advantage of the opening. He turned and stared at the conflagration behind him.

The blue fireball dissipated. Liliana slumped to her knees and fell over. The Silent Knight was gone.

The monster with the sword turned and looked past Garrick, who whirled and saw the killer with the bow kneeling a few feet away. Levinia sat up next to him, looking terrified.

Before anyone could react, the two magical assassins turned to vapor and flew off to the east. Liliana moaned. By the gods, was she still alive?

Garrick rushed to her. He dropped his sword and knelt to examine her.

"What the hell happened?" Levinia asked. Garrick ignored her.

"Liliana," he said, "are you okay? Are you okay?"

Her hand went to her throat as she coughed. After a second, she felt her neck desperately.

"Oh, no," she wailed.

"What?" he said.

"Oh, no," she repeated. "Oh, no, my amulet. They've destroyed my amulet!"

CHAPTER 30:

Silent Escort

V ICIA LEFT THE KREM at midday. She would have preferred an earlier start, but she'd slept a little late before her meeting with Kremdor, and then she'd made sure to supply herself well. She put up the hood of the thick, fur cloak she'd taken from her chamber, and it was sufficient proof against the wind.

Kremdor dispatched two of his strange, otherworldly soldiers – the Dread he'd called them – to escort her to Twin Falls. She didn't like them. Vicia was no stranger to odd creatures and weird rituals, but the warriors spooked her. They exuded a palpable wrongness she couldn't identify, but they seemed to be an affront to the natural order of things. Like the sentries at the gate last night, their hoods were up, and even in the bright sunshine, she could detect nothing underneath except the feral, blue eyes that glowed with sinister, preternatural light.

They rode alongside her in utter silence. Her own horse whinnied in protest and tossed its head fearfully. Meanwhile, the jet-black steeds the Dread rode walked as though their very purpose was to carry these fiends to their destination.

After winding down the rocky path from The Krem, they turned northward and followed the river. It bubbled happily by, making Vicia think it had no idea about the way things really worked in the world. A thin layer of snow coated the ground, but the river was too rapid and the air too warm for ice to form on its surface.

As the sun was getting low in the sky, they came at last to the source – Crystal Lake. The enormous body of water spread away to the east, west, and north. Vicia could not see the other side of it, formed by the falls that guarded the city she aimed to rule.

At the shore, the two Dread warriors dismounted. One of them withdrew a staff from a sheath on his saddle and then walked to the edge of the water. He reached out and dipped the end in the lake, stirring a few times. Then he stepped back and waited.

Vicia watched as the water started to boil. A moment later, a small ferry rose out of the waters. Carved whole from what must have been an enormous tree, her prow was shaped like a bat head, and her hull was fashioned to resemble batwings. Runes and sigils ran along her gunwales. Vicia shook her head. Kremdor loved his bat imagery.

"Come," the soldier with the staff said in a voice that made her shiver.

Vicia swallowed hard and spurred her horse forward.

"Leave your mount," the soldier said. "You will need it no further."

She shuddered at the idea of leaving the best method of escaping these monsters behind, but she supposed there was nothing to be done about it. The ferry didn't really look large enough to carry the beast. And Kremdor had said the goblins would escort her into the city secretly from behind the falls.

Patting the horse's neck, she dismounted, collected her saddle bags, and proceeded to the water's edge. The Dread warrior held the ferry for her as she climbed aboard. Then he boarded himself.

A moment later, he put the staff into the water and pushed off from the shore. The vessel swung around neatly, and her strange companion poled the ferry out into deeper water.

Vicia looked back and saw her other escort leading his partner's mount and hers back to The Krem. Her horse pulled at the reins fearfully. She felt a little sorry for it.

The ferry picked up speed out in the open water. The pilot kept his staff in the blue depths, but he ceased poling. He held it now like a tiller, and Vicia was certain it was enchanted to propel the vessel north.

They'd only been journeying an hour when the light failed. The sunset was spectacular on the waves, but it didn't last long, and Vicia soon found herself in inky darkness, with only the sounds of the ferry cutting through the black water and the light of her pilot's two fearsome eyes, which glowed with terrible intensity at night, to keep her company.

She pulled her cloak tightly about her, and sank into the ship's bow, keeping as much distance between her and her escort as the boat would allow. With her hood up around her ears, she slipped into an uncomfortable and troubled sleep.

She awoke just after dawn. The weather was overcast, and the grey light threw a gloom over the boat and the water.

Her pilot did not appear to have moved at all. He stood like a statue in the stern, holding his pole still in the waters. She could not discern if his eerie, blue eyes were watching her or gazing off into the distance, but they made her shiver.

She got to her feet and was punished by sore muscles unfurling for the first time in hours. Cramps and bruises from the hard wood of the barge assaulted her and made stretching agony. She massaged away her hurts as best she could.

"Morning," she said to her escort.

"Yes," he rumbled. "It is."

Vicia stared at him for a moment. This time she was convinced he was looking off in the distance. She shuddered again and decided against making further small talk with him. Not only was he not any good at it, his unnatural voice disturbed her.

She dug into her saddlebags and pulled out some bread and cheese for breakfast. That and the wine she'd brought took the edge off her worry.

Journeying across Crystal Lake remained dull, though. There was little to look at, and the weather was depressing.

The light was fading when she could at last perceive the lake's far shore. At first, it was only a grey blur on the horizon. As they got nearer, though, she could make out the cliff face and the hint of Twin Falls atop it.

The sky was nearly black when she heard the roar of the falls for the first time. It was too dark to see them, though.

They continued their otherwise-silent voyage for more than an hour after nightfall. Once again, her mysterious pilot took on a more sinister aspect in the dark. Vicia found herself desperate to escape the barge. She wanted away from the thing Kremdor had dispatched to get her here. She had no love for goblins, but she was certain she preferred their company to the Dread.

At last, the ferry skidded ashore. Vicia practically leaped from the bow to the rocky beach. She grabbed her saddlebags and staff and took two steps away before she realized she didn't exactly know where she was going.

Her silent escort strode confidently by her. He gave no instructions, just walked up the beach. Vicia followed, unsure what else to do.

The falls was not far away. Its roar was practically deafening. The Dread led her up a winding path that twisted ever closer to the thundering water. He stopped just shy of it.

Behind him, Vicia could perceive tiny lights. They came closer.

"Lord Vicia?" a squeaky voice called.

"Who's asking?" she replied.

An orange globe of light emerged from behind the falls, and she saw it was a goblin with a lantern.

"I am Wurg," he said. "My king, Gursh, has sent me to fetch you."

Vicia looked him up and down. He was about half her height, with green skin, large, pointy ears, and an enormous, round nose that covered half his face. Two yellow eyes glinted in the darkness, and he wore an animal-skin tunic with a small, curved sword belted to his hip.

"Very well, Wurg," she said. "Take me to your king."

"Please follow me, my lord," he said.

Vicia moved as quickly past the Dread warrior as she could manage without appearing to be scared of him.

"Thanks for the ride," she said.

Her escort didn't reply. She took one quick look back and saw him descending the trail as silently as he'd climbed it.

Wurg turned and led her to the waterfall. A small crevice in the rock face enabled them to slip behind the tumbling river. Wurg managed it easily, but Vicia was struck in the shoulder by the icy water. Her foot slid, and she tumbled into the falls and towards the edge of the rocky outcropping.

She panicked, certain she would be cast down into the lake and smashed against the rocks, but Wurg snatched her cloak and yanked her back before she could pitch over the precipice.

Wurg drew her through a portal behind the water. Within was a cavern, wherein gathered five more goblins dressed like Wurg. Some of them snickered at her misfortune with the water, but Wurg backhanded the closest.

"Silence!" he cried in his squeaky voice. "This is the honored guest of the king. You will treat her with respect!"

They all bowed their heads deferentially. Vicia was in a foul mood and didn't enjoy being mocked.

"I would hate to report to your king I was dissatisfied with my treatment," she scolded.

She was greeted with several muttered apologies. No one would meet her gaze.

"This way, Lord Vicia," Wurg said.

He led her through a twisting series of caves. Within minutes, Vicia was hopelessly lost. She could never have found her way back to the secret entrance by the falls. There were too many turns, too many switchbacks and forks in the path, for her to keep any sense of direction. She could only perceive they were constantly going up. Wherever their ultimate destination lay, it was far above the lake somewhere deep inside the cliff.

Vicia puffed heavily after about an hour of climbing. Few of the grades were steep, but she'd been walking uphill since landing on the rocky shore, and despite his diminutive size, Wurg was swift. She had to walk briskly to keep up with him and the rest of the escort. He seemed not to notice she was tiring. He kept up his quick pace, never slowing or offering to let her stop and rest.

At last, he brought her to a larger chamber, occupied by numerous goblins. Most were armed with swords or spears, and one had a club. A few appeared to be courtiers, for they had no weapons, but Vicia couldn't be certain. She didn't know enough about goblin tribal culture to know if it resembled human city-states.

An ornate set of iron doors stood on the far side of the room, and guards with spears stood at attention on either side of it. Everyone stopped talking and stared when they saw her.

"Wait here," Wurg said with a broad smile. "I will announce you to the king."

He turned and moved rapidly to the doors. He nodded to the guards, who seemed to know him, knocked twice, and then pushed one door open and slipped inside it. It shut behind him.

Vicia realized as she stood waiting that her back was sore. The caverns she'd been traversing were made for goblins. She'd had to stoop to navigate them, and even this large antechamber had too low a ceiling for her.

Pair after pair of yellow eyes studied her. They looked on her curiously. None seemed afraid. Clearly, they didn't have a good idea whom she was.

A minute later, the doors opened, and Wurg motioned for her to come forward. Vicia nodded to the goblins closest to her and then went in for her audience with the king.

Through the chamber doors was a cave at last large enough she could stand fully erect. She stretched her back, and her vertebrae cracked and popped in relief.

Approximately thirty goblins were staged around the room. Ten were armed. The rest seemed to be courtiers. They all wore animal pelts for clothing, and the courtiers appeared to have nicer ones than the soldiers, although they were all dirty and greasy.

At the back of the cave, on a large, wooden throne, sat a big goblin with an iron crown on his head. He was broad-chested but also had a considerable stomach. The crown was dull grey, but its spires were jagged and sharp. It looked like a weapon itself.

To the king's right stood a frail-looking goblin with a short staff topped with a skull. In every way, he was the physical opposite of his monarch.

"Lord Vicia," the goblin with the crown boomed. "I am Gursh, King of Goblins. Welcome to my home!"

"Thank you, Your Majesty," she said.

"This is my chief advisor and magician, Kraven," he said, indicating the goblin with the staff.

"Lord Vicia," Kraven said with a bow. "It is an honor to make the acquaintance of one so steeped in sorcery."

Vicia nodded to him. He must have been the fool who had messed up the crucifixion ritual.

"How was your journey?" Gursh asked.

"Unpleasant," she said.

"I am sorry to hear it," he replied. "May I offer you sustenance?"

"Please, Your Majesty," she answered. "That would be both kind and appreciated."

Gursh clapped his hands, and servants appeared with plates of unidentifiable meats and tankards of ale. They brought Vicia a chair and a stool on which they set her meal. The ale was bitter and the meat foul. She struggled to eat it.

"How soon can you get me into the city?" she asked.

"That depends on your desire," Gursh replied around a leg of some animal she didn't recognize. "It isn't safe for us to be seen in the daylight. If you want to rest, we'll have to wait until night falls tomorrow. But there is time to get you there tonight if you wish to forego sleep."

Vicia was exhausted. Sleep beckoned to her like an old friend desperate for a reunion. But she didn't think she would rest well in a goblin warren, and she did not wish to delay this close to her ultimate goal. Her dreams were within her grasp. She could wait no longer.

"I prefer tonight," she said. "The sooner we move the operation forward, the better."

"Agreed," Gursh said.

"Gruul has labored too long in his chains," Kraven commented.

"Yes," Gursh agreed. "I'll have Wurg and his troops escort you to the surface. Once you're inside the city, you can go about claiming the throne. Once you're crowned, we'll be in touch to start the next phase."

"How will you know when I'm crowned?" she asked.

"We have spies throughout the city, Lord Vicia," Kraven said. "We know everything that happens. Especially in the court."

"When we're ready to move, here's what we'll do," Gursh said.

Vicia listened as he explained in perfect detail what was to happen after she became duchess. She nodded several times. Vicia liked the idea of bringing Eldenberg to its knees with goblins. The Elders would gnash their teeth over being defeated by her and a dark god.

"And now I think it's time we part company again, Lord Vicia," Gursh said. "Wurg will escort you into the city. We'll await your coronation eagerly."

Vicia stood and bowed. Wurg came forward.

"I look forward to the next time we speak, Your Majesty," Vicia said. "Soon, Twin Falls and more will be ours."

"Soon, Gruul will again stride the earth," Gursh said. "And our enemies will tremble before us."

Vicia liked the sound of that a lot. She smiled, nodded to Gursh and Kraven, and allowed Wurg to lead her out.

Once again, she found herself winding through an elevating series of twisting tunnels. Like in the first caves earlier in the night, she quickly lost all sense of direction. She couldn't have found her way back to Gursh's lair if she'd had a map.

Wurg, though, seemed to know exactly where he was going. He moved with the same alacrity with which he'd brought her up from the falls, and she struggled again to keep up with him. Exhaustion was getting the better of her.

At last, they came to a stop on a large seal. Sigils were carved all over it. Vicia could see right away the goblins had labored over it lovingly, ensuring every detail was right. Gursh and his minions may have let Garrick Tremaine escape and failed to kill Liliana Gray, but they had managed this part of the operation magnificently.

"This is where the final ritual will be conducted," Wurg said.

Vicia rolled her eyes at the unnecessary explanation. He ascended a ladder carved into the stone wall without further comment. Vicia followed him.

At the top was a small chamber. Wurg went to the far wall.

"Wait here a moment," he said.

He slid a panel aside, revealing a pair of eyeholes. Then he put his head to it and looked out, not moving for nearly a full minute.

"Okay," he said at last. "It's clear."

He moved to his left, doused his lantern, and then touched something Vicia couldn't see. A moment later, an aperture opened in the stone.

"Go quickly," Wurg hissed. "I'll be in touch."

Vicia didn't wait. She slipped through the opening and found herself in an alley just off Twin Falls's central market. In the early hours of pre-dawn, the streets and stalls were abandoned.

As soon as she was through, the wall behind her slid shut. Afterward, she couldn't have said where the door had been.

The cool, night air felt good on her face. Her heart rate quickened. The time was upon her. Destiny was at hand. By this time tomorrow, she would be Duchess of Twin Falls.

CHAPTER 31:

Something Wrong

"I DON'T LIKE IT," Calavan said as he stormed around Zalachorus's office. "Something isn't right."

Zalachorus sighed patiently. The general was a paranoiac. Zalachorus supposed having a suspicious mind was natural for a security official, but it made him troublesome to deal with.

"General," he said, "there is plenty for us to worry about with the situation as it is, but I just don't see how this matters."

Calavan whirled on him, his sky-blue cloak swishing in the air. He came forward as though he meant to beat Zalachorus.

"No one on the watch reported her entering the city," Calavan said. "At either gate! And yet here she is, in Twin Falls, with the Blessing of the Fey, ready to claim the throne. That doesn't worry you in the least?"

"Of course, it worries me," Zalachorus said. "I trust no one but you or I to rule Twin Falls, and I trust that witch from Eldenberg least of all the other competitors.

"But what can we do, Blake? She has the boon necessary to ascend the throne. Bismarck has authenticated it. He plans to crown her at dawn

JOHN R. PHYTHYON, JR.

tomorrow. Are you going to revolt? Is it to be civil war? And what's your excuse? That your men couldn't account for her at the gate?

"That's a pretty flimsy platform for a *coup*, Blake. Even if you could get the army behind you, you'd never have the support of the people."

"And if I were to put you on the throne in place of her?"

Zalachorus sat back and stroked his beard. He hadn't expected the general to make that sort of an offer. Technically, he hadn't made any offer at all, but he had at least considered the possibility. An alliance between the sorcerers' guild and the military would be formidable.

All that was immaterial, though. Zalachorus had his own agenda. A partnership with Calavan was coincidental and unnecessary. Still . . .

"Are you proposing we ally against Duchess Vicia?" Zalachorus asked.

"She's not duchess yet," Calavan spat. "And who said anything about a revolution?"

"I believe you did."

"No, Zalachorus, I did not. *You* asked me if I would revolt. I did not propose it.

"I may be a soldier, but I am interested in neither war nor revolution. I would prefer to see a peaceful transition from Evonin to his successor."

"I sense a 'but' coming," Zalachorus said, his eyes glittering.

"I am a patriot, Zalachorus," he said. "If Vicia Morrigan is the rightful successor to Duke Evonin, then so be it. My sword and my heart are hers.

"But she is an Eldenberger. Furthermore, she is a disgraced murderer and a defrocked Elder of the Council. I do not believe she desires Twin Falls for anything other than her own ambition. I fear what will become of us if she is crowned."

Zalachorus steepled his fingers and tapped them gently together. All that Calavan said was true. Vicia was no friend to the city. She saw it only as a tool for her revenge.

But was Calavan the stronger ally? Could he actually oppose Vicia and win? Was it possible for Zalachorus to wait to see which of them would emerge victorious? And even if it was, could he still accomplish his own aims if he didn't pick a side now?

There was much to consider and little time to decide.

"Why are you so convinced she means us harm?" he asked.

"I didn't say she meant to harm us, Zalachorus. I said she cares nothing for Twin Falls. I don't know how she obtained the Blessing of the Fey, but I do not believe she did so honorably."

"What makes you say that?"

"Zalachorus," Calavan said, staring at him as though he didn't recognize him. "She was the first of the contestants to leave the city. Two more left after her, but the watch reported both of them appeared to be following her.

"In her absence, four contestants were murdered by mysterious, mystical assassins. Lindsay Grunvilio was cut down before my eyes by these fiends. I don't know why you and I were spared, but I can guess. Whoever rules Twin Falls will need the support of your guild and the military. The others can be bought off or ground under, but the next duke must have swords and magic to maintain his legitimacy, and he cannot purchase either.

"Now, Vicia Morrigan returns to the city with the verified Blessing of the Fey in hand. Except no one knows how she got in. I instructed the gatekeepers to inform me if any of the three contestants who left returned to Twin Falls. None of my watchmen report seeing her enter through either gate. Yet here she is, and the other two aspirants remain away.

"Doesn't this seem strange to you, Zalachorus? Don't you feel deep in your bones that something isn't right here?"

He did. Vicia may have made an alliance with him, but there was a whole host of things she hadn't told him. And Calavan's nose was getting awfully close to sniffing out what was really at work here. With an effort, Zalachorus calmed the beating of his heart.

"Blake," he said, "have your men never made a mistake before?"

The general stood up straight. His eyes flared at the suggestion.

"Yes," he answered. "But not on something of this magnitude. Even if the gatekeeper interviewing arrivals missed it, *someone* should have noticed her. My soldiers all know whom she is and why she is important. The entire shift could not have missed the arrival of an aspirant to the throne."

Calavan came forward and put his hands on the desk. He leaned in until he and Zalachorus were eye to eye.

"She's here by some other means, Zalachorus," he said. "Whether magical or mundane, she got inside the walls by some method that didn't involve walking through the gates."

Zalachorus pursed his lips. Calavan was right. Vicia wasn't playing the game by the same rules as everyone else. That made her dangerous.

"What do you propose we do?" he asked.

Calavan sighed and pushed himself off the desk. He turned and wandered away, pacing the room for nearly fifteen seconds without answering.

"I don't know," he said at last. "I'm trying to determine how she got into the city. I suspect that information would answer much.

"Perhaps you and the guild could engage in a little divination, see if you can figure out how she got here and what her intentions are."

"I will," Zalachorus said, nodding. "We need to know what she's up to, if anything."

"She's up to something, Zalachorus," Calavan said. "We need to know what it is before it's too late for Twin Falls."

No, you don't, Zalachorus thought.

The last thing Twin Falls needed was Blake Calavan discovering what Vicia had in mind. His reaction would be predictable and unfortunate.

But Zalachorus didn't like the implications of the tale the general had spun. How *did* Vicia get inside the city? And what did she mean to do once she opened the seal?

She'd been vague about all this and how Zalachorus and the guild would benefit. He intended to find out. *Before* the crown of Twin Falls was resting on her brow.

CHAPTER 32:

Back to Twin Falls

GARRICK STARED AT LILIANA in the dim light of the magically enchanted stick. She huddled on her hands and knees, sobbing. Confusion covered his face.

"I don't understand," he said.

"They destroyed my amulet!" she shouted.

Anger and tears flooded her expression. Garrick turned to glance at Levinia, but her face told him she understood Liliana's cryptic exclamation no better than he did. He faced Liliana again.

"Liliana," he said as gently as he could. "I don't understand. You've never mentioned this before. How is the amulet important?"

"I need it to work my magic," she said, weeping.

Garrick exchanged another a glance with Levinia; she continued to look as puzzled as he.

"I thought you were a sorcerer," Levinia said.

"Not exactly," she replied.

"I still don't see—" he began, but Liliana cut him off.

"I'm a wild magician, Garrick!" she screamed. "Remember? I can't control the magic without the pendant! With it, I can do almost anything.

Without it, all my magic fails. It goes off-course and makes a mess of everything! I explained all this to you before!"

He felt stupid. Of course she'd explained it to him. The night they'd opened up to each other before reaching The Enchanted Forest.

His heart was breaking. Seeing her in pain, seeing her overcome with loss hit him with the force of a mallet to his chest. He struggled to breathe.

"At least, you're still alive," Levinia said. "If that arrow hadn't hit your amulet, you'd be dead."

"I wish I were!" she screamed. "I'd be better off dead! Now, I'm worthless!"

She dropped her head to the ground. Huge, wracking sobs shook her.

"I'm no good," she wept. "I'm no good to anyone now."

Garrick didn't know what to say or do. He'd seen this sort of thing before. Warriors who lost limbs and couldn't fight anymore suddenly lost their will to live. Their entire purpose was tied up in their service, in their sense of duty. When they could no longer work as a soldier, they saw no point to being alive.

It seemed Liliana was suffering a similar malady. She'd struggled her whole existence to master the magic that flowed through her. Gothemus Draco had given her an amulet to make it possible. She'd become one of the most powerful women in The Known World. And now it was all gone, ironically snatched away by magic and chance.

What could he say that would soothe her? What comfort could he give that would have any meaning?

"Liliana," he said, hardly realizing he was speaking.

"What?" she sobbed.

"I love you."

She lifted her head slowly and stared aghast at him with tear-streaked eyes. Garrick's heart stopped. He hadn't known he would say that, hadn't realized it was true.

But he'd said it. Like the kiss, there was no taking it back.

Liliana's mouth fell open. Horror gripped her face.

She said nothing, though. She only stared for a few moments longer.

Then she lowered her head again and covered it with her arms. Her shoulders shook as she resumed crying.

Garrick tried to speak further, but no words would come. Liliana was inconsolable. He felt as worthless as she did.

He woke the next morning to discover Levinia up and around. She walked stiffly, but it was clear the healing potion had mended her broken leg enough that she could get around on it. A tiny ray of hope shone in his heart. If Levinia were better, perhaps they could increase their speed and make up some lost time.

"Good morning," she said. "I hope you don't mind, but I went through your saddlebags to get rations so I could make us breakfast."

"Not at all," he said, sitting up.

Although he did mind. There was nothing in his gear he would worry about her finding, but Levinia was a criminal. It made him nervous to have her going through his things.

He supposed, though, he was going to have to learn to trust her. She was his ally now, and he needed her. Whether he liked it or not, a certain amount of faith was required.

Garrick got up and stretched and wandered over to Levinia's makeshift kitchen. The rations weren't special – just dried meat and some hard bread, but Levinia had added seasoning to the meat that improved it a shade, and she had strawberry jam for the bread. She must have brought those herself. At least in this regard, she was making herself a good partner.

"How's Liliana?" he asked.

"See for yourself," Levinia replied, flicking her eyes in the direction of the woman he'd confessed to loving.

Garrick looked, and a fist of sorrow seized his heart and squeezed. Liliana sat against a tree, with her knees pulled up tightly to her chest and her arms wrapped around them in a bear hug. Her eyes focused on nothing, and ghosts of shame and loss danced behind her irises. Garrick had known her only a short time, but he'd never seen her like this.

"Has she slept?" he asked.

"I don't know," Levinia answered. "I passed out again after last night's . . . incident. The sedatives in that healing salve are potent.

"But she's been like that since I awoke. She doesn't speak. She barely acknowledges you're there. I tried to get her to eat, but she refused. She only shook her head when I offered her breakfast."

Garrick wanted to weep. This was the worst scenario he could imagine. He loved Liliana. He couldn't express why, and he didn't know

JOHN R. PHYTHYON, JR.

when his feelings matured from curiosity to friendship to desire. But love her he did, and seeing her like this was paralyzing. He'd lost her at the very moment he'd realized how he felt. Not only was it unfair, his heart broke at the pain that consumed her.

His personal feelings aside, the timing of Liliana's descent into madness was bad. Whether she could work magic or not, he needed her. She'd spent time in the court of Duke Boordin. She knew how to handle politics. Garrick was completely ignorant of that sort of thing. He was a soldier, not a courtier. He needed a trusted advisor.

Moreover, Liliana had been driving this cart from the beginning. It was she who believed in Garrick's destiny as Duke of Twin Falls. She was the one who had pushed him to participate in the Contest of Succession. She told him what to do and plotted each of their moves.

What was he to do without her advice? How could he manage all this without her insight, her strategy? He was no politician, but he knew ruling was a lonely job. He needed a friend. He wanted her.

And that brought him back to his love for her. Had he broken her completely by revealing it? Last night, after the amulet was destroyed, she'd been distraught, but she was speaking. But once he told he loved her, she'd become catatonic. Had he himself pushed her over the edge into permanent, unhealable madness?

He sighed. The salty, hard meat toughened. The jam lost its sweetness. He found himself having no more desire to eat than Liliana. Regretfully, he forced himself to choke down his breakfast. He suspected he would need his strength today.

"We'd better get going," Garrick said as he stood. "Can you ride today?"

"I think so," Levinia said. "I certainly mean to try. I appreciate you not leaving me behind, but being dragged behind your horse was a kind of travel I'd like never to repeat."

"Then let's get packed up," he said. "We've got a lot of ground to cover if we're going to make up any time on Vicia."

Levinia nodded and began stowing their supplies. Swallowing hard, Garrick walked over to Liliana.

"Liliana," he said gently.

She didn't reply. Her gaze continued to travel off into the distance, haunted and frightening.

"Liliana," he said again. "We need to get going."

She rose wordlessly and wandered past him like a lost ghost. Absently, she saddled Percy, then untied him and mounted. Garrick blinked back tears and went to assist Levinia in getting the supplies packed and the other horses ready.

Levinia needed assistance climbing into the saddle, but once astride, she declared herself fine. Garrick didn't believe her; she grimaced as she adjusted herself. But he supposed he didn't have much of a choice. They'd never catch Vicia if Levinia couldn't ride, and if she wanted to try, he saw no reason to stop her.

Besides, he was going to need someone to talk to. There was strategy to discuss, and it was plain Liliana wouldn't be participating. With another heavy sigh, he spurred his beast, and they were off.

Garrick had forgotten it was winter. They'd been enshrouded in the magic of The Enchanted Forest for days, and it came as a shock when they emerged from the trees to find snow on the ground and the temperature roughly forty degrees cooler. They stopped briefly to don warm cloaks before resuming their journey north.

He set a fast pace for them. Levinia was able to ride well enough they could spur the horses to a trot. He worried about Liliana falling behind, but she kept her mount just to the rear of theirs, never trailing so far that they would have to stop or slow for her to catch up.

The weather was cold and clear, and they were able to make good progress the first day. Garrick was certain they'd make the turn east for Twin Falls before noon tomorrow.

Levinia took the opportunity to familiarize him with the basics of her operation and how she planned to use it to support him. One aspect of the strategy that hadn't occurred to him was that he would need the backing of the court. Levinia had a number of thugs she thought could be employed to lean on key nobles.

"Most of them are pretty soft," she said. "A few well-made threats will bring them in line."

Garrick shuddered at the idea of strong-arming people to do what he wanted, but he supposed that was part of being a ruler. He much preferred the concept of threatening weak-willed nobles to go along to Levinia's second contingency, which was assassinating any of the more stubborn ones who tried to make trouble. As a military man, Garrick understood eliminating enemies. However, he wanted to rule justly or not all. He wouldn't want to serve a duke who murdered his rivals, so he felt he shouldn't *be* that kind of monarch.

"I understand," Levinia said, when he expressed his reasons for resisting the idea. "But this isn't going to be a simple walk through the daisies. People *will* oppose you, Garrick. If you don't make it plain you will tolerate no dissension, you'll sow trouble for yourself down the line.

"Think of it as a military decision. A commander cannot have rebellion in the ranks. Everyone has to obey orders, or there'll be disaster in battle. It's the same with court. Everyone has to understand that you're in charge, and they are to submit to your rule. They don't all have to like it, but they can't be harboring any belief that they could change things."

He grimaced. Was this really worth it? He could go back to Lord Malach and re-enlist as a soldier, forget all this.

If he did that, though, he'd be dishonoring Liliana. She'd sacrificed everything to put him in this position. By helping him, she'd put herself in the sights of whomever was controlling the Silent Knights. She'd lost her amulet and thus her power and mind. He owed her to see it through.

They rode until night had fully settled. When the last rays of the sun had finally vanished to the west, Garrick called a halt, and they moved the horses off the road.

As they made camp, Liliana dismounted, unsaddled Percy, and made him lie down. She gave him a feedbag and then huddled against him just as Garrick had found her this morning. Grief seized him anew.

They broke out rations, and he brought her some cheese and bread. She simply shook her head.

"That's not acceptable, Liliana," he said.

She ignored him. Her gaze drifted off to the west.

"Liliana, look at me," he ordered. She continued to ignore him, so he shouted. "Look at me!"

At last, her eyes traveled up to his face. They were wet and threatened to bubble over into a steady stream of tears. Garrick bit his lip and deliberately hardened his heart.

"Now, listen," he said. "We will be riding for close to three more days. We will be going as fast as we can manage. I cannot have you slowing us down or getting ill. Therefore, you *will* eat. Do you understand me?"

She didn't say anything. Her watery eyes just continued to stare at him.

"If you want to feel sorry for yourself, that's fine," he continued. "If you don't want to speak, that's also fine.

"But I'm not leaving you behind, and you're not going to slow us down. So eat."

She raised her hand without a sound. Garrick waited for a moment to see if she would do anything else, say anything, but she just waited. He thrust the bread and cheese into her hand.

Her fingers closed around the rations, and she brought them down to her lap. Then she returned her gaze to the west. Garrick stood over her, watching. Silently, she ate the meal he gave her.

When he was satisfied she'd eaten enough, he turned and went to the fire Levinia had built. Black sorrow gripped his heart. He hated seeing anyone like this, especially the woman he loved. Worse, he'd had to be rough with her. He'd have done the same thing to a soldier under his command, but he didn't want to have to treat Liliana that way. He longed for her strength and wisdom to return.

The next day brought inclement weather. Wet snow fell from the sky, and a strong wind from the north drove it into their faces. Despite his desire for speed, Garrick could not set a swift pace. The horses lowered their heads and trudged forward, but they refused to move faster than a walk.

At midday, they made the turn east as the road wound around the rising ridge that would grow to a tall precipice by the time it reached Twin Falls. That offered some small relief, because at least they weren't moving against the wind anymore. But the sharp breeze still whipped the snow into their sides, and even with hoods up, their faces were chilled.

There was little shelter that night, and no one slept well. Garrick couldn't recall a time in his life when he'd been more miserable. His grief and his worry combined with the wind to make him disconsolate.

The following morning, the snow had ceased, but the wind had not. They endured another wretched day of travel in which hardly anyone spoke.

They had to shield themselves from the howl of the wind, and most of their focus was devoted to wrapping cloaks tightly and holding hoods in place.

By the end of the day, Garrick's muscles were sore and cramped from hunching against the cold. However, they had at least made it to the scattered trees where he and Liliana had been attacked by goblins on the way out. Though the tall pines were not as thick as The Enchanted Forest, they did offer shelter and a windbreak, and Garrick was grateful for the small comfort they provided.

"When last I was here, we were attacked by goblins," he said. "We'd better set watches tonight."

Levinia's leg had improved markedly, and she volunteered to watch first. After they'd built a small fire to warm themselves and had eaten, Garrick bedded down to get some sleep. Exhaustion took him quickly, and it seemed that only minutes had passed when Levinia woke him four hours later to relieve her.

Mercifully, they were not ambushed. Whomever was running the goblins seemed to have given up on abducting him.

That thought was worrisome. Why would they cease wanting him? He couldn't believe they didn't know he was on his way back to Twin Falls. Vicia would surely know, and it only made sense that she had some connection to the goblins.

So if they had decided they didn't need him anymore, then something had changed. Garrick didn't like the idea of that. He feared it meant Vicia was already Duchess of Twin Falls and that whatever plan she had was in full swing.

Desperately, he wished for dawn, so they could resume their journey.

When it came at last, he woke Levinia and Liliana, and they ate a quick breakfast before burying their fire pit, packing up, and moving on.

For the first time in three days, traveling was easy. The wind had either ceased or couldn't penetrate the trees enough to make them miserable. Garrick was able to push the pace, and they made good time.

At midafternoon, they emerged from the trees and beheld Twin Falls standing tall and proud across the Winding River. The roar of the falls filled their ears, and the city's blue-and-green pennants snapped sharply in the breeze.

"Once we're inside, we'll get to my people," Levinia said as they approached the drawbridge. "We'll need to establish a plan and get you shelter before we can proceed."

"We also need to find out what's happened in our absence," Liliana said.

Garrick's head whipped around in her direction as she spoke for the first time in days. A spear of hope lanced through his heart, but it passed quickly when he saw she continued to stare flatly ahead.

"Even if Vicia hasn't claimed the throne yet, we need to know what the situation is," she continued.

"Good point," Levinia said.

As the horses clopped across the bridge, Garrick could tell something was wrong. Guards stood at the gate, which was closed, he noticed, with polearms crossed, blocking the way. There had been soldiers when he and Liliana had entered the city from the east almost two weeks ago, but not as many and not as determined to bar entry.

"Halt!" a solider cried before they'd finished crossing. "State your names and business in Twin Falls."

"Has passage to the city ever been barred before?" Garrick asked Levinia. She shook her head.

"No," she answered. "Not during the day. Something is up.

"We are residents of the city," she shouted to the guard. "Merchants who have returned from trade with Lord Alavair. Why is the gate barred?"

"Twin Falls is under martial law by order of the duchess," the soldier returned. "Give your names if you desire entry."

Garrick's heart fell. Vicia had indeed beaten them back and claimed the throne. Now, things were going to be difficult.

"Your duchess is a false ruler!" Liliana cried. Garrick whirled in her direction. Before he could ask what she was doing, she spoke again. "I have here Garrick Tremaine, descendent of Duke Evonin and rightful heir to the crown!"

Levinia and Garrick both gaped at her. What the hell was she doing? For a moment, no one spoke.

"Seize them!" the guard shouted.

The watch charged towards them across the bridge. Garrick yanked his sword from its sheath.

"Never mind that!" Levinia shouted. "Run!"

She wheeled her horse about and spurred it back across the bridge. No sooner had she done so, than Garrick understood why. A rain of arrows came down from the parapets. Liliana waved her hand, and they turned to snakes.

"Damn it!" she cursed.

Garrick didn't know what she'd intended to do, but it was obvious she hadn't wanted to shower them with serpents. The surprised reptiles fell on them and snapped. Garrick's armor protected him from their fangs, but one of them bit his horse on its hind quarters. It reared up in fear, nearly throwing him.

Praying that the snakes weren't poisonous, he pulled hard on the reins and urged the beast back across the river. It didn't argue, moving quickly to a full gallop, driven by fear and pain. Garrick put himself low in the saddle and held on tightly as his mount raced to safety.

Liliana was right behind him. She waved her hand again. Garrick heard an explosion, and then the river leaped up into the air and doused their pursuers with icy water. Spray inhibited the aim of the archers and a second volley of arrows fell short.

Following Levinia, they made it off the bridge and galloped into the trees. The watch did not pursue.

CHAPTER 33:

No One's Pet

"HOW COULD YOU LET them escape?" Vicia nearly shouted. She was furious with Calavan, and she genuinely feared the potential repercussions of Tremaine and his sorcerer friend eluding capture. But she did enjoy how her voice rang off the walls of her throne room.

General Calavan stood before her, a look of controlled fury marring his complexion. He did not drop his eyes deferentially to her as most of the courtiers did. This man felt confident looking his duchess in the face. His posture and expression suggested potential rebellion. She was going to need to keep very close track of him, especially with what she and Kremdor had planned.

"With respect, Your Highness," he said, "there was little opportunity. The watch captain did not recognize them on sight. As soon as Tremaine's sorcerer announced his identity, we attempted to apprehend them. But Ms. Gray's magic was too formidable."

Vicia didn't understand how that was possible. Kremdor had told her he'd taken care of the situation. Why was Liliana Gray still alive? And how was she every bit as powerful as before? It wasn't like him to make that kind of mistake.

But he had lied to her about rescuing Peaseblossom. Perhaps he hadn't been truthful about neutralizing Gray.

"Why didn't you pursue them, General?" she asked. "You told me they got off the bridge and fled back into the trees. Why didn't your men go after them?"

"Begging Your Majesty's pardon," Calavan answered, just barely respectfully, "but that would not have been wise."

"Why not?"

"Gray's magic already proved dangerous out in the open," he replied. "In the woods, she and her companions would have had cover. A pursuit would have ended in the needless deaths of my soldiers."

"And not having them in custody may prove disastrous to everything else," she snapped. "You said yourself he claims to be the true heir to the throne. If he is out there, he may try to convince others that is true. If he's successful . . ."

She let her voice fall away and aimed a glare at Calavan. He bristled.

"If it is a false claim," he said, "Her Majesty has nothing to fear."

"Oh, that's bullshit, and you know it, General," she said.

The court gasped at her coarse language. To hell with them. She had a precarious position to protect, and she didn't have time for niceties.

"People believe what they choose to," she went on. "If enough of them believe Garrick Tremaine deserves to be on the throne, they'll attempt to put him there, regardless of his legitimacy."

"You have the Blessing of the Fey, Your Highness," Zalachorus ir-Bedlam Donovian said, stepping forward from the crowd. "*Your* legitimacy is not in question."

She looked him up and down. She wasn't convinced she'd made a good decision allying with him. He was highly intelligent, but he'd become obsequious since she'd appointed him her chief advisor.

"It doesn't matter how legitimate my claim is," Vicia said. "Nor does it matter how illegitimate Tremaine's is. If he convinces others he has a case, if he gains allies, he can force a war of succession that this city does not need.

"That's why he needs to be in the dungeons or dead. He can't sow sedition if he's under our power.

"So find him, General. Bring him and his sorcerer servant and criminal ally to me. If you can't do that, bring me their heads. In fact, I'd prefer the latter. But find them and neutralize them before they cause more trouble."

"Yes, Your Majesty," Calavan said, sounding unhappy.

He bowed and then turned on his heel and went out. Vicia watched him go. Damn Kremdor anyway for not fulfilling his part of the bargain.

"Zalachorus," she said.

"My Duchess," he replied.

She waved him over to the throne. He glided over, smiling like an idiot. When he was at the arm of the throne, she leaned closely to him and lowered her voice.

"How far can I trust General Calavan?" she asked.

"You may rely on him completely," Donovian answered. "His loyalty is to the throne."

"But not to the person sitting in it," Vicia said.

"Correct," he replied. "So long as he believes you are acting on behalf of Twin Falls, he will give you his life. Should he lose faith, he will act accordingly."

She nodded. That fit with her reading of the general. She would need to spin the next piece of the operation carefully, or she would need to find a new commander-in-chief.

Vicia rose, clutching her staff tightly. She had questions she wanted answered now, and she couldn't do that with witnesses.

The court all knelt to her as she left the dais for her personal quarters. She smiled as she went. In Eldenberg, she had been one member of a nine-Elder council, and she had not been its president. She'd had to maneuver and dicker and supplicate herself before Lord Vestran to get what she wanted. Here, she was treated as a god. It was fit and proper.

She swept from the throne room and down her private hallway, followed by attendants who sought to appease her. At her royal suite, she shut the doors behind her before anyone could follow. As much as Vicia enjoyed being waited on, she didn't want to waste any time. She needed to know why Liliana Gray was still in play.

Vicia bolted herself into her dressing chamber and stood before the full-length mirror. She smirked at the sight of herself resplendent in gold-laced purple and the ornate crown of Twin Falls on her head. She might never tire of this. She could hardly wait for Vestran and the Council to see her before she ground them under her heel.

"*Spatium loqui*," she said, turning her mind to business and pointing the end of the staff at the mirror.

Silver sparkles enchanted the looking glass. Smoke filled it.

"Lord Kremdor, Lord Kremdor, I call out to thee," she chanted. "Lord Kremdor, Lord Kremdor, show thyself to me."

A moment later, she was gazing into Kremdor's laboratory. He walked closer to his scrying fire until his image filled her looking glass.

"Duchess Vicia," he said, cocking his head. "This is a surprise. I wasn't expecting to hear from you so soon."

"And I wasn't expecting to hear from Liliana Gray at all," Vicia retorted.

He tilted his head again. As usual, he wore his helmet, so she couldn't see his face, but she was willing to bet he looked confused.

"What do you mean?" he asked.

"I mean, you said you 'took care of her,'" Vicia said. "And yet she landed on my doorstep again this afternoon."

Kremdor didn't say anything at first. Vicia tapped her foot impatiently.

"I still don't follow what you are telling me," he said at last.

Vicia sighed and scowled. Once again, he was reminding her of her previous alliance with the gnome, Elmanax. The memories were not good.

"Liliana, along with Garrick Tremaine and presumably the head of the thieves' guild, returned from The Enchanted Forest," she said, making an effort to stay calm. "I had ordered the watch to arrest them if they dared show their faces here.

"The captain didn't recognize them, but when he asked for their identities, Liliana declared she was here with Garrick Tremaine, the true heir to the throne. He attempted to arrest them, and Liliana – whom you said you had 'taken care of' – cast a spell that completely defeated my guard and allowed them to escape into the woods.

"So tell me, Lord Kremdor, if you took care of the problem like you claimed, why I am still dealing with it?"

For a second time, Kremdor didn't answer right away. He stood silently, considering what she had told him. Anger rushed through her blood and quickened her heart.

"It isn't a trick question, Kremdor," she growled. "You shouldn't need to think about your answer."

"I'm not attempting to deceive you, Your Highness," he said. "I'm contemplating the implications."

"Answer my question first!" she demanded.

218

"As I told you," Kremdor said, "I sent the Silent Knights to dispatch her as we'd agreed. I also sent Isadore to observe in case something went wrong.

"The Orange Knight garroted Liliana Gray and held her fast, so the Yellow Knight could slay her. He loosed his arrow as planned. Gray was wearing a pendant, and the arrow struck it instead of piercing her heart. The amulet was magical, and it exploded when the Yellow Knight's arrow penetrated it. The Orange Knight was engulfed in the blast and destroyed."

"But she wasn't?" Vicia asked.

"No, but . . . Isadore, perhaps you can tell Duchess Vicia what you reported to me."

A giant bat dropped into view and landed on the worktable. It faced the scrying fire.

"The sorcerer's pendant exploded when the Yellow Knight's arrow struck it," the bat screeched. "She and the Orange Knight were engulfed in a ball of blue fire. When it dissipated, the Orange Knight was dead, but the woman was not. She fell to the ground and put a hand to her throat. She discovered the stone had been destroyed, and that's when she started weeping. The other Knights fled.

"When Tremaine asked her what was wrong, she kept saying, 'They destroyed my amulet.' Neither he nor the other woman understood what she meant.

"She explained she is a wild magician – she does not need spells to wield the forces of the universe."

"What?" Vicia whispered.

It wasn't possible. No human could control magic without sorcery.

"She needed the pendant to control the power," Isadore went on. "Without it, whatever sorcery she attempts goes awry. Gothemus Draco gave her the stone, which was enchanted to enable her to master the wild magical energy. Without it, she claimed to be worthless. She cannot work magic, because she cannot control the eldritch power without the amulet."

Vicia's mind reeled. Liliana Gray was a wild magician? Gothemus had given her a magical pendant to enable her to use her power? But without it all her spells went wrong? That explained why she'd come to Eldenberg a bumbler and emerged from Gothemus's tower a formidable wizard.

"So you see," Kremdor said. "Based on Isadore's report, I thought Liliana Gray was powerless. In my view, she'd been 'taken care of.'"

Bile exploded in the back of Vicia's throat. Kremdor was playing games with her again, and it was pissing her off.

"Damn you, Kremdor," she said. "You had Gursh tell me she'd been neutralized. I assumed that meant you'd killed her! Why didn't you tell me she wasn't dead?"

"According to Gray herself, she is a wild magician," Kremdor said. "Without the amulet her former master made for her, she cannot control the magic she summons. It is, if you'll forgive the expression, too wild."

Vicia wanted to scream at him, but what he'd told her paralyzed her tongue. No wonder Gray could undo any spell, could act at the speed of thought. She could actually shape magical energy. She didn't need sorcery to subjugate the universe. She could simply bend it to her will.

But not anymore. Without Gothemus's pendant, Liliana Gray was nothing more than a freak of nature. She was a wildfire that could not be focused into any sort of useful tool.

"General Calavan reported that she was able to use her magic to thwart the pursuit of his men," Vicia said. "If she can't control her powers, how is that possible?"

Kremdor nodded and thought. He crossed his arms and shifted his stance.

"When Isadore told me Gray claimed to be useless without the amulet, I believed she was powerless," he mused. "I assumed she needed it to both summon and shape the magic. It seems the former is not true."

Vicia swore. Once again, Kremdor had underestimated the threat Liliana Gray represented. He'd failed to eliminate her, and he continued to jeopardize their plans as a result.

"That's terrific, Kremdor," she said. "So we have a rogue threat to both my rule of Twin Falls and your master plan. What are we going to do now?"

"I believe we should accelerate our timetable," he replied.

"Are you crazy?" she exclaimed. "I've only been on the throne a day and a half. I am still establishing my legitimacy. The guilds aren't happy, and General Calavan is just barely loyal. If I give him any reason to doubt me, he's likely to turn, taking the army with him."

"What about Zalachorus ir-Bedlam Donovian?"

"*He's* happy," she answered. "He's the only one who is."

"But he's not a general, Kremdor. He won't be enough against Calavan and the other guilds if they oppose me."

"The Illustrious Guild of Sorcery and Wisdom is a formidable organization, Duchess Vicia," he countered. "You of all people understand the worth of a large conclave of sorcerers. Should Calavan choose to make an unfortunate decision, it can be blunted by the judicious application of magic."

"Maybe," she said. "But the situation is still tenuous, Lord Kremdor. I need to establish myself as custodian of a complex city. If I don't, we risk an uprising, and I can't help you if I have to suppress a rebellion."

"On the other hand, if you successfully handle a crisis, you'll be seen as a savior," he said. "And if General Calavan is one of the casualties of this cataclysm, he won't be in position to inspire a revolt."

Vicia stroked her chin. There was something to that. What Kremdor had in mind could in fact eliminate one of her rivals.

"What about Tremaine and Gray?" she said.

"This is why I propose we move forward immediately," Kremdor said. "At present, they are outside the city, their location unknown. If Gruul rises and a new order forms before they can make it inside the walls, it will limit their ability to cause trouble."

Now Vicia was the one nodding. If she could wipe out Calavan and put Kremdor's plan into action before Garrick Tremaine could spread his sedition in Twin Falls, she might have the stranglehold on the city she needed to fulfill her own ambition after all.

"All right, Kremdor," she said. "We'll play it your way. But I am tired of surprises, and I'm really sick of failure. Gursh had better fulfill his role, and you better be able to deliver everything you've promised. You'll like me much better as an ally than enemy."

"Don't threaten me, Vicia," he said. "You're duchess due to me. I hold your chains."

"I won't be duchess long if you screw it up with your incompetence," she retorted. "And without me, your grand vision amounts to nothing. I am *no one's* pet. Forget that at your peril.

"Tell Gursh to signal me when he's ready. I'll make the necessary arrangements on my end."

Without waiting for a reply, she ended the spell. She wanted to throttle Lord Kremdor. His miscalculations threatened to bring them both down, and she despised the inference that she was his slave. One day, she would disabuse him of that notion – with prejudice, if necessary.

In the interim, she had several problems. The first was Liliana Gray. Calavan needed to be on the lookout for her and for Tremaine. She wanted them dead or in custody as quickly as possible.

Then she needed to deal with the good general himself. She would speak to Donovian. He could be relied on to take care of that problem. He'd probably enjoy it.

"Damn you, Vestran," she said aloud. "I am going to make you pay for all the stress you've caused me. You and every Elder of the Council are going suffer."

CHAPTER 34:

No More Surprises

"YOU WANT TO TELL me what the hell you were thinking?" Levinia practically shouted.

Garrick looked back. He wanted to be certain they were indeed not being pursued before Levinia lit into Liliana.

He saw nothing but trees and the steam from their mouths and those of their horses. The only sound was Levinia's voice ringing off the frosty ground. There were no yells from soldiers, no hooves pounding the earth between the river and the edge of the woods.

"Gathering information," Liliana said, as though it should be obvious.

"What!" Levinia cried, her voice raised even higher.

Garrick shared her incredulity. His mouth hung open in stupefaction at Liliana's reply.

"I told you as we reached the city that we needed information on what had happened in our absence," Liliana said. "So I got it."

"What you got was us nearly killed," Levinia said.

Anger poured off her like steam from a cookpot. She looked as though she might murder Liliana where they sat.

"You identified us when we were trying to sneak into the city," Levinia went on. "Then you caused it to rain snakes on us. One of them bit me on the neck! Fortunately, it wasn't poisonous."

"Liliana," Garrick said, trying to defuse the situation, "perhaps you could explain some things to us. First, I thought you said you couldn't work magic without your amulet."

She hung her head shamefully. Her shoulders slumped, and she returned to the pitiful woman Garrick had known for the past four days.

"That's not what I said, Garrick," she replied. "You're not listening very well. You're going to need to get better at that if you want to be a good duke."

"A *good* duke?" Levinia exclaimed. "He's not going to be any kind of a duke at all the way things are going. How is he going to claim the throne if he's dead or locked in Vicia's dungeons, Liliana?"

Garrick raised his hand to silence her. He shared Levinia's frustration, but shouting at Liliana wasn't going to get them anywhere. With a heavy sigh, he swallowed his anger and tried once more.

"Please explain to me again," he said.

"Manipulating eldritch energy is beyond the ability of most human beings," she said. "That's why sorcerers use spells. They invoke specific effects.

"*I* can tap magical energy without having to cast a spell, but unlike a sorcerer, I can't control what happens. Gothemus figured out how to solve that by giving me a special stone. As long as I wore it, I could focus magical forces, make them do whatever I imagined. When the pendant was destroyed, I lost the control, not the ability.

"On the bridge, I saw the arrows coming, so I tried to turn them to flowers. They turned to snakes instead. I tried to create a wall of fire on the bridge, so we couldn't be pursued, but instead I caused the river to rise up. I wanted to help. I'm sorry the two of you got hurt."

Garrick's heart ached. He imagined what it must be like to be in her position, to be powerful and then suddenly rendered impotent. What if someone turned his sword to a rope in the middle of a battle? He'd still be armed, still have something to fight with. But he wouldn't know how.

It must be the same for Liliana. The magic was there, still flowed through her. But she couldn't use it. No wonder she was distraught.

"That still doesn't explain why you identified Garrick to the watch," Levinia said.

"I told you," Liliana said, "I was attempting to gather information, and I was successful."

"How?" Levinia said, her voice rising again. "We're still outside, and we had to flee before we could learn anything."

"By provoking the watch into attempting to arrest us, I learned that Vicia is afraid of Garrick," Liliana said.

"We could have learned that after sneaking into the city," Levinia said.

"I disagree," Liliana said. "Think about it. The soldiers did not recognize us on sight; they hailed us and demanded our identities. I only gave them Garrick's name, not yours and not mine. As soon as they heard it, they attempted to arrest us."

"What does that prove?" Garrick asked.

"Several things," Liliana answered. "First, Vicia is afraid of you. She has established herself as duchess, because the watch captain said the city was under martial law in the duchess's name. Levinia and Vicia were the only two female aspirants, so Vicia must be wearing the crown.

"However, her rule is tenuous, or she wouldn't need martial law. She has the city effectively locked down and barred to newcomers. That means she fears someone from the outside. Given that they attempted to arrest us when I gave them Garrick's name, she is attempting to prevent his return.

"That raises the question of why she would be worried about it. She won the contest. She has the throne. Why does it matter if Garrick comes back?"

"Because I'm the true heir," Garrick said.

"Exactly," Liliana said. "But Vicia shouldn't know that. Peaseblossom didn't reveal you were the heir until after Vicia had departed. So she either knew your identity before rescuing the dryad, or she discovered it after returning. Either way, she knows you can make a legitimate challenge to her authority, so she was dead set on preventing you from entering the city except in chains."

No one said anything for a moment. Garrick sat stunned. As usual, Liliana had pulled facts seemingly from thin air, but he couldn't deny their validity.

"It's possible she's just being thorough," Levinia said. "She was trying to have the Silent Knights kill all her rivals."

"It still doesn't explain why she would care now," Liliana countered. "She's on the throne. She's duchess. Garrick and the other contestants are no threat to her anymore."

"Except that Garrick actually is," Levinia said, a thoughtful tone in her voice.

"And Vicia knows it," Liliana said.

Levinia nodded. Garrick's mind reeled. He still didn't comprehend how deeply this conspiracy ran. Why did everyone seem to know more about him than he did?

"She must have known beforehand," Levinia said.

"Why?" Garrick asked.

"Because someone's been trying to abduct and kill you since before you arrived in Twin Falls," Liliana said.

"Before?" Levinia said.

"Yes," Liliana said. "I met Garrick on my way to Twin Falls, two days before the Contest of Succession officially opened. He was being crucified by goblins. I rescued him just before it was too late.

"Since then, we were attacked by goblins once inside the city walls, once on the first day of our journey to The Enchanted Forest, and once inside the forest itself, when you were injured, Levinia. We also were attacked by the Silent Knights before we could leave, although on that occasion, they seemed to be more interested in me than Garrick.

"But it seems pretty clear, someone has been trying to keep Garrick from fulfilling his destiny as heir to the throne of Twin Falls, and since it's Vicia wearing the crown now, we have to assume it was her."

There was another thoughtful pause as everyone considered the ramifications. Garrick sighed. He still had questions.

"Why would Vicia be involved with goblins?" Garrick asked.

"She clearly was using them as assassins to get rid of you," Levinia answered.

"Right," Garrick said, "but what's in it for the goblins? They hate humans. They avoid venturing into human territory because we slaughter them. Why would they want to work with one, especially a woman as callous and cruel as Vicia? What do they get out it?"

"I don't know," Liliana said. "I can't figure that part out. But you're right, Garrick, goblins wouldn't work as hired goons. There's something in it for them too. Somehow, they benefit from Vicia becoming duchess."

"Did you say you were attacked by goblins *inside* the city?" Levinia asked.

"Yes," Liliana answered. "On our way back from the feast."

"Hmm," Levinia said. "We'd heard rumors about goblins being in the city, but we couldn't corroborate them, and I didn't really think they were true."

There was yet another pause. Liliana's revelations and conclusions were so extraordinary, Garrick barely knew what to make of them. His mind still struggled to grasp that he had been nothing more than a soldier a month ago. Now, he was heir to a usurped crown.

And as rattling as all that was, he was equally off balance from Liliana's sudden return from catatonia to wise advisor. His heart leaped with joy while his mind shook from yet another earth-shaking turn of events.

"So what do we do next?" he asked.

"We need to get into the city," Levinia said. "We can't do anything from out here."

"Agreed," Liliana said. "We need to find out which of the other aspirants remain alive and whether they can be turned to our cause. We particularly need to learn if General Calavan is still in charge of the army and if he is Vicia's pawn or not."

"You think she's murdered the other contestants?" Garrick said.

"She tried to kill me," Levinia said. "It stands to reason she eliminated the others."

"Wouldn't that mean she's killed General Calavan then?" he asked.

"Possibly," Levinia said. "But I doubt it. As we've discussed, Calavan is a patriot, so unless something strange happened, he'll accept the result of the contest. On top of that, she needs him to control the army. Without the military, she won't be able to hold the throne, and they're loyal to him."

"Given that she's ordered martial law to secure her claim, it's a good bet he's still alive then," Liliana said.

"How are we going to get back into the city, though?" Garrick asked.

"I haven't figured that out yet," Liliana replied. "Maybe we should sleep on it tonight. It's getting late, and we won't be able to get in after dark anyway."

"That's fine," Levinia said, "but two things. First, no more surprises. We make a plan, and we stick to it. We might not know everything we know now, but we'd be sleeping at *Res Nostra* headquarters if we'd lied about our identities.

"Second, I'm sorry, Liliana, but I think you need to refrain from magic until we can figure out a way for you to control it again. It's too unpredictable. Your spells ended up not hurting us today, but we can't be sure the next one will be as benign."

Liliana hung her head. Then she nodded. Garrick wanted to weep at the sight of her. She was defeated and ashamed, not at all the vibrant, quirky woman he'd come to love.

"I agree," Liliana said.

Levinia sighed and nodded herself. Then she dismounted and led her horse to a tree, tying it up.

"Come on," she said. "Let's make camp."

CHAPTER 35:

News from the City

GARRICK PULLED HIS CLOAK tighter around himself as he huddled by the fire. He watched as Liliana dreamed fitfully. After Levinia had made her promise not to use magic, she'd returned to her state of near-catatonia. She would answer if she were spoken to, but otherwise, Liliana Gray had withdrawn back into her mind.

He wished he knew what to do about it. When they'd approached the city, it was as though the spell she'd been under had snapped. The real Liliana broke out of the chains of depression weighing her down. But now, she'd sunk back into an abyss of self-loathing, as though madness were water saturating her clothes and pulling her into the depths of darkness.

Her face twitched, and her expression turned stressful. Whatever dreams besieged her were unpleasant.

Levinia, meanwhile, slept peacefully. She lay on her back with her head pillowed by her pack and her hands folded across her chest as though she were in final repose. Were it not for the steady rising and falling of her chest, Garrick might have believed death had claimed her.

It seemed impossible to him he had come so far. He'd journeyed from Lord Malach's fortress to Twin Falls to The Enchanted Forest and now back to the city. Death had beset him at every turn. From Kaladriel, Benmark, and Marcus to Levinia's minions in the forest to Liliana's mind, destruction and doom seemed to dog his every step. If indeed it was his destiny to pursue this quest for the crown of Twin Falls, it felt like a curse rather than a blessing. A month ago, he was happy. He served a powerful warlord, he had friends, and he was successful. It was everything he could want from a soldier's life. He longed to go back to it.

Off in the distance, a twig snapped, startling him out of his reverie. He was on his feet in an instant. A second later, he'd bared his sword.

His eyes searched the darkness, seeking some sign of movement, some clue to what broke the stillness of the night. No further sounds approached him.

Garrick moved swiftly to Levinia and shook her awake. When her eyes popped open, he put a finger to his lips, then jerked his thumb in the direction he'd heard the twig break. She nodded, understanding, and crept out of her blanket towards her own sword.

Swiftly, he stole across camp and roused Liliana, repeating the warning he'd given Levinia. She too understood at once and rose carefully from her bed.

"Hail!" someone called from the darkness. "I seek Levinia Mordecai of Twin Falls. Is she in your camp?"

Garrick turned towards the sound of the voice. He pointed his sword in its direction and searched the night. Despite knowing the location of the newcomer, Garrick could see nothing. He had no idea how many friends this person had with him or what sorts of armaments they'd brought.

"Who's asking?" Garrick called back.

"Jet Orlander," came the swift reply.

"Jet?" Levinia said. "Show yourself."

A man dressed in the black garb Garrick had become accustomed to seeing on the members of *Res Nostra* stepped forward from the shadows directly in front of Garrick. He had medium-length, black hair that stuck out in all directions and a dirty face. He looked dangerous and ridiculous all at once.

"Master Levinia," he said. "Is it you?"

"By the gods," Levinia said. "Jet!"

She rushed forward and embraced him. He smiled at the warmth of her reception. Garrick lowered his sword, but he didn't sheathe it yet. There'd been too many deadly surprises on this quest for him to fully let down his guard against someone he didn't know.

Levinia withdrew and turned to Garrick smiling.

"It's all right," she said. "This is Jet; he's one of my chief lieutenants. Jet, this is Garrick Tremaine and Liliana Gray."

"Hello," Liliana said.

"Greetings," Garrick added. He still didn't trust the new arrival.

"So," Jet said, looking Garrick up and down. "You're the one the duchess is after."

"So we've discovered," Garrick said.

"What do you know about it?" Levinia asked, putting her sword away.

"She's placed a bounty on his head," Jet replied. "She's offering a hundred gold to anyone who can bring him in. It's twenty-five gold just for information that leads to his capture."

"That's a lot of money," Liliana mused. "She must really be desperate."

"And are you here to collect?" Garrick growled.

"Certainly not," Jet said, smiling broadly. Garrick realized he was young, perhaps not even eighteen yet. "I'm no lapdog to the throne."

Levinia smiled broadly at her compatriot. She clapped him on the shoulder and drew him into camp.

"Come and sit down," she said. "Have something to eat."

Garrick put his sword away begrudgingly. He supposed he needed to trust the boy since Levinia did and they were allies. He had questions he wanted answered, though. He and Liliana seated themselves by the fire across from Levinia and Jet.

"What happened to the others?" Jet asked.

"Dead," Levinia said. "Someone's been trying to kill us since we reached The Enchanted Forest. They've been partially successful."

"What are you doing here?" Garrick asked.

"Looking for you," Jet replied. "More specifically, looking for Master Levinia."

"But how did you know to come searching?" Levinia asked.

"News of your misadventure this afternoon got around quickly," Jet said. "Our spies at the gate indicated that, in addition to the fugitive, Garrick Tremaine, there were two women in the party. One of them was a sorcerer. The identity of the other wasn't known.

"Since you both left the city on the same day, seeking the same thing, Master Bryant and the cabal entertained the possibility that you had

JOHN R. PHYTHYON, JR.

returned together. They sent me to determine if Master Levinia was the other woman."

"Good thinking," Levinia said.

"Please," Liliana said, "we need news of the situation in the city. Obviously, Vicia has been crowned duchess. What of the other aspirants?"

"Most of them are dead," Jet replied. "Mysterious black-garbed assassins with magical weapons picked them off one by one."

"The Silent Knights," Levinia said.

"Lindsay Grunvilio was cut down while he was begging General Calavan for protection," Jet said.

"What about General Calavan?" Liliana prompted. "Is he still alive?"

"He is," Jet answered. "He remains in his post, although there are rumors he detests the new duchess and will not serve her long."

Garrick rubbed his chin. Calavan was alive but rebellious? On the one hand, that seemed good. Perhaps he was as approachable as they'd been hoping.

But if one of the aspirants was murdered before Calavan's presence while he still lived, was it possible *he* was the one running the Knights?

"Are all the others dead then?" Liliana asked.

"Zalachorus Donovian is still alive," Jet said. "He's joined the duchess's court and become her chief advisor. But the rest were murdered. The two of you are all that remain."

Garrick rolled possibilities over in his mind. If Zalachorus was one of Vicia's advisors, it stood to reason he was not the person running the Silent Knights. If he had been, it made little sense for him to ally with Vicia. He could have just had her killed too.

But Zalachorus was also extremely full of himself. It seemed strange he would willingly accept a role as a subordinate to Vicia. There was another piece of the puzzle missing here. Just as the goblins were unlikely to serve as minions, Zalachorus was not the kind of man who willingly bowed to anyone. Vicia must have promised him something.

So the question was, who controlled the Silent Knights – Vicia to eliminate competition, or Calavan in a failed attempt to take the crown himself?

"We need to get into the city," Liliana said. "We need to be able to approach General Calavan."

"Why?" Jet asked.

"Garrick is the rightful heir to the throne," Levinia answered. "He's a blood relative of Duke Evonin. That makes Vicia a usurper who needs to be deposed."

"And we need General Calavan's support to make that happen," Liliana added. "If we're going to stage a *coup*, we'll need the military on our side."

"Are we sure Calavan isn't the one running the Silent Knights?" Garrick said.

"What do you mean?" Levinia asked.

"Well, Jet just told us Grunvilio was murdered while begging Calavan for protection. The Silent Knights were there and Calavan was a contestant. Doesn't it seem strange that he is still alive?"

No one said anything for a few moments. They all chewed on the possibilities.

"I don't think so," Liliana said at last.

"Why not?" Garrick asked.

"Calavan didn't leave the city to get the Blessing of the Fey," she answered. "He stayed behind. The most likely reason is that he didn't know he had to go to The Enchanted Forest to get it.

"When Vicia returned with the blessing – which was a favor from Peaseblossom, a physical thing – he could have had her murdered. There are two Knights left. He could have assassinated Vicia and taken the token – and thus the crown – for himself. He didn't.

"Even if he opposes Vicia's rule, he clearly doesn't have the means to do anything about it. He wouldn't be following her orders if he could."

"Are we sure he's following her orders?" Garrick said.

"The city is under martial law, and the watch attempted to arrest us when I gave them your name," Liliana replied. "Calavan has control over those things, so I'd say, yes, he's definitely doing what she tells him. At least for now."

Everyone nodded. Garrick relaxed a bit. If Calavan wasn't making a power play, he might be approachable after all.

"I don't understand," Jet said. "If you're the heir, why didn't you say so at the feast?"

"He didn't know then," Liliana said. "We didn't find out until we met the dryad, Peaseblossom, in The Enchanted Forest."

"Can you get us into the city, Jet?" Levinia asked.

"Of course," he said. "That's why I was sent – to find out if you were here and to bring you back in if you were."

"But how can you get us in?" Garrick asked.

"Same way I got out, I reckon," he said.

"Wait," Levinia said, "you didn't leave through the gate?"

"No," Jet said, smiling. "That's another thing. You know how there were rumors about goblins inside the walls?"

"Yes," Levinia said.

"Well, they're true," Jet said. "After you left, we discovered tunnels beneath the city."

"Different from the sewers?" Levinia asked.

"Yes."

"We use the sewers to get around unseen," Levinia explained. "There's a vast underground network of them, and it makes it easy to move from place to place without anyone knowing – if you know where the exits are and how they all fit together. We do."

"Right," Jet said. "But these tunnels are not part of the sewer system. Most of them are not worked. They're natural caves. They come up in various parts of the city, and a few, including the one I used, lead outside the walls."

"That explains it!" Liliana said.

"What?" Levinia asked.

"As I told you, I found Garrick being crucified outside the city," she said. "I assumed there must be some sort of den in the woods. But we were also attacked *inside* the city and again outside to the west instead of the east. It must be the same tribe, and they have access to these tunnels. They're probably lairing beneath Twin Falls itself."

"Which is how Vicia is running them?" Levinia prodded.

"That would be my guess," Liliana said.

"The duchess is in league with goblins?" Jet said.

"Yes," Levinia replied. "Although we're not sure why yet."

"Can we get into the city tonight?" Garrick asked.

"That would be wisest," Jet said. "The entrance to the caves is covered, so it's not obvious it's there. But it can be seen from the walls. If we were to enter during daylight, there's a good chance we'd be spotted."

"Then let's get going," Garrick said. "I'll feel better the sooner we're locked away in your safehouse, Levinia."

"I agree," she replied.

They packed up their things quickly and set off. Garrick's heart pounded. He wasn't sure where things were headed, but he could feel this strange quest drawing to a close. Fear and relief coursed through him and competed for control of his mind. Whatever happened, at least it would be over soon.

CHAPTER 36:

Res Nostra

GURSH FELL OUT OF his bed onto the rough stone when Kremdor's voice resounded in his chamber. He shook his head as his concubine rolled over to see what had happened to him.

Gursh, I command you to speak with me!

"Just a damned minute," he muttered as he got up and crossed the room.

He walked to the brazier smoking against the wall and threw some of the magic dust on it. The flames roared up hot and bright. Gursh had to step back. A moment later, the familiar image of his master flickered in the fire.

"How many I serve you, Lord Kremdor?" Gursh said.

"It is time," Kremdor replied. "I have received word from Duchess Vicia that she is ready. You may begin the ritual."

A cruel grin broke across Gursh's face. He giggled maniacally in anticipation of the screams and the chaos.

"Yes, Lord Kremdor," he said. "I will have Kraven begin the arrangements immediately."

He turned and went to his gong, banging it with enthusiasm. The smile would not leave his face.

"Does this mean you won't be coming back to bed?" the concubine said.

"Silence!"

A soldier appeared a second later. Gursh had to suppress another giddy laugh to speak to him.

"Inform Kraven the time of the ritual is at hand," he said.

"Yes, my king," the soldier said, saluting.

He turned and went out. Gursh threw his hands up in triumph.

Poor Twin Falls. The humans were about to get a lesson in real power.

Jet led Garrick and the women through the tunnels cautiously. They were colder than above ground, which surprised Garrick some. He'd have thought being out of the wind would be better.

Regardless, stalactites and stalagmites emerged from the earth above and below at random intervals throughout the twisting passages, and the ground was rocky, forcing them to step with care.

They'd had to leave the horses behind. The entrance was too narrow. Liliana had been extremely upset about abandoning Percy, but Garrick didn't see what they could do about it. Levinia promised to send someone for the beasts once they were safely inside the city.

Iridescent lichens clung to the rock-face, casting a dim and ghoulish light over the cavern. Garrick had suggested they employ a torch, but Jet refused, saying the goblins would see it.

They crept through the strange passages for the better part of an hour before Jet froze for a moment. Then he signaled for everyone to take cover. They huddled behind two large stalagmites and waited.

Before long, Jet's instincts proved correct. A patrol of four goblins entered from a tunnel opposite Garrick's position and came towards them before veering off to the left and disappearing down another passage. They spoke in their guttural language, and Garrick could not understand.

"Damn," Jet whispered. "That's the tunnel that leads under the city wall they just went down. We'll have to be careful."

He made them wait almost ten minutes before they moved on again. The new tunnel was darker than the previous passages, and it was difficult to navigate. They had to go much slower to avoid tripping or running into obstacles. Liliana stubbed her toe painfully on a stalagmite that was wider than it appeared. Still Jet refused to let them light a torch.

Three more times he called them to a halt and ordered them to hide. Two of those occasions were false alarms, but the third yielded another patrol, this one larger.

Cold, weary, and stressed, Garrick's patience wore thin. He longed to get to their destination and was starting to think a fight with the goblins would be preferable to trying to avoid them.

At last, though, Jet motioned for them to stop. He put his back to a large stone and pushed. It rolled with only slight effort. He turned back to them when he had it moved about three feet.

"This way," he said.

He slipped past the boulder into another chamber. Garrick let the women go before him and then followed. After walking through a short tunnel, he found himself in total darkness. The sounds of dripping water reached him.

There was a flash, and then Jet had a torch lit. When his eyes adjusted, Garrick saw what he presumed was Twin Falls's sewer system. Large archways and aqueducts spanned the roof overhead. A river flowed tranquilly past the ledge on which they stood.

"Wait here for a moment," Jet said, handing the torch to Garrick.

He disappeared back down the small tunnel through which they'd come. Garrick heard the stone rolling back, and then Jet re-emerged.

"We should be fine now," he said. "If the goblins are here, they won't want to be seen. They'll be hiding from us."

He led them through the sewers, occasionally telling them to watch their step and always knowing exactly where he was going. Levinia, too, looked at home here, Garrick observed.

Jet brought them to a large, stone staircase that went up. He ascended without comment and came to a metal door at the top. Checking a peephole first, he opened it and motioned them through.

"We're on the street level now," he explained as they came into a small room. "This is an access chamber not far from *Res Nostra* headquarters."

Ten minutes later, he was knocking on the door of a tavern, The Bull's Horns. They waited in the darkened street for only a moment before an innkeeper opened the door looking furious, saw Jet and Levinia, and broke into a smile.

"By the gods, you've come back to us," he said.

He stood aside so they could enter and then drew Levinia into a hug once she was inside. She smiled at him.

"Nice to see you too, Kruk," she said. "My companions and I haven't had a decent meal in over a week. Would you put something together for us, while I have Jet fetch the masters?"

"It would be my pleasure, Master Levinia," he said.

Thirty minutes later, they were seated around a large table in the inn, eating the most delicious stew Garrick had ever had. He wasn't certain what all was in it – he thought it might be beef, and there were definitely potatoes, onions, and carrots – but it was aromatic, hot, and deeply satisfying, particularly with bread.

Three other masters sat at the table with them. A tall and portly man with a hairline that had long since beaten a hasty retreat to the back of his head, listened intently to Levinia's story while watching Garrick with brown eyes that looked deep enough to drown in. Next to him sat his exact opposite – a thin and spindly man Levinia had introduced as Bryant, who didn't look strong enough to wield a knife, let alone a sword. Finally, an older woman with silver hair and worry lines etched across her face sat with her arms folded and nodded regularly as Levinia laid out Garrick's noble heritage.

She finished bringing the other masters of the guild up to date, and Garrick found himself feeling sleepy just as he was expected to contribute to the conversation.

"Do I understand correctly," Bryant said, his voice squeaky, "that you intend to support Mr. Tremaine's claim to the throne? That you intend to set *Res Nostra* against the duchess?"

"Yes, Bryant," Levinia answered. "I do."

"But why?" the large man inquired.

"Because, Saulick," she replied, "*Res Nostra* has always been a part of the guild system here in Twin Falls. We may be a criminal organization, but we are part of the governmental structure and have enjoyed the protection of the crown."

"So why oppose the new duchess, then?" Bryant asked. "Why risk earning the enmity of the government?"

"Because Vicia Morrigan is a usurper," Levinia said. "Garrick has the true and proper claim to the throne.

"Moreover, she is an outsider. She's an Eldenberger, not a Twin Faller. She sought our position only because she was run out of the Council of Elders. I do not believe she will act in the best interest of Twin Falls or its citizens. She serves only her own agenda."

"But he will rule better?" Saulick said with a sweep of a pudgy hand toward Garrick. "He's an outsider too."

"True," Levinia said. "But I've fought by his side. He's honorable and brave. And I believe he will uphold our principles."

"Let him speak for himself," the woman said, her voice strong and husky.

Garrick cleared his throat and sat up straighter. He didn't know these people, so he wasn't certain what he should say. But he was also tired of being discussed as though he weren't there.

"Masters," he said, "you're right that I am not from Twin Falls. I had not set foot in it before a few weeks ago – on the very day the Contest of Succession became official. I entered only because my companion, Liliana Gray, told me it was my destiny.

"However, I came here because Duke Evonin appeared to me in a dream and told me to come meet with him about my future. And the dryad, Peaseblossom, identified me as an heir to the throne when we sought her favor – the required Blessing of the Fey – for the competition.

"As Levinia says, we've fought side by side. I forged an alliance with her. Should I be crowned duke, I will honor those terms. *Res Nostra* will be treated as a friend, and the people of Twin Falls shall be my family."

The masters of the guild nodded thoughtfully. They conferred silently and then looked to Levinia.

"Very well, Guildmaster," Bryant said. "No one opposes this decision. We support Mr. Tremaine's claim."

"So now what do we do?" Jet asked.

"As honored as I am to have the full support of the thieves' guild, I need more," Garrick said. "I need the military too."

"That will make for a strange alliance," Bryant commented.

"We need to speak with General Calavan," Levinia said.

"And how do you propose we do that?" Saulick asked.

"That's what I'm asking you," Levinia replied. "I've been away for weeks, and things have changed. How do we approach him?"

"I don't see how we can," the woman said. "Duchess Vicia is tightening her grip on the city. She has Calavan cracking down on anything that looks like resistance, and taking a meeting with Vicia's former rivals is unlikely to be well received."

"But there has to be a way, Sheena," Levinia said.

"Short of kidnapping him, I don't see what it is," Bryant said.

"Well . . ." Levinia said.

The masters considered quietly. Garrick's eyes flew open wide in alarm. Were they really talking about kidnapping the general of the army?

"Wait a minute," he said. "Are we sure that's a good idea?"

"I agree," Liliana said, speaking for the first time. "I don't believe General Calavan will be too receptive to our pleas if he's a prisoner."

"Perhaps not," Sheena said. "But how do you plan to get him to listen at all if you can't get a meeting with him?"

"Or if Mr. Tremaine is hanging from chains in the dungeons?" Bryant added.

"How would it be accomplished?" Levinia asked.

"General Calavan regularly checks on the watch," Jet said. "Especially since Duchess Vicia ordered martial law. His route is known to us. We could take out his escort and nab him."

"Absolutely not!" Garrick said. "We are not killing soldiers just to make an appeal to their commander. My becoming duke isn't worth that."

Bryant chuckled. Garrick glared at him, but the man's expression was warm and appreciative.

"It seems your faith was well placed, Levinia," Bryant said. "Mr. Tremaine is not clouded by ambition."

Garrick softened. He hadn't intended to prove he was the right man for the job. He was just trying to make certain no innocents were harmed. It was nice to have Bryant appreciate his position.

"That doesn't change the fact that there is only one way to speak to General Calavan," Saulick said. "Mr. Tremaine may be ambitionless, but he's going to have to make some hard decisions if he wants to rule."

"We don't have to kill the soldiers," Jet offered. "We could drug them. That would render them unable to stop us without harming them."

"How would you accomplish that?" Garrick asked.

"We have a number of toxins at our disposal," Levinia answered. "Some of them cause unconsciousness rather than death. A weapon coated with one of these – say, a dart – could take out General Calavan's escort."

Garrick leaned back in his chair. It was better than killing them.

"I still think it's a bad idea," Liliana said. "If you do this, Garrick, the general is unlikely to trust you."

"Perhaps," Garrick conceded. "But it may work to our advantage too. As I've told you, I plan to reason with him as one soldier to another. I can certainly explain that I specifically ordered his men not be killed, that I only wanted to talk to him and meant no harm. As a tactician, he should understand that."

"Is it a go then?" Levinia asked.

Garrick sighed heavily. Liliana was right. It was still distasteful.

"Yes," he said. "But make certain no one gets hurt. I just want to talk to Calavan. I don't want any sacrifices."

"I'll make all the arrangements," Jet said.

"You'd better get some rest, Garrick," Levinia said. "We've traveled all day, and you haven't slept yet. You'll need your wits about you when we have General Calavan in the fold."

Garrick agreed wholeheartedly. He was exhausted. He longed for sleep, and he was certain he wouldn't get much of it.

"Very well," he said.

"I'll show you to your quarters," Sheena said. "This way."

Garrick and Liliana got up and followed her downstairs. He was a little surprised not to be going up into the inn, but he supposed that wouldn't be very secure with Vicia hunting for him.

"I hope you know what you're doing," Liliana said.

"Me too," he replied. "Me too."

CHAPTER 37:

The Essence of Royalty

BLAKE CALAVAN STRODE AWAY from the western watchtower at a brisk pace. His escort matched step with him perfectly. He adored the men and women who served under him. They were great soldiers – disciplined and fierce.

Which was among the reasons he was irritated with Vicia. Check that. Duchess Vicia. He needed to remember to place the honorific in front of her name, no matter how it galled him.

Was this really the way it would be? This outlander was actually going to rule Twin Falls?

Frustration quickened his gait. What had Duke Evonin been thinking when he crafted his mad Contest of Succession? Offhandedly, Blake wondered if Vicia had somehow ensorcelled the dying duke, if she had arranged the whole thing so that she could ascend the throne. He wouldn't put it past her ambition, but he wasn't certain she was a powerful enough sorcerer to pull off such a scheme.

Not that he was any expert on magic. The mysteries of harnessing the energies of the universe were lost on him. Blake understood steel and strategy, not sorcery.

But if he couldn't gauge Vic— Duchess Vicia's skill at wizardry, he was in perfect position to judge her grasp of strategy. He found her wanting.

Locking down the city right after being crowned did nothing to endear her to the people she desired to rule. No one ever appreciated martial law, not even the military commanders who ran it.

Moreover, this fruitless hunt for Garrick Tremaine was foolish. She was duchess. He had not returned to Twin Falls with the Blessing of the Fey. The chancellor had not declared him the winner and had not transferred royal privilege to him. Vicia had it all. There was nothing to fear from a failed aspirant to the throne, especially one from outside the city.

Of course, Vicia's strategy only looked stupid if there actually was nothing to fear from Tremaine. Certainly, it didn't appear as though he had means to undermine her claim.

But if Vicia wasn't the fool she appeared to be, if her tactics had some basis in legitimate concern, then they made sense in a disturbing way. Why would Duchess Vicia be worried about Garrick Tremaine's return to Twin Falls? Why was it imperative he be detained at once?

She'd ordered Blake to send a search party after him at first light. He'd relented to her insistence he oversee their recruitment and departure personally. What was so important about Garrick Tremaine that the newly crowned duchess wanted him found? So far as anyone knew, Tremaine was only a soldier previously employed by Lord Malach.

If he, a failed aspirant, was dangerous to Vicia, why wasn't Blake? He'd declared for the throne. Why wasn't Zalachorus? He was the most ambitious of all the contestants, and Vicia had made him a trusted advisor. Was she an idiot, or was something else at work?

Blake deeply feared it was the latter. He couldn't put his finger on what was actually happening with the crown, but he knew something wasn't right. Tremaine and Mordecai had left the city. The rest of the contestants had been murdered by those mysterious assassins. He and Zalachorus had been spared. Tremaine had returned, possibly with Mordecai, and Duchess Vicia wanted him arrested and imprisoned.

What games were being played with the throne of Twin Falls?

Blake didn't know, and he had a terrible feeling that not finding out quickly enough would be disastrous. He doubted the patrol he'd sent out to search for Tremaine and his companions would find them. If Vicia was afraid of him, he wasn't stupid enough to just wait around in the woods for his enemies to arrive. He would take more aggressive action.

244

One of Blake's escorts cried out, put a hand to his neck, and fell over. Blake stopped cold and stared, ripped from his reverie.

Three more low whistles signaled they were under ambush, and the rest of his escort fell to the street as incapacitated as the first.

Blake yanked his sword from its sheath and whirled, brandishing the blade in as many directions as possible.

"Show yourselves, cowards!" he cried.

A sharp sting pinched his neck. His hand flew to the sensation and discovered a tiny dart embedded in the flesh. He had no time to panic as his vision swam, and the world seemed to turn upside down.

He realized he was lying on the ground. How had he gotten here?

Someone grabbed him roughly. A bag went over his head, and he couldn't see anymore. It was hard to breathe. His heart raced.

Then he knew nothing.

Kraven rubbed his hands in excitement. He'd been plotting this for years. Every goblin shaman dreamed of being the one to release Gruul from his celestial prison. Oh, he could hardly wait to hear the gnashing of the gods' teeth, when they realized their prize was free!

Sixteen priests gathered around the seal. Kraven had overseen its carving and painting to Lord Kremdor's exact specifications. Everything would unfold just as designed.

When the priests circled the seal as he'd directed, Kraven raised his rod and turned to the assembled army that stood behind Gursh awaiting orders. He made himself as tall as possible and spoke in his most ominous tone.

"When the great seal of the gods is cracked, the mouth of Hell shall open up and spit forth our great god, Gruul," he said. The warriors cheered. "His chains shall be broken, and he shall once again walk the earth, bringing terror before him."

Another cheer.

"Escape from Hell must be purchased in blood," Kraven went on. "He must have plenty of it to sustain his new manifestation. So you will follow Gruul and the death-shades up to the surface. You will slaughter the frightened humans, and you will feed them to Gruul. Do you understand?"

The soldiers roared in assent. Kraven grinned wickedly at them.

"Bring forth the sacrifice!" he cried.

A priest led forward a fatted ox stolen from the humans. The poor beast lumbered out onto the seal, blissfully unaware it was about to become fuel for dark magic. Kraven turned back to the seal, where the ox was encircled by the priests who would help him cast the spell.

"Begin!" he shouted.

Drums played, and the priests began their ritual dance. It was underway. Soon, Gruul would rise.

Garrick yawned despite himself as he watched Calavan get pulled into the bare room. A black bag was draped over his head, and his wrists were bound. Garrick didn't think that was going to do much for his willingness to listen.

He reminded himself that it couldn't be helped. He stole a glance at Liliana, who was grimacing. He knew she didn't like this either, and seeing the general bound did little to help. Levinia stood stoically to Garrick's right and waited.

Two of Levinia's thieves dragged Calavan to a chair and sat him in it. They drew back, and at a nod from Levinia, one of them pulled the bag off the general's head. Then they went out.

Calavan shook his head as his eyes adjusted to the light. He brought his still-bound hands to his face and rubbed his temples.

"Greetings, General," Levinia said.

He looked over his hands in her direction. Garrick watched as his eyes struggled to focus. Then recognition lit up his features.

"Levinia Mordecai," he said. His gaze traveled to Garrick and Liliana. "And Garrick Tremaine. Now there's an unexpected alliance."

"I apologize for the method by which you were brought here, General," Levinia said. "Time is of the essence, and Mr. Tremaine is wanted by your soldiers. I had to devise a quick means to arrange a meeting."

"Well," Calavan said, leaning back and feigning forgiveness, "when you're in a hurry, anyone would understand being drugged and having his escort murdered."

"Your guards were not killed," Garrick said. "I specifically ordered that."

"They were drugged like you," Levinia added.

"*You* ordered?" Calavan said. "So you're running the show here, Tremaine?"

Garrick frowned. He had to be careful. Calavan was already suspicious. Garrick needed to make sure he didn't completely alienate him.

"Yes," he said. "General, I need your help."

Calavan hung his head for a moment. Then he laughed softly.

"You need my help?" he said, meeting Garrick's gaze. "You attacked me in broad daylight, drugged my escort, and knocked me out. You brought me . . . wherever the hell we are against my will, and now you want me to help you?"

Garrick looked to Levinia, silently asking her what to do. He didn't know how to undo Calavan's suspicions.

"General," Liliana said, "please believe me that neither Garrick nor I wanted to meet with you under these circumstances. If Twin Falls were not under martial law, if Vicia had not ordered Garrick's arrest, we would have entered the city like regular travelers and sought a meeting with you more formally."

"I don't know about formally," Levinia said. "But we wouldn't have resorted to kidnapping."

"But the circumstances being what they are," Liliana went on, "we had to move quickly and discreetly. After we've spoken, I promise you'll be released. We're looking for an ally, not a hostage."

Calavan studied them for a moment. Garrick put on his most sincere expression and willed the general to believe her.

"Why would you need an ally?" Calavan asked. "What is it you're planning to do?"

"General," Garrick said. His throat closed. He couldn't figure out how to make the claim. "I'm . . ."

"Mr. Tremaine is the legitimate heir to the throne, General," Levinia said.

"What?" Calavan said. He looked as though they'd told him the grass was purple.

"It's true," Liliana said. "The Blessing of the Fey was code for a favor from the dryad, Peaseblossom. She is the fairy who originally helped establish Duke Evonin's line.

"Vicia knew this. Peaseblossom was imprisoned in The Enchanted Forest by some means unknown to us. I suspect Lord Vicia was involved somehow, and this was an elaborate setup to gain the throne.

"Regardless, Vicia beat us to Peaseblossom and secured the favor she would need to win the contest. We appealed to Peaseblossom for a favor for Garrick in hopes of beating Vicia back to Twin Falls. But the dryad said there was no need because Garrick is a blood relative of Duke Evonin."

Calavan turned and looked on Garrick. He scanned him, searching, Garrick supposed, for some recognizable physical feature he could match to the late duke.

"Have you got any evidence to support such a claim?" he asked.

"No," Garrick said, shaking his head. "I'd never been to Twin Falls before a few weeks ago. I had no idea I was of royal blood, and given that my father was an undertaker, I suspect I am, at best, a distant cousin."

"But that's still more of a claim than Vicia can make," Liliana said.

"It's *Duchess* Vicia," Calavan said. "You people need to remember that. And she doesn't need to make a claim. Duke Evonin decreed there would be a Contest of Succession. She won it. She's the duchess. Specious claims to being a long-lost relative don't matter anymore."

"By the gods, Calavan," Levinia swore, "will you listen? Vicia doesn't belong on our throne. She's an outsider, an Eldenberger, and she was expelled from the Council of Elders. This whole contest was likely manufactured by her just to get the crown. She's power mad! If Evonin had known about Garrick—"

"But he didn't know," Calavan said cutting her off. "So he devised another means to determine a successor. You and I were part of it, Ms. Mordecai. We tried for the throne too. We lost; Vicia won. That's the end of it."

"It doesn't have to be," Levinia said.

"So what?" Calavan said. "We're going to be traitors now? We're going to overturn the duke's will, reduce Twin Falls to war?

"This is madness, Ms. Mordecai! Duke Evonin didn't know he had an heir. If he had, he would have provided for him to succeed him. Instead, he found another way."

"I'm not sure that's actually true," Liliana said.

"What?" Calavan said, looking flustered. "Which part?"

"The part about Duke Evonin not knowing he had an heir," Liliana said. "The duke came to Garrick in a dream and told him to come to Twin Falls to sort out his destiny."

Calavan's head snapped back to Garrick. He nodded at the general.

"It's true," he said. "That's why I'm here. I only left Lord Malach and came to Twin Falls to learn the answers to the vision I had."

Calavan dropped his gaze and shook his head again. When he looked back up, his face was a mask of disbelief and anger.

"You people are crazy," he said. "You want to start a civil war over an unsubstantiated claim and a *dream*. You can't do that! There's no legitimacy in it, and without that, you can't expect to rule. Vicia may be an outsider, but she fulfilled the prescribed obligations to ascend the throne. People will support that. They'll *respect* it. What you're offering is nothing."

"Damn it, Calavan," Levinia said. "You're not seeing the whole picture."

"On the contrary, Ms. Mordecai," he said, "I am. Perhaps being a criminal, you don't understand the need for a lawful succession. It doesn't matter if I don't like Vicia Morrigan. She's the duchess."

"You know this isn't right!" Levinia shouted.

"What I know is that I've been kidnapped by the thieves' guild and that its master and a failed aspirant to the Contest of Succession are spinning a mad plot based on a dream to start a civil war.

"Cut me loose, Ms. Mordecai. You promised you would not keep me as a hostage. Show me there is indeed some honor among thieves."

"Maybe we should," Liliana said.

"Maybe we should what?" Levinia snapped.

"Maybe," Liliana answered, "we should let him go."

The priests were sweating, their green skin glistening in the torchlight. Kraven sang the prayers at the top of his lungs as the drums reached a penultimate tempo.

Kraven stopped, standing rigid as the dance continued. He raised his rod.

"Now!" he cried.

The priest who'd led the ox to the center of the seal, charged into the circle, an enormous sword raised above his head. It glowed brightly red with the energy of the spells Kraven had been casting upon it. He brought the blade down with tremendous strength and, empowered by Kraven's magic, beheaded the giant beast in a single stroke.

Blood gushed from its neck, its knees buckled, and it collapsed to the stone, pouring more of its precious, red *vitae* out onto the seal. The blood caught fire instantly, setting the seal ablaze. The priest who had sacrificed the ox was himself sacrificed, immolated as soon as the animal's blood turned to flame. He died with a terrible scream.

Kraven brought his rod down, and the dance and the drums ceased. The fire roared in the circle, and Kraven delighted in the way the heat scalded his skin.

"Bring me the Essence of Royalty!" he shouted.

Another priest, this one a woman, came forth with a stone pitcher that was tapered with a thin handle and was stoppered at the top. She bowed before Kraven and handed over the elixir that would finish the spell.

Kraven returned his attention to the seal. He held the pitcher aloft and spoke the dark words Lord Kremdor had taught him.

The fire increased in intensity. Even Kraven could barely stand the heat of it.

The sixteen priests surrounding the seal began chanting again. The flames swirled and danced to the rhythm of their song. When the ox's carcass was wholly consumed, it would be time to release Gruul on the world.

"Liliana, what are you talking about?" Levinia asked.

Garrick was certain she had some trick up her sleeve – she usually did. But he couldn't guess what it was.

"General Calavan clearly has no intention of listening," Liliana explained. "So we're wasting our time. We can't keep him as a hostage. Even if we hadn't promised him we wouldn't, there's no tactical advantage to it. He means nothing to Vicia, and he's a soldier, so there's a hierarchy to replace him.

"We'll just have to do the right thing by letting him go and then find another solution."

No one said anything. Garrick, Levinia, and Liliana simply stared at General Calavan, who glared back, practically defying them to ignore Liliana. Levinia sighed.

"I suppose you're right," she said. "It would have been easier if we'd had the support of the military, but there are other ways to get what we need."

She withdrew a knife from her belt and walked towards Calavan. As she bent to cut his bonds, Garrick put up his hand.

"Wait," he said.

Levinia and Liliana both turned to him.

"General," Garrick said, "give me one more chance to make an appeal to you. If you won't listen, I'll release you as promised. But I haven't had a chance to make a case yet."

Levinia stood aside. Garrick stared into Calavan's eyes, held him with his gaze.

"You're wasting your time, Tremaine," Calavan said. "But make your pitch."

Garrick exhaled. He hadn't realized he'd been holding his breath. He wasn't entirely sure what he was going to say, but at least he would get a chance.

"General," he began, "you're a soldier like me – a warrior, a tactician. Of all the people who entered the Contest of Succession, you were the most qualified to win."

"Flattery isn't going to turn my heart to your cause, Tremaine," Calavan said.

"I'm not flattering," Garrick retorted. "If all it took were that, I wouldn't want you as an ally. The facts are that you know Twin Falls back and forth. You know its ins and outs, its nooks and crannies. The pulse of this city fills your veins.

"You're also a strategist. You know how to make a plan and execute it. You know how to adapt it to changing battle conditions.

"That's how I am too. I'm like you. I'm a soldier. I don't go in for dreams and claims that can't be supported with evidence. That's shaky strategy that gets you routed.

"I've come to trust these people, though. Liliana has pushed me through every step. I did not believe I had a destiny, despite what the dreams said, until the dryad told me I was heir to the throne. I've never wanted to rule. I only want to serve.

"Levinia was my rival. She has a vast network I can't tap. She has no real motivation to throw in with me. But she has. She is willing to support my claim over her own ambition.

"I believe in you too, General. I believe you love Twin Falls and that you will defend her with your last breath. So I desire your support. If I have the military and the thieves' guild, I'll have a strong power base to stake and enforce my claim on the throne.

251

"But Vicia Morrigan is a usurper. I don't know why she wants to be duchess. Perhaps she just wants power. But I do not believe she cares for Twin Falls or its people, and based on what others have told me, I'm willing to bet you don't believe in her either.

"I have no personal desire to rule. All of this has been thrust upon me. I'd be happy commanding a unit in a peacetime military.

"Yet I can't ignore the call of destiny. I can't ignore the cries of the people whom I'm certain Vicia would oppress. I can't ignore the people who believe in me.

"If you believe in the Twin Falls I think you do, throw your support behind me. I'll deliver the monarchy you want. If I turn into a tyrant, then take my head and the throne for yourself."

Garrick fell silent. There was little else for him to say. If Calavan was close-minded after that, there was no wooing him. They'd have to move on without him.

Calavan didn't respond. He sat quietly and chewed on Garrick's words.

"Cut him loose, Levinia," Garrick said. "I promised the general his freedom after he listened. He can have it."

Kraven's heart raced as the last of the ox was consumed. It was time.

He said a quick prayer that there was enough of the Essence. Lord Kremdor had assured him there was, but they were supposed to have taken all of the human's life force. He worried that the meddlesome sorcerer had left them with too little to complete the ritual when she interrupted the crucifixion.

There was no time for hesitation, though. The seal had been prepared. If he waited any longer, the fire would die, and they would miss their opportunity.

"For the glory of goblins!" he shouted as he unstoppered the pitcher. "For the doom of humans!

"Rise, Gruul! By the power of the sacrifice and with the Essence of Royalty, I unseal your tomb! I break your celestial chains. Rise!"

Kraven poured the Essence onto the fire. Liquid, sparkling silver flowed from the stoneware and fell into the flames. They turned silver at once. Every goblin in the chamber began chanting.

"Gruul! Gruul! Gruul! Gruul!"

"Rise, Gruul!" Kraven screamed. "Rise!"

Blake watched as Levinia sawed through the ropes that bound his wrists. When her work was done, she stood back.

"I'll have someone escort you out, General," she said.

Blake stood slowly. He stared around the room. Each of them looked disappointed, but no one adopted a threatening stance. So far as he could tell, this wasn't a trick.

"You're clearly a man of honor, Mr. Tremaine," Blake said. "And you seem to have chosen your companions well, although I confess I wouldn't have believed it possible for Levinia Mordecai to be among them.

"I think— Tremaine, are you okay?"

He very definitely was not. Tremaine brought a hand to his head, as though he were feeling faint. Then his expression went totally blank. He collapsed to the floor.

"Garrick!" Gray yelled, and ran to him.

Mordecai stood rooted to her spot. Gray shook him, but he didn't respond. She rolled him over.

Blake's mouth fell open. Tremaine's face had turned ashen. His eyes were a hellish shade of yellow.

"Rise, Gruul," Tremaine said in a voice that was not his own.

CHAPTER 38:

A Dark God with a Bloody Purpose

THE SILVER FIRE ON the seal went out, temporarily blinding Gursh. The torchlight was dim compared to the conflagration Kraven's ritual had caused, and it took a moment for his eyes to adjust.

There was a deep rumbling from the floor. The earth shook beneath the entire goblin horde, and fear swept through the assembled army. Even Gursh was taken aback, worried Kraven had perhaps made some sort of mistake.

The seal cracked three times, each more deafening than the last. Malevolent, red rays shot up from the rifts and bathed the ceiling above.

All the goblins – from the priests surrounding the seal to the army behind Gursh – stepped back, giving room for whatever would happen next. The ground shook again.

Then, the seal exploded. Red-black light burst out of it like water from a geyser. The roof above them was obliterated in the blast. Dust and stone fell in around the seal and hit a few of the priests.

Gursh stood in awe as ebon forms – death-shades – rocketed out of the abyss up into the world, seeking souls to feast on. Against his will, he shook with fear as they cackled wickedly.

And then the red light turned a sickly green. It quickly took form and solidified. Gursh's mouth fell open as he beheld the great god, Gruul, standing before him, larger than life.

He recovered his wits swiftly, tearing his eyes away and turning back to his soldiers instead of staring in awe at the deity.

"Now!" Gursh cried. "Up to the surface. Slay every human you find and feed them all to Gruul!"

The horde roared its approval and charged past him to clamber up the ladders. Gursh grinned maniacally. The world was about to change.

Liliana stared down at Garrick. He shivered in her arms, obviously sick. What was wrong with him?

"Did he say, 'Rise, *gruel*'?" Calavan asked.

"I think so," Levinia replied.

The answer hit Liliana like a thunderbolt. She suddenly felt very stupid.

"Of course!" she said. "That's it!"

"What is?" Calavan asked.

"That's what this has all been about," Liliana said.

"Liliana, what are you talking about?" Levinia asked.

"We've been trying to figure out how the goblins are tied to all this," Liliana answered. "This explains it."

"What explains it?" Levinia asked, sounding irritated.

"When I first found Garrick, he was being crucified by goblins," Liliana said. "But it was no ordinary crucifixion. There was dark magic involved. Some sort of ritual was occurring.

"The goblin god, Gruul, was bound in Hell hundreds of years ago for offending the Celestial Order. I don't remember the exact crimes, but it had to do with attempting to conquer the world and putting goblins above other races including humans.

"To free him required a sacrifice of blood and the Essence of Royalty. Garrick is of royal lineage. So the goblins ambushed him on his way to Twin Falls and cast a dark magic ritual to pull his essence from him.

They attempted to kill him by crucifixion, because it takes a long time to die that way and they could therefore get more of his essence for their attempt to raise Gruul.

"I rescued him before they could finish the job."

Levinia and Calavan stared at her as though she wasn't making sense. Liliana couldn't understand what they failed to grasp. It was so obvious!

"So what's happening now?" Levinia asked. "If they didn't get his essence, what's happening to him, and what's that got to do with us?"

"I didn't say they didn't get his essence," Liliana replied. "But I stopped them before they got it *all*. They must have stolen enough from him to attempt the ritual, and because it's Garrick's soul they've tapped to bring Gruul into the Known World, it's making him sick somehow."

"Liliana," Levinia said, "are you telling us the goblins have summoned a god here in Twin Falls?"

"Not just any god," Liliana said. "A dark god with a bloody purpose."

"How do you know all this?" Calavan asked.

"I was apprenticed to Gothemus Draco," she answered with a shrug. "He made me read all sorts of things on magic, the gods, and mythic enchantments."

There was a pause as Levinia and Calavan absorbed what she said. As gently as she could, Liliana laid Garrick's head on the floor and stood up.

"So how is this connected with Vicia?" Levinia asked.

Now Liliana stopped and considered. There was still some piece of information she was missing.

"I'm not sure," she said. "But I know they're related. We know now what the goblins have been up to. They've been trying to free their god. They needed Garrick for that – royalty. Somehow it all relates to Vicia usurping the crown. Otherwise, why would she be so interested in having him captured after she became duchess?"

"Because he has the legitimate claim to the throne," Levinia answered.

"But at the moment, there's no way to prove that," Liliana countered. "That's always been the weakness in *our* plan – proving Garrick is a blood relative of Duke Evonin. And given that Garrick was kidnapped and nearly murdered *before* he arrived in Twin Falls and that Vicia almost certainly knew whom he was before the contest began, there has to be a connection. Vicia is getting something out of this, and it's probably more than ruling Twin Falls.

"We've got to find where this is happening and stop it."

"Wait a minute," Calavan said. "Are you suggesting we need to battle . . . with a god?"

"Yes, General," she said. "That's exactly what I'm saying. It's the only way to save the city *and* Garrick."

"Blood," Garrick said softly, still sounding like a demon instead of a man. "Bring me blood."

"What the hell does that mean?" Levinia said.

"Gruul must need living beings to sustain his manifestation on this plane," Liliana said. "The quickest and easiest way to do that is to give him blood."

"How much?" Calavan asked.

"Probably a lot," Liliana said. "He's a god, and he's been imprisoned for centuries. I suspect the goblins are going to need to a sacrifice a lot of people to pull this off, especially since they didn't get all of Garrick's essence."

"Maybe that's the connection," Levinia said. "Vicia delivers the sacrifice to complete the summoning."

"She doesn't need to," Calavan said. "It's midday. If they summon him in the central market, there'll be thousands of people they can feed to him."

"By the gods," Levinia said. "You're right."

"We had better get going right away," Liliana said. "Before it's too late."

"What about Garrick?" Levinia asked.

"We need to bring him with us," Liliana said. "We might need him there to draw his essence back from Gruul."

Levinia called for Jet to summon their best fighters and a stretcher for Garrick. Liliana tried not to panic. She couldn't control her magic. How would she be able to save this man who trusted her, who loved her? And what if, just possibly, she loved him in return?

She had to find a way to bend the magic to her will again, even without Gothemus's amulet. Otherwise, everyone was doomed.

CHAPTER 39:

A Disturbance in the Central Market

VICIA LOOKED UP IN surprise when a messenger burst into the throne room. He had a look of panic on his face, and she had to bite her lip to suppress a smile. He could almost certainly only be bringing good news.

"Your Highness," he cried, rushing towards the throne.

Two guards stepped in front of her and pointed halberds at the messenger. He skidded to a stop on the marble floor, suddenly terrified at the threat to his life.

"Your Highness," he said again. "There is a disturbance in the central market!"

Vicia hid a grin with a deliberate scowl. She was willing to bet it was much more than a "disturbance."

"What do you mean?" she said.

"There was an earthquake," he said. "A giant sinkhole opened in the street. Then demons and a colossal goblin some forty feet tall emerged from it. After that, a horde of regular goblins came out. They're butchering everyone!"

At last. Gursh had done his part. Gruul was here. Kremdor's plan was working.

"Where is General Calavan?" she shouted, feigning alarm.

"No one knows," the messenger said. "He was last seen briefing the watch at dawn. Neither he nor his escort has been seen since."

Calavan had disappeared? Vicia didn't like that. What was he up to?

She didn't have time to worry about it now, though. If she was lucky, it would strengthen her final play.

"Sound the alarm," she said. "Order the army to the central market to combat these fiends. In fact, order the wizards' guild in too. If there are demons, it'll take more than swords to dispatch them.

"Fetch my guard. I'll be going too. My sorcery may be needed."

Everyone saluted and snapped into motion. Vicia stood.

"Zalachorus," she said. "A word."

He detached himself from the mob of frightened courtiers and came over immediately. Vicia's eyes darted back and forth to make certain they weren't being spied upon.

"Do you know where Calavan is?" she asked.

"No, Your Highness," he replied. "If something's happened to him, I'm not aware of it."

"I'm less concerned about his well-being and more worried that he's up to something," she said.

"If he's turned against you, I'm unaware of that also," Zalachorus said.

Vicia nodded. She believed him. She had what Zalachorus ir-Bedlam Donovian wanted. Blake Calavan did not. There was no reason for Zalachorus to hide anything about Calavan.

"Very well," she said. "Stay by my side through this. If General Calavan does show up, make certain he suffers an heroic death in defense of the people of Twin Falls."

"Yes, Your Highness."

They turned as one and left the throne room. Vicia's heart was racing. She had the crown. Now she would lock it tightly on her brow and secure the means to avenge herself on Lord Vestran and the Council of Elders once and for all.

Liliana stared in horror at the scene in the central market. It was absolute chaos. Goblins raced in every direction, keeping the crowd hemmed in and slaughtering as many of them as they could.

Death-shades, black demons she'd read about in her studies with Gothemus, zoomed back and forth in search of souls to devour. Some of them feasted on the spirits of the people the goblins murdered, but just as many attacked living targets, digging into their victims' mouths with sharp claws and dragging out the souls forcibly.

And in the center of it all stood Gruul. He was forty, maybe fifty feet tall. He looked like a giant goblin, with green skin, feral, yellow eyes, and long, greasy, black hair. He was clad in a bearskin loincloth. He roared his savage delight to the sky as the goblins tossed carcass after carcass at his feet. Gruul lifted the bodies several at a time in his monstrous hands and stuffed them into his mouth.

"More blood," he growled between bites. "Bring me more blood."

"How the hell are we supposed to fight that?" Levinia said.

"First things first," Calavan replied. "We need to cut off his supply of fuel. Take out the goblins."

"Right," she said. "Bows first, everyone. Let's get as many as we can before we have to engage closely. Half of you with me; half of you with General Calavan. Try not to hit the innocents. Goblins only.

"Liliana, see if you can do something about those . . . whatever they are."

She waved her hands at the death-shades. Liliana nodded fervently and tried to recall what she'd read about them.

"Let's go!" Levinia cried.

Liliana watched as the thieves charged off after their respective leaders. Within moments, arrows were flying into the fray.

At first, it worked. The goblins were taken by surprise when they were counterattacked. A number of them fell with arrows embedded in their chests and backs.

But they quickly moved behind the panicked humans, using them as shields. Levinia's people started unintentionally felling innocents, and the death-shades raced to the freshly slain and stole their souls.

Calavan raised his sword and called for his archers to cease shooting. Moments later, he led a charge into the thick of the nearest pack of goblins. Levinia did the same.

Liliana tried to think of something to do. It had been so easy, so obvious how to help Calibot the last time she was involved in a massive battle. She'd had the amulet then. She could make the wild magic obey her commands. What could she do here?

She told herself not to panic. She gathered eldritch energy to her and directed it towards Gruul.

A ball of green flame flew from her hand, sailing towards the goblin god's head. When it reached him it exploded.

But instead of doing him any harm, it showered lovely pink sparkles down on the battle. They had no effect on anyone or anything, especially not Gruul.

"Damn it!" she swore.

Think, Liliana! she told herself. *How did you make it work when you had the pendant to control it?*

She wracked her mind. The energy had been the same. Shooting it at Gruul had been the same as when she had loosed her red arrows at goblins. What had she done differently?

Gruul shook his head and stared in her direction, a disgusting smile sliding up his face. He took a step towards her, then stopped. His yellow eyes lit up with recognition.

"Essence," he drawled, and Liliana was horrified to hear the word come both from his mouth and Garrick's.

Gruul started forward again. He took two gargantuan steps and then reached down.

"No," Liliana said, when she realized what the dark god intended to do. "No!"

Unthinking, Liliana summoned magic to her hand and blasted it at Gruul. A stream of sparrows flew towards him and dispersed. She cursed and tried again. A gentle rain fell on his shoulders.

She screamed her frustration and flung more magic at the goblin god. His skin turned pink, then blue, then purple.

Gruul ignored it all. He reached down and plucked Garrick off the stretcher as Liliana beat ineffectually at his fist.

With his prize in hand, he lifted Garrick into the sky and brought him towards his mouth.

CHAPTER 40:

The Final Piece of the Puzzle

B LAKE GAPED AT THE sight of the goblin god lifting Tremaine to
his mouth. The would-be heir didn't resist. In fact, his eyes seemed
to glow with the same wicked delight as Gruul's. They blazed an
unholy shade of yellow, and he opened his mouth, mimicking the fiend who
would eat him.

A goblin leaped at Blake, lunging towards him with his spear. Blake
dropped into a defensive stance and slashed with his sword to parry the
blow. His superior strength and size sent the fool careening past him. Blake
drove his blade between his foe's shoulder blades.

"Garrick!" Liliana screamed. "No!"

Blake barely turned to look. He snatched up the felled goblin's
spear, balanced it quickly, and then whirled and hurled it with all his might
at Gruul.

The weapon struck the god in the cheek, embedding in the soft flesh.
Gruul roared in anger.

Blake's tactic worked, though. Distracted by what amounted to a
sting to his cheek, Gruul ceased attempting to eat Tremaine and reached for
the spear. He pulled it out quickly and discarded it.

Before he could resume his grisly snack, though, Liliana waved her hand. Orange sparkles surrounded the fist holding Tremaine. The goblin deity's flesh, which had turned a bright shade of purple at some point during the battle, burst into flame.

Gruul howled and dropped his prey. Blake panicked, uncertain if Tremaine would survive the fall. He fell with a thud to the cobblestones and didn't move.

Blake started cutting his way towards him, killing any goblin who attempted to get in the way. If he didn't hurry, Tremaine wouldn't get the chance to prove his claim was legitimate.

Garrick ached everywhere. He tried to move and agony wracked his entire body.

What happened? Where was he, and how did he get here?

He attempted to move again.His muscles struggled to obey. Pain and weariness assailed his mind, wiping out the will to force himself to get up. He hadn't felt like this since . . . since he'd awoken after his near-crucifixion. What was going on?

He lay facedown on cobblestones. All around him he heard screaming and the sounds of battle.

Summoning all his strength, he rolled over and examined the situation. Goblins and humans were fighting. Black ghosts whirled around the battlefield. And a giant, forty-foot-tall goblin was screaming in pain and trying to extinguish the fire on his right hand.

He still couldn't make sense of it. Where were Liliana and Levinia and Calavan? How had he gotten here?

The only answer he got was a goblin wailing a war cry as he charged Garrick, a spear raised above his head. Bloodlust filled his yellow eyes as he came, determined to gore Garrick where he lay.

Garrick struggled to move. He knew he couldn't stay where he was, but he couldn't find the strength, the will, to get up, to even roll out of the way. Despondent, he realized he was about to die.

When the fiend was only three steps away, the look on his face changed. It went from savage glee to horrified shock. Garrick barely saw the arrow embed in the goblin's chest before his attacker fell to the ground dead.

Garrick turned to look behind him. Levinia stood, still aiming a bow at where the goblin had been.

"Thought you could use a hand," she said.

"Thanks," he croaked, barely able to speak.

"Come on," she said, lowering her weapon and coming towards him. "Let's get you to safety."

She bent down and got her shoulder under him. A moment later, though, she struggled to get him up.

"Can you help me?" she asked.

"I'm trying," he moaned. "I'm so weak. I've never felt so drained in my life."

"Damn," she swore after another attempt. "You're too heavy. I need help."

Levinia and Garrick both looked around. There was no one. Everyone they saw was engaged in battle. Levinia nocked an arrow in her bow.

"If I can't get you out of here, I'll defend you until help arrives," she said.

Garrick despaired. He'd never felt more worthless.

Blake slashed at another goblin. Where had they all come from? He'd never seen so many. He couldn't get to Tremaine. One green-skinned thug after another blocked his path. It was all he could do just to fight them. They were clever and savage, and they barred his way.

If something didn't change soon, the battle was going to turn against them. Levinia's goons were brave, but they were not warriors. The goblins and the demons were overwhelming them. Where were *his* soldiers?

As if in answer to his mental query, a horn sounded. His heart surged as he recognized the song. It was the battle cry of the Twin Falls Army.

Blake risked a look over the shoulder of his foe and saw a phalanx of soldiers crash into the fray. Behind them were wizards, flinging spells at the demons. And was that Vicia with them? The duchess had had the courage to come to battle too?

With a grin, Blake renewed his efforts against the goblin in front of him. There was cause for hope. The invaders may have been clever, but they were outnumbered now. The tide was turning.

Vicia smiled at the sight that greeted her when they made it to the square. It was absolute chaos. People were screaming and panicking. A battle raged with a force she didn't recognize opposing Gursh's army.

She supposed that was just as well. She'd been planning on riding to the rescue herself, but when she and the watch arrived, Gursh's people clearly had the upper hand, and no one knew what to do about Gruul or the death-shades that had emerged from Hell with him. There was still plenty for her to accomplish.

With a deafening blast of their horn, the soldiers flung themselves into the fight. Vicia didn't think it would take long for their superior numbers to repel the goblin invasion.

"Those are death-shades," she shouted. "Magicians, destroy them. I'll handle the god."

At her order, sorcery cascaded into the fray. Most of it was ineffectual. She'd expected that. A swarm of demons was no easy foe to fight, and Kremdor had warned her they could only be fully dispatched with the spell he had taught her. And even if the guild's spells were effective, the portal to Hell remained open. More death-shades kept arriving. That would keep everyone busy while she dealt with Gruul.

The goblin god stomped about in agonized fury, his right hand ablaze. Cobblestones cracked, and people – both humans and goblins – were squashed in his mindless rage. Vicia smiled. For a deity, he wasn't terribly sophisticated.

"*Extinguere!*" she cried, summoning eldritch energy with her staff.

She aimed an ice-blue ray at Gruul, and it struck him on his burning hand. A moment later, the flames went out.

Vicia gave him a moment to recover. Then she summoned more magic and sent a harmless blast of yellow light at him, hitting him in the shoulder.

Gruul turned to see who had attacked him. Vicia raised her staff and stared into his yellow eyes, so there could be no mistaking whom had attracted his attention.

She drew a pattern in the air with her staff and chanted another incantation. Blue energy formed in the air between them, shaping itself into the sigils on the seal that had summoned him.

Gruul grinned wickedly. He nodded to her once and then vanished.

The final piece of the puzzle was now in place. Vicia had the goblin god as her ally. Once the dust settled, she'd be in position to exact her revenge on Eldenberg.

CHAPTER 41:

The Mightiest Magic

LILIANA HAD NEARLY MADE it to Garrick's position when Gruul disappeared. She couldn't help but stop in midstride, gaping at the sudden absence of the goblin god in the middle of the market.

She turned and stared at Vicia, who was looking very pleased with herself. What had the usurping sorcerer done? Her first spell had appeared to backfire, putting out the flames Liliana had unintentionally lit when she'd tried to magically restrain Gruul's arm. Vicia's second attack had been wholly ineffectual.

But what runes had she drawn with her staff that had vanquished the deity? Liliana assumed it had to be possible to do something about a rampaging god, but she didn't recognize Vicia's spell. It was strange.

There were bigger problems at hand, though. First, she needed to check to make sure Gruul was indeed gone, that the major danger had passed. Second, she was concerned about Garrick. Levinia stood over him, defending him with her bow, but what condition was he in? Had he survived the fall from Gruul's hand? If he was injured, were his wounds fatal?

The goblins were shocked by the disappearance of their god. Many of them looked fearful, as though they had thought they were going to conquer the entire city only to find themselves disarmed midway through the siege. Consequently, Liliana had no trouble getting to Garrick and Levinia.

"Are you okay?" she asked him.

He was propped up on one arm, half-leaning against Levinia's leg. His face was ashen.

"Define 'okay'," he said.

Warm relief spread through Liliana's chest. Garrick was clearly still ill from his essence being used to revive Gruul, but his sarcastic humor was still there. His personality was returning.

"What happened?" Levinia asked, still aiming her bow from position to position in search of trouble.

"I'm not sure," Liliana replied. "Vicia did something. She cast some sort of a spell, and he disappeared. But I don't know what it was."

Before Liliana could say more, a death-shade dived at them. Levinia loosed her arrow at it, and it was on the mark. But the wooden shaft passed harmlessly through the demon's magical body. It cackled with demented glee as it swooped for her.

Liliana sent a blast of eldritch energy racing towards it, hoping to conjure her magic arrows. Instead, a ball of lightning crackled around the shade, engulfing it in electrical doom. The fiend screamed in otherworldly agony and then fell to the ground before melting away.

"Thanks," Levinia said.

"Not what I intended but effective," Liliana commented.

"I'll take it," Levinia replied.

"I don't understand," Garrick rasped. "If Vicia banished Gruul, why am I still so weak? Why haven't the demons been sucked back into Hell?"

Those were excellent questions. Liliana decided to learn the answers.

"Wait here," she said.

"No problem," Garrick quipped.

Liliana dashed over to the enormous hole in the street. Hellish, red light emanated from it, and death-shades continued to rise into the air. As she neared the lip of the crater, a shade came zooming straight at her. She whirled away from it and fell to the ground as it howled its horrid delight at being free on this plane of existence.

Liliana rolled onto her stomach and crawled back to the edge of the hole. Biting her lip and holding her breath, she peered into it.

She gazed straight into the mouth of Hell. Red, rocky cliffs burned with lurid, orange fire. Unfathomably evil things danced in some dark celebration. And one after another, death-shades rose out of The Abyss and invaded the realm of the living.

The problem was obvious. Vicia may have banished Gruul, but she hadn't closed the portal to Hell the goblins had opened to release him.

Something had to be done. But what?

Closing an interdimensional portal took powerful magic. Because she didn't know much about how this one had been opened, she was uncertain how to reverse the process.

Think, Liliana. There has to be a way.

She started with what she knew. The goblins had created a seal, then cast a spell over it. They'd used Garrick's essence to empower Gruul to break his celestial chains, but that wouldn't have been enough to open a gate. They would have needed something more. Given that death-shades were claiming lives, stealing the souls of those who were being sacrificed to feed Gruul's manifestation, she suspected it was blood.

That was it! Gruul needed blood to maintain his corporeal presence. It therefore stood to reason blood had been used to open the portal. And if it was the key to opening the gateway, then it could also be used to close it.

But whose *vitae* could she use? She couldn't kill an innocent to close the door to Hell. That would be wrong. Something was missing here.

Suddenly, the words of Devon Middleton to Calibot came floating back to her mind: *Love is the mightiest magic there is.*

Simple words from a man who was no sorcerer. Devon had only ever been a soldier – like Garrick – not a wizard. But the profound truth of those words had broken Gothemus Draco's sinister *post-mortem* spell. They had saved Calibot. Now, they would save Garrick.

She did love him. He was a remarkable man – so strong and brave. She regretted she would be unable to see him fulfill his destiny and rule Twin Falls. She got to her feet and drew her dagger.

"Garrick!" she shouted. He met her gaze. "I love you!"

Then she sliced the knife across her stomach, wincing at the searing pain it caused. She looked down, making certain she saw blood on her abdomen.

"Liliana?" Garrick said.

She looked up and smiled at him. Then she turned towards the pit and summoned all the wild magical energy she could muster. With her body bleeding and crackling with power, she leaped over the edge.

"Liliana!" Garrick shouted. "No!"

A white-hot explosion engulfed her. Then, she knew nothing more.

CHAPTER 42:

The Duke's Proper Heir

VICIA PUT HER HANDS to her eyes to shield them from the
sudden blast. Despite the fact that it was midday, white light burst
from the crater so intensely she was dazzled.

What the hell had happened? Death-shades had been pouring from
the aperture, because she hadn't closed it. She'd been waiting for the
situation to become truly desperate before she invoked the spell Kremdor
had taught her to close off the dimensional gateway. She wanted to look as
heroic as possible.

With that in mind, she acted. She waved her staff and uttered a
closure incantation. She didn't expect it to do anything, but in case
Zalachorus or any of his wizard friends were listening, she wanted them to
think her spell was authentic.

Next, she turned her attention to the death-shades whirling around
the market. The wizards' guild was making a poor show of dealing with
them. Only a tenth or so of their spells were effective. She raised her staff
again.

"*Vox magna,*" she said, casting magic on herself to enhance her
voice. Then she called to mind the spell Kremdor had taught her.

"Ventilabo daemones!"

Vicia's voice echoed off the cobblestones, off the buildings, indeed off the heavens. It shook the earth with its authority.

Searing white beams jetted from the end of her staff in every direction. Each made contact with a death-shade and caused it to scream with terror. They all froze in space, flung up their incorporeal arms and writhed in pain.

Then, with a violent, white flash, every death-shade on the ground and in the air disintegrated. Their passing reverberated through the noon sunlight and made the day seem brighter.

Several moments of stunned silence hung over the market. Then, an enormous cheer rose up from the crowd.

"Hail Duchess Vicia!" a soldier cried.

Vicia smiled broadly as his praise was echoed. She'd done it. She'd secured the crown, and now she'd bought the admiration of the masses. Moreover, she'd acquired a god for an ally. Total victory was hers.

"Wait!" a voice shouted as the applause died away.

Vicia's face fell. It was a woman's voice. It couldn't be her. It couldn't!

"Vicia Morrigan is an accomplished sorcerer," the voice went on. Vicia searched for its source. "But she is not the rightful heir to our throne."

Murmurs started working their way through the crowd. Vicia scanned left and right, trying to pin down the source of the treason.

"Show yourself!" Vicia cried. "You who would oppose me, who would set yourself against the crown, show yourself!"

A woman stood up on a cart near the pit from which Gruul had emerged. Vicia breathed a small sigh of relief. It wasn't Liliana Gray. She couldn't quite make out whom this short woman was, but she could see it wasn't the hated wild magician.

"That's Levinia Mordecai," Zalachorus said, sounding stunned. "I wouldn't have expected her to make a move like this. She prefers the shadows."

Levinia Mordecai? The head of the thieves' guild?

"Hear me, people," Mordecai went on. "Vicia Morrigan is not our true ruler. She 'won' a rigged contest to put herself on the throne of Twin Falls. She is a manipulator and a usurper. I have the duke's proper heir with me."

"Arrest this traitor!" Vicia shouted.

Soldiers looked confused, but they started to move towards Mordecai's position.

"Wait!" a new voice called.

Vicia turned her head in its direction, and her heart sank. General Calavan stepped out of a crowd.

"Let Guildmaster Mordecai speak," he ordered. "Her accusations are bold and even treasonous. But these are strange times. Let the people hear her."

Vicia cursed as the soldiers listened to him. He still commanded their respect. Something needed to be done.

"I thought I told you to kill him," she hissed at Zalachorus.

"I didn't see him until just now," he whispered back. "I didn't know he was here."

"Vicia Morrigan is a deposed and disgraced Elder from Eldenberg," Mordecai said. "She was thrown off the Council! She came here looking for a new place to rule.

"The Contest of Succession was a sham. Vicia arranged it all. She knew the answer to the riddle before it was asked. She has systematically eliminated all competition just in case someone could beat her to the chancellor. She set all this up in advance. She has stolen our throne!"

"Ha!" Vicia laughed. "A thief accuses *me* of robbery. It's ludicrous."

"The contest was legitimate. It was organized by the chancellor under instruction from the duke. I battled goblins and an elemental to free the dryad, Peaseblossom, from imprisonment in The Enchanted Forest. She gave me her blessing, and with it, I rightfully claimed the crown. It's all very proper, Ms. Mordecai. I'm sorry I was able to accomplish it before you, but I am afraid you will have to live with coming up short."

"I'm not advocating for myself," Mordecai shouted. "I've no more right to the throne than you, Lord Vicia. The true heir is Garrick Tremaine. He is a blood relative of Duke Evonin."

Vicia cursed to herself. Kremdor had failed her again. He was supposed to have all this taken care of. Tremaine was supposed to be the sacrifice to give life to Gruul. He was supposed to have been out of the way multiple times, but still he haunted her.

"The duke had no heirs," Zalachorus said. "That is why he devised the contest."

"None that he *knew of*," Mordecai countered. "Tremaine discovered his link to the duke's line while attempting to garner the Blessing of the Fey."

"Oh, very convenient," Zalachorus said, his voice covered in sarcasm. Vicia could have kissed him. "He fails to win the contest but suddenly 'discovers' he should have been the duke all along.

"Duchess Vicia earned the crown fairly. She drove off the monstrous goblin. She vanquished the death-shades. She put herself at risk, first to win the throne and then to defend the city. And now a thief and a stranger would claim the title? What kind of duke would seek the backing of the city's most notorious criminal organization?"

Vicia watched as a lot of people nodded. She needed to remember to reward Zalachorus richly for this. She knew he was doing it to protect his own position, that he desired the throne himself and that she had promised it to him after she conquered Eldenberg. But he was manipulating the crowd masterfully, and because he had a reputation as a self-interested, pompous ass, his testimony on her behalf was even more powerful.

"That thief and her criminal organization were the first ones on the scene here," Calavan said. "Long before the army and the wizards' guild and the duchess arrived, Levinia Mordecai and *Res Nostra* battled goblins and death-shades in an attempt to protect the innocent. Duchess Vicia may have vanquished the fiends, but I will not hear the thieves' guild disparaged. They fought with honor."

"Enough," Vicia said. She felt she needed to take control of the situation while she still had the upper hand. "Where is this Garrick Tremaine, that he would challenge me? Levinia Mordecai speaks on his behalf. If he would be duke, why doesn't he make the claim himself?"

Another murmur went through the crowd. More heads nodded. Tremaine would have to show himself now. Then she could eliminate him.

There was movement near Mordecai, shuffling. Then two men came forward with a third draped between them.

"I . . ." the man in the middle gasped. "I make my claim."

Vicia barely recognized him. It hardly seemed possible this could be the warrior she fought in The Enchanted Forest. There was virtually no color in his face. His beard was scraggly and showing of grey. His cheeks were hollow, his eyes sunken. He barely looked alive.

She wanted to clap her hands in delight. Kremdor had said they'd gotten enough of his essence to raise Gruul, and the god's presence in the market this morning was proof of that. But apparently resurrecting him had negatively impacted Tremaine. With his essence stolen by Gruul in the awakening, Tremaine could barely stand.

"You . . . are a fraud, Vicia," Tremaine went on, his breathing labored. "You engineered . . . the contest and this incident. Liliana . . ."

Tears streamed down his cheeks, and he couldn't go on. Vicia seized the opportunity.

"Look at him," she said. "He's too weak to stand, to even speak. This is our duke? Someone as sickly as Evonin before his demise? So Garrick Tremaine ascends the throne, dies in a few weeks, and then what? Another contest?"

"Listen to the duchess," Zalachorus said. "We have our rightful ruler. Let this pretender and his criminal entourage seek their undeserved fortune elsewhere."

A rumbling of support went through the crowd. Vicia had them now. All she needed was to close the deal.

"What do you want?" she cried. "A duchess who drove out demons when they attacked, or an also-ran, a pretender who can't even make a claim for himself?"

"Vicia!" someone shouted. A chant went up from the assembled, "Vicia! Vicia! Vicia!"

She raised her hand for silence. After a moment, she got it.

"What say you, Levinia Mordecai?" Vicia asked. "Do you yield, or do you persist in this treason?"

"I support the true heir to the throne," Mordecai said without hesitation. She jerked her head in Tremaine's direction.

"And you, General Calavan?" Vicia said.

Calavan shifted from one foot to the next. He looked at Tremaine for a long moment. Then he returned his gaze to her.

"I am sorry, Lord Vicia," he said. "Until we can confirm or deny the legitimacy of Tremaine's claim, I cannot support you. If you will not yield the crown to Chancellor Bismarck until an enquiry can be completed, you have my resignation as general."

There was stunned silence. No one could believe the staunchly patriotic Calavan would make such a statement. Vicia needed to act fast.

"As you wish," she said. "Seize the traitors!"

No one moved at first. They were still surprised.

Then the soldiers snapped into motion, but it was too late. The hesitation was all Mordecai needed.

She threw something to the ground, and there was a small explosion followed by a giant burst of smoke. Vicia saw Mordecai leap into the pit, and the two men carrying Tremaine followed after her. Several more thieves jumped in before the smoke dissipated enough for someone to get near.

"After them!" Vicia cried.

Several soldiers went into the hole. There were shouts. Then the sounds faded away.

Calavan stood firmly and proudly. Two soldiers held him, but Vicia sensed they didn't need to. He would happily walk to the gallows to defend his principles.

And that was exactly what she intended for him.

CHAPTER 43:

A War of Succession

BLAKE STEPPED OUT INTO the sunlight from the tower surrounded by guards. They all looked on him grimly. He smiled.

Ordinarily, executions were held within the prison itself, but Vicia had ordered his be done in the central market. She wanted to make an example of him.

Blake couldn't help but grin to himself, despite the fact that he would be dead soon. Vicia had proven herself a tyrant. He'd been uncertain about her from the start, and her treatment of him, her refusal to investigate Tremaine's claim to the throne, was all the proof Blake needed to know Vicia Morrigan served only her own ambition.

His trial hadn't lasted long. He'd proclaimed his loyalty to Twin Falls. He'd suggested he would happily serve whomever could demonstrate they were the true, worthy successor to Duke Evonin. Vicia asserted she was. Blake exhorted her to disprove Tremaine's claim. She'd refused and demanded he swear fealty to her or face the consequences.

It was all perfectly simple to Blake. Vicia knew Garrick Tremaine indeed had a legitimate and superior claim to the crown she wore. Otherwise, she'd have happily engaged an enquiry. But she knew she wouldn't be happy with the result, so she refused. She needed to solidify her position, and that meant silencing anyone who challenged her.

Soldiers in the tower brought him news. Vicia had ordered *Res Nostra's* headquarters sacked and burned. They'd been found abandoned. Levinia, Tremaine, and the rest of the thieves' guild had gone to ground. Vicia stripped the organization from the city's Charter of Guilds and made being or harboring a member a capital crime.

That was another violation of Twin Falls tradition. Evonin's line had long ago recognized the thieves' guild, preferring to keep as much criminal activity above board as possible. Blake had never trusted them, but at least he knew more or less what they were up to, and they didn't cross certain lines.

No, Vicia was no Twin Faller. She had no respect for their customs or their history. She only wanted the throne.

Zalachorus had testified against Blake. He supported Vicia's claim and certified the legitimacy of the Contest of Succession. Blake couldn't figure that out. Zalachorus was every bit as ambitious as Vicia. Why had he suddenly become her lapdog?

She must have promised him something. What could have been big enough to feed the ego of Zalachorus ir-Bedlam Donovian?

Blake supposed it didn't matter. Within half an hour, it wouldn't be his problem anymore. He wouldn't have any more problems at all.

He walked with his head held high through the streets as the drums beat out his death march. The sun felt warm on his face, and he thanked the gods for a pleasant day. If this was the last time he was to lay eyes on his beloved Twin Falls, he wanted it to look as he remembered it.

Offhandedly, he wondered if it would hurt. At his sentencing, he'd requested a headsman. He told Vicia that the traditional penalty for treason was beheading. Partially, he was afraid to hang. He didn't want to lose his dignity as he danced before a crowd.

But he also wanted his death to be as grisly as possible. He wanted to send a message that Vicia Morrigan was no just ruler. She would spill the blood of Twin Falls's most loyal citizen in horrific fashion. Hopefully, that would help inspire rebellion.

They turned onto the main street leading to the market. A large throng was gathering to watch. Vicia had made sure everyone knew today was the day the traitor would lose his head.

They'd gone a hundred yards, when there was a disturbance up ahead. Blake couldn't make out what it was, but there was shouting.

His escort signaled a halt. Blake looked at them curiously, but they all showed the same surprise. Whatever was happening was not part of his scheduled execution.

The guard nearest him flinched and put a hand to his neck. Then he collapsed as his partners stared at him in astonishment.

In quick succession, the other three guards suffered the same fate. Blake grinned. He'd seen this before.

Six people in black cloaks and hoods burst from the crowd and rushed him. One of them threw an identical cloak over Blake, and they dragged him out of the street and into the crowd.

Startled, the onlookers parted to allow them through. More shouts and cries went up, but Blake couldn't see what was happening.

With a savage yank, he was pulled into an alley, where a sewer drain with the grate pulled off was waiting. One of his benefactors produced a large set of shears and sliced through the chains of his manacles.

"Quickly!" another of them said. "Down the shaft."

Blake was practically pushed in. He was barely able to grab the ladder and descend properly. At the bottom, two more black-caped men were waiting for him.

"This way, General," one of them said.

He was whisked down the sewer as the drain grate was pulled into place overhead. Blake and his rescuers raced down several winding tunnels. He was thoroughly lost when they at last came to a stop at a steel door.

One of his escorts produced a key, fitted it into the lock, and turned. He pushed the door open, beckoned for Blake to enter, and shut it behind him when they were all in. Levinia Mordecai sat in a chair on the far side of the stone room.

"Welcome back to the land of the living, General Calavan," she said.

Blake cocked his head, uncertain what to say. It had all happened so fast, it had been so surprising, he hadn't had time to really think about what was going on.

"Thank you," he replied. "Pardon me for sounding ungrateful, but why am I here?"

Mordecai smiled and laughed. She stood up.

"Well, I didn't think you wanted to be separated from your head," she replied. "And since I don't have any influence with our usurping duchess, I had to take matters into my own hands."

"That much I can see," he said. "I mean why did you rescue me in the first place?"

She frowned and cocked her head. Then she shook it.

"Ah, General," she said, "your loyalty never ceases to amaze me. You'd have walked up to the chopping block willingly just to prove your patriotism."

"Of course!" he said.

"Well, I have a better way for you to serve the city," she replied. "And so does our true duke. I rescued you because Garrick wanted me to. We need allies and people willing to stand up for what is right. The duke requests you serve as his general. He values your patriotism and your wisdom."

"Where is he?" Blake asked.

"I've got him secreted away in one of our fortresses," she answered. "He's not well, Calavan. The goblin god stole much of his life force, and his heart is broken over Liliana's sacrifice."

"Liliana? What happened to her?"

"It wasn't Vicia who closed the gate to Hell," Levinia said. "Liliana did it. She saved the city by spilling her own blood.

"But Garrick lives, and we are searching for a means to heal him. In the interim, we're establishing an underground, and we'd like you to be our chief military officer."

Blake nodded. He didn't like this. Sneaking around and acting like a spy was neither the sort of thing he excelled at nor what he thought of as proper warfare.

But it was war – a war of succession – and at the moment, his side was at a disadvantage. They needed to do something to gain the upper hand.

Moreover, he was pleased Vicia's tyranny would be opposed and he would get to join the resistance. He could hardly wait for the day he would see her ambition unravel. This was a much better alternative to the death he'd been facing less than an hour before.

"Very well," he said. "I accept. How do we get started?"

EPILOGUE:

Strange Magic

K REMDOR COULDN'T HELP BUT smile at Vicia's troubles. He knew he should be irritated, even worried about the fact that she was dealing with an underground resistance now. He knew the fact that they were talented enough to snatch a condemned criminal from her custody in broad daylight meant they were more dangerous than Vicia admitted.

But he just couldn't help it. Vicia was so arrogant, so convinced of her own greatness, that every one of these little setbacks amused him. She needed the reminders that she was not the grand demigod she thought herself to be.

Of course, it was still a problem. As long as Vicia was fighting a rebellion in her own backyard, she couldn't turn her eyes to Eldenberg, which was part of the overall scheme.

It wasn't a total loss, though. Vicia was still in power, and in a worst-case scenario, Kremdor would send units to support her. He did need her help with Eldenberg in the long run, after all.

But he also could now turn his full attention to Sothernia. Until and unless Vicia needed his help holding onto Twin Falls, she wasn't his problem at the moment. Eldenberg could wait.

Besides, he had something far more interesting to think about.

As if on cue, there was a knock at his door. Another smile lit his face behind his mask.

"Come in!" he called.

The door to the *sanctum* swung in, and Esmerelda stood in its frame.

"Gursh, King of Goblins to see you, my lord," she said.

"Show him in," Kremdor replied.

Esmerelda stood aside and Gursh marched triumphantly into Kremdor's lab. A twisted, toothy grin lit his face, and four more goblins followed him in, carrying a body wrapped in a shroud.

"Greetings, Lord Kremdor," Gursh said.

"Hello, King of Goblins," Kremdor returned. "Welcome to my abode."

"I am honored to be in your presence," Gursh said. "I bring the gift I promised."

"Excellent," Kremdor said. "Bring it here."

He indicated an empty table with a sweep of his hand. The goblins brought it over and heaved it somewhat unceremoniously onto the wooden surface.

"We found her lying face down in one of the caverns," Gursh explained. "She was unconscious and bleeding. We stitched her wounds, and I had Kraven enchant her as you instructed."

"And you say you found her beneath the seal?" Kremdor inquired.

"Two levels down," Gursh said. "It shouldn't have been possible. She would have had to have passed through some thirty feet of stone. But yes, she was directly beneath the seal."

Kremdor nodded. There was strange magic at work here. Even he wasn't sure what it was.

But he was very pleased. He felt certain this was going to be a huge boost to his overall plan.

He drew back the shroud and gazed on the sleeping face of Liliana Gray.

THE END OF *THE CROWN CONTEST.* THE USURPERS SAGA CONTINUES IN *THE KRAKEN BONE.*

ACKNOWLEDGEMENTS

A S ALWAYS, WHILE AN author's name goes on the cover of a book, he doesn't reach the publication stage without a lot of help. The following people were instrumental in bringing *The Crown Contest* to publication.

Jill Jess – Everything starts and ends with her. She makes my authorial career possible. This life I live is because of her, and I'm grateful she wants me as a partner and companion. And of course, if she hadn't inspired *The Dragon Sword*, this novel would never have been written.

Knute and Diane Pittenger – When I needed shelter and friendly ears, they were there. A personal crisis broadsided me in the middle of writing this novel, and they helped rescue me. Truly, I am lucky to know them and have their friendship.

Shawn Inmon – Not only is Shawn an exceptionally helpful member of the BookGoodies Authors' Group and all-around great guy, his 120 Club proved really inspirational for making sure I was hitting my word count every day. I'd never have finished this book on time without him.

Bryan Cohen – *Bryan has been a fantastic mentor on the business side of being an author. This relaunch of* The Usurpers Saga *with new covers and content is due in large part to his success and advice. I'm grateful he has a few spare moments to offer guidance to little guys like me.*

My parents – They too provided shelter when I needed it during the writing of this book. And their support of my dreams helped put me on this path.

My children – This book is neither about you nor for you, but I hope you'll remember its most important lesson: Love is the mightiest magic of all. May you understand its transformative power, and feel it from me.

ABOUT THE AUTHOR

 *John R. Phythyon, Jr.* wishes he were a superhero or a magician, but, since he has not yet been bitten by a radioactive spider or received his letter from Hogwarts, he writes adventure stories instead. He is the author of the Wolf Dasher series of fantasy-thriller mash-up novels, several modern fairy tales, a two-act comedy, and a series of humorous memoirs about his childhood in the 1970's (the "True-Life Adventures" series). Prior to becoming a novelist, he was an award-winning game designer.

He lives in Columbus, Ohio, with his wife, their children, a dog, and a cat. It is rarely quiet, but it's often entertaining. His current projects include world peace, desperately wishing for the Cincinnati Bengals to win a Super Bowl, and acquiring more cool socks.

Connect with John online at his website, www.johnphythyon.com, on Twitter at @JohnRPhythyonJr, and on Facebook at www.facebook.com/johnrphythyonjr. Or email him at john@johnphythyon.com. He writes back.

Volume I: The Dragon Sword – Calibot hated his father. The world's most powerful wizard had little time for a son interested only in poetry. But when his father is murdered, Calibot is bequeathed the legendary dragon sword, *Wyrmblade*. Enchanted within the sword's steel are the secrets to unlock even greater power, perhaps even mastery of The Known World itself. But using its magic could cost Calibot his soul. Worse, this may have been his father's intention all along.

As he struggles to complete the mad last wishes of the father he loathes, everyone with a stake in The Known World's future will try to stop him – his power-hungry uncle, the murderer, even an earth fairy bent on revenge. If Calibot fails, he dies. If he succeeds, he'll lose everything he's ever loved . . . including himself.

Volume III: The Kraken Bone – T'Lenn Dartha yearns for freedom. A shapeshifter who's been coerced and enslaved to serve others' insidious purposes, he's no longer certain of his own identity. But he can be free forever if he'll just commit one more crime – help Zod the Fearless usurp the throne of Sothernia.

Zod was supposed to be King of The Known World. But after his brother betrayed him, he is a broken man, purposeless and depressed. But if T'Lenn Dartha's offer is genuine, Zod can reclaim his former glory.

Sailing for a distant island from which no one has ever returned, T'Lenn and Zod seek the Kraken Bone, a legendary artifact that can fulfill their dreams. Surviving the journey is only the first challenge. With the fate of The Known World riding on the outcome of their quest, they'll discover there is more at stake than they imagined. And neither one knows the ultimate betrayal still lies in wait. . . .

Made in the USA
Middletown, DE
05 August 2023